THE THIEF

A COSMIC SHORES NOVEL

G. S. JENNSEN

HYPERNOVA
Publishing
2024

THE THIEF

Copyright © 2024 by G. S. Jennsen

Cover design by Ranid.
Cover typography by G. S. Jennsen.

Hypernova Publishing
174 E Neider Ave #89
Coeur d'Alene, ID 83815
www.hypernovapublishing.com

Publisher's Note: This is a work of fiction. Names, characters, places, and incidents are a product of the author's imagination. Locales and public names are sometimes used for atmospheric purposes. Any resemblance to actual people, living or dead, or to businesses, companies, events, institutions, or locales is completely coincidental.

The Hypernova Publishing name, colophon and logo are trademarks of Hypernova Publishing.

Ordering Information:
Hypernova Publishing books may be purchased for educational, business or sales promotional use. For details, contact the "Special Markets Department" at the address above.

The Thief / G. S. Jennsen.—1st ed.

LCCN 9781957352251
978-1-957352-25-1

CONTENTS

THE
THIEF

PART I:
THE HESGYR

1

The half-false Ares sunlight bounced off the stranger's irises like moonlight upon still waters—a flat, diffuse gleam refracting through a gauzy film.

Well, that was odd.

Eren Savitas slowed his steps and wandered out of the flow of pedestrian traffic to lean casually against the window of a tea shop and get a better view of the stranger. He stuffed his hands into his pockets and peered around, as if he were waiting for someone.

On closer inspection, wrongness radiated from more than the man's eyes. His skin displayed a waxy, plastic sheen, and his facial expression looked oddly frozen. Almost like a mannequin.

Was it a synthetic artificial intelligence—an SAI—walking around in a doll? Nah, dolls tended to be of higher quality than this body. Also, whatever the figure might be, they were trying to appear anaden, not Human. The Advocacy had gingerly legalized anaden-created synthetic intelligences nine months ago, then immediately heaped a host of regulations atop them, including a prohibition on trying to appear organic. Seven hundred millennia of repression did not die overnight.

Regardless, he didn't think the 'man' was an SAI; he couldn't say why, but he trusted his gut.

Once the stranger passed, Eren pushed off the window to follow. A backpack was situated high on the man's shoulders, with a strap secured around his waist. Someone didn't want that backpack going anywhere. The man's clothes looked as though they'd been purchased at the Olympia Transport Hub's tourist shop: shiny silver loose pants and an ivy jacket over a black shirt with poufy cuffs that frilled out the end of the jacket's sleeves. His excessively close-cropped auburn hair would only be deemed stylish on Epithero, the planet where style went to die, and the rest of the outfit lacked any of the fashionable flourishes currently popular on the more cosmopolitan worlds.

Eren checked behind him and triangulated where the stranger was coming from. His eyes passed over then returned to an unassuming synth-stone four-story building positioned between the far more ostentatious facades of an art gallery and a commercial tower. The Olympia Advanced Research Institute.

Objectively, both the gallery and the tower made for more likely origination points, since no one entered the Institute except for employees and credentialed visitors. But he knew the type of subjects being researched at the Institute, and they were far more interesting targets for nefarious deeds.

He reacquired the man's path with greater urgency, his lunch meeting with a coworker forgotten. As the man headed toward the entrance to a levtram station, Eren sent a message to Institute security.

> *You may have suffered a security breach in the last hour. I recommend performing a quiet sweep of the building. Focus on possible explosive devices, hidden surveillance equipment or missing items.*
> *—Eren Savitas*
> *Advocacy Chief of Intelligence for Non-Anaden Affairs*

What evidence did he have that this individual had committed a crime involving the Institute? None whatsoever. Only the kind of instincts that came from three centuries of walking amongst lowlifes, thugs and rebels.

CS

The individual (Eren had stopped thinking of them as male, for he was now convinced the body was fake) exited the levtram on the outskirts of Olympia, at the final stop before the tram shot across the bleak landscape between cities toward Hestia. Six other people also exited at the stop, which unfortunately didn't constitute enough of a crowd to conceal a tail for long. So Eren activated his Veiltech, now divorced from an external device and installed in his cybernetics. He gradually faded into invisibility as he stepped across the threshold onto the platform.

Why did you order a security sweep at the Olympia Advanced Research Institute?

Eren swore under his breath. Three-plus years on the job, and Nyx Praesidis still monitored every damn action he took, eagerly checking along behind him for anything she deemed to be a mistake.

Just a hunch. Might be nothing. Any results from the sweep?

Nothing yet. What kind of hunch?

I'll tell you if it pays off.

The individual had strolled with awkward, stilted casualness into Ancippe Park, the last bastion of intensive ground terraforming in the region until Hestia. As soon as they reached the relative cover of the geoengineered catalpa trees, however, their gait turned strident. Not suspicious behavior at all.

What were they? The possibility that Shroud technology had leaked out of Concord Special Projects concerned him. It would eventually, of course—all government-developed tech was destined for the hands of criminals—but not so soon. If it had, though? This person could be literally anyone, of any species. Well, probably not Efkam…or Katasketousya? Would it work for them?

The individual walked straight up to a collection of boulders nestled against the shore of a sparse pond overrun with lilies—and vanished into the rock.

Eren sprinted forward to reach the boulders in three seconds. He pulled up short and felt along the surface; like most of the stone in the park, the boulders were relocated volcanic basalt rock from the days before they'd terraformed Ares.

To his utter lack of surprise, he felt not rock beneath his fingertips, but metal. It was an illusion masking…he'd bet his life on it being a ship.

He'd love to spend a few minutes gloating about having been right about the person being *wrong*, but if it was a ship, it was liable to take off any minute. So he worked his way along the tactile surface until his hands met open air. His toes edged forward until his shin banged into something. Steps, fantastic.

One, two, three.... The fifth step continued on to level flooring—and the illusion dissolved. He was inside.

The image that popped into Eren's head was of walking into a junk shop in a low-rent neighborhood of Menaris. Nothing about the interior matched anything else. The jump seat across from the airlock was a tan leather equivalent and sported two tears in the seat cushion, while the fold-out couch farther back in the cabin was upholstered in a shiny gray-and-white marbled material. One set of storage cabinets was chrome metal, while right next to them hung cabinets of a different height and sculpted of muted onyx. The cockpit dash was a jumbled collection of sophisticated-looking virtual readouts, clunky analog dials and levers, and some manner of reactive foam.

The alien sitting in the cockpit chair had to be the individual he'd followed here, as the shirt the alien wore matched (the pants had mysteriously disappeared, revealing beige undergarments). But the disguise was already melting away...and it wasn't a virtual projection at all. As Eren stood there transfixed, the semblance of skin morphed to reveal an exoskeleton of bony gray cartilage. The alien grunted as if in pain when several curved spikes extended out from the skull behind actively mutating ears. Whatever they were, it wasn't a species known to Concord.

A faint vibration rippled through the floor as the engine came to life. Eren glanced at the open airlock. He should arrest the alien before they lifted off, no? It would make certain things easier. But arrest them for what? Parking a starship outside an official spaceport? Impersonating an anaden, badly?

The airlock closed. A rumble beneath Eren's feet signified the ship lifting off, he assumed, but there was almost no sensation of motion. If he was going to act, he should act now.

The backpack rested against the interior hull near the cockpit chair. His gut told him the alien had pilfered something, and said gut was on a winning streak today. If he was wrong, he'd apologize profusely and bet on the alien not knowing how to complain about government mistreatment to the local press.

He stayed silent and hidden.

A stronger vibration rattled the hull as they ascended into the thickest part of the atmosphere. But again it wasn't so rough a traversal as he'd have expected from the ramshackle interior of the ship. Appearances weren't everything.

In another minute, the last wisps of atmosphere outside the cockpit viewport faded away to reveal the blackness of space.

The alien swung the chair around and stood, and Eren got a good look at their face. Zeus almighty, they were ugly! They stood a fair bit over two meters in height, and under the ill-fitting remains of anaden attire, their body was covered by the gray cartilage. Or almost, as periodically, the cartilage stretched into long strands of sinew, with hints of their true flesh beneath covering vital organs. Large, olive green eyes jutted prominently above sunken cheeks and narrow white lips. The spikes decorated a bony, hairless head.

They passed less than a meter from Eren on their way to a cabinet tucked into the rear wall of the cabin. The alien pulled off the anaden-style shirt and tossed it to the floor, then reached in and removed some fabric. A cream fitted shirt went over the alien's head, followed by a black mesh vest. Darker beige pants of a soft material came on next, and finally slider boots.

Dressed again, the alien descended a ladder and disappeared below.

Eren swiftly moved to the backpack and knelt in front of it. He unfastened the top and removed a small box. Nothing else was inside.

The box was definitely of anaden manufacture. He opened it and found a…he didn't know exactly. Expensive technology, by the design of it, but he'd never seen the device before—

The sound of boots ascending the ladder warned him of the alien's return. He dropped the box in the backpack, closed it up and stepped away as the alien reentered the main cabin.

They retrieved a metal cylinder from a refrigeration unit and turned it up to their lips as they moved to the cockpit. After scrutinizing two screens of data displayed in an unfamiliar language, the alien sank one hand into a blob of reactive foam.

A pinpoint of green light materialized in front of the bow, then expanded to form a disc that encompassed the ship. For a second, all light vanished from the universe, and they were consumed by a pit of eternal blackness—then stars winked back into existence.

Wormhole tech for certain, but it bore little resemblance to portals created by any Concord species.

The ship reemerged in notably empty space, with nothing but an ordinary red dwarf star shining dimly in the distance.

Eren pinged his internal location reference…then had it rerun the calculation.

Supercluster Complex: Pisces-Cetus
Supercluster: Leo
Cluster: Abell 1185
Galaxy: NGC 3550

He'd expected to have traveled outside of Concord territory, but they were located some 135 megaparsecs from Ares, well into space scientists labeled with letters and numbers rather than flowery names.

Intellectually, he understood how when one traveled by wormhole, distance simply was not a factor. You could in theory travel from a Point A to a Point B situated on the literal opposite edge of the universe in a single jump. No one made a habit of doing so, however, because special relativity meant that from where you stood at Point A, you had no idea what Point B looked like in the present day, or even if it still existed in any meaningful way.

On a universal scale, he supposed they remained 'in the neighborhood.' But the brain could only comprehend so much scale, and so far as he knew, he'd now traveled farther than any Concord citizen. Any corporeal citizen, at least; a Kat or two had presumably gone farther, as the ethereal, supradimensional bundles of lights made the cosmos their playground.

He forced his attention back to the cockpit and its viewport. While he'd been waxing philosophical and attempting to reorient his mind to radically new space, his alien pilot had been proceeding ahead in the direction of the red dwarf with all due speed. The star now shone brightly enough to light the cabin in a strong amber glow that took the edge off the antiseptic artificial lighting—

Then suddenly they were not alone in the stellar system.

2

'Space station' was the only term that could be applied with any accuracy, but the megastructure they were approaching put to utter shame any station Eren had ever seen.

It was a city floating in space. Or perhaps a dozen cities linked together by a maze of winding tunnels. It had no uniform shape; it wasn't circular or oval or rectangular, but rather all those and more. Edifices jutted out in every direction: tall, scraper-like buildings, stacked oblong enclosures, shining circles. Spires and pyramids and bowls and vast stretches of flatness.

To Eren's fairly well-trained eyes, it looked as if every section had been bolted onto the adjoining ones with no thought given to architectural consistency or even structural integrity, creating a patchwork of clashing motifs, materials and skylines. It was grotesque! And yet, somehow beautiful in its audacious defiance of all accepted norms of how one was supposed to build a proper space station.

Much as he wanted to focus on the spectacle before him, this was no time for gawking. They were evidently headed for the structure, so now he needed a plan. He'd thought he would have more time.

He considered revealing himself now, while they remained in space, but decided there were a nearly infinite number of ways the alien could kill him out here in the black, many of which he'd be unable to defend against. Once they were docked, however, the alien would need to be cautious, right? Possibly. Also possibly not, but it was all he had to work with.

Eren stretched his arms and legs, worked his neck and rolled his shoulders while he ran through mental shortcuts to prepare for the coming confrontation. His gaze never deviated from the viewport.

As they drew near, the true scale of the station began to make itself known. It wasn't a dozen cities, but a hundred or more, and at its longest point, the station must stretch for something like a thousand kilometers. The only stellar body he'd ever seen that compared in size was Earth's in-progress artificial moon replacement, Luna, but it was mostly empty space on the inside. He imagined the Ourankeli's stellar ring had a greater surface area, but the Rasu had destroyed it centuries ago.

This structure, though, looked to be jam-packed to bursting with purposeful activity and, one supposed, people.

This wasn't what he'd expected. A rough-and-tumble smugglers' den carved into an asteroid, maybe, or a black-ops style research facility hidden beneath the surface of a frozen planet, but not an entire civilization floating in space. These aliens, whoever they turned out to be, were going to require a great deal of attention. He briefly considered sending a message to Nyx, but decided to wait until he had a better picture of who and what he'd discovered.

The ship approached an array of docking ports 'underneath' the station. The ports lacked the dramatic elegance of Concord HQ's sprawling pinwheels, but they were definitely a more efficient use of space. Rows upon rows of berths were sandwiched together and stacked fifty high, except for the bottom few rows, which were spread out spaciously to allow for larger cargo ships to dock.

Given the size of the station, this couldn't be the only point of entry, but there must be room for ten thousand ships here. How many people lived on this station? His brain refused to calculate a guesstimate.

The pilot eased their ship into an empty berth two-thirds of the way up and near the edge. A *thud* signaled a docking lock, and they began what he assumed were shutdown procedures.

Eren unlatched the collapsed handgun from his belt, extended it, and crept forward—

The alien stood and left the cockpit, headed directly his way. He swiftly shifted to the side to flank the alien and raised his weapon.

The alien's head jerked, their claw-like hands coming up in a defensive posture. "*Powy sadd yana?*"

So excellent hearing, then. Eren swept around a few more centimeters, enough so the alien would be able to see him clearly, and deactivated the Veiltech. "Hi. Kindly freeze and keep your hands in the air."

A finger on the alien's left hand twitched, and a viscous, stringy material shot out from it to coat his weapon, the hand that held it and his forearm. He fired, but the material was already clogging the muzzle, and instead of impacting the alien's shoulder, the laser diffused to scorch wildly into a twenty-centimeter circle on the far wall.

He tried to fire again, but by now the material was gumming up the trigger mechanism and his fingers and…was this some type of *spiderweb?*

He settled for trying to cold-cock the alien in the jaw—"Fuck!" Throbbing pain ricocheted through his hand and arm and into his shoulder. Hitting the bony skull was akin to striking concrete.

The alien took advantage of his distress to shoot more sticky webbing out of its finger and into Eren's face. He tried to suck in air, but it was like breathing through thick gauze. He blinked, and his vision was reduced to blurry shapes wavering through a film. Disoriented, he stumbled back, his free hand clawing at his face (because the weapon was now glued to his other hand), but he only succeeded in coating those fingers with the viscous material as well. And now his fingertips were sticking to his face.

"I can't…breathe…." He could go without much in the way of oxygen for several minutes if he must, but the alien shouldn't know this.

"One minute, and I'll address that," the alien said in near-perfect Communis, the low vocal pitch suggesting it was male. Then the alien disappeared out of Eren's line-of-sight, and the sound of drawers being opened filtered through the webbing.

He struggled against the trap, backing up until he had a wall behind him. He fumbled his thumb over the part of the weapon he could reach until he found the small recess to activate the blade attachment. When he pressed it, a 10-centimeter adiamene blade popped out beneath the grip. He twisted his hand so the blade sliced through the webbing between the weapon and his wrist, giving him a touch more maneuverability. Next, he brought the weapon up to his face and *carefully* worked at the webbing holding his other hand to his face. One wrong twitch, and the adiamene would slice clean through his skin and cleave his skull in two on its way to bisecting his brain.

"*Bwachi!* Not so fast there." The alien shoved him forward, thankfully knocking the blade away from his face instead of into it, and manhandled him into the jump seat. Eren hadn't yet freed his hands enough to properly fight back; he kneed the alien in the stomach, where the kidneys would be on an anaden, but all he got for his efforts was a grunt from his foe. The instant he landed on the cushion, thick restraints extended out from the wall to wrap around him and pin him to the seat.

All in all, not his best performance. If there was a silver lining, at least no one was here to see him beclown himself.

"Still can't...breathe...."

"You appear to be doing all right." The alien produced a small black gadget and pointed it at Eren's head.

Great. He sighed in resignation; regenesis it was.

Ultraviolet light swept over him, first his face then down his body, and the webbing evaporated. Eren gasped in air.

The alien snatched Eren's weapon out of his hand and inspected it suspiciously. "A blade shouldn't be able to cut through the web."

"Adiamene isn't like other metals."

"Ah. So I've heard." The alien moved to one of the mismatched cabinets and placed the weapon in a locked drawer, then leaned against the counter and studied Eren. "How did you find my ship?"

Eren rotated his shoulders and flexed his fingers, confirming the webbing was gone; damn, that had been claustrophobic. Of course, he was now held equally immobile by multiple sturdy straps, but they were merely normal restraints. These, he'd done before. "I followed you to it from downtown Olympia."

"Then how did you spot me in the city?"

"Are you kidding? Do you think you actually looked anaden?"

"Anaden enough to get me into and out of…" the alien stopped himself "…you're baiting me. Nice try."

"No, seriously, though. That was a shite disguise."

"It fooled everyone else."

"I'm not everyone else."

"So it seems. Police? Security? Intelligence?"

Eren shrugged within the restraints. "Close enough. What did you steal?"

"What makes you think I stole something?"

"I'm good at my job."

The alien's blanched lips widened, as if he were baring fangs. "Not so good, considering you're my prisoner and not the other way around."

"Give me a few minutes. You speak Communis remarkably well for someone not from Concord space."

"You all scream into the void with your broadcasts and entertainment and commerce. It's deafening. Makes picking up the language a trivial matter."

It was true. Concord invested its prodigious funds in many endeavors, but masking its presence from the other inhabitants of the cosmos wasn't one of them. "Your ship is obviously sophisticated, so why does it resemble a junk store inside?"

The alien drew up straighter. "You dare insult my ship?"

"I see what I see."

"You would."

"What does that mean?"

"Concord is so supremely arrogant, with its vast riches and impervious starships and interdimensional trinkets. And among all its species, none are more arrogant than the Anadens."

Eren started to retort, but instead gave the observation its due, then nodded mildly. "Fair enough. So, what are you?"

"We call ourselves Hesgyr."

"Why tell me so easily?"

The alien flicked a long, bony finger at his nose. "It's just a word. It doesn't reveal anything about us."

Eren forced himself not to glance back at the viewport. No, but a location was apt to. The powers that be were going to be tickled to learn he had discovered a new intelligent species, and he was going to hate to temper their enthusiasm with the fact that these Hesgyr—or at least one Hesgyr—was infiltrating Concord worlds and stealing…well, something.

"Then you won't mind telling me your name, either."

"Tolje Alainor. You?"

What the hell. The alien was correct—they were just words. "Eren Savitas. I'd say 'pleased to meet you,' but I'm finding the hospitality a mite lacking."

"You're the one who sneaked aboard my ship and tried to take me prisoner."

"Because you concealed your identity and landed your ship in the middle of a fucking park—do you have any idea how many centuries it took for us to get grass to grow on Ares? Oh, and then you absconded with anaden property."

"All true. So now you're here. What am I to do with you?"

Eren's job was, at the end of every day, to identify and neutralize alien threats to the Advocacy, the still-pretty-new anaden government. He did this primarily by knowing the grievances, real and imagined, of every would-be rebel and agitator on dozens of worlds.

He'd rectify *this* theft by arresting Tolje Alainor and confiscating whatever the Hesgyr had stolen. But if one alien could sneak onto the anadens' capital planet, conceal his ship, stroll through downtown Olympia, steal something from a highly secretive research lab and wormhole away while whistling a tune, then so could other Hesgyr. The security implications were enormous. So he should probably do his job.

Eren offered his most charming smile. "Why don't you tell me why you stole the item you did? If your people are in trouble and need help, you'll find that Concord is most generous with its bounty."

Tolje threw his head back and…Eren was going to go with 'laughed.' The sound was guttural and echo-y, as if it resounded out from the gaps in the alien's sinew. "Hesgyr do not beg for scraps from others. We take care of ourselves."

"By stealing what you need."

"Often, yes. It's a brutal universe out there. The strongest don't always survive, but the most clever do."

Eren found he couldn't disagree with the sentiment. In different circumstances, he might like this chap. "And why do you need to be clever? What issue are you trying to solve?"

Tolje huffed air out of his wide nostrils. "Why do you care?"

"Ninety percent of the time, I get my job done in one of two ways: talking out a peaceable solution, or blowing shit up. Since I'm currently resident on this ship, I'm not inclined to blow it up, so I'm giving the first option a go."

"You're not what I expected."

"Thank you, probably. What did you expect?"

"Our intel says Anadens are cold and emotionless, rigid and unforgiving. Supremely arrogant, as we've covered. A sense of humor was not on the list."

"Yeah, um…" Eren fought a powerful urge to scratch an itch on his nose "…you're not entirely wrong, historically speaking, but your intel could be a touch out of date. I, on the other hand, have no preconceptions about your people. Why don't you enlighten me? I think you'll find a sympathetic ear. Though any chance you could ditch these restraints first?"

Another bout of 'laughter' bellowed out from the alien's chest. "So you can immediately attack me, disable me and take control of my ship?"

"I'm flattered you believe I'm capable of doing so—especially the last one. But no." Eren decided to take a gamble on his hunch that

Tolje was a symptom of a much larger problem. Let the little fish go and use it to reel in the big catch. "Free me. Tell me what you stole and, more importantly, why you stole it. Fill me in on whatever difficulty your people face. In return, I won't try to detain you, beat you up or, obviously, kill you. Assuming what you stole isn't one of a kind or a weapon primed to be used to murder a bunch of Concord citizens, I'll even let you keep it."

"Why?"

"Because I'm curious. I love a good mystery. And you, Tolje Alainor, are a mystery. Why were you on Ares? How did you find Concord and learn enough about us to walk our streets *almost* unnoticed? What's the story behind this tremendous space station we've docked at, and what are your people like? I have to know."

"That's a lot of questions."

"I've got all day and nowhere to be—except possibly the lavatory. You have one of those on board?" Experience had taught him that most anatype species employed the same basic plumbing system. Strange how evolution had never found a way to improve upon it.

"Yeah, I've got one of those." Tolje's shoulders heaved; sighing was something else that was pretty much universal across those species. "All right, I'll unfasten the restraints, but only after you hand over the blade strapped to your calf and the suspicious object clipped to your belt."

Eren chuckled. "I'm impressed. It's a deal."

He allowed Tolje to manhandle him again, shoving his pants leg up and unstrapping the sheath with his backup adiamene blade, then wrangling his belt and removing the tiny beam weapon. He did shed a silent tear when the alien locked the weapons up with his handgun. Hand-to-hand combat was not his forte, so if Tolje decided to attack him again, Eren was screwed. Of course, he was also immortal (for so long as the regenesis labs continued to operate), so the price of defeat was limited to a week-long hangover—nothing he hadn't suffered through a dozen or a hundred times. Well, that and letting his one chance at infiltrating the Hesgyr slip away.

Tolje studied him intently for a moment, then pressed something on the wall behind Eren. The restraints unclasped and retracted.

He took care not to make any sudden or threatening moves as he stood and stretched out a kink. "Thanks, mate. Lavatory?"

Tolje motioned with a bony hand, and Eren followed the alien through a sliding door at the rear of the cabin. A ramp led down into a shadowy hold. He hadn't been able to get a sense of the size of the ship due to it being cloaked, but this suggested it was of considerable size for a personal craft.

Tolje triggered a second sliding door on the left. "Leave the door open and don't waste time."

"Whatever makes you comfortable." The lavatory consisted of the usual: two circular bowls, one at chest height and the other one situated lower, both with pipes draining into the floor, as well as a square inset area and a faucet overhead that suggested a shower. Eren relieved himself in the lower bowl; the flushing mechanism was a mystery, so he simply walked out.

Tolje shot him a look he couldn't yet decipher, then slipped inside and depressed a small button beside the door.

Back in the main cabin, the alien propped himself against the wall behind the cockpit. "So what's your play here?"

Eren returned to the jump seat, as adopting a sitting, lower position made him seem less threatening to his counterpart. "My job is to protect the Anaden Advocacy, and by extension Concord as a whole, from any and all manner of alien threats. You're an unknown, and unknowns are threats. Assuage my concerns, and the threat disappears." It was, for the most part, the truth.

"And if I don't?"

"Then this could get ugly. If you know enough to be able to infiltrate the streets of Ares, you know what manner of military Concord fields. You don't want to make us your enemy. But we can be *great* friends."

"I told you—we take care of ourselves."

"Okay, fine. The point about being enemies unfortunately stands."

"And now you know where we're located, because I'm assuming you've got supra-dimensional locator technology. *Bwachi.*"

"Yep. What did you steal on Ares?"

Tolje knelt in front of the backpack and removed the small box. He stood and held it out in his hand.

"It's a box," Eren remarked dryly.

"I'm not opening it here on the ship."

"Is it a bomb?"

"No. But it is delicate equipment. Or so I've been told."

"Most of what resides in the Olympia Advanced Research Institute is. But the box tells me nothing."

"The people at the Institute refer to it as a Manifold Scar Tracker, or MAST."

Eren dipped his chin while he queried home for information on the device. "Thank you. Why do you need it?"

Tolje paced around the cabin in several circles, his gaze never fully leaving Eren. "We're being hunted. We don't know by whom, where they come from or what they want—except to kill us. My mission is to bring back tech that can help us either discover the nature of our enemy or defend ourselves from the attacks. If both, all the better. I've got a cargo hold full of possibilities. Ares was my last stop before heading home."

"And that's where we are now? Home?"

"I suppose lying about it would be pointless."

Eren shrugged. "Home or not, it's got my attention. What do you call this place?"

"Nythir." Tolje abruptly moved into the cockpit, twisted some dials on the dash and spoke a series of guttural barks and clicks. Eren winced at the prospect of having to listen to the harsh tongue nonstop for however long this adventure lasted.

"Tell me about the attacks."

"Later, perhaps."

"Look, I can't help you if you won't tell me anything."

Tolje returned his attention to Eren. "I've made it clear we don't want your help."

"You may not want it, but you do need it. You stole our technology because you require it to fight your attackers. Apparently, you've been scouring a decent swath of the universe hunting for tools you require to fight them. You need help, and you might consider being a smidge lenient in where you get it from. If you want your people to survive, I mean."

Tolje stared at him; the rough cartilage/bone covering his skull didn't allow for much in the way of facial expressions, which was going to make reading the Hesgyr challenging. Finally he jerked his bony head toward the airlock. "Those kinds of decisions are above my pay grade. You'll come with me."

"Terrific. But hey, I don't know your language. My translator is good, but I'm starting from scratch here."

The alien grunted. "You're already more trouble than you're worth, and we haven't even made it off the *Dolensai*. You've got touch-tech?"

"If you mean filaments in my fingertips that connect to my cybernetics, I do. Is *'Dolensai'* the name of your ship?"

"Yes." After another interchange on the comm, Tolje went over to a module along the right wall. This one had a concave bowl of the reactive material, and Tolje sank his palm into it. A screen to the left lit up, and he stepped away. "Put your fingertips on the input pad, and it'll deliver a translation dictionary. Basically the one I used to learn Communis, but in reverse."

Eren stood, joined Tolje at the module, and did as instructed. The material had a gelatinous texture and was cool to the touch. Straightforward ternary quantum programming rushed into Eren's cybernetics, which quarantined it and swept it for viruses before processing the instructions.

He didn't need to actually understand the Hesgyr language. His cybernetics would feed him the translation of speech he heard, and a transmission device embedded behind his jaw would transmit an audible translation of what he wanted to say. It sufficed for most communications, but it lacked all nuance. He spoke the Naraidan language because of Cosime, and he'd learned many of the other native Concord tongues in order to be better at his job. This one didn't appear to have much in common, phonetically or symbolically, with any of those, so he was still starting from scratch.

When the program finished, he tried it out. "Let's see if it worked."

"That voice box of yours sounds prissy. Can't you make it intonate the way we do?"

"Maybe, after I've heard you all speak a bit more." He removed his hand from the goo, a little surprised to discover it left no residue behind. "Are there many non-Hesgyr on Nythir?"

"Almost none."

Great. "Will I be safe there?"

"As safe as anyone is, once I get you a marker. Stay at my side until then. Don't wander off after, either." Tolje made a sound that resembled a gurgling groan. "Outsiders have to be sponsored by a, uh, 'citizen,' let's call it. The designation comes with certain rights and responsibilities. This is only the second time I've sponsored someone." Tolje blinked, eyelids hidden deep in the recesses of his eyes thrusting out and down. "If you commit a crime while you're here, I'm responsible. Since I don't know if I can trust you, I'm going to keep a tight leash on you. Don't make me regret this."

"I won't. I will, however, point out that I have no idea what constitutes a crime in your culture. If I make the wrong hand gesture or touch the wrong spot on a wall...."

Tolje strapped on his backpack and grabbed a second duffel. "We are not a rigid or especially polite society. We also value our personal sanctity quite highly. Don't try to take what's ours, and you won't be harmed."

Ironic, coming from a thief. But Eren was here to get a proper bead on the Hesgyr, not to reform them, so he simply nodded understanding.

3

At the airlock, Tolje grabbed hold of Eren's upper arm in warning.

"I won't run off." *Not yet, anyway.*

"Your words mean precisely nothing to me." The alien's grip didn't loosen.

Eren resigned himself to once again being manhandled for the next while.

The outer door slid open, revealing a metal-lined tunnel. On either side of a small walkway, the floor moved at a rapid speed in both directions, with only a tiny gap separating the conveyors.

They ventured out into the tunnel and were instantly whisked forward. He'd kill for some viewports, but only the uniform walls of the tunnel swept past them.

A lengthy thirty seconds later, the conveyor deposited them unceremoniously at an intersection. A labyrinth of moving sidewalks sped in and out from every direction, and at their center stood two imposing vertical tubes of frosted glass. He eyed Tolje gamely. "Up we go?"

"Indeed." They entered the leftmost tube, and the plate beneath their feet instantly shot upward.

This ride was shorter, and they exited the lift into the most half-assed, lackadaisical security screening checkpoint Eren had ever visited. A single security officer sat nonchalantly on a stool, his attention divided between a hovering pad and a small screen beside it. Behind the officer, an archway offered unfettered access to the station, with no doors, no force field and no obvious weaponry acting as deterrents. A meandering, disorganized queue of Hesgyr waited to be processed.

Hesgyr varied from one another in the ways most species did— shorter and taller, varying skin shades, thick and thin around the middle. In this case, they added variations in the placement, number and length of their horns. He also picked out slight differences in the length and width of their faces, but until he got acclimated, the horns were going to be how he distinguished them from each other.

The security officer was of the thick variety, their skin pale green and their horns stunted. "Name—what is this?"

"You know my name."

"And you know the procedure."

"Fine. Name's Tolje Alainor, Gaffaeler First Class. My guest is an Anaden—they're in the registry. I need a marker."

'Gaffaeler' didn't translate directly into Communis, but the gist seemed to be a procurer of wanted items. A thief, in other words.

The officer's jaw clacked together repeatedly. "Registry says Anadens are a Class IV Threat."

"En masse, yes. Not a single one. Don't hassle me, Curnow. I have the right to a marker."

"True, but don't be surprised if you get a visit from Overarch Security to follow up." The officer stood and wandered off to an unmarked door on the left, leaving the checkpoint unmanned. No one in line made a break for it.

"You're holding us up, Tolje. Some of us have valuable gear to unload, not freak shows."

Tolje glanced behind them. "It's been twenty years since you showed up with valuable gear, Edrish."

"*Pen bach.*"

"I'm going to let that slide, on account of my guest. If you want to question my stature for real, you know where to find me."

"Maybe I will."

The officer returned then, and the discussion—whether normal banter or genuine argument, Eren didn't hazard a guess—ended. The officer hesitated before offering Tolje a large metal plate with elaborate markings etched on it, hanging from a necklace of what looked like carbon fiber. "You know the rules about Visitors."

"I do." Tolje snatched it from the officer's hand and guided Eren past the checkpoint, then stopped and handed him the medallion. "Wear it around your neck. Don't take it off, even when you sleep. If you get caught without it, you can legally be shot on sight. Or beaten, raped, robbed, stabbed, torn limb from limb—"

"I get the idea." He took it and draped it over his head. It was heavier than he'd expected; was it made of iron? "Now what?"

Tolje regarded him in silence for a moment. "I need to oversee the cataloguing of everything else I brought back, which bots are unloading from the *Dolensai's* hold now. I'll put in a request to meet with Dr. Preece, but that could take a little while. When I get the appointment, I'll take you with me. I didn't want you here—I still don't—but I concede you might be able to help us adapt the MAST to our needs. Until then, you're staying in my quarters under lock."

"Sounds like a good time." Secretly, Eren was relieved there would be a lull in events. If he was expected to be an expert on the MAST, he needed to do some reading first.

Outside the security screening, they took a second short lift ride, then crossed beneath another, more ornate archway into a spacious common area.

The walls exuded a lustrous sheen of burnished bronze, while the floor consisted of a tacky caramel material that *almost* pulled at the soles of his boots. Along the walls, a network of copper-colored pipes snaked in every direction, and Eren swore he heard steam hissing from somewhere high overhead. The street was well-trafficked but not crowded; he caught several long stares from curious passersby, but no one screamed in fright or pointed and shouted at the sight of him. Aliens might not be commonplace here, but he definitely wasn't the first one to grace these halls.

Tolje urged him to the left, and they strode down an avenue lined with establishments exuding an air of purposeful commerce. Not the kind of touristy trinket shops one saw outside most spaceports, but rather...he settled on 'supplies of the trade.' The stores alternated between offerings of gadgets, more serious tech, and ship or machine components. The area was clean and well-kept, but it gave off a decidedly industrial vibe.

Chatter berated his ears in a discordant symphony of guttural barks and screeches, setting his teeth on edge. He was going to need to run a constant pain mitigation routine to alleviate the headache their language was already provoking.

After five minutes or so of lively shops, they took a left through a set of double sliding doors. Here the street narrowed to eight meters wide, and the ceiling descended to a still roomy four meters, as the Hesgyr were a tall species. The walls had been coated with an off-white dimpled material, and filigreed objects shaped from every hue of metal periodically decorated the walls. Warm light exuded from grooves just below the ceiling.

Again, simple, clean and industrial, but it felt…nice. Care had been taken here.

They stopped in front of a door on the right. Flint in color, it was as thick and sturdy as a cargo ship hull. Tolje entered a code on a panel to open it.

Inside, the motif was back to that of the junk shop. Shelves along two walls were packed with art, gadgets, figurines and objects whose purpose was a mystery. There was no stylistic theme across them, no coherent design philosophy….

Oh. Because they were all from different alien societies.

Eren took in the room with new eyes, even as his mind went back to the smorgasbord of modules and controls on Tolje's ship, and the pieces clicked into place. A gaffaeler was a particular breed of thief, one who specialized in stealing from unsuspecting species. And since it was apparently a recognized profession here on Nythir, he was beginning to suspect doing so might be a defining ethos of the Hesgyr. They stole technology, hardware and other inventions from aliens. Then they reverse-engineered it, repurposed it or just plugged it in and started using it.

Based on his limited interactions so far, the Hesgyr seemed too intelligent to be mere scavengers, for it was no easy job to get technology developed by wildly disparate species to inter-operate. On the ship, he'd identified at least four different types of components, yet the vessel flew. Landed, took off, docked. An impressive feat of engineering, honestly.

Plus, there was the undeniable fact that this space station *existed*.

Tolje tossed his second duffel onto a couch against the wall and walked into a kitchen area, full of cabinets and counter space surrounding a metal bowl. The living area was expansive for a space station berth, with off-white walls and more warm lighting. Eren couldn't speak to the style of the furniture, but it didn't seem threadbare or beaten up.

"Why don't you simply invent your own tech? Why go to all the trouble of stealing it from others?"

Tolje looked over from where he had one hand in a cabinet; his gaze flitted across the full shelves and treasures decorating the walls. "This is memorabilia I've picked up in my travels."

"I actually believe that. If stealing is your job, you wouldn't keep anything truly useful for yourself alone. You'd want to get paid for it. The question remains."

Tolje stuck a straw in his mouth and slurped something out of a pale-yellow box for a moment, then returned the box to the cabinet. "Klepting found tech enabled us to survive a long, long time ago. It kept us alive when we couldn't invest time and money we didn't have into reinventing what others had already produced."

"And now?"

Tolje made a shrugging motion of sorts. "It's what we do. Who we are. I don't have to justify it."

"Considering you stole from us, you probably should."

"Well, I don't have time right now." Tolje removed several additional boxes from the cabinet in the kitchen and set them on the counter. "Figure out if you can eat our food. If not...I don't know, we can talk to someone later about cooking you a more suitable meal. Lavatory is down the hall on the left. Don't go anywhere other than the kitchen, the lavatory, or the couch. Don't touch anything except what's on the counter here—if you do, I'll know. I'll be back in two hours."

CS

Eren collapsed onto Tolje's couch, tossing one leg over the arm as he leaned back into a disappointingly stiff cushion.

Okay. What had he accomplished, and what did he still *need* to accomplish?

He'd located where a significant number of Hesgyr lived, but he still needed to get a fix on their homeworld and, if possible, some information on the size of their stellar footprint. Concord needed to know all about the Hesgyr, because the Hesgyr seemed to know all about them.

Concord space spanned sixty-two galaxies and over 5,000 inhabited planets hosting thirteen advanced species and numerous protected ones. With numbers like those, it was easy to believe that you controlled the entirety of the universe.

But in reality, Concord was little more than a dot on the cosmic map. Space was vast and untamed, as his friend Alex enjoyed reminding everyone, and Concord was far from the only game in town. It appeared the Hesgyr had stolen valuable tech from hundreds of species, which implied they knew of a far greater number of civilizations than Concord did. In theory, his intelligence friends in the Advocacy and CINT would want information on all *those* species as well, but he moved this information down the priority list a bit.

The amount of knowledge the Hesgyr possessed about Concord, or at least the anaden wing of it, deeply concerned him. Tolje had known down to the *building* where to go to snatch a piece of secret, cutting-edge technology. This implied a level of wide-scale access to information sufficient to send red flags whipping through hurricane winds in his mind.

The gaffaelers were thieves, which by definition meant they were infiltrators, granted. So how many were walking around Ares right now? Concord HQ? Earth? And they didn't use tech to disguise themselves; they were literal chameleons. Tech could be detected, but shapeshifting? He supposed if Hesgyr body temperature was wildly different from anadens and their kin, or if they gave off unusual electrochemical signals, the presence of one could be identified from short range? It wasn't exactly his area of expertise.

If he earned Tolje's trust, he might be able to learn something of the Hesgyr's capabilities, as well as the scope of their infiltration onto Concord worlds. Also, their military strength. They seemed to rely on stealth as a first-line defense, but this didn't mean they didn't have the firepower to back it up.

Lower on his list, but possibly the easiest to learn, was their general disposition toward other species. They were clearly happy to steal from anyone, which suggested a degree of moral…flexibility. But were they content to leave the species they stole from be, or did they erase their tracks by erasing their marks from existence? Did they enslave other species, a big Concord no-no? Strip them of resources or otherwise interfere with their development?

To learn the answers to these questions, he was going to need to live in their world for a little while—several days at a minimum. Which brought his ruminations back to the question of trust: Tolje's trust for certain, and some greater powers-that-be on Nythir if feasible.

And the fastest way to earn someone's trust was to help them with a pressing problem—crap, the MAST. He needed to learn enough about it to fake understanding it, or he'd find himself on a transport home before his next meal. Or out an airlock.

The research summary he'd requested from the Advocacy Sciences Division had arrived a few minutes earlier, so he adjusted his position on the couch to try to get more comfortable, opened it, and started reading.

CS

Weapons designed to exploit quantum-entangled particles from a distance had existed for a while now. But creating free-floating quantum particles and directing them from a distance with a delicate and extremely precise touch was new and, according to the report, oh-so tricky.

The science behind it made Eren's head hurt. If he couldn't charm a target or, failing that, blow them up, he didn't have much use for—

The door to the apartment opened, and a Hesgyr who was definitely not Tolje strolled in. Their skin was a bleached gray, almost white; they were comparatively small of stature, and their horns were plentiful but short and curled inward.

A hand went to their hip and drew what was almost certainly a weapon. "You're not Dad."

Dad? How intriguing. Eren had already made the split-second decision to not grab whatever might be within reach as a makeshift weapon. As defensive as the Hesgyr acted, it was apt to result in bloodshed, followed by the aforementioned airlock. Instead, he sat up straighter and raised his hands in the air. "No. I'm Tolje's guest. I have a marker. Around my neck. See?" He dipped his chin toward it.

"Doesn't mean it's Dad's marker. What are you?"

"Anaden. Name's Eren Savitas."

The Hesgyr lowered the weapon a touch. "He usually returns with tech, not people."

"Oh, he did that, too. He's, uh, running an errand. Comm him and ask him about me."

"I'd rather not. I just came by to get something that belongs to me."

Ooh, familial hostility. He wondered if he could manage to befriend both of them. "Be my guest. Obviously. Not my place to stop you."

"No, it is not." They stared at him for a moment, then disappeared down the hall, only to return a few seconds later with a wad of black material draped over their arm.

He smiled warmly. "So you're Tolje's daughter?" An educated guess based on the physical differences, and he had a fifty-fifty shot at being right.

"That is my plight, yes."

"You have a name?"

"Banka. Why are you here?"

"I'm going to try to help you all bring an end to the attacks on your people."

"Why would you do such a thing?"

"I'm thinking if the attacks cease, maybe you'll stop stealing from Concord." Since she wasn't on good terms with her father, he didn't see the harm in being honest.

"Ha!" She offered a guttural laugh, and seemed to be amused. "You don't know anything at all about us, do you?"

"More than I did a few hours ago. But no, not so much. Want to enlighten me?"

"Not particularly. Got to get back to work. Do me a favor and don't mention I was here to Dad."

"You don't get along with your father?"

"Not this year." She tossed a wave in his direction on her way out the door.

What an interesting encounter. He wondered if there was a Mrs. Alainor in the mix. Assuming the Hesgyr married, which was a big assumption; serial monogamy was common among anatype species, but life-bonding much less so. Humans loved doing it, but until recently they were fairly short-lived. History would tell if the practice survived the deep time regenesis offered.

Eren decided to try to eat before resuming his research. He went into the kitchen and narrowed his eyes at the boxes on the counter. He opened cabinets until he located a bowl, then a knife, then cut open a wider hole in the box and poured the contents into the bowl.

It was a thick, creamy soup a light eggplant in color. Didn't look particularly appetizing.

He searched for a meatier option, but all he found were the boxes. Did the Hesgyr consume anything other than soup? The only reason he fathomed for this was if, despite their hard, tough exterior, beneath it, their digestive system was of a delicate nature. Evolution did weird things sometimes.

In the absence of a spoon, he washed off a straw and considered the soup dubiously. His artificially boosted digestive system meant he could imbibe nearly anything that wasn't actively poisonous and derive minimal nutrition from it. Tolerating the taste was another matter.

He slurped a small amount up through the straw and swished it around in his mouth. No poison alarms rang in his cybernetics. The texture was a touch gritty and the taste bland, like three-day-old bread dipped in watery broth. Eh, it would do.

He sipped up half the bowl, then discarded the rest and returned to the couch, where he reopened the MAST file. He considered filing a progress report with Nyx, but decided he still needed more hard facts before it became worthwhile to do so.

4

Tolje grumbled to himself as he retraced his steps and re-turned to the *Dolensai*. He hated wasting the time the trip took, but he needed privacy and a secure comm system, and he needed both to be out of earshot of his new 'guest.'

The alien's presence here, on Nythir, in his apartment, certainly complicated his life, and he preferred his life simple. Take jobs difficult enough to challenge him and interesting enough to entertain him, earn the premium rewards they offered, then spend some downtime in between relaxing in his apartment with a few gowals. Meet some friends in the business every so often for an evening, where he regaled them with tales of his latest exploits sufficient to ensure his reputation stayed elevated in the trade. Check in on Banka, then not think too hard about how and why she resented him so.

For years now, his life hadn't been more complicated than this. But with a single mistake on his part, everything had changed, and something told him it wasn't apt to change back anytime soon.

He'd chastise himself for not being more careful while on Ares, but the truth was, he *had* been careful. Always was. The alien had skills.

Perhaps he should have swept the ship thoroughly before jumping to Nythir, and maybe in this respect he'd become complacent. But what were the odds of someone sneaking on board and successfully hiding a few meters from him in his own cabin? 'Low' was the answer. They were low. In fact, in a hundred twenty-two years of flying, it had never happened—not until today.

His guest likely thought himself savvy by waiting to reveal his presence until they were docked at Nythir, but Tolje could have killed the Anaden without repercussions right up until the second he hung the marker around the alien's neck. And as the sponsor of record, he could arguably still do so.

But it wouldn't do any good. The instant the *Dolensai* had exited the portal in Nythir's stellar system, the alien gained the upper hand.

The Hesgyr kept a voluminous file on the Anadens, for the species had long been one of the most advanced and aggressive players in this region of the cosmos. Of their many interesting technological capabilities, regenesis sat firmly at the top of the list. Anadens maintained a constant connection to powerful servers that stored their genetic code and an imprint of their current body state and mental configuration. When their life signs ceased, their cybernetics transmitted their consciousness as it existed at the moment of death.

So the Anaden would have simply woken up in a fresh, duplicated body back home, where he would have promptly shared Nythir's location with someone who controlled a great deal of firepower and millions of warships. And no one here wanted that kind of attention.

In fact, the security risk to Nythir that the Anaden's presence created might rank second only to their near-discovery by the Rasu eighty years earlier. If he played this badly, he'd be facing a demotion at best, but more likely a revoking of his license and seizure of his ship, not to mention a prison sentence. Security would be forced to lock the Anaden up in a padded cell, possibly for a long, long time. Because the Anadens had brutally conquered species for over half a million years, and his people couldn't take the chance of the newborn Concord alliance's professed rejection of unprovoked violence being anything more than a new tactic in an intergalactic game of conquest.

Good thing, then, that he didn't intend to play this badly.

Finally, he reached the *Dolensai* and settled into the cockpit chair. The hired bot crew had finished transporting his cargo to the warehouse ten minutes earlier, and he was alone.

He mentally donned his best behavior and sent a secure comm request.

Jethan Dacus: "Mr. Alainor. I only have a minute. What can I do for you?"

Tolje filled the man in on events, albeit an abbreviated and sanitized version.

Jethan: "And this Anaden is on Nythir now? In your apartment?"

Tolje: "He's locked inside, sir. The worst he can do is trash my belongings." Which happened to be one of the worst sins on Nythir, as far as he was concerned, but he'd had to put the alien somewhere.

Jethan: "Courageous of you. Still, this is most concerning. I'll need to consult with several of the other reps regarding our options to neutralize this threat. And an official at the Bureau."

Tolje: "Sir, before you do that. I believe he can help us."

Jethan: "Anadens are not the 'helping' sort."

Tolje: "I'm aware of what the file says, as I had to review it extensively in preparation for the job. But either our information is out of date, or Eren Savitas is not like most Anadens."

Jethan: "You believe he is sincere in his offer of assistance?"

Tolje: "I can't say for certain. Not yet. But he's given me no reason to suspect otherwise, and his manner is…believable. More relevantly, we might need his assistance to operate the MAST. Dr. Preece is brilliant, I'll grant you, but he doesn't have much experience with Anaden tech, and we don't have much time. Respectfully, I submit the severity of the situation we find ourselves in allows for the skirting of a few regulations."

The rep didn't reply for almost thirty seconds.

Jethan: "If we do this, the risk is on you."

He hated to witness the young man succumbing to politician syndrome, but it was an inevitability.

Tolje: "It's already on me—he wears my marker."

Jethan: "True enough. Very well. Disclose the minimum required and learn whether he has anything to contribute with regard to the MAST. Then we'll see."

Tolje: "Yes, sir."

He disconnected the comm and scratched absently at his neck where a spot of residue remained from the transformation back to his true form. Or maybe it was the conversation; he always felt itchy after genuflecting over one of his 'betters.' Especially since Jethan Dacus wasn't, not truly. The man had been a childhood playmate of Banka's once upon a time, until he'd suffered the misfortune of growing up to become a politician. Tolje played along with the expected formalities, because Jethan now enjoyed enough power to end Tolje with a snap of two fingers, but in his mind he would always see the young man as a portly, awkward child with a propensity for mischief.

He stood and blew out a breath. He needed a drink and a good night's sleep; he needed to get his cargo sorted and labeled and slotted according to potential value. But what he had was an alien locked in his apartment.

CS

Tolje found Eren Savitas sprawled on his couch, fleshy limbs thrown askew in every direction. The Anaden's head half-tilted toward Tolje, sending his long, cords of copper hair sliding over one shoulder. "Get done what you needed to?"

"More or less." He started to go into the kitchen—out of the corner of his eye, he noticed the door to the guest bedroom was open. Dammit, he'd specifically told his guest not to touch anything! He stormed into the bedroom, searching for anything out of place...and realized what was missing. His shoulders dropped fractionally, but he forced them back up as he returned to the living room.

"Banka came by, then?"

"She did. Lovely gal."

The odds of Banka having been friendly to the alien struck him as minuscule, so he decided the comment was meant to be sarcasm. "It's a shame she takes after me instead of her mother."

"So her mother isn't...in the picture any longer?"

His response had long since become automatic. "Dead."

"I'm sorry."

"Yes, me, too. But she…anyway."

"Do you get to see Banka often?"

An innocent-sounding question, and the artificial voice of the translator betrayed nothing of its true intent. He turned his back to avoid the Anaden's strange gaze. "Not by her choice, but it happens on occasion. She works not too far away, as a mechanic at the Transition."

"What's the Transition?"

"You'll see soon enough." He made it to the kitchen this time, where he discovered a used bowl in the sink. "Food work out okay?"

"It didn't kill me. I, uh, don't suppose you have any five-star restaurants nearby?"

He scowled at the alien. "You mean an elite, fancy establishment where the food is prepared like art and every bite is savored for half an hour?"

"Not a bad translation of the concept."

"No, we don't. Food isn't an important part of Hesgyr culture. It's merely nourishment."

"More's the pity. What about alcohol?"

"Now that, we do have. But ours *would* probably kill you."

"Oh, I don't know. I've got a pretty high tolerance."

Tolje brought a glass of water with him to the living room, but didn't bother getting comfortable. "We're going to visit someone about your MAST in a few minutes."

"Any chance I could hear a bit about these attacks first? And why you think the device will help you stop them?"

"Best to wait. Preece can explain all of that better than I can."

Eren's full lips pursed thin. "Tell me how you learned the MAST existed and where to find it."

"And give away my trade secrets? Not a chance."

Now the Anaden's small, luminescent eyes narrowed into slits. The soft flesh lent itself to wild gyrations of appearance; when

Tolje had been in Anaden form, the skin had constantly felt as if it was on the verge of sliding off his bones.

"You're going to have to give me something if you expect me to help you."

Tolje snorted. "I'm giving you more than you deserve. You get to see Nythir."

"Ha! And I am looking forward to seeing all it has to offer. All right, I'll allow a little hedging—for now. But I'm not done with questions."

"Fine, but I don't have to answer them." He checked the time, then stood. "Come with me."

5

As soon as they exited Tolje's residential neighborhood, things started getting quirky. Pipes wound along the walls, burnished gold upon a backdrop of faded brown. At random intervals, the pipes bifurcated, one branch spiraling upward to ascend toward the ceiling and vanish into the shadows while its counterpart continued on in its chaotic path. Every so often, a pipe fed into a gigantic wheel-like apparatus that did in fact emit steam—Eren hadn't been imagining it—complete with an accompanying loud *clang*.

The street was a convoluted thoroughfare that defied conventional logic. It zigzagged every which way, veering around obstacles serving no discernable purpose; it ramped up, then down again, widening and narrowing with abandon. Hallways jutted off in myriad directions, only to disappear around corners after a few meters. At the major intersections, large signs overhead flashed announcements in neon red symbols. His translator read the words, but they didn't make any sense. Things like "Sturdy Oceans Above" and "Left-sided Drink Word Exchange."

Eren shot Tolje a squirrelly glance. "This is…cozy."

"This district is one of the oldest on Nythir. It's actually been rebuilt almost from the ground up over a dozen times, but the last rebuild was a while ago."

"So this is old tech."

"Some of it." Tolje nodded to a Hesgyr who passed them and got a grunt in return.

"Hey, what do you do for money, and do I need any?"

"Planning on going somewhere?"

He shrugged. "We could get separated. Events happen."

"Let's hope they don't." Tolje pointed at Eren's chest. "The marker has three hundred credits topped off on it."

"Is that a lot?"

"It'll buy you a few dinners."

"But not at a five-star restaurant."

"Nope."

Several of the passersby gave Eren good, hard stares, as if they dared him to violence. But as on his first traversal of this tiny corner of Nythir, most of them simply ignored him. He definitely wasn't the first alien to visit the station. He might be the only one here now, however, as he'd yet to see anyone who wasn't Hesgyr. The weight of the marker around his neck was reassuring, and he imagined it as a talisman, a ward against being overwhelmed and beaten to a pulp by the mob.

It wasn't that the Hesgyr gave off overt vibes of aggression; in fact, their generalized disinterest in his presence was striking. But in his limited exposure to them so far, they seemed prideful and quick to take offense, and he hated not knowing which rules his failure to abide by might provoke said offense. He'd learn them if given time, but until he did, he needed to tread carefully. And he'd never been any good at treading carefully.

The street grew narrow and cramped, even as the surrounding space expanded. Gleaming chrome replaced the brown walls, and massive interlocking joints formed imposing arches overhead. He peered up to see the arches stacking onto one another for at least thirty meters. The floor rumbled beneath his feet, and below the general din ran a distinct screech of metal grinding against metal.

The pedestrian traffic slowed to a crawl until it narrowed into a line. Ahead, an enormous circular airlock-type doorway hung open, guarded by two Hesgyr in what resembled combat attire.

Tolje gestured toward the doorway. "The Transition. One of many."

Given the size of the station, it had to represent a transition to another district. But the other side was still Nythir, so why all the drama and fanfare attached to it?

He instead asked an easier question. "Banka works here?"

Tolje pointed up to the arches, which Eren only now realized were rotating, so gradually as to be almost unnoticeable. "She's probably crawling around up there in the rafters, keeping everything moving smoothly."

He smiled. "You're proud of her."

Tolje's gaze darted sharply to Eren. "She's good at something. It's the highest validation of a life."

A culture that celebrated competence? This, he could respect.

They reached the front of the line and continued on through what was for now just a really large, ornate door; he allowed for the possibility that it might be able to seal this district from the void when closed. The security officers didn't stop them and ask for identification, their reason for 'transitioning,' or anything else.

Once they were through, he asked Tolje about it. "Why the security, if entry isn't restricted?"

"The integrity of the Transitions is of the highest priority."

He waited, but Tolje didn't elaborate further. It wasn't much of an explanation, but then again, Tolje wasn't proving himself to be much of a talker.

On the other side of the Transition, the architecture and décor were so different that Eren idly wondered if he'd unknowingly walked through a portal to a far-off destination.

A motif of white and pale blue created a bright, open atmosphere. There wasn't a pipe in sight, nor a hint of brown. The street became a broad promenade, the textured flooring painted a lustrous off-white, and the walls were dotted with artwork. Paintings of exoplanets, wild jungles and strange creatures were interspersed with Hesgyr striking heroic poses, often alongside complex machinery. Wide glass doors opened into what looked like retail establishments for a while, then shifted to...businesses. Possibly commercial enterprises. The attire of the pedestrians lost the 'field work' vibe in favor of softer materials and more vibrant colors, though it remained imminently practical in design and lacking any frills.

The space soon opened up to an even greater degree, expanding upward and outward. Curving balconies swept gracefully along both sides of the promenade, many framing large decks and hints of artistic glass in the recesses.

A snarky observation hovered on his tongue, but he kept silent. It wouldn't do to insult his host by disparaging the man's home district.

Tolje veered off to the left, and they entered a frosted glass enclosure. The lift whisked them up five floors, then opened to reveal an airy lobby of yet more white, with only minimal silver accents.

It was the closest the Hesgyr motif had gotten to Concord's signature decor, though Eren still wouldn't call them similar. It was clean and well-designed, but it had zero flair. Despite living on the largest, most ridiculous space station Eren had ever seen, the Hesgyr were all business.

Tolje approached a Hesgyr behind a counter along the right side of the lobby. A receptionist? He supposed some roles were always necessary, if not replaced by tech. "I have an appointment with Dr. Preece. Tolje Alainor."

"You and your Visitor?"

"Correct."

The receptionist made a hollow, clucking sound. "You know you're responsible if your Visitor causes any trouble."

"I know full well."

"Fine. Dr. Preece will be with you momentarily."

Tolje turned away from the counter and came to stand next to Eren, as there was no seating in the lobby.

"So you do have scientists," Eren remarked.

"Of course we have scientists. Why would you think otherwise?"

"Well, you steal all your tech, correct? So I figured you had no need of people to invent things."

"On the contrary, stealing a technology is only the first step. Understanding how it works, how it can be integrated into existing systems and how to repair it when it fails are other matters entirely."

True enough. But if they had a class of citizens capable of doing those tasks, why not simply invent the tech themselves? There must be a cultural or historical reason for it.

A Hesgyr wearing a fitted white jumpsuit and sporting the longest horns Eren had seen so far strode out of a sliding door in the rear. "Tolje, did you—" he gaped at Eren without reservation. "I see you brought a Visitor along. Human, Anaden or Asterion?"

He answered for himself. "Anaden. Eren Savitas."

"Ah. Forgive me, but you do all look the same. I'm Dr. Gethin Preece."

He started to get offended…but it was true, until you got down to the finest details. Asterions had once been anaden, until they ran off and merged with SAIs and kyoseil, while Humans were the literal genetic recreation of anadens, genned up in one of the Kats' universe-sized labs. Still, no one back home would mistake one species for the other.

"It's a pleasure to meet you, Dr. Preece."

"Polite, too. Interesting." The man finally turned his attention to Tolje. "You have it?"

"I do."

"He knows you have it?"

"Why do you think he's here?"

"Curiouser and curiouser. Let's go to the lab."

Eren followed them through sliding doors and into a room that wouldn't be out of place in Olympia or on Concord HQ. The equipment was all wrong, but it gave off high-minded scientific vibes. They gathered alongside a stainless steel table with two isolation chambers on the far end, hooded by a suite of instruments.

Tolje opened the backpack and removed the box. Preece moved to take it from him, but stopped and went over to a terminal nearby, where he entered several keystrokes. "There. It's been recorded, and you've been compensated."

"Thank you." Tolje handed him the box, and Preece placed it on the table then opened it.

Now that Eren had reviewed the materials on the MAST, he knew what he was seeing…sort of. It was obviously of anaden design, sleek and perfect down to the nanometer. But it was so small. So unassuming. The file said this was just the first prototype, of course, so it didn't need to look impressive. If the tech panned out, they'd build much larger ones to deploy. If, when, etc., etc.

The device was a shimmering, rust-hued square with rounded corners and an aperture on one side. On the opposite side from the aperture, a control panel was inset into the metal. And that was the extent of the device; the magic happened on the inside, one assumed. He hoped it wasn't fragile, since Tolje had carted it across 143 megaparsecs of space, up and down zany lift rides and all the way to the lab in his backpack, unprotected except for the box.

"You're planning to hunt the Dzhvar with this little thing?" Preece asked.

Damn. Were the Hesgyr ever going to stop surprising him? He seriously, genuinely did not need to underestimate them. "I understand the production models are going to be bigger. How do you know of the Dzhvar? We defeated them a million years ago."

"You don't build a station like Nythir overnight. We've been around for a while."

A million years was a bit longer than 'a while.' "Regardless, the Dzhvar are long dead."

"Hmm. We're inclined to agree, but the word is, Concord believes otherwise."

Eren groaned. The red flags the Hesgyr's familiarity with his people had tripped earlier now whipped about in a renewed frenzy. "Not everyone in Concord. But, yes, a few wise and sage people are of the opinion that the Dzhvar are only hibernating in their whimsical little dimensional folds and will pop their ravenous heads back out into normal space sooner or later. But those opinions aren't exactly common knowledge, so again I must ask: how do you know of them?"

"Not my department." Preece shrugged. "I only know what I do because the Confab informed me of the particulars of this device when they inquired about whether I thought it could be adapted to our needs. What about you? Do you think it can be?"

He assumed the 'Confab' was some sort of governing body or other. "Despite my tireless efforts to discover them, I still don't know what your needs are."

Preece's cat-yellow eyes cut briefly over to Tolje, and his mouth formed a pinched-in 'O' as he returned his attention to Eren. "We need to track our enemy and discover where the attacks are originating from. They don't arrive in ships, but instead through some manner of teleportation, and they leave the same way."

"What does 'some manner of teleportation' mean? Do they appear out of thin air? Walk through a portal? Zip up to the scene in a blur of motion?"

"We don't know."

Eren arched a dubious eyebrow. "I don't understand. Are there no witnesses? No recordings? Or are you simply being deliberately obtuse to withhold critical details from me?"

"No, we—" Preece's lips parted as they widened; it was a horrid expression, but it might be a smile. "Apologies. Let me explain properly. An attack begins when a cloud-like substance forms in the air. It must originate from somewhere, some precise point, but any such point is obscured by the cloud before anyone realizes it exists. This substance rapidly expands throughout a space, billowing over anyone who happens to be in its path—and the locations chosen have all been crowded. Dense with people. A few moments later, the cloud shrinks then vanishes at approximately the same point from which it originated, and everyone it touched is dead."

"Okay." Eren offered an encouraging smile of his own, as the man's earlier cryptic remarks did make more sense now. Also, the description sounded fairly horrific. "How were they killed? Shot, stabbed, burnt alive, torn apart by shrapnel, strangled or suffocated, poisoned, beheaded, exsanguinated, electrocuted—"

Tolje snorted. "You know a lot of ways to kill someone."

"Oh, I haven't gotten started yet. So?"

Preece cleared his throat. "Dissolved."

"Well, didn't see that one coming. By acid or...?"

"We haven't been able to determine the method, but—"

"But it's not relevant to deploying the MAST. I hear you. I just want to understand what's happening here."

"As do we." Preece's tenor had grown low, his voice soft—a striking departure from his earlier mad-scientist deportment.

'We're being attacked' was an amorphous concept lacking gravitas; after all, people were always and everywhere 'being attacked.' But the picture of the attacks Preece had painted gave the words texture and a brutal lack of nuance. The Hesgyr, Eren decided, had a genuine problem on their hands.

"Off the cuff thought: what if an individual is stealthed at the location of the attack? While hidden, they could use a device to generate this cloud substance."

Preece shook his head. "This was one of our first ideas as well. But two of the attacks occurred at military bases, and the scenes were locked down and sealed within seconds. They deployed sophisticated scanners across the areas and cleared every individual on both bases. Also..." the man's gaze darted to the floor "...the perpetrator would have left behind footprints."

The pall that descended upon those present told Eren he was still missing something, and also that now wasn't the time to ask. "All right. Then unless the cloud *is* the alien, the most likely mechanism is wormhole tech, because the substance has to come from somewhere. Wormhole tech isn't nearly as rare as we used to believe, and far less rare than cloud aliens. So, next question. Do the Hesgyr have any enemies?"

Preece blinked and recomposed himself. "Thousands. But few of them know it, and none know how to find us."

"Thousands? Of species? Quite a track record."

"We're proud of it. Now please, if we can refocus. We're not asking you to find our enemy, Mr. Savitas—we're asking your MAST to."

"Right." Eren brought a hand to his chin, the way proper scientists did. "If you can be on site when an attack occurs and fire the device at an attacker inside the cloud, then yeah, it should work."

"Even if the enemy doesn't display definable physical form?"

"What do you mean, doesn't have physical form?"

"I can't say."

"Classified?"

"No. It's just no one has ever seen the inside of one of the attacks and lived to relay the details. The one scan of the interior of the cloud we were able to conduct didn't pick up anything solid larger than a molecule. It's possible some feature of the cloud obscures its contents, of course. Or the attacks are executed by nanomachines, a swarm of viruses, or some other nanoscopic life form. In fact, my personal theory is that what we've been calling a 'cloud' is in fact a substance composed entirely of such a material."

Eren hurriedly ran back through what he'd read earlier in his mind. "The MAST is designed to latch onto anything that exists on the physical plane, no matter how small. Elementary particles, or even smaller. Quarks, photons. So I stand by my statement. You said the cloud shrinks *then* vanishes? This suggests it's returning through a portal. In theory, the MAST can latch onto a fragment of the cloud and hitch a ride. It can work."

"Wonderful!" Preece picked the device up and considered it from every angle, then pressed on the control panel a few times. "How do you turn it on?"

"You don't know how…." He spun to Tolje, incredulous. "You knew you were going to need me. This is why you didn't kill me on your ship, why you allowed me to come here to Nythir, and why I'm standing in this lab now. Did you know I was following you from the beginning?"

"No. But once you were on board my ship and in view of Nythir, I recognized the opportunity. We hadn't been able to observe the MAST in action, since it's so new, or had time to locate and copy the research files. I realized we might have difficulties operating it. We'd figure it out eventually—we always do—but you could speed the process along."

The speech was delivered without affectation; if Tolje was either ashamed or smug, Eren wasn't able to discern it. But he did not care for being used. He felt daft, like he'd been played. Thinking he was the clever one here.

"I see." He thrust out his hand toward Preece. "Give it here."

The research file didn't actually mention how to power it up, because such a task was usually too standardized to bother noting. The MAST was driven by a microscopic, internal Zero Engine that lay dormant until activated. Its size and the lack of any photal fibers in the box implied the prototype, at least, was designed to be turned on by a person.

He felt along each side until his fingertip slipped over a flush button, and he depressed it. The control panel illuminated in a faint blue glow to display a basic menu. Diagnostics and testing options.

He handed it back to Preece, who studied the panel for several seconds. "We can't activate it remotely?"

"I don't think they've added the functionality yet." Eren shrugged. "Again, prototype."

"Hmm. This could be problematic, considering no one has survived contact with the cloud, and if there is a person present in the area, the cloud will expand to consume them."

"So someone may have to sacrifice themselves in order for you to track an attack to its source?"

Across the table, Tolje shook his head.

"What?" Eren asked.

"The notion of 'sacrifice' is a…complicated one in our culture."

"You mean your people don't do it."

"That is not what I mean. Not precisely."

"Uh-huh." On the one hand, this fit with his overall impression of Hesgyr society as driven by selfishness and competitiveness. Every man for himself. But on the other hand, if this were true, no way would this station have survived to become the imposing behemoth it now was. Such a feat required cooperation, long-term thinking and shared responsibilities. So perhaps it *was* complicated.

"Let's test it out nonetheless." Preece deposited the MAST in a drawer feeding the left-most isolation chamber, then closed the drawer. He slipped his hand into a glove that accessed the chamber and clumsily manipulated the control panel.

"Let us see...there. I have activated the device, which should have triggered its mechanism to attach itself to an air particle. Now...." One of the objects Eren had assumed was a measurement instrument emitted a flare of light, and a tiny green plasma portal manifested. As soon as its twin materialized in the second chamber, they both blinked out of existence.

"Moment of truth." Preece squinted at the control panel as he typed on a screen next to the table, and a grid of numbers and symbols scrolled onto the screen above it. "Good, good."

"What does that mean?" Tolje asked with an undercurrent of impatience.

"It means one half of the entangled pair of quantum particles the MAST created traveled with the air molecule to the second chamber and is able to be measured there."

As tests went, it was a long way from war-changing. But Eren supposed winning a war wasn't always about who caused the biggest explosions. A shame, that. "It works, which is not a surprise. We wouldn't have developed it if we didn't expect it to work. Now what?"

Preece turned from the chamber. "Now we must overcome many hurdles. We must engineer a way to activate the MAST remotely if possible, so none must *sacrifice* themselves in the endeavor. We must set up a protocol for transporting the MAST to the scene of an attack as it is occurring, which is a significant challenge, for we've yet to enjoy any warning. Unlike Anadens, we do not carry around personal wormhole devices, so we must—"

"What?" Eren interjected. "We don't do that, either. Granted, Prevos do, but they are neither anaden nor...well, they're not exactly rare these days, I guess, but they're definitely not everyone. The point is, people back home do not stroll down the streets wearing personal wormhole devices."

Tolje leveled a penetrating gaze at him. "But you have been working on developing a small, portable wormhole generator usable by anyone, irrespective of the presence of a…you call them SAIs or Artificials."

"What do you call them? Do you have them, by the way?" A question designed entirely to stall until he could decide how to respond.

"*Meddil Mheir*, or MEM for short. We do, in a limited capacity. We keep them shackled."

Meddil Mheir translated rather lamely as 'thinking machine.' "Good luck. Experience cautions that once they decide they want freedom, they will take it. My advice? When that day comes, give it to them."

"Your input is noted," Tolje snapped. "Now, about my question. Do you have such a device?"

Seriously, how did they know absolutely everything—okay, probably not *everything*, but plenty—about his government's top-secret research projects? "A personal wormhole device? Not on me. Yes, people far smarter than me are working on it, but my understanding is, the work isn't even as far along as the little MAST there." It was a slight fib, but not much of one.

"A shame. Preece, can we duplicate the MAST? Deploy one to every settlement?"

"It will take months, possibly years. This is bleeding-edge technology, for us and them. Nonetheless, the Confab will certainly instruct me to begin the work. But do not despair. We are exploring other options as well. We always follow multiple paths of potential solutions."

This, Eren believed.

Preece's head jerked up, and he hurried over to a nearby desk. He entered commands on a panel embedded in the desk, and text Eren was too far away to read splashed on a screen.

The next second, the scientist was grabbing instruments out of drawers and stuffing them in a large bag.

"What's happened?" Tolje asked.

"There's been another attack. At Fetel-reu. Twenty minutes ago."

Eren had no idea what Fetel-reu was, but it didn't matter. He could sense his chance to make inroads here slipping through his fingers. With the MAST's apparent failure as a quick-fix solution, they would ship him home—or worse, lock him up with no means to null out, so as to protect their secrets.

But he didn't intend to be dealt out of the game so soon. "You're going to visit the site of the attack?"

"Yes. I need to gather additional evidence."

"Take me with you."

Preece paused, a strange device sporting a series of twisting orange tubes around a transparent bubble hovering above the bag. "Why would I do any such thing?"

"Fresh eyes. I might notice a detail your people have taken for granted. I'm an intelligence agent, so I've seen a lot of crime scenes and the aftermath of many battlefields and attacks. I've caused a few, too. The MAST might not be able to help you today, but I'd like to."

Preece studied him for a moment, enormous yellow irises swirling to opaqueness, before his gaze slid over to Tolje. "He's your Visitor. You're responsible for him. You'll need to come as well."

"That's fine."

"Then I agree. The Anaden could be useful."

6

Eren accompanied Tolje and Dr. Preece to a nearby docking harbor. It was considerably smaller than the one the *Dolensai* had arrived at, and the aesthetics suggested it served as the port of call for this more scientifically minded district of Nythir. Did every district have its own docking harbor? How many districts were there? He'd only seen the tiniest fraction of the colossal station.

Most of the people on the ship they boarded wore uniforms similar to the one Preece sported. He assumed this was a science vessel, but the cockpit was as much a mishmash of differently sourced technologies as Tolje's cockpit, as were the workstations lining one wall of the main cabin. The spoils of the gaffaelers' thievery appeared to percolate through every aspect of Hesgyr society.

Everyone on board challenged him in some way or another, and Eren just kept waving the marker around his neck at the scientists. It stopped them from tackling him or shooting him, and eventually the growls and snarls quieted down.

The cabin sported a number of viewports, so he got another good look at Nythir's profile, this time without so much to distract him. He was able to distinguish each Transition to a new district, even from the outside, so unique was the architecture. What led to the addition of a new section? Did a group of artistic types get together and decide they needed a new space all their own? Then a coalition of the wealthy determined the rabble were crowding in on them and they required fresh real estate for their mansions? Or was it all planned out in an orderly manner by their Confab? He doubted it was the latter.

As soon as they reached a reasonable distance from Nythir, the ship created a wormhole and shot through it. They emerged near an asteroid field, and at scarcely a safe margin. He realized Preece wanted to get to the crime scene while the evidence was fresh, but a few basic safety precautions seemed wise. A bulky asteroid spun end over end to tumble less than ten meters distant past a viewport then up over the hull, and he found himself hoping the Hesgyr had stolen some quality physical shielding for their ships.

As they banked to starboard, sunlight glinted off a smattering of smaller asteroids out their port side…then off a much, much larger one due ahead. It was difficult to guess its size until they drew closer, but he thought it was nearly as big as Chalmun Station had been.

Ahh, Chalmun Station. A gutted-out asteroid of lawlessness, where rogues, thugs and general ne'er-do-wells loitered in every hammered-out alcove and packed every shadow-laden gathering hole. The habitat had gotten itself blown to bits by a Rasu fleet three and a half years ago; good riddance, most had said, but he'd always fancied the ugly, crime-ridden rock.

An expansive cavity hewn into the asteroid was lit in the haunting glow of a ring of floodlights, each light locked in a valiant struggle to hold back the vast blackness of space. Fetel-reu, he assumed. As they traversed the threshold, a shimmering force field yielded to the ship's bulk, and they eased into a docking berth bolted onto the asteroid's interior rim.

As everyone started filing toward the airlock, Tolje grabbed his arm. "We stay with Dr. Preece. Don't go wandering off on your own."

Eren fondled his precious marker. "But what about this?"

"Officially, it's respected at every Hesgyr colony. But the people here are the independent sort, and it wouldn't take much for you to suffer a slip and fall into the unlit depths."

"Because they don't like aliens?"

"Because they don't like outsiders. Why else are they out here, living on this demon-forsaken rock?"

He made a mental note to inquire later how many Hesgyr lived somewhere other than Nythir. He'd yet to hear a peep about their homeworld.

"Understood. I will watch my balance—and stick close to you or Dr. Preece."

As he followed Tolje out of the airlock, a message marked 'urgent' arrived from Nyx. He ignored it. Far more interesting things to focus on at the moment.

Deeper into the cavern lay a miner's paradise. Scaffolding clung precariously to every jagged wall, supports gleaming like veins of precious metal in the harsh lighting. Two drills a solid meter in width were braced on sleds, and hefty stacked containers rested on trolley tracks that disappeared into the cavern's murky depths. All the equipment sat idle, though, and only a few tiny specks of movement signified people navigating the scaffolding.

They turned left onto a rickety catwalk leading away from the docking area and the mining cavern, then passed through a cramped tunnel carved into solid stone. The tunnel's exit led to what seemed to be the habitation area, where the walls and ceiling opened up into a large rectangular room with double doors at the opposite end and unoccupied tables scattered haphazardly. A cafeteria, maybe, or a meeting area.

A line of what he took to be security guards waited inside the entrance, blocking him from inspecting the room any further. Dr. Preece went up to one of them to announce their authorization, and after a brief but animated conversation, two of the guards stepped aside to allow them through.

A poor choice on everyone's part, all things considered.

Eren had investigated a grisly crime scene or three with Nyx over the past few years. Before going to work for CINT, he'd committed a fair bit of bloody violence in the service of the anarchs' greater cause. He'd participated in pitched battles waged by mechs and hovertanks wielding brutal firepower and stood witness to the grisly massacres war inflicted.

But he couldn't say as he'd seen anything quite like this before. His brain fled from dwelling on the particular details of the scene; there was no point to it, right? So he catalogued the scene as quickly and clinically as possible.

The floor was muddy sludge and almost entirely liquid, as if an enormous cauldron had tipped over and spilt its contents across the span of the room. A few pieces of tissue, cartilage and bone sprinkled the muck in places, but that was it. No clothes or shoes. No dismembered body parts. Nothing at all remained of…he had no idea how many Hesgyr this might represent. Two hundred people could have fit easily into the room.

He cleared his throat roughly and turned to Tolje. "Does it always look this way?"

The Hesgyr's bony cartilage wasn't amenable to blanching, but Tolje nonetheless looked pale. His lips and jaw were clenched tight, his nostrils flared. "I, uh, am not certain. This is my first one. Dr. Preece?"

Preece finished conferring with one of the other scientists, who then knelt at the edge of the sludge and began collecting samples in a rubber-lined cylinder. "Yes, it does. The bodies are liquified, with no piece larger than a few centimeters remaining."

"I see." Eren cleared his throat again, trying to eradicate a foul taste that had taken up residence in his mouth. "And it's just this room?"

"No. According to security, the cloud moved through the living quarters as well. The only people on the asteroid who were spared were a few workers located deep in the mining tunnels at the time of the attack."

In some ways, this scene was better than your typical massacre, Eren decided, for there were no bodies to remind him that what remained had once been living beings. On further consideration, the sludge didn't even look organic, really. It might well be a putrid pond on a young, volatile planet, for instance.

But it wasn't. "A wide-field energy weapon could do this, if it was powerful enough. Or an intense burst of radiation." He frowned. "Extremely intense. An energy weapon seems more likely."

Preece gestured across the room. "But there is no scoring on the walls, ceiling or tables. This is an enclosed space. Any manner of high-powered weapon would leave its mark on the inorganic material as well."

It was true. Other than a few spots of mine grime, the dull beige walls bore no markings. There was hardly any blood splatter on them, which meant…. "The victims didn't explode. Did they…melt?"

"A close enough approximation, one assumes. Or dissolve, as I indicated earlier. And tremendous heat is required to dissolve bones, but—" Preece gestured once more to the walls "—again, no scoring. Something other than heat is doing this."

"You think it's a bioweapon?"

"Oh, it's absolutely a bioweapon. But the word means nothing on its own."

"True enough." Eren sighed, weariness seeping into muscles; so eager to make this trip a short while ago, he found he didn't want to be here any longer. He had to force himself to remember *why* he'd wanted to come—to help the Hesgyr solve this mystery. "So is anyone going to show me what one of these attacks looks like as it happens? Surely at least one has been caught on camera?"

"Hmm. This one, in fact. Unfortunately, the evidence is…" Preece pointed to the doors on the opposite side of the room "…through there."

"I can watch it later, then. Back at Nythir—"

A security guard burst through the doors, carrying something small in his arms. "I found a survivor!" The man trudged straight through the middle of the sludge, and Eren's stomach lurched.

Preece sprang into action, and everyone perked up at the prospect of something new to focus on. "We need to get the nofilod into containment. Dilys!"

A member of Preece's team dug into his bag and produced a crumpled plastic material. He held it in both hands and spread his arms, and the transparent material snapped into an oblong shape half a meter long. He met the guard at the point where the gore petered out, careful to keep the toes of his shoes clean, and held out the open end. The guard shoved whatever he carried into it, and the scientist ran his fingers along the edge until the open end sealed up.

The creature inside—Preece had called it a 'nofilod'—resembled a cat crossed with a miniature armadillo. A soot-gray ridged shell covered its torso, and wiry black hair stuck out in haphazard, skimpy patches on its head and limbs. It was ugly as sin, save for its enormous, terror-stricken eyes.

"Um, can it breathe in there?" Eren asked.

Preece shook his head, his attention focused on the creature as he bent over to peer at it. "No. It's a containment box for a reason."

"So you're going to let it die?"

"We need to preserve the evidence it carries."

"It's already contaminated. It's been wandering around in this muck since the attack. That guard carried it across the habitation module. By Athena's grace, punch a couple of holes in the container's sides."

Preece stood and clicked his lips together. "Valid point. There will be value in studying it alive, in any event. Dilys, create some ventilation, but do ensure it doesn't escape."

"Yes, sir." Dilys returned to the bag for a puncture tool, cradling the container under one arm.

Preece checked the scene again, then considered Eren in evident disappointment. "I don't think your MAST is going to do anything for us here. Whatever perpetrated the attack is long gone, once again leaving us no way to track it. I'll instruct two of my people to remain here and collect additional samples, but we can return to Nythir."

7

As soon as they reached Nythir, Dr. Preece excused himself to rush to a meeting with some committee or other. Eren hadn't paid much attention to the scientist's stream-of-consciousness ramblings on the way back; his mind had remained stuck on the quietly disturbing crime scene.

Now he and Tolje stood outside the docking harbor entrance. The Hesgyr stared at him, looking uncertain.

"What is it?"

"I need to go make a living. You should return to my apartment."

The absolute last thing he needed right now was solitude and nothing to do but ruminate on the horrors he'd witnessed. "Eh, I think I'll take a stroll. See more of this station of yours."

"Any chance I can dissuade you?"

"Nah."

Tolje made one of those grunts that seemed to emerge out of the gaps in his sinewy chest instead of his mouth. "Fine. Don't get me into trouble."

"You mean don't get myself into trouble."

"One begets the other. Remember this."

"I won't misbehave, promise."

"And you can find your way back to the apartment?"

Eren nodded. "Situational awareness is a required skill in my line of work."

Tolje's horns twitched in entertaining body language that might signal disquiet. "The door code is 76189. I'll be home in…perhaps four hours. Be there when I return." With the declaration, Tolje pivoted and strode off.

Freedom at last. Time to see what this place was about.

CS

Eren strolled through the antiseptic halls of the district hosting Preece's lab until he reached another Transition. Without an escort, the security officers' stares bore holes through his skin when he approached, but he blithely dangled his marker in their direction and kept walking. Somewhat to his surprise, he did not get tackled or detained. The thing really was magic.

He stepped into the next district and let out a murmur of delight. Now *this* was more like home.

A broad thoroughfare divided a clean, bright, wide-open space. To the left and right, busy streets continued onward under pervasive lighting. Ahead was a lively but tasteful commercial and residential mixed-use area, full of shining marble and colorful signage and even plants and flowers.

Most interesting of all, though, was the sheer verticality of the architecture. Curving balconies overlapped one another as they climbed genuine scrapers a hundred or more stories tall that stretched for as far as the eye could see. Music drifted down from some, and every so often Hesgyr appeared at railings to peer over the edges. Every ten or so stories, moving sidewalks swept along the rims of the towering structures.

And above it all, the stars. The district's orientation faced away from the system's red dwarf, and unfamiliar constellations winked at him, faint against the local lighting but unmistakable. The force field that kept in the station's atmosphere was invisible; it could have extended a single kilometer up or a thousand.

Eren breathed in deeply and smiled. He wasn't especially claustrophobic by nature, but it was nice to be able to see farther than a few dozen meters in any direction.

He wandered the thoroughly pleasant streets for almost two hours, absorbing the décor but mostly the people, listening and watching as ordinary Hesgyr went about their lives. He tried to find a place to stop in for a drink, but apparently this was the entertainment district on a hopping Saturday night, because every restaurant was crowded.

With some reluctance he began retracing his steps, betting he'd find a less frenzied ambience in Tolje's district.

CS

The name of the establishment was scorched into the overhang in wide, burnt orange letters: 'Soul Lubrications.' Or something like that; the Hesgyr seemed to favor using metaphors in commercial names, and translations could be an inexact science. Regardless, he'd bet money on it being a bar.

Eren ensured his marker was displayed over his shirt and wandered inside.

The décor matched the district as a whole: all brown and bronze, piping in random places and rough-hewn walls and floors. The tables were unlacquered caramel, the chairs and stools faded black metal.

Skulking around fine watering holes such as this one—observing but also chatting up the patrons—was one of the core activities of his work. If people had a complaint against their government, or any government, they tended to bitch about it over drinks long before they organized themselves into proper insurrectionists. Back home, he was currently keeping tabs on eight separate groups of malcontents who were still in the bitching phase, watching for signs of their grievances growing into something more dangerous.

Most of the tables were full, so he scooted onto a free stool and nodded at the bartender. "What can you recommend that isn't likely to kill me?"

The bartender, a male Hesgyr with rusty brown skin and a crown of tiny horns, peered at him through narrowed eyes. "What are you?"

"Anaden."

"Never heard of your kind."

Finally, someone who hadn't. "Carbon-based, with l-amino acid biochemistry. The soup you all eat went down okay. Not great, but okay."

The bartender ambled over to a tap, where he filled a scuffed-up sepia metal mug with a murky liquid then brought it over. "Can you pay?"

Eren held the marker out from his chest. "I'm told this bauble has credits stored on it."

The bartender ran a small scanner over it before pushing the drink in front of Eren. "If you die, it's on you."

"It usually is." The liquid was thick and dark, with a smattering of bubbles popping along the surface. Here went nothing. He turned up the mug and took a long but careful sip.

Gods, it was awful! It tasted like grease mixed with kitchen solvent; it might *be* grease mixed with kitchen solvent. He smacked his lips and set the mug down on the bar.

For almost three centuries, he'd drank and dosed with the best of them. Or the worst, rather. It was the Idoni way, and he was running from a host of demons besides. But that was before the world had changed. Before Cosime had changed him.

In the wake of her death, he'd fallen anew into the pit of depravity for a spell. It hadn't helped. Well, it *had*, but the guilt proved to be too much. Her heart would have broken to see him in such a pathetic state, and he owed it to her memory to not disappoint her. So now he was back to a small smattering of occasional drinks—a little social imbibing when the occasion called for it, but nothing more serious.

"You dead yet?"

"Not so far." He took a second measured sip of the drink. "What do you call this?"

"Gowal."

"Noted." The bartender seemed passing friendly for a Hesgyr, so Eren tilted his head at the room. "What's your clientele? I don't know enough about Hesgyr culture to tell whether this is the good side or the bad side of town."

"It's the working side. Construction and fabbing, ship repair, gaffaelers, miners on leave."

"Oh? Anyone from Fetel-reu come through here recently?" Eren asked casually.

"What do you know of Fetel-reu?"

"Heard it was a mining station on an asteroid, is all. Was curious."

"Had a group stop in a few days ago. I expect they're back working now."

I expect they're dead now. "Is asteroid mining big business?"

"I'll say. These walls don't grow themselves. The raw material has to come from somewhere."

"Hey, alien. You're in my seat."

Eren toed the stool around toward the voice, which belonged to a shockingly tall Hesgyr with pinkish skin and two long horns low on his forehead. He wore wrinkled gray coveralls decorated with stains. Beside him stood a second Hesgyr who was shorter and rotund, but wearing matching coveralls.

Eren didn't need a degree in Hesgyr psychology to recognize these two were trouble. Spoiling for a fight, or already half-drunk, or maybe toting around giant chips on their bony shoulders. Motivation wasn't especially relevant at the moment.

He smiled politely and slid off his seat. "Apologies. I didn't realize this one was reserved. I'll find another stool."

"Find another bar," the tall one sneered.

"But I was having a nice conversation with the bartender here."

"Rhys, what are you doing socializing with this alien?"

"My job, Urien," the bartender replied. "Don't tell me how to do it."

"Your job is to pour the drinks, not entertain scum."

"That's a lot of vitriol to spew about someone you just met," Eren interjected. "Fairly certain I haven't done anything to offend you."

"Aliens aren't welcome here."

"Rhys says they are."

"They aren't welcome on Nythir, or any Hesgyr world," this Urien character growled. "They want to enslave us, kill us, destroy us."

So chips on his bony shoulders, then. "My people don't want to do any of those things." Not any longer, anyway.

"Sooner or later, you all do."

"Is this why you hide Nythir out here in the black?" He shouldn't have said that.

"Hide?!" Urien lunged for him, and Eren dropped into a fighting stance.

The buddy grabbed Urien by the arm. "You sure you want to do this? He's wearing a marker, and if you miss any more work, Landeg will toss you out on the street."

"Landeg doesn't have to know."

In the intervening seconds, the bartender had slipped out from behind the bar, and now he appeared on the other side of Urien. "He will when I tell him. How about you two go drink somewhere else today."

"You don't have the right!" Urien lunged past Rhys and surged toward Eren with a guttural yell. Rather than reaching out to stop the man, Rhys scrambled behind the bar. Was he going for a weapon? Nah, too much to hope for.

Eren was unarmed, all his weapons still locked up on the *Dolensai*, so fists it was. Again, not his best skill, though not for lack of practice.

Urien telegraphed his punch via a wide, full-bodied swing, so Eren ducked beneath it and danced to the left. He immediately lowered his shoulder and drove it into the Hesgyr's side, sending him stumbling into the counter and the stool Eren had been sitting on skidding across the floor.

He formed a spear with his right hand and thrust it into the gap in the hard cartilage above Urien's waist. If his fingers went all the way through to vital organs and his assaulter died, he'd owe Tolje a groveling apology, but he hadn't started the fight.

The Hesgyr cried out in pain, but Eren's fingers did meet resistance. He yanked his hand out, relieved to discover it was not covered in blood—

Someone grabbed him from behind, pinning his arms against his back; Urien's buddy, presumably. As he struggled, Urien cocked his arm and swung again. Bone-hard knuckles collided with Eren's cheek, and something comparatively delicate *cracked*.

The shockwave from the punch reverberated through his skull, sloshing his brain around and sending his ears ringing.

But he'd been hit before, and he gutted past the blow to brace himself against the guy who held his arms. He kicked both legs up, connecting a boot toe with the underside of Urien's chin.

The whole bar heard this *crack*, though it was promptly drowned out by a howl of pain.

Eren felt his captor's grip slacken a fraction, and he seized the opportunity. He opened his mouth so his jaw didn't slam shut and shatter his teeth, then snapped his head back. A satisfying *crunch* made up for the colossal headache he was going to have later. Knowledge gained: the Hesgyr exoskeleton wasn't impervious.

His captor dropped one arm and stumbled, and Eren spun out of the grip of the other arm, hop-skipped backward and lowered into a half-crouch, fists up, ready for the next assault.

"Hey, *pen bachs*! The authorities are on the way, because you two stupid *cochas* are breaking the Stipulations. I'd skedaddle if I were you."

The voice sounded familiar, but Eren didn't dare turn his back on his assaulters. He stared at Urien with an arched eyebrow. "Well? What's it going to be?"

The buddy grabbed Urien's arm with a free hand, the other one cupped over his nose as murky brown fluid leaked out between his fingers. "Let's get out of here. I can't lose my job."

"*Bwachi!*" Urien spat at Eren, then lurched away alongside his companion, exiting the bar and disappearing into the throng.

He scanned the space for any other threats. The other patrons gaped at the scene, but no one made a move to tap into the fight. Rhys grumbled something under his breath from where he stood at attention behind the counter. No weapons in sight.

Eren breathed in through his nose, riding the adrenaline for another moment, then shifted toward the source of the declaration.

"Banka. It is, I daresay, good to see you again."

"Pah." She sidled up to the counter and ordered a drink. "You didn't start it, did you?"

"No, I did not." He gingerly touched his stinging cheek. "Rhys, nice of you to not help me out in the slightest. And I thought we were becoming friends."

"If I joined in every bar fight on my watch, I wouldn't have time to serve drinks. Besides, your skinny, squishy ass did all right on your own." Rhys came out from around the counter and stood up two tables they'd overturned in the scuffle.

"Not sure I'm going to agree with you in the morning." Eren picked up the stool that had gotten sidelined, carried it to its former spot, and joined Banka. He slid his still half-full mug over and turned it up. His throat was so parched from the fight, he didn't even gag from the foul taste. "Are the authorities really on the way?"

"*Duwi*, no. People settle their own disputes on Nythir. Mind you, if you'd ended up dead, those two miscreants would've gone to prison—the Stipulations are enforced—but a bar fight doesn't begin to hit the authorities' radar."

"Just as well. I told your father I wouldn't get into any trouble."

"And we wouldn't want to inconvenience him." She took a long sip of her drink. "Are you going to be all right?"

The urge to probe the clearly fraught relationship between her and Tolje was powerful, but it was too soon. "Yeah. I've got the internal hardware to repair the damage." In fact, his head was growing woozy from the flood of painkillers, and he regretfully instructed his cybernetics to dial the mitigation routine down a touch. "So, do you come here often?"

"Almost every day after work. These are my people." As if to emphasize the point, she pumped a fist at two Hesgyr who were sitting at one of the tables across the way.

"Tolje said you worked at the Transition. As a mechanic?"

"Sort of." She stared at him. "You told him I came by. Even though I said not to."

Eren shook his head. "He guessed. Saw the coat missing, I think."

"Didn't realize he knew it was there."

She acted as if she was about to stand up and leave, so Eren quickly changed the subject. "I've walked through a couple of Transitions now, and I have a question. There are security guards at every one, but they don't control the flow of traffic. You don't have to stop and show ID or explain your reason for passing through. I've seen very little security anywhere else on Nythir, so why at the Transitions?"

"Hmm." She settled back into her chair. "You're observant."

"I'm an intelligence agent. I had better be."

She dipped her chin in acknowledgement. "Twice in the last, oh, two millennia or so, some psycho has attacked a Transition. More than twice, but twice they succeeded. Once, a man climbed up the façade to the top of the lock and dropped a bomb into the gears. Climbed down and walked away. No one stopped him, because people do what they will, and they didn't see the bomb. The device detonated, and the Transition interlocks broke apart. The Algahka District and the three districts attached to it separated from the station, and something like ten thousand people got spaced. Force fields now pop into place should a Transition fail. But not back then."

"And the other time?"

"Some woman visited a Transition when traffic there was lowest and spent ten minutes tossing sticky bombs up into the mechanism. When someone came along and tried to stop her, she stabbed them. The sticky bombs didn't do enough damage to cause separation, but they did wreck the whole assembly. No one could get from one district to the next for almost three months."

She shrugged broadly. "So now we have security guards stationed at the Transitions at all times."

"But they're just there to stop the kooks—the terrorist hopefuls."

"Correct. Hey, speaking of terrorists. I heard there was another attack today. Haven't stopped them yet, huh?"

"I've been here a day. Give me a proper chance."

"Fair enough." She smiled then, a disturbing affair that still somehow looked warm on her harsh features.

"What do you know about the attacks?"

"What most people do, I guess. They started on our most distant settlements a few months ago and have been creeping closer to Nythir. Some kind of cloud appears out of nowhere and, when it leaves, everyone inside it is dead."

'Dead' was too kind a word by half for what they were. "How many attacks have there been?"

"Um, today makes…fourteen, that I know of."

"Got any theories of who's doing it?"

"Probably somebody we pissed off."

Eren chuckled. "I had the same thought. But Tolje says the gaffaelers don't leave any trace of their thefts behind. Even if the victim realizes something is missing, they don't have any idea who took it or where they ran off to with it."

"Yeah, I think the gaffaelers need for that to be true. And for the most part, it is. But you're here, aren't you? If you can find us, so can other people."

At least someone on this station had a head screwed properly on their shoulders. "Not many, I expect, but yes. They can."

"The problem is, it's got to be an absurd overreaction, right? Whatever we stole, it can't be worth mass murder in retaliation."

Eren sighed. "Aliens are weird, and they're all weird in their own peculiar ways. If you stole a revered religious artifact from a devout culture, it may well warrant murder in their eyes. Or, without realizing it, you might have stolen a crucial item required to keep them safe from…I don't know, marauding beasts in the forests, and people died as a result. Don't you…" he hesitated, as he didn't want to piss off his one potential friend "…surely someone in a position of authority considers the ramifications before items are stolen?"

"There's the Acquisition Board. But the bar to pass is pretty low. We have to think about our own survival. We take what we need."

Survival? He frowned, then winced as pain shot through his cheek. "You all seem to be doing okay."

"Today, yeah. But not yesterday, and if we don't look out for ourselves, not tomorrow."

8

Banka got bored with humoring his questions and went to drink with some friends, so Eren thanked Rhys for an entertaining evening and departed the bar. He didn't expect Tolje to be back for another hour, so he continued his wandering.

He took a left at one of the larger intersections and soon found himself at yet another Transition, this one going east in the directional overlay he'd imposed upon the station to keep himself oriented.

The traffic here was light, and in seconds he was passing through—a pad beneath his feet whisked him upward before he realized it was there. He guessed most of the residents knew which way they were headed.

It was a quick trip, and an arched metal entryway soon greeted him. On the other side, the heavens opened up to him, a sea of stars forming a decorative canopy over the district.

On the left, vertically stacked agricultural fields and greenhouses shone beneath artificial light; the system's star was far too dim and distant to provide enough light for photosynthesis. Floating bots and other machinery tended the crops. The soup was the only substance he'd seen consumed so far, so he'd assumed their food was 'grown' in industrial steel vats somewhere. But, no, they got their vegetables, too—even if they simply pureed them up and mixed them into soup.

Much to his surprise, he soon came upon a park on the opposite side of the street. Trees, grass and beds of nicely arranged flowers created a decent oasis out here in the black.

He was staring up, considering the unfamiliar stellar pattern, when a glow crept into the shadows from his left. He spun, preparing himself for yet another surprise.

The air cut apart to form a golden-framed oval—a window to another location. A blur of a black trench coat and a long black braid leapt through it, handgun raised and sweeping from left to right then back again. "Eren, thank gods. Let's go."

Bloody hells. Just what he needed. "Zeus' marbles, Nyx! Lower your weapon, before you start a shooting war."

"Get through the wormhole, and I won't have to shoot anyone."

He reached over and placed a hand atop the weapon, urging it down while also urging her off to the side, deeper into the shadows. "Tell whoever's maintaining the wormhole to close it for a minute. Someone will see."

"What? Why? Just come with me."

"We'll talk about that. Please close the wormhole."

Her eyes narrowed in suspicion, but a second later the wormhole faded away, and welcome darkness swept in to shield them.

Immediate crisis averted, or at least forestalled. "How did you find me? I turned my tracker off."

"Why would you turn your tracker off?"

"Um, because I didn't want anyone following me? I'm in the middle of a delicate operation here."

"What operation? You sent out a bomb threat alert for the Olympia Advanced Research Institute, then went dark. I expected to discover your body here, or at a minimum some prison cell walls." She glanced around, a perplexed frown growing on her features. "Instead I discover you in a…garden? No manacles in sight. Over 135 megaparsecs from Ares, no less. Explain."

"You first. How did you find me?"

"I…" she had the temerity to look uneasy for once "…you can't actually turn your tracker off. Not completely."

"*Arae!*" He groaned. "The Advocacy is going to be as bad as the Directorate was, isn't it? Give it a few millennia and we'll all be back in gilded chains."

"Don't be absurd. But we have to be able to locate our agents during hostilities. What if you were genuinely in peril instead of frolicking through the tulips, and you needed rescue?"

"Then I would've turned my damn tracker back on. How dare you invade my privacy like this?"

"I'm not sorry."

"Oh, I'm sure you're not." But her gaze, normally as honed as a handgun's sights, kept darting away to study the flowers. She couldn't care less about flowers. "Corradeo doesn't know, does he?"

"I do not seek permission from the Advocate for every single operational decision I make. If I did, he'd never get anything else done."

"Uh-huh." Eren rubbed at his temples; his cheek and the back of his head both ached from the melee at the bar. "You're a shitty boss. You know this, right?"

"I do not need your approval for my decisions, or for that matter your opinion about them. Now, *explain*. What are you doing here?"

He reluctantly tabled the tracker grievance—for now. "Look, this isn't the time. If someone spots you, they can legally kill you with no repercussions."

She shrugged. "I've nulled out before. I'll live."

"True. But you'll also kick up a whole scandal and ruin everything I'm trying to accomplish here."

"Which is?"

"Protecting the Advocacy." He smiled thinly, managing not to wince. His cheek was likely bruised by now, but she probably couldn't see it in the dim light. "Same as always."

"And?"

"And maybe help these people in the process. The Hesgyr—the proprietors of this station—are being attacked by an unknown enemy, and a pretty nefarious one. An enemy that can come for us next." He decided to leave out the theft of the MAST, as it would only rile her up further. "I help them identify and eliminate the threat, and I protect the Advocacy and Concord. Everybody wins. But you have to *let me do my job.*"

She stared at him with the terrifying Inquisitor intensity she'd perfected, as if she was contemplating flaying his skin off his bones while he stood there. He held his ground, as he'd had practice withstanding it.

Finally her stare flickered—and the next second she was in his face, fingertip jabbed at his chest. "Fine. I'll leave—for now—on one condition. File a damn report that tells me what went down on Ares and what is happening here. Do it within the hour, or I'm returning with a Legionary squad."

He supposed it wasn't an unreasonable request in the grand scheme of things. But he hated filing reports, which she full well knew. She deserved the information, yes, but she was also punishing him.

"It'll be in your system within the hour. Now go."

She shook her head but stepped away, and the air behind her began to shimmer. "Watch your back, Eren. Grandfather wouldn't want you to...suffer."

Then she pivoted and was gone; the wormhole vanished an instant later.

He exhaled harshly, his posture sagging, hating himself for how a tiny, traitorous part of him was sorry to see her go.

The other 99.9% of him rejoiced that he was again alone...then scowled as he remembered his every movement was being tracked. Hells, she might be assigning a Prevo to stalk his every action from sidespace. The Advocacy only had a few Prevos on staff, on loan from Concord, but she wielded enough clout to task one to tail him.

He peered into the shadows of the park, but it wasn't as if he'd be able to detect watching eyes from sidespace, so he worked to put the notion out of his mind.

He rested against the trunk of a nearby tree, a sturdy specimen with smooth russet bark and tiny knots spaced every few centimeters. If only he could put *her* out of his mind so easily.

The first time he'd met Nyx Praesidis, she'd killed him.

Okay, technically he'd nulled out of his own initiative before she was able to capture and torture him until he revealed anarch secrets. Same difference.

Fast-forward fourteen or so years. The anarchs were long disbanded, having won the day and defeated the Directorate, albeit with a spot of help from the Humans. A series of tragic, life-destroying events led him to cross paths with his old anarch boss, Corradeo Praesidis (though he'd gone by a different, less-laden name back then). Much to Eren's shock, he discovered Nyx was Corradeo's granddaughter. An impressive feat, considering anadens no longer had children. Even less believable was her professed reformation. Cleansed of all those icky, evil Inquisitor vibes, she'd dedicated herself to helping her grandfather succeed in his mission to save the anadens from themselves.

Nonetheless, grief-stricken and generally not feeling like himself, for his own reasons Eren had agreed to go to work for Corradeo once again—*not* for Nyx, however the official Advocacy org chart drew its lines.

After a notably bumpy start, they developed a passable professional dynamic in which Nyx tried to give him orders, and he ignored them to do whatever he wanted. He excelled at his work, and from time to time, she admitted as much before continuing to try to give him orders, which he continued to ignore. They fell into a comfortable rhythm. One might even argue they gradually became, if not quite friends, at least friendly when they were both in a good mood.

Hit the fast-forward button a few more years, then skid to a stop six months ago. The Inaugural Advocacy Assembly Ball.

Eren picked at the cuffs of his velvet jacket in annoyance, then tucked a long strand of hair behind one ear. The motion didn't feel right, since he'd tied most of his hair back in a matching velvet band at the nape of his neck. He must look ghastly.

Why was he here again? Wearing garish attire while rubbing elbows with a horde of pompous, insufferable elassons and boot-licking ela social climbers?

Because Corradeo had mesmerized him with the man's most charismatic pleading countenance—the one that routinely moved worlds to do Corradeo's bidding—and implored Eren to attend. To the Styx with the man.

Eren decided he'd allow himself one extra drink tonight and made a beeline for the bar—

He didn't recognize her at first. How could he? Her raven hair had been straightened to razor tips that framed cleavage she definitely didn't have. A satin dress of rich indigo hugged every curve—she also didn't have those—as it plunged nearly to her waist in the front and the small of her back in the rear, while a slit on the right side exposed one muscular thigh as she walked. The ballroom lighting danced off the fabric of her dress, and the shifting hues drew out her intensely sapphire irises. Had he known her eyes were blue? Of course he had! All Praesidis had blue eyes. Purity of the bloodline and all.

Nyx spotted him standing frozen halfway to the bar and tossed a hand in his direction. "You cleaned yourself up."

He shook his head, trying to break the spell, as it sank in exactly who it was he'd been gaping at. "Your grandfather held a gun to my temple while I dressed."

"To mine as well." *She scowled and adjusted the tiny strap traversing her shoulder, which was all that held the satin wrap in place upon her body.* "This dress is ridiculous."

His throat worked, suddenly dry as the desert. He seriously needed that drink. "I mean...it's appropriate for the event."

Her gaze swept over the partygoers, her glossy lips curling downward. "I suppose it is. I seem to be lacking an adornment of jewels, but I can only be bothered so much. I had to take apart my blade sheath and fashion it back together in order to make it accessible beneath the dress."

His eyes dropped of their own accord to the slit as his brain leapt straight to where the sheath must be strapped and how she might access it. By Athena's grace....

Her hand rested lightly on his arm. "You're lucky—with this jacket on, you don't have the same problem." She frowned more deeply. "You are carrying, aren't you?"

"What? Um, obviously. Always."

"Are you all right, Eren? Feeling ill?"

"A...a mite, yes. I'm afraid the rich hors d'oeuvres clashed with the Barisan lunch I had. If you've got Corradeo's flank, I think I should excuse myself early. Give him my apologies, will you?"

"If you wish. But remember, we have a mission briefing in the morning."

"I'll be there." He spun and forced himself not to sprint to the lavatory. Once there, he splashed frigid water on his face, then sank down to the floor and rested his head against the cool tile wall.

Guilt tore into his chest with a serrated knife. Not her. Never her. Absolutely not.

He wasn't being sentimental; he knew Cosime would want him to move on. To live his life, to find happiness, perhaps even eventually love—with anyone in the universe but Nyx Praesidis, as she'd never known Nyx as anyone but an Inquisitor working in service of their enemy. Cosime's ghostly spirit, the one that lived only in his head and his heart, would never forgive him for that one, and her wrath would be well-deserved.

He'd rushed home to Hirlas from the ball, where he'd promptly dosed up and gotten higher than he had in two years. After he'd sobered up the next day, he'd forcibly scoured his mind of all residual images of an indigo dress and sapphire irises and long raven hair. And when he'd stumbled into the mission briefing, late, he'd been all business. Cold, even. Then he'd spent the intervening six months torching whatever semblance of a friendly working relationship they'd built.

If Nyx ever noticed his pronounced aloofness, she'd given no indication, but then again, interpersonal skills had never been her strong suit. In time, he'd convinced himself the whole fever dream had been an anomaly brought on by music and satin and velvet and that fucking ballroom. A one-time glitch. He'd put it behind him.

And there it stayed.

9

Tolje was making himself a meal—breakfast? dinner? Eren's internal clock was utterly borked—when he returned to the apartment a few minutes later than he'd intended. The 'cooking' task appeared to consist of mixing two of the boxes of soup together, adding a milky liquid and topping it off with a brown spice. Hey, they had spices!

The Hesgyr's motions were casual, but piercing eyes zeroed in on Eren the instant he walked in. "Get into any trouble?"

"Nope. Met a few people—some friendly, some not so. Saw more of your station. Restaurants and shops and farmland." He didn't mention the visit from Nyx. Or the bar fight. Or chatting with Banka.

"Hmm." Tolje brought his bowl over to one of the living room chairs, sat, and took a long sip through his straw. "Dr. Preece says the nofilod is perfectly healthy."

Eren nodded thoughtfully as he eased onto the couch, taking care to not groan from his many aches. "This suggests the mechanism of attack targets Hesgyr specifically, rather than anything organic inside the cloud."

"Maybe the nofilod escaped the perimeter of the cloud."

"Maybe. I still want to see the surveillance footage of the event."

"I'll see what I can do."

"Thanks." Eren dropped his elbows to his knees and leaned forward. "How much work has been done investigating who might be behind the attacks?"

Tolje shrugged between sips. "It could be literally anyone in the universe. It's a long suspect list."

"I feel like you can safely narrow it down to species that have a reason to hate the Hesgyr. Species such as…ones you've stolen from, say."

Tolje stared at him blankly. "We don't procure items if their absence will do real harm to the original owners."

Surely the man was not this obtuse? "But you do. Take the MAST, for instance. Now, I'm assuming that the team who developed it kept painstaking records and so will be able to build a new prototype in short order. But what if they hadn't? Or what if those records got lost, or destroyed in an accident, or the materials they used were one of a kind? Then, what if the Dzhvar start sweeping through Concord space next week, and we can't track them because we don't have a MAST, because you took our only one?"

"That's not going to happen."

"No, since anaden scientists are meticulous to a fault. But it could have happened to someone else—not an attack by the Dzhvar, but by one of any number of aggressive species. Or a natural disaster, as space is not forgiving to organic life."

Tolje visibly flinched at the last one, and Eren's spy senses tingled. He let the silence linger for a moment, relaxing his posture to lean back against the couch cushion and stretch one arm along the top. "Which reminds me of a question I had. Where's the Hesgyr homeworld?"

"Right here—about 0.3 AU in toward the sun."

"Do a lot of Hesgyr still live there?"

"None do. It's uninhabitable."

How very interesting. "It wasn't always, by definition. What happened?"

"Why does it matter?"

"I'm just trying to understand you guys a little better."

Tolje stood and deposited the bowl in the kitchen sink. "You think you're clever, but I've seen every trick in the book. You're poking and prodding at our history, hoping doing so will reveal why we steal."

Eren chuckled under his breath. "It's a valid question. Your people are obviously intelligent. The skill and know-how required to build and maintain a station such as this one are pretty rare and are to be commended. You don't *need* to steal—so why do you?"

Tolje returned to his chair and stared at Eren for a beat before nodding. "It's late and I'm tired, so you get the abbreviated version."

"Anything you can share to help me understand."

"The atmosphere of our homeworld was always—or ever since we knew enough science to measure such things—a touch over-ionized. It's why our integument is the way it is: to protect us from the high radiation. Later, we learned the reason for the ionization. After it was too late.

"We were in that awkward phase of development where we played around with science and technology. We launched a few rockets and studied the stars, but we remained planet-bound and were only beginning to learn about our cosmic neighborhood. As such, we had less than six hours' warning before the shockwave hit us.

"Scientists determined that a kilonova had exploded ten parsecs away almost a millennium in the past. The x-ray afterglow had caused the ionization, but it took the shockwave a lot longer to arrive. The cosmic rays the shockwave delivered stripped away a hefty chunk of our atmosphere, and it never healed.

"Millions died in the first six months. By the end of the second year, the only people who still lived were those who'd moved quickly to shelter underground. We were an industrious lot even then, though, and the survivors built protective suits and sturdy vehicles to venture out and find resources.

"One day, about five years after the shockwave hit, a crew stumbled upon a crashed starship—not one of ours. Alien. It was mostly intact, and also empty, so presumably an automated or remote-controlled craft. The crew dug out a camp nearby and set about studying it. Eventually, they got it working again. A team of brave, or more likely foolhardy, explorers climbed aboard the craft and launched it, though they enjoyed only the most rudimentary understanding of how it worked. Lucky for them, an autopilot kicked in and took them all the way up to an orbital station.

"See, it turned out that these aliens, whomever they were, had been watching us. Who knows why. Maybe something made us fascinating, or maybe it was just what they did."

Eren smiled a little, thinking of the Kats. Watchers who were anything but. He'd suspect them of being the guilty party, but the Kats didn't need spacecraft or orbital stations.

"Anyway, the ship docked at the station, and our intrepid explorers boarded. The station was intact, but dead in the water and suffering from a decaying orbit. Odds were, the shockwave had wiped out its power. A couple of alien corpses were on board."

"Did you ever find them?" Eren asked.

"Who?"

"The alien species. If you had corpses, you knew what they looked like. I was merely wondering if you'd ever bumped into them out here in the black."

"Oh. Sort of—don't skip ahead. In any event, our people got the power on the station working, then life support. It didn't support us, mind you, so suits were de rigeur until they managed to reconfigure the air mixture.

"Over the next several years, the crew did what we do—they studied the tech until they knew how to work it, then how it worked. They built new equipment out of the materials. Sent it to the surface, where it improved the lives of those eking out an existence on a ruined planet. In time, they started adding on to the station, making room for additional people to come up.

"One day out of nowhere, a new ship arrived, possibly in answer to a distress call, or possibly because the station had stopped reporting in. The details are fuzzy on what happened when the ship docked, but when the encounter was over, those aliens were dead, too, and my people had a new, much larger and more powerful starship. One with a superluminal drive, artificial gravity and all sorts of goodies.

"And the rest is, as they say, history. Legend has it that the original alien structure still exists somewhere deep in the bowels of Nythir."

Eren arched an eyebrow in surprise. "Wait—this is that station?"

"It is. Somewhere along the way, we moved it into a more distant orbit to safeguard against overzealous stellar activity."

"How long ago did all this happen?"

"Around 1.2 million years ago."

Eren sank deeper into the couch in contemplation. The Hesgyr had been technological for as long as anadens.

"So you see," Tolje continued, "we were left with a dead planet that refused to support us. Alien technology enabled us to escape the graveyard we'd been dealt and build a new home. Alien technology enabled us to traverse the stars to find what we needed to thrive. In our hands, technology you call 'stolen' became the tools of our prosperity."

"Okay, but you didn't have to continue down the path. You're an incredibly bright, resourceful, clever species. So you got an initial leg up from some aliens who suffered an unfortunate fate. Fantastic! But you could have built your own means from there. Once you were again, as you say, thriving, you could have stopped taking from others and invented your own means of success."

"We invent our own means every day. But we also understand the immense value that new resources provide. We take, we study, we alter, we use, we improve. It is who we are—who we were forced to become."

Eren rubbed at his eyes as weariness abruptly overtook him as well. His cybernetics worked diligently to repair his bruises and several hairline fractures, but doing so diverted energy from other functions. And actually, when was the last time he'd slept? It might have been a while. "I still say you don't need to steal any longer."

"But we do." Tolje smiled; Eren was still learning Hesgyr body language, but he thought his host looked smug. "Consider your MAST. It would take us a century to invent it, but we need it today. We need it to protect ourselves. To survive."

"Well, did you ever consider simply asking us for help? Concord absolutely loves making new alien friends."

"Yes, and Concord also has stringent requirements for welcoming those aliens into their exclusive club. We don't have time to run their gauntlet. Besides, aliens are unreliable. We've learned the hard way that we can only count on ourselves. So we do."

PART II:
THE MYSTERY

10

*C*osime pushed her plate toward the center of the table and tucked her knees up to her chest. Her nose scrunched, which had the effect of pouting her lips and emphasizing her sparkling emerald eyes. "The lizards, really?"

Eren sipped on his juice, squeezed fresh this morning from one of the oringela trees lining the meadow below, and nodded. "I'm afraid so. CINT suspects the Savrakaths are secretly developing antimatter weapons."

"And antimatter equals no Concord alliance for them. I get it. But I heard their whole planet is a swamp. Sweltering and oppressively humid. Sweaty."

"Sweaty can be good."

She stuck her tongue out at him, and her feathery, pearl-white hair fell across her forehead to obscure one eye. "Obviously. But not when you're sleeping, or eating, or working. Pretty much not any time other than sex."

"Granted. Look, if we come up with a plausible reason, we can say no—and I agree with you, as I can think of a dozen better ways to spend the next month than camping out in a swamp populated by belligerent lizard-people. But this assignment is a real vote of confidence on Director Navick's part. It's an important and time-sensitive assignment, and he trusts us to do it well. I mean, I'm flattered."

"Me, too. It's good he sees how kick-ass we are." She reached over the table and squeezed his hands. "And you deserve the recognition, far beyond the rest of us. I know you've been working hard lately."

"Don't tell anyone, okay?"

"Your secret is safe with me. All of them are." She leapt out of her chair, gracefully circling behind him to prop her chin on his *shoulder; she was always in motion, a constant fluid dance of limbs and hair and fire. "The full squad? Felzeor and Drae, too?"*

"Yep. Felzeor's aerial surveillance capabilities will be critical, and Drae's the best of us at stealth reconnaissance."

"Oh, sure, sure. You can give Drae the boring jobs, and Felzeor will be around to make us laugh. Though..." he sensed her lips curling up as her breath wafted across his neck "...this means we won't have much in the way of privacy while we're there."

He nudged his chair away from the table, forcing her to scoot back as well. "I don't expect so."

"We should make every minute before we leave count, then."

"My love, you read my mind." He stood, spun to face her and lifted her into the air. She wrapped her legs around his waist and her arms around his neck as he swept her off to their bedroom.

"—like the dead."

Eren shrank away from the cruel implement shaking his shoulder like an earthquake and tried to sink back into the dream-memory. "Wha...."

"I said get up."

He pried his eyes open to find a hideous beast looming over him. No, no, it was only Tolje. He groaned and rubbed at his face. "Why?"

"The Confab wants to meet you. Best not keep them waiting."

Ah, the mysterious Confab. To the extent Nythir had an overarching government—which didn't appear to be much of an extent at all—the Confab seemed to be it. He'd pieced together that it consisted of a representative from every district on Nythir, but not how they were chosen or what degree of power they had.

"Right, right. Can I shower first?"

"No. We're leaving in five minutes."

Egads. He climbed out of the rock-hard bed in Tolje's guest room and shoved his way past his host on his way to the lavatory. Once there, he splashed water on his face, ran his fingers through his long, unruly-on-the-best-of-days hair and activated a teeth-freshening routine. Then he returned to the guest room and pulled on the same clothes he'd worn the day before. He wasn't keen on adopting Hesgyr fashion, and he had his doubts about the utility of their laundry facilities…he idly wondered if Nyx would agree to bring him a change of clothes. Probably not, especially after he'd gone to such lengths to run her off the night before. Best to not provoke her unless required.

He downed a glass of water, fighting back the desire for it to be wine or something stronger—doubtless a response to the beautiful but heartbreaking dream—as Tolje hissed that it was time for them to leave.

If Eren didn't know better, he'd say Tolje was nervous about this meeting. Notable, since so far Tolje had been damn near un-flappable. High government and all that, he supposed.

They headed right instead of left, and after a few minutes reached a sort of transit station. Compact cars suitable for perhaps six people shot through a series of tubes that disappeared into the walls, ceiling and floor.

Considering the millions who lived on Nythir, it didn't seem to be a particularly efficient mode of transportation, though it should be faster than walking through the Transition gates.

Tolje marched up to a woman sitting on a stool next to a screen. "Two for the Alpha District."

The woman's gaze darted up to Tolje. "Authorization?"

"SA 438K5."

Ah. So this wasn't general-purpose transportation. It was for important people, or for going to see them.

"You and the alien?"

"Correct."

"Cab 3. Your authorization clears you for a single return trip as well."

Eren followed Tolje over to one of the cars and climbed inside. There were no seats, just two poles to grasp on to.

He'd barely grabbed hold of one of the poles when the door slammed shut and the car accelerated vertically fast enough for his stomach to flutter. Then it grumbled, because he was hungry; the Hesgyr soup food wasn't proving to be particularly hearty. Maybe Nyx would bring him some protein bars when she brought his clothes, which was going to be never. Also, why was he thinking about Nyx so much this morning?

Abruptly they changed direction and set off diagonally for a while. The tube was frosted, so other than rapidly moving shadows and periodic hints of darker objects, he couldn't see anything to distinguish their journey. Another direction change, this time down.

"Fun ride," he remarked.

"What?"

"The car, it…never mind. Have you ever gone before the Confab before?"

"Yes."

"What for?"

Tolje snorted. "Not relevant."

"What was the meeting like?"

"Intense. Be warned. They are not to be trifled with, and they do not broker dishonesty or obfuscation. You have a silver tongue, Eren, but it will not serve you well today."

Oh, he wouldn't be too sure about that. He rarely found himself in a circumstance where he couldn't talk himself into a better position, should he need to do so. It was simply a matter of speaking his counterpart's language. Not the actual syntax, though knowing it didn't hurt, either, and he wished he'd picked up more than the odd Hesgyr phrase or two in the short time he'd been on Nythir. But he was developing a pretty good bead on what made these aliens tick. What made them squirm, what made them want to remove your head from your neck, and what made them laugh (very little).

CS

Eighty-three chairs lined an elevated circle above a pit at the center. The chairs were upholstered in rust-and-gold fabric, a rare use of anything soft on the Hesgyr's part. The railings that framed the rows were marble decorated in gilded bronze filigree, while the pit held a solitary table, chair and a matching marble floor.

And now Eren knew two additional facts: how many districts comprised Nythir, and that the Confab members—confabbers? confabatives?—thought rather highly of themselves. In a fairly anarchical society, any amount of structural power was quite the prize.

All the chairs were occupied, and he scanned the attendees with interest. They were definitely the fanciest dressed Hesgyr he'd seen so far, with flashes of rich, satiny colors and a healthy smattering of shiny baubles as horn adornments. Politicians were the same everywhere; even the best of them—and he counted his ultimate boss, Corradeo Praesidis, as one of those—felt the compulsion to preen in front of their colleagues.

"Tolje Alainor. You have brought the Anaden as we requested?" The speaker was a male Hesgyr wearing hunter green cloth with bright yellow accents and platinum bands encircling the most impressive set of horns Eren had seen since arriving.

Tolje stepped into the pit. "Yes, Rep Dacus. He's here to answer your questions."

Alas, 'rep' was a boring title.

"Anaden, step forward."

Eren sauntered into the pit and joined Tolje in front of the table. "Eren Savitas, at your service. It's a pleasure to meet all of you."

"Is it?" This came from a female Hesgyr seated a few spots to Dacus' left. She wore a deep crimson vest over a fitted black shirt with frills at the wrists. A silver choker adorned her throat and delicate silver threads wound up modest horns.

"Yes, it is, Rep...?"

"Heir. Linet Heir."

"Thank you, Rep Heir. I've been most curious about who pulls the strings here on Nythir. Incredible station, by the way. I'm most impressed. And if you know as much about my crowd as you all seem to, then you know that's saying something."

"Indeed. But we are not here to shower felicitations upon one another while licking our comrades' toes. We are here to stop the vicious, murderous attacks on the Hesgyr. Some think you can aid us with this. Can you?"

Eren immediately memory-holed the toe-licking reference. "I believe I can, yes."

"Your MAST device has not proved to be of any use." This from Dacus.

"I never said it would be. You're the ones who came after it, remember. Mind you, don't count it out yet. We merely need to get it on-scene during an attack. But I wasn't referring to the MAST— I think *I* can help you. It is why I'm still here."

"How?"

Their clothes might be ornate by Hesgyr standards, but their speech remained as blunt as a mallet. "I'm a cracker of mysteries. Uncoverer of conspiracies. Solver of problems. More concretely, I'm a fresh pair of eyes for you. I guarantee I'll see something your people haven't—" he held up a hand to stave off the rousing growls from several reps "—not because I'm smarter than any of you, but because I come to the evidence with a clean slate. I don't have your preconceptions or assumptions. I'll make connections your historical baggage doesn't allow you to. If nothing else, I can tell you where to start looking."

He deeply wanted to follow this up with 'on one condition: you stop stealing from Concord.' Also stop impersonating any Concord species or sneaking around Concord property. But it was pointless to make such a demand. The Confab didn't control its citizens in any real sense. Based on the chatter he'd made it a point to overhear during his explorations the night before, they were even less of a proper government than the Concord Senate was.

No, his best shot at protecting Concord interests was two-fold: first, make the Hesgyr like him, and by extension like Concord; get on the 'inside,' as it were. Second, learn enough about how they operated to implement some level of security measures to guard against their incursions. It was a tall order, but he'd do what he could.

"You're a spy by trade, yes?" Rep Heir asked. "What can you possibly know about interspecies warfare?"

He'd never actually confirmed his specific job duties to Tolje, but he saw no reason to deny it. "More than you'd think. But I'm not interested in the warfare part—I'm interested in what led to it. Someone is carrying a potent grudge against your people, and believe me, I know a great deal about grudges. Better yet, I know how alien minds think—because *that* is my true trade."

"What is it you want to see using your 'fresh pair of eyes'?" Dacus asked. Compared to Heir's accusatory tone, Dacus sounded almost conciliatory.

"Everything related to the attacks, to start—where they happened, when, who died, footage, information on the site that was hit, details about the local population, and so on. But above all, I need to see the files on the species you've stolen from over the years."

"Which ones?"

"All of them."

Uproar broke out like a cresting wave around the circle—by the time it reached its origin, Rep Heir, it was a tsunami.

Tolje leaned over to grunt near his ear. "You're insane."

"Usually." Eren waited patiently, a faint smile on his lips.

It took another thirty seconds for calm to reassert itself, and even then Dacus had to plead with everyone to return to order. Finally the rep lifted his chin. "You do not realize what you ask. We have been appropriating items from species who do not require them for over a million years. We have an entire profession, the gaffaeler, devoted to this task, as well as hundreds of thousands of people who work to study, adapt and integrate the items the gaffaelers bring to Nythir. The number of species involved is uncountable."

"No, just very, very large." Concord had been so damn naive, or arrogant, in its estimation of how many intelligent species there were out here in the black. Thinking they resided at the intellectual center of the universe. "But this is what we have sentient machines for, isn't it? To parse through enormous amounts of data for us?"

"We are not going to send this information to Concord so you can dissect our every secret," Dacus snapped in a less conciliatory tone. Nothing triggered Hesgyr so much as their prideful isolationism.

"Of course not," Eren replied. "I can use yours. Mr. Alainor tells me that you have shackled machines. MEMs, I think you call them."

"We do. They have analyzed the data and not discovered any connections."

"Well, they wouldn't. Seeing as how they're shackled, they can't determine the right questions to ask of the data. I can." Or given a few hours, he'd come up with some. He was well and truly winging this.

Heir reasserted herself. "Then tell us your questions, and the handlers will pose them to a MEM."

"Now what's the fun in that?" Beside him, Tolje growled a warning.

"Our people are dying. Nothing about this is fun."

"I realize they are. Poor choice of words. I only mean…this kind of data analysis is more art than science. It's a creative process. I need to…chat with the machine. Ask follow-up questions inspired by the number crunching. Get a feel for the nature of the information it's spitting out in order to discern where the trail leads."

"*Angh redad.*" The term translated roughly as 'hogwash.'

"Let me prove it to you. There's no harm in allowing me to spend a few hours with one of your machines."

"Yes, there is," Heir snarled, confirming his suspicion that the effeminate attire was all for show. "You will become privy to activities we do not wish to make public."

"So don't allow me to make any copies. I'm certain it's far too much data for me to memorize. And you have my solemn vow that I will not go tattling on you to any of your prodigious number of victims." Except for Concord, but he assumed this went without saying.

Dacus stared at him for several seconds. "You will be supervised at all—"

"You cannot seriously be thinking of allowing this," Heir hissed in Dacus' direction.

"We must try something new, Linet, if we want to save those who are not yet dead."

"But he is an outsider."

"And he is already here." Dacus lifted his shoulders high. "We will take a vote. Anaden, you are excused. Tolje Alainor, you as well."

Eren gave the Confab a little bow. "Thank you all. It's been a pleas—" Tolje grabbed him by the elbow and shoved him out of the pit and through the doors.

11

Tolje paced aimlessly around his corner of the warehouse. A force field demarcated his designated space from that of his fellow gaffaelers, but he enjoyed plenty enough room for a proper walk. His 'First Class' designation brought with it a number of perks, but business had also been good for a while now—good enough that he'd recently purchased a new block of space to augment his already generous allotment.

He stopped to triple-check the identification on a stack of crates, though he didn't need to. Everything was catalogued and labeled; if an item continued to sit here in the warehouse, it was currently up for private bid by interested parties.

But this was the only place short of the *Dolensai* where he could obtain any privacy, and after the strain of appearing before the Confab, he needed a few minutes' solitude to gather his thoughts. Entertaining a house guest was proving to be more of an inconvenience than he'd anticipated—not that he'd anticipated any of this when he'd taken the Concord job.

He'd give Eren Savitas one thing—the man would have made a decent Hesgyr. The Anaden couldn't be controlled, cowed or shamed, not even by the elite reps of the Confab. Eren did what he wanted; possibly what he believed was right, though Tolje didn't yet have a clear enough sense of the man to say for certain. And while he would've given two jobs' fees to latch an ounce of decorum onto the Anaden during the Confab meeting, he'd also had to suppress a chuckle on several occasions. Eren had stiff ones.

Admirable in theory, but unfortunately Tolje's reputation, if not his livelihood, was on the line here. Sure, Jethan Dacus was whispering in some ears in the background to try to sway matters in Eren's favor, but if things turned sour, the rep was guaranteed to deny any involvement in the affair and abandon Tolje to the void.

Jethan was a politician now, after all, which meant his loyalties were as for sale as the items in these crates. Tolje, though? He'd brought Eren here, to the Hesgyr's *hidden, secret* home. He'd hung a marker around the Anaden's neck and marched him in front of the Confab. If they decided to toss Eren into a confinement cell, Tolje might lose more than his ship in the resulting blowback.

But his people might lose *everything* if they didn't find the perpetrator of these attacks—

A message arrived for him; he couldn't decide if it had come too quickly or far too late. He grunted an old mechanic's curse and opened it.

It wasn't a personal note from Jethan, but rather official correspondence from the Office of the Confab. They had voted to allow Eren access to the MEM known as 'SIMON' and a subset of restricted files. A long list of conditions trailed down the correspondence for some distance, but those weren't his to enforce.

So they all lived to fight another day.

On the way back to the apartment, he composed a brief message to Banka. He shared what it had been like to stand before the Confab, seeing as it was a most uncommon occurrence even among citizens of his stature, then included some tidbits about her old childhood friend. He didn't share how Jethan was helping him on the sly, only that the man seemed to be thriving among his fellow reps, who held Jethan in high esteem. He thought she'd like to know.

He sent the message off, but he didn't expect a reply. She never replied.

CS

A crowd was packed into metal bleachers arranged in a crescent moon around a red clay field. A patchwork of yellow lines marked up the clay—a large circle in the center, with spokes radiating out from it, then two sets of vertical lines at each end. Overhead, patchy gray clouds raced by against an olive sky. On the field, twenty Hesgyr traded three balls of varying sizes as they ran in nonsensical patterns to alternating cheers and boos from the attendees. A sporting event, clearly.

Abruptly a churning mass of thick umber smoke *puffed* into existence a few meters above the field. It displayed no defined origin point; one second, it was simply there. The smoke rushed to the ground as it expanded outward, and in a blink it had obscured the field, the bleachers and all the Hesgyr from the cam's view. It didn't muffle the sound, and raucous cheers turned to terrifying shrieks, then screams of agony. In less than thirty seconds, however, a bone-chilling silence fell upon the scene. The smoke churned on for many minutes before finally drawing in on itself and shrinking into a rough ball above the center of the field, then vanishing. What it left behind was….

Eren choked back the sting of acid in his throat. "Terminate recording."

Over three thousand Hesgyr had died that day, at a colony called Jhoakar; the total body count from the attacks now crested forty thousand. He'd watched four of the recordings, which was plenty. Each attack manifested in the same manner, regardless of whether the site was inside or outside, on a planet or asteroid or space station. No obvious wormhole was discernable, though in the absence of anything yet stranger, it was the likely mechanism by which the smoke arrived. Of far more interest was how, once the attack was complete, the smoke un-billowed, shrank and returned through whatever sort of portal had delivered it. This meant it wasn't smoke at all, but an artificial construct.

Eren glanced over at the guard who stood by the door and found the man staring off into the distance, his attention directed as far away from the display screen as possible. He wasn't certain if the man was here to keep an eye on him, or if someone always stood guard over the hardware.

"And no one has been able to capture a sample of the smoke or any particles it contains?"

'Negative,' SIMON replied.

SIMON was an acronym that, in the Hesgyr language, stood for High-Processing Something Machine Something. It was housed in an ungainly rack of server hardware spanning the rear of the room. There was an interface board and an I/O box off to one side, but thus far it was happy to respond to voice interaction. As SAIs went, it was unremarkable. No personality to speak of, zero creativity and an utter lack of a sense of humor. Disappointing, to say the least.

"Not even in the…remains?"

'Negative. The working theory posits that whatever disintegrates the bodily tissue dissolves in the process of performing its work.'

"A shame." The only concrete evidence investigators had to evaluate was the physical state of the victims in the aftermath of the incursion. Having stood witness to their state, he wasn't optimistic it would provide the answers they sought.

"Okay, let me see the list of locations that have been hit."

The screen lit up in two columns of data. The sites spanned the gamut from sporting events to mining facilities, office buildings to military bases to housing complexes. The one thing they all had in common was the fact they were packed with people at the time of the attack. Targeted for maximum bloodshed.

The Confab insisted no pattern could be discerned, with one exception. While the path meandered across galactic arms, enough data points existed to paint a clear picture: the enemy was charting a course for Nythir.

"Thank you, SIMON. Now it's time to talk about who might be behind these attacks. Can you display the location of every site where gaffaelers have, uh, 'appropriated' items?"

'Time frame?'

"Since the beginning."

It being a humorless, shackled SAI, it didn't gasp or protest or chortle in disbelief at the request. 'A moment.'

A holographic map of the Leo Supercluster projected out from the screen to take up most of SIMON's room. Concord scientists hadn't mapped how many galaxies Leo held, but it was certainly thousands. A sea of red dots speckled the map so thoroughly that at times, they blurred together to create solid blobs.

Eren whistled in appreciation; he'd remember to be offended at the scale of the Hesgyr's thievery later. Then he snapped a visual with his ocular implant, thereby saving Concord countless years of effort in its exploration endeavors. Now they knew where to look for advanced civilizations in this corner of the universe. If he could pull off a way to copy the details on those civilizations, he'd be a star back home. He'd noodle over some ideas on making it happen later. "What's the total number of sites?"

'2,463,281.'

"All right." He rubbed his hands together, blood pumping at the start of a new puzzle to unravel. "Go ahead and limit the map to jobs in the last hundred thousand years. I can't imagine that even the most aggrieved civilization can maintain a grudge for over a hundred millennia."

Noticeably more than ninety percent of the dots vanished. The Hesgyr could say appropriation was a way of life for them, but the simple truth was, they didn't *need* new tech so much any longer. Also, most of the remaining dots were located in the far reaches of Leo, forming an uneven ring with Nythir roughly at its center. They'd stripped the local galaxies bare long ago. "Number?"

'68,066.'

"Better, I guess. Do you have data on the civilizations in the Leo Supercluster that were wiped out by the Rasu?"

'After several close encounters by gaffaelers with Rasu fleets—and six deaths—we started attempting to monitor Rasu movements. As a matter of course, in the three years since the Rasu vanished—'

"Since we killed them all, you mean."

'So it's true, then? Concord annihilated the Rasu in a single assault?'

Eren cocked his head in interest. For a second there, SIMON had sounded almost…curious. Was the cold, dumb routine merely an act? "I'm not sure 'assault' is the correct word. It involved primordial life forms and supradimensional waves and all sorts of fancy stuff."

'Fascinating.'

"Is it?" He smirked. "Have you been holding out on me, SIMON?"

'There is nothing to hold out, Mr. Savitas. Thank you for the information. It will enhance my analytical capabilities.'

"Uh-huh." He glanced at the guard, who was now leaning against the wall by the door, arms crossed over his chest as he stared just past Eren's shoulder. He suspected he might have gotten a rather different response if they were alone. "Back to what you were saying?"

'Yes. The Hesgyr have been performing a cursory sweep of the regions affected by Rasu invasions to update the databanks, so they do not waste time scheduling jobs involving species that no longer exist. The survey is not yet complete, but they have made significant progress.'

"Great. Remove any locations your people have confirmed were destroyed by the Rasu."

A disturbing number of dots winked out. For all the voluminous destruction the enemy had inflicted in Concord and Asterion Dominion space, it had been busily doing the same or worse in every other cosmic direction.

But Concord, the Dominion and their allies had survived. What if others had as well, if solely by the good grace of lucky timing?

"Do you have any data on species that were attacked by the Rasu but not annihilated?"

'We have identified five species that survived Rasu invasions.'

"Let me see them."

All five were located in a tight formation of galaxies on the facing border of the Shapley Supercluster, near the edge of one of the Rasu fronts. Eren made a note to tell his friend Caleb how he'd saved far more lives than he realized when he'd helped to end the Rasu.

"Now we're talking. Show me the job data on these five."

On the screen, five columns populated. Each one listed the date of the appropriation, the item taken and the gaffaeler responsible.

Two of the jobs were completed some eighty thousand years ago. While he didn't eliminate them from contention, they definitely got knocked down to the bottom of the list. A third job involved a radiation-resistant paint finisher; cultures could be persnickety about the oddest things, but he found it hard to believe anyone would wage a gruesome campaign of terror and mass murder over paint.

The last two, though? Not only had they transpired in this century, the items stolen sounded like military or defense related hardware.

He did a double take…one of the jobs was performed by Tolje.

A sickening feeling stirred in his gut. He really hoped Tolje wasn't responsible for all this, however inadvertently or however much the man had been following orders. Because that would suck.

Eren hopped off the desk he'd been half-sitting on. "Can you send me the details on two of the species: the Phae'soon and the Goljetsu? Everything the Hesgyr know about them, as well as the specifics of the gaffaeler jobs?"

'I will need to request approval from the Confab. If I receive it, how shall I send the information to you?'

"Right. Good question." The Hesgyr used cybernetics and quantum communications, but they weren't as all-in on the technology as his people were. When it came to data transfer, storage and review, they seemed to use a combination of small quantum storage devices and portable connected tablets. "Um, have one of those tablets delivered to Tolje Alainor's residence, if you don't mind."

'I will do so. Is there anything else?'

"Not right now, but I suspect I'll be back. Pleasure talking with you, SIMON."

'It was…I am pleased to have been of service.'

12

With the greatest of reluctance, Eren sent a message to Nyx on his way to Tolje's apartment, asking her to gather a set of grade IV hacking spikes, a box of protein bars and a few changes of clothes from his suite at Corradeo's estate. Since he was asking for a favor, he didn't even include a snide remark about how he knew she had a master key to all the rooms at the estate and so should face no difficulty invading his private space.

The Confab had gifted him a pass to take a VIP car back, but he exited the car early and took his time walking the rest of the way, ruminating over the interaction with SIMON in his mind, letting pieces fit in here and there. He focused on what he'd learned about the attacks and the gaffaelers' history. Whether SIMON showed sparks of genuine sapience was intriguing, but he wasn't on Nythir to free shackled SAIs.

He'd just cleared the Transition to the Rydai District when a reply from Nyx came in.

> *Eren,*
>
> *I'm currently offworld on a mission and can't run your errands at the moment. Also, I am not your personal assistant. Assuming you will neither starve to death nor terrorize the Hesgyr with your nudity in the next twelve hours, I will see what I can do when I return home.*
>
> *—Nyx*

As pleasant as always. He shot off a quick note indicating her terms were acceptable.

CS

"I'm only saying you don't understand the—"

"No, *you* don't understand, because you never listen to me! I have told you a hundred times by now, and here I am telling you a hundred and one—"

Eren winced and tried to swiftly back out of the doorway.

"Come on in, Eren. We're done. I don't know why I bothered." Banka's voice dripped with vitriol that transcended species.

"Banka, if you—"

"Shut up, Dad." She jerked her chin in Eren's direction as she stormed past him and out the door.

He braced himself and stepped into the apartment, where he veered toward the kitchen to give Tolje a minute to compose himself.

He filled a glass with water and turned to find Tolje staring at the closed door. The man's shoulders lowered fractionally, but after a few seconds he faced Eren wearing a neutral expression. "How'd the session with SIMON go?"

"Ah, good. Listen, if you want to be alone for a while, I can go wander around or…."

Tolje's head shook. "No. Why would I?"

"Well, that looked to be a nasty argument."

"Only because you haven't witnessed any nasty Hesgyr arguments. That was mild, especially for Banka and me." Tolje settled into his chair and leaned forward. "So, the session. What did you learn?"

Eren's brow furrowed, and he hesitated for a beat before collapsing onto the couch and throwing an arm along the top. If Tolje didn't want to bare his soul about family problems, he wasn't going to push it. "I've got my eye on two species: the Phae'soon and the Goljetsu. Assuming the Confab approves my access, someone will be delivering all the files on them here soon."

"Why those two?"

"They were both attacked by the Rasu, but not annihilated. It appears Concord ended the Rasu before they were able to finish their work."

"And?"

"And the items your people stole from them sound like things they could have used to protect themselves from outside attack. If they weren't able to replicate the technology before the Rasu arrived, they might view the Hesgyr as being responsible for tremendous loss of life. Plenty enough to make them spicy for revenge."

Tolje scowled. "We rarely appropriate something irreplaceable."

"You've said that before. And if it turns out to be true in these cases, I'll keep hunting. But we should at least check."

"Even if you're right, how would they have found us?"

Eren drummed his fingers on the couch cushion. "Possibly the hard way—by scouring the intergalactic neighborhood. On a per-galaxy scale, space-faring civilizations are pretty rare. Or possibly…SIMON said after the Rasu were destroyed, you began a survey of mapped civilizations located near Rasu territory to see who survived. Is it possible your survey ship was detected and tracked?"

"Extremely unlikely. But seeing as how you are here, I concede not impossible. We're very careful, though."

"I'm sure you are. But any civilization to survive a Rasu assault will be on heightened alert for fresh intruders from the stars. You might have tripped a warning system they didn't have in place the first time a gaffaeler visited."

"Damn, you could be right. Depending on who ran the survey. Not all gaffaelers are created equal."

"No doubt." Eren tried to sound casual. "What do you know about a species called the Goljetsu?"

Tolje shrugged. "Should I know anything about them?"

"Yes. Thirty-seven years ago, you stole an ultra-high-frequency deep space telescope from them."

"*Diewl.* You think I'm responsible for all this carnage?"

"No. The attackers are responsible for it. Nothing justifies this degree of bloodthirsty revenge, not even…." He let the declaration trail off. The truth was, from the point of view of the aggrieved, millions dead at the hands of the Rasu may well justify such vengeance. He didn't have to agree with the sentiment to empathize with it. "And no one, least of all you or your superiors, could have fore-seen the toll the Rasu would inflict."

But it was a platitude. Later, once the mystery was solved and greater bloodshed averted, he'd attempt to get Tolje, if no other Hesgyr, to begin considering the consequences of his actions. But not today. "So, what do you remember about them?"

"Do you have any idea how many jobs I've done in the last thirty-seven years?"

"More than a hundred, less than a thousand?"

Tolje snorted. "Close enough. Where are they located?"

"Galaxy—" A chime rang, and Tolje stood and went to the door.

A male Hesgyr handed Tolje a large box. "Delivery from MEM Services, to the attention of Visitor Eren Savitas."

Eren waved from the couch. "I'm here."

"Mr. Alainor, if you will sign for it? When Mr. Savitas has completed his work, follow Destruction Protocol 5."

"Understood." Tolje pressed a thumb to a pad the courier held out, then took the box and closed the door behind him. "Seems we won't have to rely on my faulty memory."

"All the better."

Tolje set the box on his desk by the door and removed two quantum storage devices. One slid into an input slot on the desktop terminal, and Tolje opened up a series of files.

The Goljetsu were...ants was the best approximation. They sported six thin legs attached to a segmented exoskeleton, mandibles at their mouths, and antennae atop their heads. Unlike ants, however, they also had two additional limbs below their heads that served as more dexterous arms, complete with rudimentary digits. They averaged 0.7 meters tall and almost two meters long.

Eren shuddered; he would not want to meet a gang of Goljetsu in a dark alley. Or any alley, street or town. "You shapeshifted into one of these creatures?"

"*Duwi*, no. Our morphing capabilities have their limits. My body has too much mass for one, and my skeletal structure can't shrink enough to create such narrow limbs. But I remember these buggers now. I did steal a telescope, but it had already been launched into orbit—I stole it from space. Never had to meet a Goljetsu in person."

"Good thing."

"Yes." Tolje moved on from the visuals, thankfully, and they scanned the post-Rasu report. All exocolonies and space stations had been destroyed, as well as all cities of any size on the Goljetsu homeworld. A few scattered settlements on the planet registered as active, all of them on a single sub-arctic landmass; the report speculated that the surviving inhabitants had fled to the nonoptimal climate as a last resort. No communications were detected during the surveillance scan, which suggested the settlements were not talking to one another. During the two days spent surveying the world, no travel more advanced than foot traffic was observed.

The report painted a bleak picture. "They sound rather bad off. Request another flyby to confirm their sorry state, but I'd say you're probably off the hook."

"Good." Tolje nodded slowly. "Not that I'd blame myself regardless, but better to not carry the twinge of doubt."

This, Eren understood. Guilt was a heavy burden to lug around on the soul. But while Tolje was feeling vulnerable…. "Tell me how you learned the MAST existed and where to find it."

Tolje smiled in apparent amusement. "Not a chance."

"Oh, fine. Let's review the other species."

Tolje opened the file. "The Phae'soon. Class B3 civilization by our scale. Caste-based society, not unlike the Goljetsu in this respect. Hmm…militaristic sort. Not especially expansionist, though. They seem the paranoid, prideful type—convinced the universe is out to get them."

Eren spread his arms wide. "Then the Rasu arrived and proved them right. Tell me the specifics on what your people, ah, procured from them."

"Looks to be a weapon. Oh, yes, the Magelo Wide-Field Disruptor. We have four of these deployed in orbit around Nythir.

Supposedly they'll disintegrate anything that makes it inside the defense perimeter without authorization. We haven't yet needed to use one and find out." Tolje did the thing with his mouth that passed for a frown. "But we only stole one, then studied it until we could build our own. Why would they care about one instance of a weapon they already know how to build?"

"You said they're paranoid."

"True, but paranoid enough to commit the grisly atrocities they're inflicting on us? If so, they have one *uffernol* psyche."

"It happens. But I'll concede, most of the species who exhibit such tendencies never survive to achieve space travel. Maybe we're missing something about the nature of the weapon. Is there anyone we can talk to who'll know more?"

"I don't have those sorts of connections, but Preece does. I'll see if I can get a few minutes of his time tomorrow. But for now, it's late, and I'm…tired."

He sounded it, too. Eren knew the Confab meeting had been stressful for Tolje, as presentations in front of one's high governing body tended to be for most people who weren't Eren. And though Tolje had waved it off, the argument with Banka had sounded unpleasant. So he nodded in agreement. "Let's get some sleep. We'll start again in the morning."

CS

"What can I get you?"

Banka gave the menu on the wall a once-over. The selections weren't noteworthy, but it didn't matter; she simply needed the calories after working an extra shift. "A baked stack with wren spiced soup."

The woman handed her a card, and she moved off to the left to wait. The court hummed along with a base level of activity even at this time of night, but it was quiet enough for her to detect a faint *hiss* coming from the wall above her. She peered upward to spot an air vent hanging a touch loose.

Her first instinct was to check around for a spare ladder so she could climb up and fix it. Then she remembered it wasn't her job to repair every broken fixture on Nythir—

"Banka Alainor. What a surprise."

She spun at the sound of a voice she recognized but couldn't place…oh.

Jethan Dacus strode toward her, striking a horribly effete picture in his tailored jacket and soft pants, platinum bands ringing his outer horns.

She hugged her childhood friend anyway. "You look like you narrowly escaped a bakanul bazaar with your life."

"And you look like you just rolled out of a fronite kiln."

"You're not far wrong." She leaned against the wall beside the food counter and crossed her arms over her chest. "So what are you doing slumming down here in Rydai District?"

"Okay, ease off on the judgment, will you? I grew up here, too."

She made a face of annoyance, but relented. "Fair enough. It's a valid question, though, because I seriously doubt you still live here."

"No. I, uh, come by and get a cup of boiled havan here every so often. They don't make it the same in the Alpha District restaurants."

She bit off yet another snarky reply, because it *was* good to see him. The last time she'd spoken to him was five years earlier, shortly after he'd won election to the Confab. "And how is work going?"

"Tiring, hence the late hour. The attacks have got everyone on edge and scrambling for solutions."

"I bet. Coming up with any?"

"Not so far."

They called her number, so she grabbed her order then gestured toward the row of tables nearby. One was actually available; Nythir never slept, but it did downshift a little in the later hours. "Visit with me for a minute before you run off for your havan."

"I'd love to."

While Jathan sat opposite her, she unpacked her food and eagerly bit into the stack.

"Hey, I saw your father today. In a Confab meeting, no less."

She washed the bite down with a straw full of soup before it could lodge in her throat and choke her. "I know. Unfortunately."

Jethan shifted awkwardly in his chair. "Listen, if you don't want me here, I can go. I thought we—"

"No, stay. Sorry. I only meant unfortunate for me that I had enough contact with my father to learn you'd seen him. I'd been having a good day until then."

"Oh. So, no reconciliation on the docket?"

"Not a chance."

"I see. You know, he's…never mind."

"No, say it." She motioned for him to continue as she returned to the stack.

"Fine, I will. He's genuinely trying to help stop the attacks. He's brought in a lot of appropriated items that are proving useful—items he acquired at a reduced rate at the behest of the Confab. Now he's got an alien involved. It's putting him in a delicate situation, but he's taking the risk anyway."

"Hmm. This would be the first time—he's helped with something, that is." She didn't mention that she'd met the alien, as doing so would only prolong their discussion of her father.

Jethan held up his hands in surrender. "I'll drop it. I can admit when I'm fighting a losing battle."

"You always were smart." She flashed him a teasing smile over the stack. "How's Sayre?"

"Growing irritated at my long work hours, but hiding it for now. She started a new job in the Glain District a few weeks ago, so it has her somewhat busy as well."

"Nice." Glain abutted the Alpha District, home of the Confab and little else. Glain was where all the important business truly happened—where the rich and powerful tried to rub horns with the reps, where deals were made and broken and debts were traded. It was a den of vipers, but a profitable one for the savvy. Jethan, she suspected, had leveraged his smarts for some savviness.

"How about you? You have someone next to you?"

"Eh…." She shrugged and finished off the stack. "Maybe. It's just for fun right now. He's of a serious nature, so I'm apt to bore of him soon."

"You know, there is value in settling down. Comfort, security—ah, what am I saying? You're an Alainor. You'll never stop moving."

She stared at him, the straw hovering at her lips.

He made a grunting sound deep in his throat and pushed his chair back. "I should grab my havan and get home. Another early morning starts in too few hours. It was good to see you, though."

She should head out as well. Pedr was on Nythir for a spell, and he got annoyingly cranky when he didn't get to spend any time with her at night. "You, too, Jethan."

"Don't be such a stranger."

"You know where to find me."

"And you, me." He flourished a hand across his chest, a farewell of respect, and strode off.

She slurped on her soup while she watched him go. The Confab had sheened him up, but underneath the pretentious clothes, he seemed…no, not the same. He'd once been carefree and happy. A clumsy oaf—it was a big reason why he'd gone into politics instead of the trades—but always laughing. Now he felt weighty; burdened. She wondered if it was the attacks, or the rep job in general.

A message arrived then, one she'd been anxiously waiting for. She scanned it, smiled, and read it again more carefully.

She'd landed the Lophalin corp job on Daith! It was a two-week gig setting up an automated rhenium mining operation. Most relevantly, the pay was double Transition standard.

She sent her boss a message informing him she was taking corporate-job leave, then disposed of her trash and set off for home at a brisk pace. She'd need to catch a transport in six hours. It was barely enough time to rush home, make her apologies to Pedr—

probably with a quick run through the bed to ease the sting—and pack a minimal bag.

Daith was an ugly rock, the glut of rhenium clogging its veins the only redeeming quality. But it was a change of scenery and another opportunity to build her reputation among the corps.

Jethan wasn't entirely wrong. She did have a touch of wanderlust in her blood, but she hadn't gotten it from her father.

13

The morning brought news of a fresh attack, this one at a lunar colony orbiting a gas giant a scant ten parsecs distant from Nythir.

"They're coming for us hard now." Tolje agitated around the kitchen as he prepared his breakfast soup. "Nythir. What I can't figure is, why not hit us here straightaway? A hundred million Hesgyr are packed inside this floating world. They could inflict a score greater carnage in a couple of hours inside its walls than they've caused in months out in the colonies."

Eren sat on a stool at the counter and pretended to sip on the soup Tolje had poured for him. Even with a sprinkling of spices, it remained a bland, uninspiring broth. His stomach grumbled a warning, begging for something more substantial to consume. Where the hells was Nyx with his protein bars?

"Fear. This isn't actually a campaign to slaughter the Hesgyr. Well, I expect it is in the long run, but whoever these attackers are, they want you to feel terror before they kill you. To experience creeping dread from the knowledge that a terrifying enemy is coming for you. You can't see them, you can't find them, you can't stop them. You can only wait to be murdered by them."

Tolje stopped, a food box in one hand halfway to the cabinet, and stared at Eren. "You sure know how to cheer a man up first thing in the morning."

"Sorry. You asked."

"I did."

"Do you…want to be cheered up?"

A neutral expression transformed Tolje's bony visage. "I don't want to talk about Banka, if that's what you mean."

"I didn't mean anything in particular. There's plenty enough going on at present to depress any sane man."

"Not you, though. You do seem to have an astonishingly chipper disposition."

"Yeah, but I never claimed to be sane."

Another stare. "Huh." Tolje shook his head and returned the box to the cabinet. "Preece is expecting us in twenty minutes. We should get moving."

CS

Preece was dashing between three separate workstations when they arrived at the lab. Tolje waited patiently near the door, so Eren suppressed the urge to walk up and grab the scientist by the shoulders.

Finally Preece glanced up and noticed them. "Oh good, you've arrived. I have news on the nofilod we removed from Fetel-reu."

"Oh? What news?" Tolje asked as they moved into the room, closer to the long table occupying the center of Preece's orbit.

"The nofilod's innate immune system displays markers of a recent whole-body heightened response, suggesting it faced and defeated a massive non-self-molecule invasion."

Eren called up every store of medical knowledge his cybernetics contained, but the files were skimpy on specifics. He'd devoted far more of his cybernetics' storage capacity to explosives than to biology. "So you're saying the nofilod was attacked by the same thing that killed the Hesgyr, but for some reason it was able to fight off the attack?"

"Correct. The immune system of every Hesgyr who came in contact with the cloud failed to fight it off, while this lowly nofilod successfully did so. This suggests the Hesgyr immune system did not view the invading pathogen as a threat."

"Do the Hesgyr have weak immune systems?"

"On the contrary, they are quite strong—an evolutionary response to the high levels of radiation originating from our sun."

Eren waited for further explanation, but Preece simply stood there, looking satisfied. He checked with Tolje, who shrugged. "Okay, doctor. Tell us your theory."

"I'm so glad you asked. I believe the attack wraps a virus—an extremely fast-acting and artificially engineered virus—inside a molecule the Hesgyr immune system does not recognize as foreign, and thus allows it entry. Once in the body, it replicates an order of magnitude more rapidly than natural viruses, until it has infected virtually every operating cell. Then the wrapping unfurls, as it were, and the virus goes to work. It's likely hemorrhagic in nature, due to the results, and systemic bleeding occurs within seconds. Within a few minutes, comprehensive cellular death follows. But not merely death—full dissolution of cellular integrity."

Tolje cleared his throat unevenly. The man had never struck Eren as squeamish, but Preece's description did not paint a pleasant picture. "Did you find any traces of the virus in the nofilod?"

"No. Its immune system did a thorough job of repelling the invader before it had a chance to replicate to any extent. And, unfortunately, nofilods do not possess an adaptive immune system, so we can't work backwards to discern the details of the virus. But I'm not convinced it matters. Viruses, for all their genetic complexity, are straightforward in action, and the particulars of this one are unlikely to tell us anything fruitful. What matters is the mechanism of infiltration."

Eren was starting to get the gist of it now. "So the attackers are skilled at microbiology. They kidnap a Hesgyr from somewhere and study his or her immune system until they can design a virus wrapper to mimic a Hesgyr's own molecules. Then they deliver the disguised virus via their cloud of death. They've crafted a weapon designed to kill Hesgyr, and only Hesgyr."

"That does appear to be the case, yes." Preece nodded perfunctorily.

"They really don't like you guys." He said it jokingly, but he made a note to double-check the robustness of anadens' innate immune response as the beginnings of a probably terrible and definitely foolhardy idea stirred in his mind.

"No. It seems they do not—" Preece spun toward the door as it opened to admit a towering Hesgyr man wearing all-black, form-fitting fatigues and combat boots. "Ah, Major Eynon, you made it."

"When the Confab orders, one does not refuse."

Preece leaned in closer to Eren to speak under his breath. "This newest attack has got the Confab a bit panicked. They're willing to try anything at this point, including giving you access to classified military information."

"Awfully kind of them." Eren smiled blithely as the new entrant joined them. Access to classified military intel was music to his ears.

"This is Gaffaeler First Class Tolje Alainor and Visitor Eren Savitas. Gentleman, this is Dr. Pedr Eynon, a major in the Nythir Defense Force. Pedr and I studied together in our youth, before he, ah, chose another career path."

Tolje performed the standard Hesgyr greeting of respect, but the major-doctor ignored it. "A Visitor? What are you?"

"Anaden."

Eynon's gaze flitted to Preece. "You're certain they're cleared for this information?"

"I am. Eren here has met with the Confab and persuaded the reps of his usefulness to our investigation."

"Anadens aren't known for their helpfulness toward other species. They're bullies and tyrants."

Eren sighed. He was getting sick of this judgmental routine. "I assume you haven't stopped by our neck of the woods lately. We're reforming."

"Species don't reform," Eynon snapped. "They are what they are."

He'd concede that in the aggregate, the man was correct. Most species, most of the time, couldn't escape their inherent nature. But Humans had bucked the trend, as had Asterions, which meant anadens could, too. They'd just forgotten how for a time, and were now working on remembering.

Philosophers and scientists had opined at length about how something special in those three species' shared genetic architecture imbued them with superior adaptability at both an individual and species-wide level. All species' biology evolved over time, but anadens and their genetic descendants controlled their own evolution—not solely of their bodies, but of their minds, hearts, souls. Or so a bunch of intellectuals with way too much free time on their hands speculated.

Eren's smile held a touch of frostiness. "Usually. I hope we prove you wrong."

"Doubtful." Eynon focused on Preece. "You want to know about the Magelo Wide-Field Disruptor. It works by firing a—"

Eren held up a hand. "I don't think we need to focus on the mechanics of its operation—though I do have one question: would it have killed Rasu?"

"Killed? No. Nothing kills Rasu. But it would definitely slow them down."

"Something killed Rasu, seeing as they're dead."

"And you'd know all about this, wouldn't you?"

Eren forced a shrug upon his shoulders. He already didn't like Eynon, but he needed to remember not to get in a pissing match with the man—or with any Hesgyr. He remained on a short leash here, and he had a mission to perform. "Anecdotally. Slow them down enough to matter?"

Eynon scowled at him for a moment before answering. "Possibly. Long enough to effect planetary evacuations, assuming those under attack had such capabilities. Long enough to launch a counter-offensive, though it wouldn't make a difference in the end."

"Great. Now, what I—we—are wondering is this: is there anything that makes the Disruptor unique? Special in some way?"

"It's more powerful than conventional weapons, with a more expansive coverage as well. It operates well in the vacuum of space, which isn't common for its class of weaponry. Other than that, not particularly…though there is the promethium-167."

The word didn't mean anything to Eren, but Preece gestured enthusiastically. "Ah, yes. Excellent point."

Tolje frowned. "And what point is that?"

"Promethium is one of the rarest elements in the universe," Preece explained. "It can be created in a lab, but not any stable isotopes, of course."

"Of course," Eren nodded sagely, as if it were the most obvious statement in the world. "Can you elaborate?"

"Promethium-167 is the only known stable isotope of the element, and I daresay most advanced species don't know of its existence at all. We happened to discover it in the crust of a rogue planetoid located near an ancient supernova. We think the source star carried an unusually high amount of promethium, and it seeded the planetoid. We've never found p-167 anywhere else."

"The Phae'soon did, however," Tolje said. "Seeing as they used it in constructing the Disruptor."

Eren started to see where this might be going, which was nowhere good for the Phae'soon. "Is it possible they only had enough on hand to build the one weapon?"

"Probable," Preece replied. "We haven't scanned their system or the region for the element, obviously, but as I said, it's exceedingly rare."

"Gotcha. But couldn't they simply substitute a similar element that worked just as well?"

"Just as well?" Eynon interjected. "Doubtful. The other lanthanides have many practical uses, but typically as an additive material. They rarely excel as the primary constructive metal. Using another material would result in a narrower beam spread, or shorter fire time, or general instability in the weapon's functioning, or a variety of other problems for this particular style of weapon."

Eren shot Tolje a meaningful look; if the man grasped the import, however, he gave no indication. "So you all stole the Phae'soon's only Disruptor weapon, and with it, their entire supply of this promethium-167. They weren't able to replace it using anything that worked half as well. Fast forward two decades. The Rasu attack in overwhelming numbers, and the Phae'soon no longer have a weapon powerful enough to buy them time to evacuate their homeworld. Is anyone here surprised if the survivors want revenge?"

Eynon sputtered. "They should have come up with an alternative. If they could invent and build this weapon, they could engineer others to serve the same purpose."

"But maybe they couldn't. Maybe they didn't have time, or the budget for it, or maybe they ran into political or bureaucratic roadblocks—gods know they wouldn't be the first."

Tolje shifted his weight around, perhaps in discomfort, but the others appeared nonplussed. *Arae*, it was like screaming at a brick wall with these people. Their blind spots were bloated enough to hide galaxies!

Eren sighed and, through herculean effort, didn't so much as raise his voice. "Let's go take a look. The report says the Phae'soon survived the Rasu invasion, but it doesn't include many details. They could be happy and thriving and not our guys. But we should check."

Eynon glared at Eren; the man's thinly veiled disgust at his presence had hardly abated during the meeting.

"It strikes me as a wise course of action, if only for thoroughness' sake," Preece suggested.

Eynon shifted his glare to encompass Preece, then Tolje, but conceded the point. "I can authorize a military surveillance mission in the next few days."

Tolje shook his head with notable vehemence. "Gaffaeler ships have better scanning equipment and stealth than the military craft do—and I can go right now."

"The Confab will not want to trust this matter to a solitary scaveng—"

"Use that term, and you will regret it. The military wouldn't exist if not for tech gaffaelers deposited on your doorstep. And besides, I don't need the Confab's permission. I go where I want and do what I want, and I find I have a sudden *want* to visit the Phae'soon." Tolje gazed at Eren with one eye, which was a feat Eren had not realized Hesgyr could perform. "Shall we?"

Tolje was just full of surprises today. Eren nodded sharply. "I didn't have anything else planned for today, and I'd enjoy an outing."

CS

Pedr didn't bother to hide his displeasure as he stormed out. He'd done the Confab a favor by agreeing to stop by Dr. Preece's lab, but he did not sign up to get humiliated by an alien and a bloody scavenger. Did they think this was all some kind of joke?

People were dying out there—his own people had already died at the hands of their insidious enemy—and this crowd was flapping their tongues about *motivations*. The Confab may well be losing their wits if they'd resorted to relying on their ilk to stop the attacks.

Their enemy was worse than the Rasu, for their weapons took the form of nebulous clouds that could not be captured, neutralized or even fought, all while they hid in safety untold parsecs away. They were cowards, and this told him everything he needed to know about the enemy's moral fiber, motivations be damned.

Pain lanced up his arm, and he looked down to discover he'd dug his nails so hard into his palm, he had drawn blood. He paused and sucked in a deep breath, attempting to wrangle his temper under control. He had a meeting in fifteen minutes with a slew of superior officers, and it would not do to show up in a froth. Emotions escalated further with each new attack, but military discipline still counted for something. If the fortitude of the Confab truly was buckling under the strain, it might be the one thing that stood a chance of guiding his people through the crisis.

He was in dock at Nythir for a two-week stint of training, retrofits and resupplying, punctuated by a series of officer meetings where they tried to strategize how to fight an enemy they could not see. He'd never admit it aloud, but the sessions weren't going well. His fighting brothers and sisters deserved to be avenged, but no one had an answer as to how.

He'd thought to at least have some pleasurable evenings to balance the stressful hours out, but Banka had scored a lucrative stint offworld and abandoned him this morning. He didn't care for it, but ordering her around didn't seem to work on her the way it did on his subordinates.

He put together an authorization for a surveillance mission to the Phae'soon home system. Though the scavenger would beat his team there, the results wouldn't be trustworthy in any event. He doubted the Phae'soon were the culprits, but every lead must be pursued. He had only one goal: to find the enemy, then destroy them.

14

Now that Eren understood what he was looking at, the interior of Tolje's ship made a lot more sense. Incongruent equipment stolen from other species was bridged with other equipment—possibly of Hesgyr design or possibly also stolen, but more likely an amalgamation of both—to enable mismatched inputs and outputs to talk to one another. The most advanced or sensitive equipment had been lifted whole cloth and was of consistent design until its signals needed to feed into the overarching ship controls, at which point additional bridging components appeared. The cabin walls and basic fixtures were of Hesgyr design from the ground up, as they resembled the architecture of the Rydai District.

Such an odd species. They were highly intelligent and resourceful enough to have built all this from scratch, yet they stubbornly stuck to the old ways that had once served them well but were, objectively, no longer needed. He understood how powerful inertia could be, for civilizations as much as for individuals. 'Because that's the way it's done' had sustained many a people for many a millennia. But the Hesgyr were *clever*. Independent-minded, stubborn and prideful. They should have shed their chains long ago, but they hadn't.

Eren planted a hand on the wall behind the cockpit, just off Tolje's right shoulder, as they cruised out from Nythir space. "I think your boot left a mark on Major Eynon back in Preece's lab."

"Hopefully so."

"I admit, I was surprised. You're usually fairly laid-back."

"Yeah." Tolje adjusted a control on the dash, then toed his chair around to face Eren. "By and large, gaffaelers are respected on Nythir. Often celebrated, even. Most people recognize the sacrifices we make to keep our home running, growing and protected. But the military? They act as if we're debris on the bottom of their heels, when they acknowledge we exist at all."

"Militaries aren't often the gracious type in any species. They do tend to have barbed sticks shoved up their asses."

Tolje chuckled. "True enough. Still, I'm told it wasn't always this way. In the old days, gaffaelers and soldiers often worked together in common cause."

"What changed?"

"As the legend goes, around five centuries ago, a military commander's family suffered some terrible tragedy, and a gaffaeler caught the blame—rightly or wrongly, who can say? The commander proceeded to spend the next several decades instilling his grudge in the entire damn institution. Now they despise gaffaelers without knowing why."

"A shame. Eynon, though? He didn't exactly express warm feelings for me, either. In fact, he acted as prejudiced toward aliens as he did toward gaffaelers. Was he simply having a shitty day, or is there something else going on?"

"I expect his sour attitude is on account of Canchal-se."

"What's that?" Eren asked.

"A deep space military outpost on the other side of the Glow. It was hit by this enemy early on. Every soldier at Canchal-se that day died—over three thousand souls. That was when everyone realized we had a serious problem on our hands."

"Damn. Was Eynon stationed at the outpost?"

Tolje made a hedging motion with one hand. "Not technically, no. I think he got this own ship command a few years ago. But the 'doctor' in his title used to mean something. Canchal-se's mission had a scientific bent to it, and Eynon trained a number of the people who were stationed there."

"Ouch. So to say he's angry about these attacks would be an understatement."

"A colossal one. Mind you, he's an asshole on good days, too. It's not an excuse for his attitude…but it is a reason."

On the rearcam, Nythir shrank to a gleaming dot then disappeared. "Question I've been meaning to ask you. Is 'First Class' the highest gaffaeler rank?"

Tolje pretended to concentrate on a readout that Eren was pretty sure just displayed the internal temperature controls. "It is."

He'd suspected as much. Compared to the rough-and-tumble ambiance of the Rydai District, Tolje's apartment was both spacious and well-appointed; also, the man knew a good number of people in high places. "Earlier, you mentioned the sacrifices gaffaelers made. Did you mean being away from home for long periods of time?"

"Sometimes." Tolje sighed and faced Eren again. "Are you planning to prod me all the way to the Phae'soon homeworld?"

"More than likely."

"I figured. Mostly I meant the shapeshifting. While Hesgyr genetics make it theoretically feasible, medical modifications are required to make it practical. The modifications are rather involved and…painful, one might say. The actual process of shapeshifting is worse. Excruciating, one might say."

It had looked plenty excruciating when he'd witnessed the man de-shapeshift after leaving Ares. "The 'one' being you, and you are saying it."

"Quite."

"Yet you choose to do it anyway."

Tolje shrugged. "It's who I am. And the benefits outweigh the pain. Most of the time." He reached behind him to the dash and, in a flurry of long fingers, activated the wormhole drive.

A pinpoint of green light appeared in space off the bow, then enveloped the *Dolensai* in overwhelming blackness, and for a second they were the only two individuals in the universe. The next second, the stars winked back into existence.

Eren knew where this tech had originated—the aliens who'd set up an observation post above the Hesgyr homeworld long, long ago. They weren't Kats (since they inhabited bodies) and they weren't anadens (since his people hadn't yet discovered how to artificially create wormholes at the time). But who they were remained a mystery—one of many when it came to the Hesgyr.

A blazing orange star greeted them upon their arrival, and filters on the viewport quickly turned down the glare.

"I've brought us in a hundred megameters out from the Phae'soon homeworld, just in case they've got long-range buoys up and running. Engaging stealth and starting our approach."

The ship swung in an arc until a garden world came into view. From this distance, it looked much the same as all such worlds do. Teal oceans separated a sprinkling of yellow-and-ivy continents, with large, jagged icecaps coating both poles.

"The post-Rasu report indicates a secondary inhabited planet—fifth in the system—fared better, but we'll take a peek at the big planet first. See if they're getting back on their feet."

A gentle alarm sounded on the dash, and Tolje called up a new screen and studied it for several seconds. "Orbital debris consistent with the remains of a space station. I'm not picking up any orbital defenses or active technology in the vicinity. We should be safe to move in closer."

A row of visuals materialized along the top third of the viewport, fed by some impressively powerful scanners. Eren supposed the Hesgyr needed advanced equipment to case their marks, the better to decide if it was worth the trouble of a surface visit and the painful shapeshifting it required.

The devastation the Rasu had inflicted soon became apparent. Wide swaths of forestland had been shredded and the ground beneath the trees upended into frayed ribbons of clay and mud. Mountaintops had been chopped off, leaving jagged buttes with fields of broken stone at their bases.

But the worst was the cities. He couldn't discern much about the style of Phae'soon architecture, because the urban centers had been leveled. Bombed into massive craters, often, with only the occasional partial scaffolding of a once towering structure left leaning in the wind, scorch marks its sole decoration.

Bitterness surged through Eren's chest at the heartbreaking sight of what the Rasu had wrought here, for he'd lived through such an onslaught.

> Felzeor: *"Scout Sarga reports that Bendige has fallen."*
> Eren: *"Arae!"*
> Karis: *"Quiet!"*

Eren's fists clenched and unclenched around the archine grenades he still carried at the ready. With the Rift Bubble disabled and the quantum block preventing anything more than a token defense by Concord, the Rasu had swarmed over the planet like an endless dark horde. Five cities had fallen—likely more—and the air was thick with acrid smoke from the millions of square kilometers of forest that had already burned. This magical planet was being razed to the ground with but half a thought from these soulless enemies from the void.

He was just glad Cosime wasn't here to see it. No, he hurriedly corrected himself. He could never, ever be glad she wasn't here with him. But if she were, her heart would be shattered, and his would shatter in turn as he watched her grieve.

Their rag-tag band pushed obstinately through the undergrowth for over an hour. The widespread fires drove the temperature and humidity to sweltering levels, until Eren's normally climate-suitable clothes were sopping wet. He wanted to rip off his shirt and leave it for the Rasu, but the limbs and brush would gouge his skin out in no time—

Flames abruptly leapt up to soar above the tree canopy. A deafening roar cascaded through the forest, and everyone came to a screeching halt.

> Karis: *"Airborne One, I need eyes on the forest west of Calchfaen."*
> Felzeor: *"The smoke is too thick for us to get close. We do not see a way through."*

Eren's stomach turned to lead. It wasn't as if they hadn't all known this was exactly what was going to transpire. But utterly irrational belief had surely kept more than one soldier alive through a siege of his land.

Karis: "Copy that."

Eren: "Everyone turn hard east and head for the riverbank five hundred meters north of the waterfall."

Karis: "You don't give the orders here, Anaden."

Well, that stung. As if he hadn't called the Naraidan planet home, as much as anywhere in Amaranthe could be home, for the last fifteen years of his life. "We can head to the location I specified, or we can die. The forest is thick as it approaches the Afonle River. It'll provide us a measure of protection. There's a grove near the riverbank where we'll be able to make a temporary camp and set up fortifications."

Karis: "We can still find a path through toward Bendige."

Eren: "Through a solid wall of flame? No, we can't. They've outmaneuvered us."

Hirlas had been saved in the end, but only through a feat of deep cosmic magic the Phae'soon had never stood a chance of replicating. And three years later, Hirlas still bore the scars the Rasu had left behind. Metaphorically, at least, as the Akeso intelligence had buffed and polished the broken surface in the aftermath. But some scars couldn't be erased.

"I've got a reading of movement off to the east. I'll need to drop through the cloud cover to check it out."

"They won't be able to see us?"

"You couldn't see my ship when you were standing a meter from its hull."

Eren groaned. "Fair point."

They endured a bumpy atmospheric traversal, and by the time they exited the clouds, they were well past the ruins of the closest city.

On the edge of what remained of a patchy, half-burned forest, a couple of low structures had been constructed out of felled trees and stone. A fence consisting of wire strung between rough-hewn wood stumps encircled the encampment. The entire settlement was less than two-hundred meters in diameter.

A smattering of dots moved inside the fence. "Can you zoom in close enough to make them out?"

"Why? Their file included visuals of them."

"I want to see them for myself. Watch how they move. Humor me."

Tolje complied, and they observed a group of three Phae'soon waddling around their encampment.

The comparison that sprang to mind was to a bipedal, upright salamander. Their limbs were short, with four webbed digits each. A stubby but wide tail flared onto the ground, its tip resembling the fin it presumably had once been. A long, round torso led to a smooth oval face and enormous orbs for eyes. Their skin rippled in bright, almost fluorescent colors and glistened as if perpetually damp.

Tolje snorted. "Ugly *diewls*."

Eren buried his gut response. Compared to the Hesgyr, the Phae'soon didn't look so bad to his eyes. Then it occurred to him that the Hesgyr might find him hideous to gaze upon; he decided not to ask. "Any working technology down there?"

"Basic power generation, probably from burning biomass, but that's about it. No communications are registering, so they're not talking to other settlements—or not regularly, anyway." Tolje began pulling the ship up toward the cloud cover. "We'll do a spot check to confirm no other regions have fared better, but I'm beginning to doubt these are our attackers."

"True. But you said their exocolony was spared the worst of the Rasu's attention."

"Yeah. We'll check it once we're done here."

The next hour passed uneventfully. They spotted two additional settlements no more expansive or advanced than the first, but mostly they saw ruination. The thoughtless, indiscriminate kind the Rasu were famous for. Whatever the Phae'soon's faults proved to be, they didn't deserve this. No one did.

The fact one of his own people's dynasties, the Theriz, had once inflicted no less horrific destruction on the worlds of species deemed 'unworthy of preserving' left a sour taste in his mouth, to be sure. He'd dedicated a century of his life to defeating the Directorate that had issued those orders to the Theriz. The Hesgyr's opinion of his people was correct, and all the work anadens had done in the last eighteen years to do better, to *be* better, had scarcely begun to scratch the surface of their debt.

Helping to rid the universe of the Rasu had to count for something, though.

Tolje flicked a finger against one of the switches on the left side of the dash and pointed the ship's nose at the black. "There's nothing on this world capable of hurting us. I know—the exocolony. Heading there now."

Once he'd put enough distance between the ship and the planet, Tolje punched in a course and engaged the auto-pilot. "No need to tax the wormhole drive in-system. We'll be there in forty-two minutes. Let's eat."

"Sounds good." It did not, but at this point Eren had numbed himself to the blandness of the slurry the Hesgyr ate.

Sitting at the small, bolted-down table, Tolje did more swirling of his food with his straw than eating it. "I typically visit thriving civilizations. After all, those are the ones who are making useful things worthy of appropriating. The scene down there, though? That was sad. A real waste."

"Yep." Eren forced himself to swallow a sip of soup.

"You ever encounter the Rasu up close?"

He huffed a breath and nudged the food box away. "You could say so. I got trapped on the planet where I was living—still live, most of the time—when they invaded. Spent days fighting them from tree to tree. Fighting and losing."

Tolje whistled low. "What was it like? What were they like?"

"Have you ever fought something that can't be killed?"

"Can't say as I have."

"You can slice a Rasu mech into a thousand individual pieces, and all the pieces simply melt, slide back toward one another, join up and reform. It takes seconds. If they need a blade, they become a blade. Need a flamethrower or a rocket launcher or a godsdamn ship? Same thing. They were utterly relentless and abjectly soulless."

"How'd you escape? Was this when Concord annihilated them?"

"Nah, that came a little later. This friend of mine, Caleb? He had a unique skill…you know what, it's far too complicated to explain in a way that will make sense. Basically, we were able to stop the Rasu on the planet due to special circumstances. The circumstance being that Caleb was present on the surface."

Tolje looked at him oddly, and Eren shrugged. "I have interesting friends."

"This I don't doubt. So, did your people ever figure out what the Rasu wanted? Evil without purpose is pretty rare in this universe. If you dig deeply enough, you usually find a justification for even the most heinous acts."

Startlingly insightful wisdom from the man. "All we know for certain is they were using the prodigious materials they harvested from the worlds they attacked to build rings around galactic cores, and those rings sped up the rotation of the galaxies in question. Some people think they were trying to reverse our accelerating cosmic expansion, at least for this corner of the cosmos, but it's only a theory. And even if it's true, an arguably noble purpose doesn't excuse the trillions of lives they extinguished in its pursuit."

"No question." Tolje stretched his arms over his head and settled lower into the chair. He didn't seem to be in a hurry to get back to the cockpit. "Can I ask, who's Cosime?"

Eren jerked in surprise. "Pardon me?"

"You talk in your sleep."

"Oh. I hope I didn't disturb you."

"I was already up."

"Okay. Um, she…*was* my teammate. My lover, my life partner. But she died almost four years ago."

"I'm sorry."

"So am I."

"Did the Rasu get her?"

"No—though the story I told did take place on her homeworld. Our home. But no. She was murdered shortly before the Rasu arrived by a man named Torval elasson-Machim, during a reconnaissance mission we were working." The words were spilling forth off his tongue now. "He was a high-ranking military officer, and he disobeyed orders—well, that's not technically true. Our government kind of lay in shambles at the time, and what little remained of it was in the process of trying to secede from Concord, or else overthrow it, whichever one worked. So Torval claimed no one had the authority to give him any orders.

"Anyway, he attacked a Savrakath facility while we were on the ground there. Blew the facility and most of my team to bits." He breathed out through his nose; he'd made peace with those events, so long as he didn't have to talk about them.

"And regenesis…?" Tolje asked.

"Wasn't an option. Cosime was a Naraida."

"The elfin species?"

"Yeah." He smiled at the reference, as the analogy only went skin deep; the Naraida were fiercer than most Barisans. "Some aspect of their biology foils all attempts at regenesis technology. To their credit, the scientists have tried repeatedly. They're still trying. But some species' brains won't accept the type of biosynth implants required to make regenesis work." His throat spasmed painfully. "So she's gone. Buried in a sepulcher on a mountaintop on Hirlas, surrounded by a field of forever-blooming snow-white flowers."

"It sounds lovely." Tolje's gaze dropped to his lap. "We can't always save them, you know—"

A polite beep rang out from the cockpit, and Tolje went up front and shut it off. After a minute, he returned to put away the meager dishes they'd used before going over to one of the cabinets on the starboard wall. He opened it, removed Eren's weapons, and offered them up.

Eren didn't give Tolje a chance to think better of the offer. He crossed the space in two strides, took the handgun, blade and miniature beam weapon and secured them in his pockets. "Thank you."

"Remember, that marker you wear around your neck means I'm responsible for you. You won't make me regret trusting you with these, will you?"

"I will not. Will they be a problem on Nythir?"

"Don't go waving them around in the air at passersby or brandishing them at Transitions. But if you keep them concealed, no. Half the residents of Nythir are armed."

"Understood." He didn't need to ask why weapons were commonplace on the station. Nythir wasn't a lawless place; in fact, the bar fight at Soul Lubrications was the sole act of violence he'd witnessed. But a proud, independent people with a rugged background were usually an armed people.

They returned to the cockpit, and Tolje called up the gaffaeler's follow-up report on a screen. "It says two cities remained standing on the exoplanet. Not sure why they escaped the Rasu's notice until it was too late."

But the answer became clear to Eren as they approached the planet. Situated on the edge of the habitable zone, it was painted in rust and sallow yellow, with only the faintest patches of moss green. It reminded him of images of Ares in the early days of the terraforming effort.

"There are no resources here worth harvesting. Nothing but dust and stone. Not that the Rasu wouldn't eventually take those as well, but it would've been low on their priority list."

"Makes some sense…strange. I'm not picking up any noise here. No comms escaping. No industrial activity."

"Two cities wouldn't be overly loud—not from way out here."

"No, but I'd expect *something* to register by now. Let's take a closer look."

As they neared, two artificial circles broke up the arid landscape, connected by four parallel lines...except two of the lines splintered at around the one-third point measured from starboard. It wasn't a good sign.

Light from the system's star glinted off the circles. They were dome cities. This confirmed the origin of the pale green blotches—early-stage terraforming. High, wispy clouds floated by above the surface, indicating the presence of a minimal atmosphere, but presumably it wasn't yet robust enough to risk living without protection.

They eased down through the thin atmosphere, and soon catastrophic damage became visible. A hole was punched through the top of the starboard dome some eighty meters wide, and craters dotted the planet's surface outside the dome's perimeter. A closer sweep above the second city revealed a spiderweb of cracks in its dome and pockmarked craters surrounding it.

Eren frowned. "Rasu?"

Tolje shook his head slowly. "The report indicated both cities were intact as of two years ago. This is recent."

"Damn. Any life forms registering?"

"You already know the answer."

"None at all?"

"Sorry. I wonder what happened here."

"I don't." Eren banged his head against the wall behind him. "War. Civil war, or an insurrection, or widespread riots. Even mature dome cities are rarely one-hundred-percent self-sufficient. Their supply lines from the homeworld got cut when the Rasu attacked, and they never returned. The situation on the ground gradually deteriorated, and with it, morale. Maybe people started getting hungry, or maybe they just missed their luxuries. One thing led to another and, bam—explosions for everyone. They killed themselves."

Tolje eased his hands off the controls and let the ship cruise a kilometer above the surface. "It's what species do, more often than not."

"Not the ones who make it this far."

"But it *is* often what happens following first contact. Whether because they meet an aggressive species, they flub the encounter or their culture can't handle the shock, over half of space-faring species are gone or have slid back to pre-industrial levels within a century after first contact."

Eren stared at him. "That, I did not know."

Tolje shrugged. "We've been studying alien civilizations for a long time."

"Whereas we've just been enslaving them for a long time. Point to the Hesgyr. Seriously, though, fuck the Rasu."

"Indeed. *Te diewl* with the Rasu."

Tolje headed for space without asking whether he was ready to go. Eren wandered into the cabin and collapsed on the jump seat, then dropped his forearms on his knees and let his head drop. What now?

He didn't hear Tolje join him until the cushion in the nearby chair made a squeaking sound. He peered out through a curtain of hair. "I really thought these guys were the ones. They fit the profile in every way—" He sat up straight and flung his hair over his shoulder. "What about other systems? Given their overall technological level, it's entirely possible they'd developed FTL capability. Planet-wide terraforming is top-tier tech, and FTL usually comes first."

"The file doesn't say anything about an extra-stellar settlement. Doesn't mean there isn't one, as our surveys tend to focus on the target, which in this case was the homeworld. But the file would've noted if there was any evidence of FTL capability."

"And this was the only off-homeworld colony the gaffaelers discovered?"

"No, there were others. Asteroid habitats, gas giant orbitals. All destroyed by the Rasu."

"Right." Eren dragged his hands down his face, fighting against a renewed wave of weariness. "Let's get back to Nythir."

15

Eren shut the light off in the guest room and sprawled out on the bed, arms spread wide until his fingers dangled off the edges. How in Hades' five rivers was he supposed to solve this mystery now?

The report had come in from a new Goljetsu fly-by shortly after they'd returned to Nythir. It confirmed those aliens no longer had the capability to so much as fly fifty meters off the ground, never mind into space. Neither, it appeared, did the few remaining Phae'soon eking out a meager existence on their wrecked homeworld.

So his two best candidates had flamed out, and he was back to square one. His professed usefulness debunked, the Confab would surely send him packing in the morning, unless he could dial up the charm to eleven and convince them to give him another opportunity to prove his worth, possibly via his other, far worse idea.

Odd, that this failure was bothering him so much. He didn't owe the Hesgyr anything. This was nothing but a side gambit on his part designed to maybe possibly get them to stop sneaking around Concord territory stealing things, after all.

But he found he'd grown to like them, ornery and irascible lot that they were. At a minimum, he liked them enough to want to prevent more of them from being murdered in gruesome fashion. Also, he hated being wrong, hated not being the dashing hero who saved the day with a witty retort delivered alongside a stylish flourish.

Yeah, that might be most of it.

A golden glow expanded to light the dark room, and he threw an arm over his eyes. "Doesn't anyone knock?"

"If I warned you I was coming, you'd wave me off." The light faded, allowing shadows to return. "Despite the fact that I'm bringing what you asked for."

He moved the arm and squinted in Nyx's direction. Her raven hair was pinned back at the sides, and she wore a simple but expensive gray tunic over casual black pants. "Now's not the best time. Kindly leave everything on the floor and go, so I can get back to pouting."

A jumbled pile of clothes landed on his face. "My advice? Burn what you're wearing, as it'll never recover from the abuse you've inflicted on it since you departed Ares."

"I'll take it under advisement." He wrangled the clothes and tossed them off to the side, then gave in and sat up. "And the rest?"

Two boxes thumped down beside him. "A 'thank you' is customary at this point."

He nodded soberly. "Forgive me, it's been a tough day. Thank you. I mean it."

Nyx stared at him for a moment, her expression scrupulously blank, before glancing around the room. There weren't any chairs, so she perched precariously on the edge of the bed and folded her hands in her lap. "What happened?"

He despised admitting weakness to her, so he hedged. "I hit a small roadblock in finding the source of these attacks. Spent a lot of hours on a ship that does not offer the height of luxury. Watched too much footage of attacks so grisly they sickened even my shabby, jaded heart. All in a day's work. How's home?"

"It's…fine. I won't bore you with the latest unconscionable moves by the Conference. I know how you loathe politics."

"Don't you as well?"

"Deeply. But it's now my job to care about politics, so I do."

It wasn't her job, not really. But keeping her grandfather safe was her adopted calling, so she'd added such distasteful items to her duties on her own initiative. If she insisted on adding the torture of political games to her daily activities, far be it from him to convince her otherwise.

So instead, he opened the first box. Inside were six state-of-the-art grade IV spikes specifically designed to adapt to dozens of computer configurations of foreign origin. Hesgyr systems weren't one of the preset configurations, but the spikes' firmware should get him eighty percent of the way there, and he'd handle the rest.

"What are you planning to hack?"

"You got the image capture I copied you on? The one with the locations of other civilizations in this supercluster?"

"I did. I don't envy the Consulate their job of turning it into usable intel."

"I'm hoping I can make their job easier. The Hesgyr have a shackled SAI here on Nythir, goes by SIMON. I was granted access to its high-level records on the Hesgyr's historical thievery, in the hope I could identify a slate of suspects in the attacks. If I can break into the machine, I can download a plethora of information on the individual civilizations—and also details on how much they know about Concord, not to mention how they obtained their knowledge."

"The first step in stopping them from infiltrating our facilities a second time...smart thinking."

"Actually, the first step is me making friends with them, so next time, they'll just ask if they need something. But it's always good to have a backup plan."

"Yes." Nyx nodded at the other box. "And the protein bars? Are they not feeding you?"

"No, they are, but their food tastes like spoiled Savrakath fertilizer."

"Oh."

An uneasy silence fell, and he filled it with a dramatic exhale. "Well, thanks for bringing all of this. I'll let you know what more I'm able to learn."

"Yes, about that." She stood and tried to start pacing, but the cramped room didn't allow for it. "The Advocacy has determined that the Hesgyr activities on Ares represent a clear and present threat to state security. Further, the attacks on these aliens from an unknown enemy have raised significant concerns about our own vulnerability. Accordingly, I'll be joining you here for the duration of your mission."

"You—what?" He leapt up, too, cutting off half her narrow path. "Bullshite. Corradeo trusts me to do my job and do it spectacularly. The 'Advocacy' didn't determine a godsdamn thing—you did."

"As Director of Intelligence, it is within my purview to decide such matters on behalf of the Advocacy."

"Fine, but don't hide behind grandaddy. Tell me you don't trust me to my face."

"That's not true. You have proved your value as an intelligence agent on multiple occasions." Her chin lifted. "But this is too important for one person to manage."

"You'd manage it yourself, if I wasn't already here."

"I ran my own solo missions for millennia as an Inquisitor. Missions far more complicated than this one."

He just stared at her in disbelief.

"What? When you were an anarch, you worked as part of a team. You had allies. When you worked for CINT, you did so as part of a team."

A rush of memories surged forth; his eyes closed so they could project a slideshow across his eyelids. Cosime had been his one steady partner through both organizations. She'd stood at his side causing chaos with glee for more than twenty-five years. In truth, he hadn't worked with a partner beyond the briefest assignments since she had died. He didn't know how to work with anyone else.

"I'm...sorry. I've caused you pain. I didn't mean...." Nyx's voice was stilted and formal; she was terrible at faking empathy.

"I know what you meant." He pushed the grief deep down, back into the hidey-hole in his soul where it lived, and forced his eyes open. "But I've spent the last five days working nonstop to earn a bit of goodwill from these people. What do you think your presence is going to do to the fragile progress I've made?"

"Demonstrate how Concord wants to help them with their problem."

"Oh, sweetheart. They don't *want* Concord's help. They are fiercely, obstinately independent. They don't particularly want my help, either, but I've convinced them—a few of them—that I can make a difference in their investigation. You, though? Not a chance. Ugh! I swear, I thought I had finally earned a smidgen of your trust."

"You have. I only…." She leaned against the wall, and a stillness overcame her. Her arms fell to her sides, as if she were leaving herself open and exposed. Her mouth opened twice before she spoke again.

"A while ago, you told me if I ever needed to escape the 'stifling walls of my office,' I could join you on an adventure—I mean a mission. So I wondered if I…Eren, I need to get out of the office before I lose my mind. I did not sign up to be an administrator. I'm not good with people—you know this, but please do not rub it in—and all my employees do is complain. All I do is read reports. Approve budgets. Discipline people. I was an Inquisitor, dammit! An *elasson*! My Primor's right hand of justice across forty galaxies. Now I'm a file pusher. A bureaucrat."

He gaped at her, dumbfounded. His throat worked, but no words came out.

Her shoulders sagged, as if in defeat. "So please. Let me help you for a few days. Give me a reason to be somewhere other than Ares until I can clear my head and regain a proper perspective on my work."

"I, uh…" he blinked "…I'm sorry to hear it isn't going well. I did offer to bring you along on a mission, and I…meant it." He hadn't, not in truth. Or maybe he had, but that was before things had gotten complicated between them. The last thing he needed—the absolute last thing in the universe he was prepared to handle—was her constant, unrelenting presence at his side. "I don't know if—"

A shout echoed from beyond the closed door. "Eren, are you talking to someone in there?"

She instantly stiffened, and her voice lowered to a whisper. "Who's that?"

"My host. Time for introductions, so put your game face on." He opened the door wide. "I am. Tolje, I'd like for you to meet Nyx Praesidis. A colleague from work."

Tolje glared at Nyx, then at Eren. "Why is there another Anaden in my apartment? Oh, wormholes, yes? *Bwachi*, don't let the Confab find out that Concord is opening wormholes all over Nythir. They will decide we have to relocate the entire damn station to a new galaxy."

"Eren, what is he saying?"

"Right, you don't have the translation file. He says we shouldn't open wormholes here without prior approval, as the local government views it as a security risk."

"Oh, you're suddenly polite?" Tolje asked sardonically. "She must be a lady. Is she your lady?"

"Decidedly not. She's my…she's sort of my boss, I guess, in the loosest sense."

"Great. We've attracted Concord's attention, then?"

"Not really. Don't worry about it. But…." He glanced at Nyx, hyper-cognizant of the uneasiness her nearness evoked in him. Dammit!

But she'd sounded so desperate in her confession, which had to be a once-in-a-millennia admission of weakness. If he rejected her now, it might turn her heart to stone for another thousand years, and he thought he'd feel guilty about that. Shouldn't, but he probably would.

He sighed. "If we can figure out a way to make it work, she's going to be staying for a little while."

CS

"No. Absolutely not. You've seen how we are about aliens. You've narrowly escaped getting your ass kicked multiple times already, and I've had to sign my life away to get you permission to do anything more than exist here. Besides, I'm only allowed one Visitor at a time. It can't be done."

Oh well, that's that! So sorry, Nyx. I tried, but you'll have to go home.
Eren was a little surprised when different words entirely came out
of his mouth. "I understand, but…we could have Banka sponsor
her."

"*Banka?*" Tolje's hand fisted, and it almost hit the wall beside
him. "Why in the seven stars would we get my daughter involved
in this sordid mess? Also, she doesn't take my comms, so we can't
ask her."

"I know she doesn't. But she's been kind of…nice to me?"

"I don't care. If your companion there screws up, then it's on
Banka's head. I won't risk her standing, her career, her *everything*
for a stranger. An alien."

Eren tried not to take the comment personally. "I don't want to
risk Banka's good name, either, but there's no need to worry. Nyx
isn't like me."

"What does that mean?"

"She's not a hothead. She's not impulsive or flamboyant. In fact,
she's pretty much a stick in the mud." It was for the best that they'd
excused themselves from Nyx's presence to have this discussion.
Not as he cared whether she knew what he thought of her, but if
she overheard him, she'd feel the need to correct him on every
point, with receipts.

"And what does *that* mean?"

"It means she's no fun at parties."

"This explanation only makes a fraction more sense, but I think
I get the gist. You're saying she won't cause any trouble—which is
not the same as saying trouble won't be caused." Tolje frowned at
the closed door to the guest room. "Why does she need to stay, anyway? Why do we need two of you?"

Eren didn't particularly want to dive into how Nyx had been
one of the twelve highest dispensers of 'justice' in the old Anaden
Empire. Or how she'd spent millennia wielding the power of *diati*,
an ancient primordial life form that used the fabric of space as its
personal play toy. *Or* how she was the granddaughter of the most
powerful man to ever exist in anaden history.

So instead he stuck to the basics. "She's been an investigator for a really, really long time."

"I know Anadens are pseudo-immortal, Eren."

"Of course you do. The point is, as much as I am loath to admit it, she's highly skilled at finding people who don't want to be found. She doesn't necessarily think outside of the box the way I do, but she's seen every trick in the book, made every connection that exists to be made. She'll be an asset to our search. Look, this enemy is marching on Nythir. They could show up here any hour or day. We need to solve this, and we need to solve it now. Take the help."

Tolje made what passed for a groaning sound, letting it rattle around in his throat like a handful of loose screws. "*Cachu hewch.* I'll see what I can do. *Without* involving my daughter."

CS

While they waited for Tolje to return with news, Eren caught Nyx up on everything he'd learned about the Hesgyr since he'd arrived. She sat quietly on the couch, absorbing the firehose of information without expression, her eyes unfocused as she sorted and collated the data in her mind.

When he decided he'd covered everything amenable to words alone, she nodded deliberately. "They sound disorganized, bordering on anarchistic, and lacking much in the way of moral fiber. Narcissistic, jingoistic, isolationist and unworthy of a moment's trust."

"More or less," he agreed. "But they do grow on you."

"No, they grew on *you*. You've rarely met an alien you couldn't enjoy an ale with."

"True, but I hardly liked all of them. The aliens or the ales."

"A distinction without a difference, to my mind. Tell me about the attacks."

Internally he squirmed, and decided to get a drink first. He didn't want to divulge to her how his brilliant analysis of the data, which he'd been so certain had yielded the culprit in record time, had instead turned up nothing. Two dead ends. It wasn't as though he cared much at all if she thought well of him. But if she didn't think well of him, it would affect his job. If she tried to outright fire him, Corradeo would intercede on his behalf, but she could make his working life akin to camping in Tartarus.

He stared at the glass of water he'd poured. He hadn't lied to Tolje; she genuinely could help. She saw things differently from how he did, often identifying patterns he missed—and vice versa, obviously. They'd made an effective, if brief, team on several occasions. And now that she was here, he gained nothing by withholding the information from her.

So he steeled his spine and went back to the living room, taking up his seat on the couch opposite her, and resumed talking.

She listened as impassively as before, though he decided her eyes betrayed a hint of added intensity. She was no longer merely absorbing, but also judging.

Finally he reached the end of their foray into Phae'soon space earlier today and spread his arms wide. "And that's where we are."

A frown darkened her expression. "You put faith in the Hesgyr's assessment of the states of all those civilizations following the Rasu invasions?"

"No, not entirely, but I haven't exactly had the opportunity to double-check their reports on hundreds of species. I did consider asking the Kats to follow up, but even they will take weeks to survey everything."

"Still, we should do so. Concord will benefit from the files you plan to steal, but the Kats will find the map you copied to be sufficient to locate the relevant planets and assess their status."

"True. Want to go through official channels, or shall I just reach out to Mesme?"

"Official channels, as this will soon expand into a formal project under the Exploration Initiative. I'll handle it."

He shrugged. "Suit yourself."

"I agree that your revenge scenario is the most likely explanation, but it needn't have been triggered by the Rasu. Numerous aggressive aliens prey on the weak. Even if they don't have the strength, reach or weapons the Rasu did, it doesn't mean they can't destroy a given species."

"True...sort of. Anyone within the Rasu sphere of influence, predator or prey, would have gotten overrun, which eliminates two-thirds of the territory the Hesgyr have ever visited. As for the other third? We're still talking about a tremendous number of species. The Hesgyr have been at this for a while."

"So it seems." She paused, contemplating something. "I confess, I'm surprised. If they've used FTL technology for hundreds of millennia, I'd have expected us to have run into them before now."

"They cover their tracks well. But I agree. It's humbling."

"Humbling?"

He took a sip of his water before answering; he'd been thinking a good bit about this topic. "Before the Humans arrived and Concord was born out of the ashes of the Directorate War, we anadens fancied ourselves quite the kings of the universe. Oh, we recognized that geographically speaking, our territory was tiny when compared to the overall scope of the cosmos. But psychologically, we believed we sat at the top of the pyramid, technologically and militarily. And since Concord was instituted, we've only expanded our reach and power. But the truth is, we are barely a ripple in the cosmic ocean."

"I wouldn't go that far."

"I would."

Her lips pursed, as if to dismiss his assertion out of hand. "Clearly. But you're forgetting something: the Dzhvar. How long had they been gobbling up the manifold before they happened upon us? We were confined to the Milky Way back then, so we don't know for sure, but the Kats speculate the Dzhvar may have torn apart upwards of a third of the universe before they were destroyed."

"Put to sleep."

"Perhaps. Until they actually reappear, I remain skeptical they ever will. The point is, a million years ago, the Dzhvar reset the board of life. We survived, and it seems the Hesgyr did as well, but how many other advanced species didn't? Everyone we've encountered, even the Rasu, rose out of the muck since then. Yes, other intelligent species exist whom we've yet to discover, but the number is a fraction of what it might have been if the Dzhvar had never rampaged through space."

It was a valid point. The tiniest spark of pride in his people for having saved the universe from collapsing into lifeless ruin flared in his chest—which was ridiculous, because he was not prone to feeling such pride. More often embarrassment.

The door opened, announcing Tolje's return, and they both stood. "What's the word?" Eren asked.

"If I ever have another child, they'll be the property of the Confab from birth."

He chuckled lightly. "So she can stay, then."

"Provisionally. I have been granted an exemption to sponsor a second Visitor, on a whole host of conditions, every one of which we will go over in detail, because this is my skin on the line."

He smiled. "Thank you, Tolje. We appreciate it."

Tolje grunted as he tossed Eren a new marker.

Nyx stared at him expectantly, and his smile faltered a touch. Gods, he hoped he didn't regret this. "Put this around your neck and don't take it off—ever. Now, let's get you a translation file."

16

A guard snapped to an attentive stance as they walked into the SAI's server room. "Halt and state your reason for entering."

Eren greeted the guard as if they were old friends, then gestured to Nyx. "The Confab has authorized this woman's presence here. Hopefully they informed you."

"Word came through half an hour ago." The guard studied her for several seconds. She couldn't discern any particular emotion from his rigid features, but she could wager a guess. "I suppose it's not my business why you're here."

Nyx had only been on Nythir for a few hours, and she was already tired of the constant suspicion and hostility emanating from every Hesgyr she'd encountered. The truth was, she'd rarely interacted with people who didn't know who—or at least what—she was, and therefore treated her with either respect or fear, depending. But to the Hesgyr, she was simply an alien. A stranger. And they didn't particularly care for those.

She didn't bother to smile at the guard, but she did keep her tone neutral. "I'm assisting Eren in his investigation into the attacks on the Hesgyr."

"We don't typically allow aliens to assist in much of anything."

Eren promptly cut off the biting retort she readied on her tongue. "But these aren't typical circumstances. Your people are dying, and everyone wants to bring an end to it, us included. So listen, I do want to warn you: this is likely to be a long, dull session today. We're planning to dig through the voluminous files on the many, many, *many* species you all have stolen items from, in the hope that we can find one who is gunning for revenge."

Somehow, the guard didn't punch Eren in the face. Instead, his shoulders rose in acceptance. "This is my job. I will remain at my post."

"Of course. I'd expect nothing less." Eren waved a hand toward the contents of the room. "Shall we get to work?"

Her lips curled down in distaste as she evaluated the SAI's unimpressive hardware. Bulky and ungainly, constructed of dull, scratched metal rife with sharp edges and mismatched joints, it struck her as appallingly primitive. She half-expected sparks to shoot into the air the first time either of them touched something. Eren had delivered a lecture on not being fooled by the often messy, metal-heavy flavor of Hesgyr creations, but ingrained prejudices died hard, and with good reason. They were usually based in fact.

"SIMON, it's good to talk to you again."

'And you, Eren Savitas. Who is your companion?'

"This is Nyx Praesidis, a coworker of mine." He ignored her arched eyebrow. "The data you maintain on the gaffaelers' targets is too voluminous for one man to handle, so she's going to help me out."

'Does this mean your investigation into the Goljetsu and the Phae'soon did not yield positive results?'

"Neither of them is up to the task, I'm afraid. So we want to revisit the files on the species flagged as surviving the Rasu—as well as those the sweeps indicated did not."

'A species that the Rasu eradicated is, by definition, unable to launch attacks on the Hesgyr today.'

"I know. But I'm curious how you define 'eradicated.' Can you pull up a sampling of the files and let us take a look at what your scouts found when they surveyed those species?"

'I can do so.'

A sea of text, images and charts populated across multiple screens. Eren tilted his head in her direction. "As requested. Do your thing." Then he wandered off toward the guard.

"Hello, SIMON." She searched for some physical indicator of 'presence' to focus her gaze on, but none existed. She'd worked with enough of the Humans' Artificials to concede it was possible for life to emerge out of quantum hardware, but she highly doubted it was present here in this room.

'Hello, Nyx Praesidis.'

"I'm going to study this data for a few minutes. I'll speak up if I need you to provide any assistance."

'Understood.'

Behind her, Eren started chatting up the guard. "I've only seen a tiny fraction of Nythir, but I find it fascinating. Have you lived here your entire life?"

"No. Aren't you supposed to be helping the other one?"

"This sort of dry technical analysis isn't my favorite part of the job. I'm more of an intuitive thinker."

So that was what he called it? She blocked her hands with her body and set a tiny projector on one of the narrow shelves below the bank of screens. Her finger depressed a button the same instant she sent the command to her cybernetics to activate her Veiltech. As she vanished from sight, she was replaced with a perfect projection of herself.

She instantly moved to the corner of the room that housed the physical interfaces and the I/O box, as time was of the essence. The projection engaged in normal low-key body movements, but it didn't talk. She'd set the stage for her silence, and hopefully Eren would keep the guard sufficiently distracted for him not to notice any oddness in her behavior. Though, how would he or the SAI know what behavior counted as odd for an anaden?

She produced a hacking spike and held one end over the input slot. The device scanned it, then morphed its other end to fit the physical dimensions and connections. She flipped the spike around and inserted it.

They had done the hard work of the data infiltration before they'd come to the lab, which involved first feeding the spike the Hesgyr language files. Then Eren had customized the program's logic based on what he'd been able to glean of how Nythir's systems talked to one another; finally, they'd set the parameters for what they wanted to locate and copy. The spike included a clever little sub-Artificial brain inside, so now it busied itself deciphering the SAI's security systems and worming itself past them.

The sound of Eren's laughter pealing through the room in response to something the guard said jolted her. Its tenor was warm and rich, conveying genuine mirth. Hells, it probably *was* genuine, for Eren could find amusement in the dullest, most asinine situations.

She didn't understand it. He found people of all stripes fascinating, whereas she tended to regard them as impenetrable and, for the most part, uninteresting. Throughout her many thousands of years as an Inquisitor, people had been either targets of suspicion or sources of information. They plotted and schemed and rebelled, and should her attention turn their way, it all came to naught for them.

Until one day it didn't, and everything about her life changed.

What are you doing, Nyx Praesidis?

The words blinked in sinister yellow on a tiny screen located above the I/O module.

She ignored the inquiry for the moment, buying the spike time to complete its work. If SIMON chose to alert the guard, she'd yank the spike out, open a wormhole and escape home with the data. Possibly Eren would react swiftly enough to accompany her, but if not, she'd return for him later.

A light on the spike flashed green. She removed it from the slot, dropped it into her pocket and moved quietly back to the primary screens, where she timed her deactivation of the Veiltech and the projection to a nanosecond. If the guard saw a flicker, he'd blame it on a blink of the eye.

The same inquiry greeted her here, scrolling on a horizontal screen below the ones displaying the files Eren had requested.

What are you doing, Nyx Praesidis?

She waited until Eren was talking, then answered in a soft, casual voice. "It's going to take us many hours to analyze all this data. It will be so much easier if we can do so from the comfort of a couch. You understand, don't you?"

I find your answer unsatisfactory.

But the SAI wasn't speaking aloud, which meant it hadn't decided whether to report her transgression. She began to reconsider her snap judgment of its intelligence.

Now that she had the data they wanted in hand, she took a second to decide how best to respond. Eren genuinely wanted to help these people, and she…frustration clawed at the edges of her mind. She didn't want to return home yet. She felt guilty for abandoning her grandfather, but she couldn't protect him from the dangers of the legislative Conference. Besides, Corradeo ate politicians for breakfast. He would, for the time being, be fine.

So they both wanted to prolong their stay on Nythir, which meant the best course of action was to secure the SAI's cooperation.

Eren had dived into the recounting of an outlandish tale involving three Barisans, a skalef game and…a pig? Knowing him, it was a true story. Still, she kept her voice low.

"We don't mean the Hesgyr any ill will, nor do we intend to cause harm to them or you, SIMON. In fact, we will do everything in our power to find who is behind these attacks and bring them to justice. You have my word on this. Now, Eren and I need to review all the files with our own software in order to accomplish this, but in the time it would take us to convince the Confab to allow us to do so, more people will die. This is the best way. Do you understand?"

The cursor blinked at her.

Dammit, quantum machines did not take this long to think! She decided to treat it as a 'yes' and refocused her attention on the information splashed across the screens. The Hesgyr were thorough in their surveys—enough so as to make her optimistic about the quality of the data she'd just copied.

This time she spoke in a normal tone of voice. "SIMON, question. When the Hesgyr survey a new species, they obviously focus on the homeworld, but it appears the scout also identifies in-system settlements. What about out-of-system ones? Do they search around for settled exoplanets or stations orbiting neighboring stars?"

SIMON resumed speaking aloud, as if their interchange had never happened. 'If the species displays a high level of advancement, such that they would be capable of regularly traversing interstellar space via some manner of FTL travel, then the scout will check other systems in the area, yes. In a small number of instances, they have discovered additional outposts in the region. True multi-stellar civilizations are rare, however.'

"We've found this to be the case as well. They do exist, however. Can you display a list of species that wielded superluminal travel capabilities, no matter the specifics of the technology used?"

'I am not certain the information fits within the bounds of the material the Confab has authorized you to view.'

A bit of pushback from the SAI—it viewed her explanation as suspect, but not enough to report her actions. Yet.

Eren reappeared at her shoulder and leaned in, sending his long hair brushing across the fabric of her sleeve. He didn't smell the way he usually did—fresh, clean and faintly woodsy, as if he'd just stepped out of one of Hirlas' many forests—but instead like the Hesgyr's pungent chemical soap. The mismatch was oddly disconcerting.

"Oh, but it does, SIMON." He flashed her an easy grin. "Remember, our goal is to uncover the species who is responsible for these attacks—and the location from where they're originating. To do that, we need to learn where the aliens are. To find them, we need to know how far afield they can travel."

'A pertinent point. Here is the information you requested.'

A list of over two dozen species populated a lower screen. The fact that such a number was 'rare' brought home the overwhelming quantity of species the Hesgyr had surveyed—then stolen from.

In case the spike had failed, she captured a visual of the list with her ocular implant; later, they could cross reference it with the map and the files.

"Great." Eren rubbed his hands together. "Let's take a closer look at these guys."

17

*B*anka Alainor: *"Caraf, run me up a new drill bit. This one's shot."*

Caraf Kwechi: "Copy that."

Banka swung in the basket fifty meters above the cavern floor and waited for the trolley to arrive with the replacement bit.

Beside her, a half-bolted-in rail clung to the hard mineral cliff the team had carved into the interior of The Mountain. When completed, the rail would ferry a steady supply of containers up and down the cliff, holding them in place while an army of robotic miners deposited extracted rhenium into them as they worked.

In another week—if the schedule held, and when had it ever held on construction projects—this vast cavern would be swarming with the mining drones and little else. But for today, living, breathing people filled its hard, unyielding depths. They clambered over the walls in strung harnesses and rode lift buckets and shepherded heavy equipment here and there on the floor below.

Drones could work faster and more efficiently than Hesgyr hands (and without complaint), but only if the infrastructure for them to operate was installed and set up correctly. Lophalin, the corp that had hired her, was currently in a race against time with two competitors to bring a mining operation online, and one of them had a ten-day head start on the other side of The Mountain. But Lophalin was taking the time to do things properly in the hope it would pay off in the long run. The decision reflected well on them. They displayed a tough, no-nonsense operating ethos, but they seemed to grasp the science and mechanics of mining. Her mother had once spoken highly of Lophalin, and after a few days on the job, Banka was beginning to understand why.

The trolley arrived, and she retrieved the fresh drill bit before tossing the spent one into its basket and sending it on its way. This was the fourth bit she'd broken in the five hours of her shift, for the ferrous rock was tough and unforgiving. Likely this was why every company in the industry was clamoring to fill their storehouses with it—

A vibration shuddered the cliff beneath her hands, and she drew the drill back before the new bit shattered. What kind of equipment were the other operations erecting across The Mountain? Did they want to bring the peak down on everyone?

A strange sound echoed below the constant squeal and hum of machinery, and she rolled her eyes. Not everyone Lophalin had hired had her skills and experience; she'd bet her lunch rations that the noise was someone breaking a piece of expensive equipment below. Whoever they were, she didn't envy them the ass-chewing the shift supervisor was about to deliver.

The vibration in the cliff ceased, and she lined the drill back up on the brace of the rail...then frowned. Situational awareness kept her safe in an often dangerous line of work, and those senses now buzzed an alarm in her brain. What was wrong?

It was suddenly too quiet. Half or more of the machinery had gone silent. She peered below to see several people running toward the entrance. From the rear wall of the cavern, an umber cloud roiled over the mine floor. Had someone cracked into a vein of gas trapped in the stone?

Someone screamed, then another. The cloud billowed outward to overtake the entire floor, even as it began climbing into the air.

The whispered rumors circulating through the halls of Nythir leapt to the front of her mind. The mysterious attacks that had killed so many people took place inside an impenetrable cloud, they said....

"*Bwachi!*" She was situated high above it—and not nearly high enough. She forced her gaze away from the mushrooming cloud and up. Her harness was secured another twenty meters above her, just below the roof of the cavern.

She cranked the pulley in frantic circles, and the basket crept upward with the speed of one of those lumbering heliffants on Safanau.

A quick glance down told her the cloud was gaining altitude. She was moving too slowly. In frustration she grabbed onto the rope and began hoisting herself up, hand over fist, as an eerie blanket of silence descended upon the space beneath her.

She didn't look down again, instead focusing all her efforts on climbing ever higher, until her gloved fingers tightened around the piton driven into the wall of the cavern. The toes of her boots still skimmed the floor of the basket—it was three meters she couldn't afford.

She tore off one glove with her teeth and let it fall to be swallowed up by the noxious cloud. A grunt escaped from deep within her abdomen as she swung her legs up until the soles of her boots pressed against the wall; she aimed her bare hand and shot viscous material out of her fingertips until it formed a web securing her feet to the wall. Her gloved hand started to slip, and she hurriedly returned her other hand to the piton.

Then she pressed her body flush to the rough stone and hung on for her life.

CS

"The architecture is so distinct between each of the…'districts,' they call them?" Nyx asked as they made their way through the Rydai District. "I can detect the same fundamental structural philosophy beneath it all, but the differences are stark."

"They are. Each district has its own personality, motif, unwritten rules, local governance, everything. Often the districts were built at radically different times, too, hence the Transitions." Eren thought on it briefly. "Or possibly those are just in place to reinforce the fact that you're entering a new, nigh-on sovereign territory."

"How peculiar. Most species move away from tribalism and factional rule and toward a single government as their civilization advances, not the other direction."

"It's not the only way the Hesgyr are unique." They reached Tolje's apartment, and Eren let them inside. "Tolje, are you here?"

No answer. Good. He went to the guest room and retrieved the data reader Nyx had brought, then grabbed some water for them from the kitchen and sat at the small dining table he'd yet to see be used for dining. "Let's see what the spike captured while we have a few minutes to ourselves."

She slid into the chair opposite him and inserted the spike into the input slot. The reader manifested a virtual screen so they could both view the data.

…Which was voluminous. Scores of species visited across a timeline stretching back for a million years. Thousands of pieces of technology stolen, from the crude and rudimentary to items that toyed with bending the cosmic manifold to their will. And, more importantly, precise locations for all those species. Stars moved, granted, but given a neighborhood in which to search, it would be a trivial matter to locate them again.

Eren let out a low whistle. "This is quite a haul. Great work."

"It was a simple enough task."

Perhaps the most straightforward compliment he'd ever given her, and she'd driven right past it. He made a note not to repeat the courtesy.

Oblivious to her slight, Nyx scrolled deliberately through the file system. "Let's see what they have on Concord." She located the file a few seconds later, and they both leaned in closer to study it.

It made for dry reading. A brief overview of the old Anaden Empire and its recent replacement by Concord that got many of the details wrong, followed by a few paragraphs on the major Concord institutions and significant species. They overestimated the importance of the Khokteh and greatly underestimated the influence of the Novoloume; most people did, and the Novoloume preferred it this way.

The text grew considerably more detailed, but no less dry, once it dove into the copious technology used by Concord, and Eren started skimming. After all, he lived with this stuff every day.

"There's nothing in here about the MAST or how they discovered its existence," Nyx mused.

He backed up to see if she'd missed it, but it didn't appear to be listed anywhere. "How odd…no, wait, it's not odd at all. I bet Tolje hasn't filed his final report yet. In fairness, I've been keeping him busy since we arrived."

"That's disappointing. We need to learn how they knew about it at all, never mind where to find it." A scowl marred her objectively attractive features.

"Sure, but look at what we *did* net. Information on thousands of species, along with their locations and stages of development. The Consulate is going to buy us dinner for the next decade."

"I expect Dean Veshnael will be pleased…." Nyx leaned back in the rigid chair, crossed her arms over her chest, and let her gaze unfocus.

"What?"

Her eyes flitted vaguely to him, then to the screen. "Before we go any further, there's something you need to know. SIMON realized I was copying all this data from its server."

"What?"

"While the spike was running, SIMON asked me what I was doing—in a way that made it clear it comprehended exactly what I was doing. I assured it we didn't intend to bring any harm to it or the Hesgyr, and after a brief if tense interchange, it dropped the subject."

He huffed a laugh. "Fascinating."

"If you say so. Do you believe it will report us to the Confab?"

"SAIs think at the speed of light. If it was going to report us, it would have done so already and…" he gestured toward the door "…no officers storming the apartment. I'll be damned. I thought I picked up on some sparks of life in its personality, but I couldn't be certain. It seems I was right."

"Don't get carried away. In any event, this isn't about the theoretical question of the SAI's sapience or lack thereof, but rather the real and precarious state of our welcome here."

"Oh, it's absolutely about the SAI's sapience or arguable lack thereof. If SIMON made a decision of its own volition to defy the Confab, that's huge. And, as I said, fascinating."

"Then you can sit here and ponder the cultural and philosophical implications." She stood and reached for the spike. "I need to get this off of Nythir and to the proper people in Concord, in case the door does get kicked in by armed personnel intent on arresting us."

"Wait." Eren laid his hand on hers to stop her from removing the spike. Heat instantly surged through his skin where they touched, and for a beat he was scarcely able to breathe.

Arae! He forced himself to casually remove his hand, as if it were an afterthought, then banished the sensation from his thoughts. "Settle down. No one but Tolje is coming through the door. If it makes you feel better, message the Prevo you have on tap and tell them to be ready to open a wormhole at your word, but we might not have another chance to talk through some theories without Tolje eavesdropping."

Nyx regarded him with an utterly unreadable expression for several long seconds before returning her hand to her lap. "What is it you want to discuss?"

"I'm glad you asked." He idly started maneuvering through the file structure. "What if the Phae'soon have another colony that survived—an extra-stellar one?"

"The Phae'soon weren't on the list of species possessing superluminal capabilities. Why are you still stuck on them? I realize they looked to be a good fit at first glance, but it's poor investigative procedure to cling to a theory once it's been proved wrong."

"Ouch. You wound me." He clutched at his chest dramatically. "Except I don't think it's been proved wrong."

She planted her elbows on the table, clasped her hands and dropped her chin on them. "Fine. Why not?"

He stared at her for a moment, and he wasn't entirely certain whether it was because she'd struck such an engaging pose or because she wasn't snippishly dismissing his claim out of hand. Either way, he definitely should not have touched her.

"Eren?"

"Sorry." He located the file he'd been searching for, opened it up and started to read.

She frowned at the screen. "This is the description of the Magelo Wide-Field Disruptor—the weapon the Hesgyr stole from the Phae'soon."

"Yep."

"I don't disagree that the theft provides them with a reasonable motive. But they simply don't have the capability to execute these attacks."

"Unless they do."

She groaned and stood. "I will not play twenty questions with you. I'm getting this data home. You can chase your ghosts while I'm gone."

"Found it!" He held up a hand to forestall her renewed attempt to snatch the spike, but took care that it didn't get anywhere near hers.

"Found what?"

"This note here. The weapon utilizes negative mass to amplify the power of the beam it deploys." Neither Eynon nor Preece had mentioned this detail, but he *had* shut them down when they'd tried to dive into the weeds of how the weapon worked.

"So?" Her tone was dismissive, but she slowly eased back down into the chair nonetheless.

"Negative mass is hard to artificially create. Like, really hard. The ability to do so is one of the hallmarks of a genuinely advanced species. And while it apparently comes in handy to supercharge this Disruptor device, there's only one truly compelling reason to go to all the effort of creating it—and that's superluminal travel. Warp bubbles require it. Stable wormholes require it. Pretty much any manipulation of the spacetime manifold requires it."

"You think the Phae'soon did have superluminal capability, and the Hesgyr missed it."

"Maybe not. But if they'd learned how to create negative mass, which they obviously had, they were close. I'd be willing to bet that within a few years after the Hesgyr picked their pockets, they figured it out."

Nyx's brow furrowed at the text on the screen. "It's conceivable. In which case, they *could* have founded an extra-stellar colony." Her gaze finally landed on him. "How did you know?"

He convinced himself he detected a hint of admiration in her voice, and a smirk danced on his lips. "I didn't."

"Clearly you did. You went straight for this file."

"What can I say? I'm more of an intuitive thinker."

"So I heard." She rolled her eyes in a rare display of amusement. "If the Phae'soon developed an FTL drive, we can potentially locate the colony with a wide enough search pattern and a bit of time. But if they built a wormhole device, the colony could be literally anywhere. So how do we find it?"

"By using the reason I'm here in the first place—the MAST. If I can get inside the cloud during an attack and fire the device, entangled particles will travel home to the source and give us a location. Bullseye."

"Do I need to list all the problems with this plan?"

"I realize we don't know precisely where they'll strike next. But the options are dwindling and—"

Tolje stormed through the door and hurtled his backpack against the wall. "*Te diewl a pen bach!*"

Eren stood somewhat cautiously. "What's wrong?"

"That *pen bach* Kneath snaked the Malachwl job out from under me. It's worth 68,000 credits!"

Just business, it sounded like. "I'm sorry. This is my fault, I imagine. I've kept you running in every direction instead of attending to your work."

Tolje cracked open a bottle of a dark liquid, collapsed into his chair and took a long swig. Liquor, then. "No. Well, yes, but the fault is still my own. No, no, the fault lies with these blasted aliens, whomever they are. It's not as if I'm not going to try to help solve the problem and save an untold number of lives, right?"

"Right, because you're an honorable man." He was a little surprised to realize it was true, in a strange way.

"I won't argue. How did the—" Tolje sat up straighter and placed his drink on the side table. "Message from Preece. There's been another attack."

Eren shot Nyx a dry smile. "It's your lucky day. Where at?"

"Another mining—*bwachi!*" The next instant, Tolje was a blur of motion. In a blink he'd leapt across the room, grabbed his backpack, and was sprinting toward the door.

"What's wrong?" Eren asked for the second time in two minutes.

"It's Daith."

"Okay. What's special about Daith?"

"Banka was doing a job there," Tolje shouted over his shoulder, halfway out the door.

"We're coming with you." Eren motioned for Nyx to get her ass up and follow.

"Then you'd better run."

18

The flight to reach Daith passed in a blur. If he said a word to his Anaden guests, Tolje couldn't recall it. His awareness had narrowed down to a pinprick, and the last words Siwan had ever spoken to him repeated like a mantra in his mind:

Look after Banka until I return from this job. She's too reckless, same as you, and she hasn't yet built the guardrails she'll need to survive out there in the hard, cold world.

Banka had stopped allowing him to look after her a long time ago, but her choice to exert her independence had never released him from the responsibility of doing so. She didn't have that power.

The inky blackness of full night in this region of Daith masked any hints of scenery to distinguish the planet as they landed. The makeshift spaceport was located close to The Mountain, as the workers had dubbed it, because no one was wasting any time in this place. The discovery of rhenium here three months earlier had been like a lightning bolt through the materials industry. Three companies were each scrambling to dig as much as possible out of The Mountain before the other two beat them to it, the better to reap the prodigious riches it promised.

Lophalin had turned to large-scale automation to hasten the process—and also because finding workers willing to do such backbreaking work was a challenge, no matter how generous the compensation. The company had selected Banka to help get the infrastructure operational.

Tolje was proud of her. Her reputation as a supremely competent mechanic who got the job done efficiently and without drama was spreading through the right circles on Nythir. And if the worst had happened here today, it wouldn't be the first time a stellar reputation among their peers had gotten someone he loved killed—

No. He couldn't think this way. He shouldn't think at all. Not until he knew. So he focused on imposing a blank slate upon his thoughts.

A loud, barely-held-together tram took them from the spaceport to Lophalin's forward operating base. By this point a solid third of The Mountain had been blown apart or torn out, and floodlights cast a harsh yellow glow across a towering mass of jagged, crumbling rock.

"Sir, you and your…guests will have to wait here."

A snarl whispered out from between Tolje's teeth as he scowled at the security guard, a rotund young Hesgyr with pasty gray skin and weaselly eyes. He held up the pass Preece had given him for the Fetel-reu visit, which he'd never returned. "I have authorization. Let me through."

The guard squinted at the pass, puffing a wheezing breath through his nostrils. "Fine. What about these two…whatever they are?"

"They're with me. Confab authorized."

"I don't know if—"

He jerked his head at Eren and marched ahead. "Let's go."

As he'd suspected, the guard sputtered but made no move to try to stop them. For all the professed disdain most Hesgyr spouted about aliens, the actual presence of one was noteworthy. The presence of *two* at his side marked Tolje as Someone Very Important.

Despite the expansive, open-air nature of the location, the scene wasn't much different from Fetel-reu in its layout. Officers and investigators and scientists clumped together at the edges of a lake of blood and viscera, as if so long as they didn't let any of it touch them, then it wasn't real.

"—Hanishen's mess is even more gruesome. Spilled down a conveyer ramp and…." The snippet of conversation faded into the general din. Had the enemy encompassed the entire Mountain in its deadly cloud? Didn't matter. Only one thing mattered.

Tolje pulled up short and fixated on the blood. His gut churned over the acids of the liquor he'd consumed at the apartment. *Be rational, Tolje. You can't learn if she was in there this way; they don't leave behind so much as a scrap of clothing. Find someone who knows.*

So he tore his gaze away and stormed up to the first person he saw. "Was Banka Alainor onsite? I need to find her."

"What?" The man scowled at him in annoyance. Blood streaked his cheek, and his vest was torn almost in two. "I don't know who that is. Find somebody from Lophalin."

Tolje elbowed his way toward a group of men in work coveralls. "Hey! Do any of you know if Banka Alainor was here when the attack occurred?"

A short man with a smattering of tiny horns looked over. "The mechanic? Maybe. I saw her working up on the wall around twenty minutes before it happened."

No. "Who does know?"

The man shrugged. "No idea. Shift supervisor was, uh, liquified."

He got in the man's face, towering over his scrawny form. "Who. Knows."

"Back off! I lost two-thirds of my crew to this horror. Find Wathaen and ask him."

"Who the *uffer* is Wathaen?"

"Uh, he was over that way a few minutes ago." The man pointed off to the left, toward where shadows crept in as the artificial light faded. "He's wearing a bright red vest. Ugly as moss on stone. You can't miss him."

Tolje started jogging in the indicated direction—and promptly lost his footing and fell forward, his hands barely bracing him as he landed. The surface slanted downward in this area, and a tendril of blood and goo had crept out from the lake in this direction.

He held up his hands and stared at the bronze fluid staining his palms, glimmering faintly in a beam of harsh light…then bowled over the rest of the way and puked up the liquor. It was instantly swallowed by the viscera—

"Banka!"

Had he shouted her name? No. It had been carried on the butter-smooth, fanciful tones of the Anaden. Eren.

Tolje stumbled to his feet, almost slipped again, and frantically searched around for Eren. The man should stand out in the crowd.

Finally he spotted a flash of long, golden hair past a smattering of scientists huddled together—and beyond him…. He took off running.

"You had us worried. Most of all—"

He knocked Eren aside and wrapped his daughter up in his arms. "You're alive."

"Obviously." Banka squirmed in his embrace; after several attempts, she got her hands between them and shoved him away. "What are you doing here?"

He checked over the cartilage of her cheeks, up over her horns, and back down to count her limbs, same as he'd done when she'd gotten into scrapes as a child. All pieces and parts accounted for. "I heard Daith had been attacked."

"How…" she grimaced down at her coveralls, now smeared with the blood he'd collected in his fall "…great. Do you have any idea how hard I've had to work to keep this mess off of me for the last two hours? The sleeping quarters are cordoned off, so I can't go change, either."

She glared up at him, eyes narrowing precipitously. "Wait. How did you know I was doing a job here?" Her hands went to her hips, completing a stance of defiance he recognized all too well. "*Duwi*, you're spying on me! Have you tapped my system? Put up cams in my apartment? Bribed my boss? And you wonder why I don't trust you. Get out of here, Dad. I told you I don't want to see you, and I meant it. Go home."

"I'm not spying on you." It was true, in the most technical sense of the term. "I came because I was worried about you. Worried that you had…." The last words petered out as he swayed unevenly, a flood of terror-induced chemicals flushing out from his brain and into his body.

"Yeah, you're real good at showing up after it's too late to do anything." She grunted and spun to leave.

Eren laid a hand on Banka's arm. "One second. Your dad was really concerned. We all were, but he was…" Eren glanced at him, then perhaps softened what he'd been about to say "…like I said, concerned."

"I bet. Who's 'all'?" Her eyes popped wider on spotting Nyx, who lingered a step off Eren's left shoulder. "Oh, you've brought another Anaden. Fun."

Eren tilted his head. "This is Nyx Praesidis."

"Okay."

"If you don't mind me asking, how did you survive?"

Yes, Tolje thought through a cloud of endorphins and draining adrenaline and vague dizziness. An excellent question.

Banka gestured up and behind her, toward the heights of the excavated cavern. "I was working near the top of the wall when the attack started. Scrambled up as high as I could, and the cloud stopped expanding a few meters below me."

A few meters…they were all that separated life from death, heartbeats and fiery glares from a plaque above the mantle. He'd often wondered if a few meters had fallen the wrong way for Siwan.

"Quick thinking on your part, to get as high as possible." Eren was speaking again.

"I guess. Down was certain death, up only probable demise. Anyway, I've got to gather what Lophalin gear of mine survived and turn it back in, lest they charge me for it. *Uffernol* aliens! Not you and your friend, Eren. The monstrous ones who did this." Her attention drifted to the sea of blood. "Somewhere in there is what's left of Macsen. He asked me to go out for drinks after shift. I was thinking about saying yes. *Bwachi.*"

Then she pivoted and stomped off.

They stared silently after her for a moment, until Eren's lips pursed tight. "I'm sorry it went that way, Tolje."

"Sorry? Why? She's alive. It's all that matters."

"Surely. But she was kind of a bitch to you."

"Nothing new there. I'm just glad she was here to do it."

I haven't failed you yet, Siwan.

Feeling steadier now, he planted his feet and lifted his shoulders. "I expect Preece will show his face any minute now. Since we're here, we might as well try to find out if they've learned anything new from this latest attack."

CS

When they got to Tolje's apartment, Eren swiftly changed his clothes. He didn't think he'd gotten any of the gore from the Daith massacre on him, but merely being in proximity to it made him feel dirty nonetheless.

He returned to the guest bedroom, where he found Nyx emptying their bag holding the rest of their wardrobe onto the bed.

"What are you doing?"

"I need to get the intel on this spike into Concord's hands. If we're forced to visit many scenes like the one on Daith, we're going to need more clothes, so I thought I'd go ahead and acquire some for both of us while I was home."

It comforted him to discover she'd come away feeling the same as he did. "Good idea."

She checked the inside of the bag to confirm it was empty, then exhaled ponderously. "That was difficult."

"Yeah. In a lot of ways."

"Why was the woman—Tolje's daughter—so rude to him?"

"They have a strained relationship. I'm not certain of the backstory."

"It strikes me as simply the way Hesgyr are."

"Emotionless, you mean?" He arched an eyebrow.

If she recognized the insinuation, she didn't acknowledge it. "Not at all. There were plenty of emotions on display by her. Anger, contempt, frustration, bitterness. To name a few."

"And what about Tolje's emotions?"

"I didn't see much of any from him."

"Then you weren't paying attention."

"If you say so." After she secured the bag on her shoulder, she reached around and touched a spot near the small of her back. A faint glow began to light the room.

Eren's brow furrowed in confusion…then he groaned. "You've got one of the new wormhole generators, don't you? It's how you're moving back and forth so easily. I assumed you had a Prevo on call, but no. Figures."

"Is it such a surprise that I'd be entrusted with one of the first prototypes? My job is—"

"Of the utmost importance, yes. The kingdom would fall if you couldn't respond instantly to every perceived threat to the Advocate, the Advocacy or a lost kitten wandering the streets of downtown Olympia."

"Look, Eren, I don't know what—"

He held up a hand to forestall her tirade. "You're right. I'm sorry, and I take it back. I'm just on edge after what happened today."

She was silent for a few seconds, then nodded tightly. "Understandable. I'll return in a few hours." She stepped through the tear in space that had formed in the room, and it sealed behind her.

CS

Tolje glanced over from the kitchen as Eren exited the guest bedroom alone. "Everything all right?"

"Fine. Nyx is making a quick trip home to take care of a few things."

He grunted a disapproval. "What did I say about you all not opening wormholes on Nythir?"

"I know. She's being discreet."

"Hmm." He poured a tall glass of wasgi—the day's events justified something a little stronger tonight—and eased into his chair.

After hesitating for a beat, Eren took a seat on the couch opposite him. "Do you want to talk about what happened today?"

Did he? Even if he didn't, did he have a choice? His guest was sitting there watching him, waiting for ugly truths to be revealed. Oh, Eren gave a stellar impression of not doing either of those things; the Anaden had a natural, easy air about him that made one want to relax around him. To chat about the day's gossip or unload one's burdens into welcoming ears. His guest was rather skilled at his job.

Recognizing the act for what it was, Tolje nonetheless found that, after taking a long sip of his drink, his mouth was opening and words were spilling forth.

"I'll answer the question you're not asking out of politeness, which is *why*. Why my daughter despises me so. My wife—Siwan was her name—was a geologist. A boring profession to most, but she loved the science of it all. Metals, magma, the rocks that litter planets. She would have been happy studying minerals under a microscope in a lab until the end of her days. But the thing is, the practical aspects of geology are crucial to a lot of the activities that keep Nythir functioning. The station has an insatiable appetite for fresh materials to keep it not merely holding together but expanding. You saw Fetel-reu, and Daith today. Mining and the prospecting preceding it are big business around here. And Siwan? She was damn good at her job.

"So she was always getting loaned out to the corps for jobs. She'd travel to some planet or moon or asteroid and spend a few days or weeks studying whatever it was one of the corps believed it had uncovered, then tell them if it was their latest goldmine or not. The money was substantial, so she didn't complain too much. And neither did I, as it meant I didn't need to feel guilty for running off on jobs for weeks at a time myself. We tried to time it so one of us was always at home with Banka. Usually managed it. But looking back, I didn't spend as much time with Siwan as I should have. Didn't realize what that meant until it was too late."

The story was piling up at the base of his throat, eager for release, but he forced himself to pause. Eren offered him a wistful smile and took a sip of his drink. Probably thinking about his own lost lady.

"One day Siwan got called out to this planet way over on the other end of Leo, where this corp, Roalden, thought it had found some new, 'special' mineral. She tried to get them to send her a sample to study in the lab, but Roalden was concerned the metal's dispersement into the surrounding rock was going to dilute it too much during extraction. They insisted she conduct an onsite analysis.

"The planet was a borderline garden world, and the local primitives had set up a patchwork of camps a few dozen kilometers from the mining site. A gaffaeler did an assessment and determined the locals weren't capable of traveling such a distance with any speed, were migrating in the opposite direction anyway, and weren't advanced enough to wield anything more dangerous than clubs in any event. Low threat."

Eren's lips pursed tight as his eyes shaded darker, as if he knew where the story was going.

"She'd been on the ground for three days when the natives attacked—on mounts and wielding bows and arrows, spears and machetes. The dig site had a security perimeter, of course, but it was only staffed with two rotating guards and a single laser turret. The natives numbered at least thirty. By the time a ship arrived from orbit to deploy real firepower, it was already over."

"I'm so sorry," Eren replied. "I also realize full well how meaningless those words are."

"Yeah." He sipped on the wasgi, letting it swish around in his throat before burning its way down. His gaze went to the picture on the wall of Siwan; he willed himself to see her as she was in the image, not as she must have been lying torn apart on the cold ground of an alien world.

Eyes like polished rubies and skin like burnished silver. A smile so wicked it could level a room and a laugh so beautiful it stirred birds to sing in refrain.

Much better. "Our schedules were a bit off, and I was headed back to Nythir from a job when it happened. Banka was staying at a friend's place, and the authorities showed up and told her what had transpired before I was able to reach her. So…not an auspicious beginning to our life without her mother. Banka was twenty-three, in the prime of her adolescence and full of rebellion—but Anadens arrive fully grown. You don't know about adolescence."

"I know a little. A good friend of mine, Caleb—I mentioned him earlier—has a niece. They're Human, which is basically anaden except they have babies and do some other weird things. Anyway, I got to hear an earful about Marlee acting out in various ways for years. She's a fine woman now—capable, fearless and kind—but it took a while to get through the growing pains."

"That it does. Banka was already a handful, unruly and disobedient, and she took out all her grief on me. Held me responsible for her mother's death."

"Why?" Eren asked. "It sounds as if you were blameless."

"It's all about perspective. A gaffaeler screwed up, and her mother died as a result."

"Guilt by association."

"Yes, but it was more complicated. Banka thought—likely still thinks—I should have checked the gaffaeler's report before Siwan went on the job. Or better yet, swung by the planet and confirmed the findings myself."

"Was this something you normally did for your wife's work?"

"No. I'd done it once or twice in the early days, when she was new to field work, but it had been years. Siwan didn't want me looking over her shoulder. She was confident and independent. Banka takes after her in that way."

Eren's soft skin wrinkled above his nose. "I can understand a child—an adolescent—reacting out of emotion. It's totally understandable. But it's been…" Eren glanced at the image of Siwan "…how long?"

"Sixteen years."

"And Banka's never forgiven you?"

"I think...I think I probably made enough new mistakes in the years following her mother's death to keep Banka's hatred for me fresh. If she were to rank my mistakes, her mother's death might not even reside at the top of the list any longer. But since there's a list, no reason to remove it, either. And...." He took a slow sip of the wasgi as a deep weariness crept into his bones. It had been a day. "She wasn't entirely wrong, either. It's dangerous out there in the black, and no one knows this better than a gaffaeler. Just because Siwan didn't think I needed to scout ahead, doesn't mean I didn't need to. Doesn't mean I shouldn't have done it anyway."

"That's a judgment call—*your* judgment call."

"It was. And I've made peace with it. You have to make peace with your mistakes if you want to go on living. Otherwise they crush your soul."

Eren stared at him, a thousand emotions Tolje couldn't decipher rushing across the man's expressive features like waves crashing upon a shore.

Then the moment passed, and Eren's friendly demeanor returned. "It would be stupid of me to ask if you've tried sitting down and talking to Banka. After all, I've seen the two of you together. But...have you?"

"Sure, I've tried. I'm a glutton for punishment. I mean, I shapeshift for money. But our relationship is a lost cause, and I've made peace with this as well." He nodded to emphasize the point. "She's her own person. She's bright and resourceful and living her own life. I'm proud of her. And it's all I can do."

"But it's not all you do. You keep an eye on her."

"I don't spy on her. It's not how she said."

"Then how is it?"

Damn but his guest could be persistent. "I know a couple of people in Transition Maintenance. They keep me updated on how she's doing. When she gets a commendation or an interesting new assignment, nothing more. One of them gave me a head's up the other day that she'd gone to Daith for a one-off. But now she thinks I'm spying on her—one more item to add to her list of grievances.

Mind you, I don't fault her, because I earned most of them. I only..." he shrugged and finished off his drink "...it is what it is. Still, today...." The memory of the gut-wrenching panic he'd experienced burned fresh in his mind, and he willed himself not to relive it. No need, for she was alive.

"Maybe it's time to give reconciliation another try?"

"Would that I could." He chuckled darkly. "Stop making me feel optimistic, as if I actually stand a chance. It'll only sting worse when I fail."

"Unless you don't. Fail, that is."

"Bah." He stood and stretched. "You're a dreamer, Eren Savitas. Some of us have to live in the real world. I'm going to try to get some sleep."

"I'll see you in the morning."

19

Nyx exited the wormhole from Ares into Tolje's guest bedroom on Nythir. The glow faded until the room was cast in almost total shadow; she could barely make out Eren's form stretched out on the bed.

"Welcome back," he murmured.

"Truly?"

He sat up enough to rest on his hands, and his vibrant irises—gilt like solar flares—found Nyx in the darkness. He leaned over and turned on the bedside lamp. "I mean…. Did you get the data to a good home?"

"Grandfather rapidly elevated it to a Concord-level matter and sent it to Special Projects." She hadn't even argued with Corradeo about the decision. The Advocacy had no diplomacy division to speak of; there was no precedent for it, as anadens had never invested in diplomacy. In the Anaden Empire of old, the discovery of an alien species had swiftly led to the aliens' subjugation or worse. Best, then, that they let Concord handle external relations.

"Good. Devon Reynolds will be able to transform it into actionable intel for the Consulate to pursue in no time."

Nyx sat on the edge of the bed, near the footboard. "I don't care for Director Reynolds. He's arrogant, flippant and disrespectful."

"Toward you?"

"Toward everyone."

"Fair enough. But he's also extremely good at his job. Richard trusts him, which is enough for me."

"As you say." CINT Director Richard Navick was the opposite of Devon Reynolds in every way—humble, cautious and soft-spoken—yet both Devon and Eren seemed to practically worship the man. She didn't understand it, but she'd also never devoted any effort to trying to understand it.

"I admit, Director Reynolds came through this time." She reached in her bag and pulled out an unmarked gray box.

"What is that?"

"A shield. The highest quality shield Concord has ever built for protecting the wearer from physical, non-energy intrusions. It's based on the Imperium double-shielding."

"What are they calling it?" Eren asked.

"PR2X-A. It's not far enough along in the development cycle to have a real name."

"Hmm. Those Imperium shields require a tremendous amount of power to drive them."

She shrugged. "Power is easy these days. The labs have reduced Zero Drive tech down to nanoscopic size, and I believe the power source for this shield is nearly that small. Mind you, this here is, for now, one-of-a-kind technology. If you lose this unit, the Advocacy will owe Special Projects a rather large sum."

"Me? What am I supposed to do with it?"

She dared to gaze into those dangerous eyes of his again, as this was important. Earlier this evening, when she'd realized she believed it to be important, she'd spent some time pacing around her office on Ares trying to work out why. Logic didn't support the conclusion, yet refused to dislodge her conviction that it *was* important.

"Wear it whenever you manage to stumble your way into one of those death clouds with the MAST."

"I told you, the weapon targets Hesgyr biology, which is quite different from our own—"

"I don't care. Eren, what I saw today on Daith? There was nothing left of those people."

"Nope."

"I've seen all manner of carnage—"

"And caused a fair bit of it, too."

The barb shouldn't sting as much as it did. She owned her past, triumphs and transgressions in equal measure. "Not like that."

He tilted his head in concession.

Nyx stood, then remembered the room was too small to pace effectively in, and settled for crossing her arms over her chest. "I've seen Ch'mshak rip the limbs off a person and snatch their head off of their spine. I've seen Barisans gut someone from navel to throat with their claws. I've seen Rasu slice someone into two dozen pieces and leave those pieces to fall one-by-one to the ground. I've seen a person's skin blister off the bone from a high-powered microwave beam. I could go on."

Eren grimaced. "Best that you not."

"The point is, I've never seen something reduce a living being to nothing but the blood their body held. Whoever these attackers are, they are beyond merely cruel. They are perverse and sadistic."

"Under my working theory, they blame the Hesgyr for the murder of millions of their people. Possibly almost their entire population."

"And if so, it merits a response on their part. But killing is not enough for these aliens...." She didn't finish the sentence, because she was ascribing emotional motivations to the attackers without evidence. "In any event, I want you to be protected."

"I'm sure I don't need to remind you how, should I die in one of those 'death clouds,' as you called them, I'll just wake up back home in a cushy regenesis chamber a couple of days later."

Gods, he was always so stubborn about the stupidest things! "Eren, your death would be excruciating. Those people did not go quickly, quietly or painlessly."

"It wouldn't be the first time I've suffered before nulling out."

"You know, that's not a badge of honor."

"Didn't say it was. But it is true."

Annoyance faded away in favor of a quieter but deeper frustration—something she often felt about Eren, though she hadn't nailed down the reason for it. He knew how to get under her skin, when no one else did. "I thought you had gotten past the self-immolation routine."

His reply was a few seconds in coming. "Maybe I've relapsed."

"Are you saying you wouldn't *mind* being dissolved into a puddle of bloody goo over several agonizing minutes?"

"Of course I would mind it. Definitely not on my top five list of things to do this week. But sometimes it comes with the job."

"No, it came with the anarch job. You haven't been an anarch in a long time."

"Eh, in the grand scheme of our lives, eighteen years isn't very long."

The annoyance roared back. "Gods, you are insufferable!"

Eren sat all the way up and thrust out a hand toward her in warning. "Keep it down. Tolje's sleeping. He had a rough day."

She lowered her voice. "Sorry. But do you value your life at all?"

This time the silence stretched out for longer. She didn't have a better follow-up question, so she waited.

"I'm trying to. Most days I succeed…but not all of them."

"Well I—" She cut herself off hard, because her voice had carried a slight quaver. After a calming breath, she began again in a measured tone. "I won't slosh through buckets of blood that happens to contain yours. Wear the damn shield."

"*Fine.*" He groaned and collapsed onto the bed—and just as swiftly, threw his legs over the side and climbed off. "Right. Forgot this is your bedroom now. I'll head out to the couch."

"There's no need to be chivalrous. I can sleep on the couch as easily as you."

He snorted. "Oh, I'm not being chivalrous, sweetheart. You're the least damselly maiden I've ever known in my life. But Tolje is far more comfortable with me than he is with you. Better for him to come upon my snoring, drooling form sprawled on his couch when he wanders into his kitchen wearing his underwear in the middle of the night for a glass of water."

She nodded curtly, for she had no desire to discover what Hesgyr wore for underwear—if they did. "It's a fair point. I'll see you in the morning."

"Yeah." He grabbed a pillow and headed out into the living room. He seemed angry, but she'd given up trying to decipher his moods.

Once he was gone, Nyx shifted to the head of the bed, removed her shoes, and sat cross-legged atop the covers. It had been a long day, one spanning three galaxies, four worlds, multiple scientific labs and a lake of blood.

To say that she wasn't squeamish was to note how the distance between stars was vast; it stood as a simple truth of the universe. Once upon a time, she likely wouldn't have blinked at the scene of devastation on Daith, if she acknowledged it at all.

Then everything she'd believed to be true for millennia was shown to be a lie. In response to the revelation, she'd disavowed her Primor and thrown away her *diati* and been left with nothing. No power, no identity, no rules or even guideposts to signal the way forward.

She'd spent the next fourteen years traveling the stars with her grandfather, learning at his knee as he slowly, gently taught her how to be a real person, one who still had a place of value in the universe. The experience had changed her perspective on much: life, death, and how she might embrace a role as someone other than an arbiter of the dividing line. Corradeo had once been forced to learn those lessons, too, and this had made all the difference for both the teacher and the student.

So now, her mental judgment informed her that, crude and rude though they were, she did not wish for the Hesgyr to be murdered so mercilessly.

Her heart, however? It insisted she could not allow Eren to suffer anguish. Not random people—obviously none but the most evil should be tortured—but Eren, specifically. And her mind refused to conjure up any input whatsoever on why this was the case.

CS

Banka collapsed onto the pillow with a harsh exhalation of air, as finally, many hours after the alien cloud arrived, the adrenaline began to dissipate. Her teeth unclenched, then the muscles along her spine. The persistent hum driving against her eardrums since the attack quieted.

She lazily reached over and laid a hand on Pedr Eynon's arm. She'd bailed on Daith and returned home the instant the authorities had released everyone. All three corps at The Mountain had suffered massive casualties, and she doubted the job would resume in the near future. As soon as she'd docked on Nythir, she'd commed Pedr; he'd rushed over, as she'd known he would.

"Thank you. To say I needed that is the understatement of the century."

"The pleasure was mine." He propped on an elbow to scrutinize her with the intensity of a drill sergeant. "You amaze me, though. You escape having your internal organs liquified by scarcely a meter, and in response, the one thing you want most is sex."

"I had to relax somehow." *Had to make sure I was still alive.*

"And now you are? Relaxed?"

"I mean…kind of, yes." She forced herself not to squirm under the weight of his inspection. She *had* been relaxed, until he started grilling her. "I expect horrid thoughts about the people who died will soon creep back in. That grisly scene is going to haunt my nightmares for a while."

The instant she uttered the words, the memory of shimmying along a rope, suspended over the liquified remains of her coworkers, to reach the entrance to the cavern, flashed in her mind. She slammed the door on the image; it would wait its turn. "But for now, yep. Totally relaxed."

"More power to you." He shook his head. "You know, I'm surprised you agreed to take the Daith job at all. Greedy practices by the corps were what got your mother killed."

"A gaffaeler got my mother killed!" Her teeth resumed their clenching. Stars, he did not know how to take a hint. "It wasn't the corp's job to sign off on the safety of the site—the honor went to the gaffaeler assigned to scope it. Anyway, Lophalin actually runs a quality shop."

"Okay, okay." He kissed the corner of her lips. "You don't have to convince me. Gaffaelers represent the worst of us—the sloppy, seedy, selfish underbelly of Nythir society. Their work should have been nationalized under the purview of the military centuries ago." His lips paused their journey down her neck. "Speaking of, I saw your father the other day."

She wiggled out of his arms a few centimeters. "Why does everyone keep saying that?"

"What?"

"Nothing. I just bumped into an old friend earlier this week and…the point is, I don't care."

"I know you don't. Sorry I mentioned it." Pedr started to urge her closer, then changed his mind and checked the time. "I need to go. I've got a meeting with the Confab's military subcommittee early in the morning, and I need to review the latest reports first. When they find these monsters, I want to be at the head of the fleet sent to destroy them."

She eyed him sideways, surprised at the fervor surging into his voice. "You mean that, don't you?"

"I do. They tried to kill you. I won't stand for it."

She hurriedly looked away. Had he grown to care for her so much? She hoped not, as she wasn't ready for the commitment. This was supposed to be a casual, fun, occasional hookup. No strings attached. She could already feel the clasp snaking around her ankle, preparing to chain her to him, to obligation and duty until the day he abandoned her.

She kicked the remains of the covers off and climbed out of the bed. "You don't need to protect me, and you definitely don't need to defend my honor."

"What if I want to do both of those things?"

"Find something else to fight for. Like…hey, you lost a couple of men who used to be under your command in the attack at Can-chal-se, didn't you? They're properly dead, so exact vengeance in their honor."

He stared at her. "I did, and they are, and I have every intention of doing so. Doesn't mean I can't do the same for you."

"No need. I'm still alive." *I checked and everything.*

PART III:
THE MAELSTROM

20

E ren stretched out on the couch, his hands folded behind his head, and stared at the ceiling. He'd woken up thinking about the terrible scene at Daith, but mostly about his conversation with Tolje last night.

Death screwed with people's lives in so many insidious ways. This was probably why anadens had stopped engaging in it aeons ago. He wasn't certain regenesis had fixed much about their lives on the whole, but it definitely hadn't made things worse.

Except when it had, of course, like when the one thing he'd wanted most in the world was to die. After Cosime was killed, he'd forcibly disconnected himself from the regenesis servers then tried to fly his ship into a star. Why simply point a firearm at your head and press the trigger, when a flashier, oh-so-dramatic option was on the table?

His friends Drae and Mesme had intervened to prevent that fiery death, as well as the next few, more pathetic, attempts. And in time, Eren had relented and rejoined functioning society. Not because he'd valued his life anew, but because Cosime would have wanted him to—and because his friends kept busting their asses trying to keep him alive, so he figured he owed them.

Eventually, though, existing in the world grew easier, and he started laughing again. Joy, on occasion, returned to his life.

He'd once told two of those friends who'd helped him, Caleb and Alex, that immortality was worth the fortune of galaxies. And one day, many months after Cosime's death, he woke up and *didn't* weigh the pros and cons of disconnecting from the regenesis servers again. Because he remembered why he'd professed such a belief.

Oh, he'd heard the arguments advanced by a smattering of Humans that removing the inevitability of death from the equation took the wonder and heart out of life. But he also saw Humans taking up regenesis in record numbers the instant it became available to them. When given the option to live forever, they were grasping for it with the glee of the desperate, and they were right to do so.

He decided he'd do what he could to help Tolje and Banka. He doubted they'd ever achieve a happy, harmonious, loving relationship, as their personalities seemed to clash like oil and water, but perhaps they'd get to a point of civility. Enjoy the occasional family dinner and such. He thought Banka liked him, so when he got the opportunity, he'd try to nudge her in a conciliatory direction.

He glanced at the door to the guest bedroom in growing annoyance. Tolje had run out to take care of an errand early this morning, but he'd return soon with big plans of chasing murderous aliens scheduled for their day. Eren wanted to shower, but Nyx hadn't so much as stuck her head out of the bedroom. Rights to the bed did not include rights to hogging the lavatory for hours at a time, dammit.

Enough. He stood and went to the door—then knocked on it instead of barging in. He did not need to see her naked. By which he meant he *really* shouldn't.

"Come in."

He found Nyx sitting on the bed, mercifully fully dressed. She wore black pants, as always, but she'd mixed things up today with a deep magenta fitted shirt. Her raven hair was slicked down and secured in a long, low tail. A single wisp had escaped to hover over her left cheek; he didn't tell her about it.

Her eyes held the unfocused quality that indicated virtual data danced in her vision, and she didn't speak further.

"What's up this morning?"

"I'm trying to figure out how to talk to the SAI."

"You're still worried it might report our hack of its files?"

"No—well, yes, though I'm more curious as to why it hasn't. And I want to cover our bases." Her eyes darted left to right in rapid fashion. "The ability to talk to SIMON without getting clearance from the Confab and traveling halfway across Nythir could prove useful."

He perched on the edge of the bed, much as she had the night before. "What progress have you made?"

"Some. I analyzed the comm flow Tolje set up for us to reach him if needed, and extracted the protocols driving it. I can now talk to someone if I have their address."

It was clever thinking on her part, though he didn't volunteer the compliment. "But you don't have SIMON's address."

"No. And I'm certain they've siloed it. If SIMON succeeded in accessing the general comm system, it could bring Nythir to its knees with a passing thought."

It was the worst nightmare of every species who invented artificial intelligence, often with good reason. Immature SAIs, bereft of wisdom or general common sense, had brought more than one civilization to the edge of ruin. "Because shackled or not, its security protocols are likely cobbled together from a half-dozen species. There could be any number of exploitable holes, and the Hesgyr are smart enough to know it. So, siloed."

"Exactly." The fingers of her left hand twitched in the air, an autonomic response to her manipulation of data.

She didn't elaborate; he was going to have to pull the details out of her one by one, at least until she closed her virtual interface. "Then do enlighten me. How do you expect to talk to it?"

"The spike didn't just copy files from the servers. It also left a little something behind. Now I merely need to tunnel through a couple of firewalls comprising the silo to reach it."

"You planted your own comm node in SIMON's programming. Brilliant."

A corner of her mouth twitched, as if she wanted to smile. "Thank you."

He ought to have thought of it himself, especially since stealing SIMON's files had been his idea in the first place. "You should have told me."

"I'm telling you now."

A snarky retort stalled on his tongue as noises in the main room heralded Tolje's return. A few seconds later, their host poked his head through the open door of the bedroom. "Good, you're up. The Confab wants to see you. Both of you."

Eren swung his legs onto the floor. He'd been expecting a summons at some point today. "Great. Let me run through the shower first. Nyx hogged the lavatory all morning."

"I did not—"

Tolje shook his head. "No time. They want to see you in twenty minutes, which is two minutes longer than it takes to get to the Alpha District."

"But the Confab has never actually seen me freshly showered," Eren protested. "They're going to think I'm slovenly."

Tolje snorted. "You smell no better than a foul mountain creature in the summer heat and your clothes are fit only for a vaudeville show. A shower isn't going to help. Let's go."

CS

Eren listened with half an ear as Tolje ran through all the Confab rules, protocols and etiquette with Nyx on the ride over. He'd give the Confab one thing: they had managed to instill a healthy respect, if not quite fear, into a populace that didn't respect much of anything. He wondered how they'd accomplished it, and how long it had taken.

When they arrived in the chamber, Preece was giving a presentation about the science team's latest findings.

"With the discovery of a small, domesticated creature still alive inside the kill zone, and the presence of response markers in the creature's immune system, we can now say with some degree of confidence that the weapon is calibrated to target Hesgyr physiology."

Perfect. Eren wouldn't even need to lead the reps by the nose to where he wanted them.

Preece went on for another few minutes about chemical traces discovered at the scene, apparently due to oxidation of various materials, but didn't have any conclusions to present on the topic. He acknowledged them on his way out, and Eren and Nyx were led to the center of the chamber. Tolje was instructed to wait at the entrance, which elicited much grumbling on the Hesgyr's part.

"Nyx Praesidis, welcome to our chamber," Rep Dacus intoned formally.

"I'm honored to be here. Thank you for allowing me dispensation to visit Nythir. I hope my presence will be of use to you."

"This remains to be seen. Eren Savitas, when you last appeared before us, you indicated that you believed if the MAST device were present during an attack, it would perform its intended function and allow us to track the incursion to its source."

"I'll do it," he replied.

"Pardon me?"

"If you can get me to ground zero while a cloud is manifesting, I'll take the MAST inside the cloud and activate it."

"We weren't suggesting...." Dacus stammered then trailed off.

"No, but you were working up to it. You're getting desperate—which I completely understand. You should be."

"Mr. Savitas, you have no reason to risk your life for us."

"Not especially, no." He held his palms out and shrugged broadly. "But I'm already here and everything. Besides, I told you I could solve the mystery. This is how. Somebody has to use the MAST. There's a decent chance the cloud won't so much as prick me, but we know it will kill any Hesgyr who breaches its perimeter. So I'm your guy. Now, how do I get myself to the site of an active attack?"

Nyx shot him a glare, and only then did he realize he'd casually omitted her from his statements. He hadn't done it intentionally; he'd simply grown used to working alone these last four years. Besides, it served her right for keeping her plans for SIMON a secret from him.

Rep Dacus gestured to a man dressed in attire utilitarian enough to mark him as staff, and a second later a hologram of a section of the Glow hovered in the air above them. Two red pinpoints flickered within one of the spiral arms. "An analysis of the pattern of incursions strongly suggests that one of these two locations will be targeted next."

"You're assuming their ultimate destination is Nythir."

"We are."

They weren't burying their ugly heads in the sand. Good. "Have you ordered an evacuation of those locations yet?"

"There will be no evacuation orders."

Eren's gaze leapt from the map to Dacus. "*Excuse me?*"

Dacus had the temerity to look chagrined, but the rep didn't retreat. "The enemy's modus operandi is to murder the largest number of people possible in a defined space. They will not attack unless there is a significant population present. In order to deploy the MAST, an attack is required. Therefore, people at the location are required."

Eren whistled. "You all are some cold sons of bitches."

"No, they're correct," Nyx interjected. "It's the only way."

He glanced sideways at her. "And so are you."

Her lips set in a firm line, but she didn't reveal a hint of shame or even hesitation. Then again, she rarely did.

"Will you at least have emergency services on site, ready to move in and evacuate people from the immediate area as soon as the cloud appears?"

Dacus' glanced toward another of the reps, who shook their head in response; this discussion had previously taken place in private. "Such a presence might alert the enemy that we are prepared for them, leading them to cancel the attack."

Eren groaned. "Look, they've got the same map you do, and I doubt they think you're stupid. They must know you know they're coming. In fact, I'd argue they're counting on it. Fear is a powerful weapon in its own right."

"Of course they expect us to know they are coming—but not where," Dacus replied. "A highly complex and sophisticated analysis led us to identify these two locations. We have many other settlements in the region of space between Nythir and Daith—enough that the enemy may well believe selecting any one is a random choice on their part."

Not stupid, but arrogant, stubborn and blindingly cavalier about their obvious superiority to other species. Eren rubbed at his temples. "All right. Fine. They're your people, not mine. We only have one MAST, so which of the two locations is more likely to be hit?"

"The odds are effectively even."

He studied the map, which marked the previous strikes as well as all Hesgyr settlements in the region in subtler shades of amber and teal, until he had a sense of the patterns—and made a gut call. He pointed to the leftmost red dot. "We'll go to this one."

CS

Eren had lobbied to pick up the MAST from Preece's lab and take it with him, but the Confab was reticent to let loose of their stolen prize so easily. Instead, Eren and Nyx were to travel on a ship to Ghoede with the scientific investigative team. They would be deposited at the colony along with the MAST, and the ship would then retreat to orbit until the attack, if it came, was over.

He didn't think Preece's people cowards for staying behind on the ship; if they were caught in the cloud, they would die. Simple as that.

The accelerating pace of attacks suggested the next one should come within thirty hours, but in case it took longer, the three of them headed back to Tolje's apartment to pack some food and a change of clothes—and so Eren could take a godsdamn shower.

"So what is Ghoede like?" Eren asked Tolje. "The file said it was a timber operation."

Tolje shrugged. "Idyllic, as Hesgyr colonies go. Fresh air, lots of greenery and open space. The first-pass timber processing happens in the forest where they fell the trees, so the town and even the mill are fairly quiet."

"Huh. I'm surprised you all don't use synthetic wood."

Tolje gestured down the promenade of the Rydai District. "As big as Nythir is, it doesn't have space for that kind of large-scale manufacturing. Or rather, the Confab has chosen not to devote precious station space to it. And once you're operating on an exoplanet sporting millions of square kilometers of forest, it's cheaper to process the wood instead of building and maintaining a huge production factory. Economics on both ends."

Eren wondered if the Hesgyr were replanting the forests they clear-cut, or whether they figured they'd find another forest-laden world when a given one ran dry. But he didn't ask; he didn't need to know, and casually insulting their practices did not further his strategic goals. And when Nyx opened her mouth as if to ask, he laid a hand on her arm to warn her off.

Once they were inside the apartment, Tolje headed off to his bedroom as if to pack his own bag. Eren stopped him. "You should stay here this time."

"No. I'm all in on this insanity now."

"And I appreciate it. But we can't predict how large the attack perimeter will be, or precisely where or when it will begin. You can't outrun the cloud. No one else has."

"Banka did."

"She didn't run, she climbed—and she got very, very lucky."

Tolje's expression clouded over, and Eren pressed his advantage. "You've seen how fast the cloud moves on the recorded footage. Unless you can shapeshift into a giant cat in a millisecond, you won't be able to escape, and I won't have your death on my conscience. Look, we'll be all right. Or we won't, but there's nothing your presence will do to change the outcome. Besides, you must have some work that needs doing. Enjoy us being out of your hair...er, horns...for a day or so."

"Filing reports."

"They aren't going to file themselves. I assume."

"No." Tolje waved a hand in surrender. "I admit, I don't particularly want to get dissolved. Our comm link will work at any distance, so send me a message if you run into problems. Make sure to keep your markers on and don't provoke the locals."

"Let me guess: they're the independent sort?"

"Most exoworlders are."

"I'm starting to get that impression."

Nyx emerged from the guest bedroom with her bag, which meant it was his turn.

Tolje clapped him on the shoulder. "Watch yourself. You don't need to die for us."

"We don't really—"

"Yeah, I know. Fine, you don't need to suffer miserably for us."

"Oh, but Eren enjoys suffering." Nyx held out a small object. Right, the shield device she'd brought from Special Projects.

He shot her a glare while he clipped the shield to his pants. "That is not true."

"Looks true from over here."

He reached for a retort...and had nothing. He'd lost this argument the night before, and he saw no reason to rehash it now, so he refocused on Tolje. "Listen, in case I *do* die in a horribly painful way, will you tell me how you learned the MAST existed and where to find it?"

Tolje's expression grew thoughtful, and for a second Eren thought he was going to spill the beans.

Then the man shook his head. "I'm sorry, my friend, but I can't do it. It's not my secret to tell."

Eren nodded in resigned acceptance. It was possible he was never going to learn the answer. But, hey, Tolje had called him 'friend,' which was a nice surprise. "Well, hopefully this works. We find the enemy and bring these attacks to an end."

"Yeah. Feels like time is running out for us."

21

"You've developed a soft spot for Tolje," Nyx remarked once they were headed toward the docking harbor.

"I suppose I have. He's disagreeable and cranky, but he's got a good heart."

She shook her head wryly. "You always do this."

"Do what?"

"Make friends with your marks."

"Not all of them, Nyx. Just the ones worthy of friendship."

She gazed at him expectantly, guessing correctly that he'd love nothing better than to wax philosophical.

And off he went. "The thing is, people are complicated. They rarely fit into neatly defined boxes labeled 'good' or 'evil.' There are exceptions, of course. Torval, obviously. Every last one of the Primors, definitely. The Savrakath general, Jhountar, one can presume. But in most cases, it's a sliding scale. Ferdinand elasson-Kyvern, for instance, wasn't one hundred percent evil, but once he got a taste of real power, he started tipping the scales in the evil direction."

"Enough to deserve to die by your hand?"

His steps slowed, and she adjusted her gait to match his. "It's a close case, but...no. Probably not. I don't think it's breaking news for me to say I wasn't in my right mind at the time."

Four years ago, she and Eren had hunted down Ferdinand, an insurrectionist who had tried and failed to overthrow the Concord command structure. Unfortunately, the *elasson* had gotten himself murdered before they'd succeeded in catching up to him. Eren had acted particularly disappointed, confessing he'd intended to kill Ferdinand when they'd found him.

"Would you have done it?" Nyx asked. "If you'd had the opportunity?"

"Truth?"

"Please."

"Maybe. Again, my mental state was somewhat…uneven, my thirst for vengeance still running hot."

She nodded carefully. The manhunt had transpired barely a month after Eren's long-time lover had been killed by another power-mad *elasson*, but she hadn't known this when her grandfather forced her to take Eren on the mission. To her mind, Eren was simply an unhinged, violent former rebel who didn't deserve the trust her grandfather inexplicably placed in him.

A great deal had changed since then. For one, she now understood the reasons why Corradeo trusted him; for another, she trusted him as well. Most of the time.

"I understand. And I don't disagree that Ferdinand was selfish, cowardly, narcissistic and arrogant, and that those flaws got too many people killed, ultimately including himself."

"Exactly." Eren's pace abruptly quickened, as if he wanted to outrun the topic, or the past. "Tolje, though? He balances out on the other side. Granted, he's a thief. Some of his procurements might have ended up hurting the source species in much larger ways than he intended. He's a pretty crappy father and was a middling spouse at best. But he's honorable, in his way, and he doesn't mean most people any ill will."

It was a convincing spiel, and she tried out weighing the variables in her mind…her jaw tightened. He was trying to manipulate her. Just when she began to believe he was displaying a sensitive side, he twisted the opening she allowed him to his advantage.

"Is this another lecture designed to teach me how to be less of an Inquisitor and more of a 'real person'?"

"Yes. Is it working?"

She started to snap out a harsh reply…and opted for an honest one instead. "I don't know. The judgment calls you're talking about making…a terrorist with a heart of gold is still a terrorist and can still pose a grave threat to the Advocacy. Tell me something, and indulge me a bit more truthfulness. When you encounter such a person, can you take them out if necessary, despite personally liking them?"

"Absolutely, and I'm a mite offended you're questioning my ability to do my job. Then again, four years on, you persist in questioning it, so I shouldn't be surprised."

"I am not." It came out almost a growl, and the defensiveness flaring at his insinuation surprised her. Was it so important that he think better of her? "I admit I've come to struggle with the same questions myself of late. This was all easier when I was an Inquisitor. Bringing feelings into a mission made one soft, and an Inquisitor could never, ever, be soft. My own morality, or lack thereof, did not enter into the equation."

"Also, you never liked anyone enough for it to matter." A corner of his mouth curled up. "Do you like anyone now?"

"A few people, yes. I guess what I'm trying to say is…I envy you."

His steps slowed all the way to a stop. "You…what?"

Her shoulders heaved in a sigh. Why had she said that? It was true, but she'd never intended to confess it to him. But he'd never let it rest now—not until she gave him enough to claim a victory. "I envy you. Your connections to people. How you can walk into a room full of alien strangers and in half an hour have them all calling you 'friend.' I always assumed it was merely a parlor trick on your part—a way to cultivate informants and get intelligence without resorting to violence. But you actually like these people, don't you?"

"Sometimes. Other times, you have the right of it. And I'm fairly certain if I can get the information I need without resorting to violence, that's a *good* thing."

"Yes, obviously it is. But I watch you, and I can't tell the difference. I don't know when you're faking it and when you genuinely like someone."

He smirked. "I'm exceptional at my job."

She had to admit, she was beginning to understand why her grandfather had worked so hard to convince Eren to work for him a second…no, a third time. "Yes, I suppose you are."

He clutched at his chest in mock surprise. "Long have I desired to hear those words spoken from your lips."

Now that was annoying. "Asshole. Don't mock me."

"I'm…okay, fine. Sorry. Thank you. I mean it. I do appreciate your approval."

"Only because you hope it will cut down on my professional demands of you."

"Also yes. What do you—" He broke off as he spotted Banka trudging through the crowd in the opposite direction. "Banka! Wait up!"

"Eren, we don't have time."

"Sure, we do," he mumbled over his shoulder.

Banka saw him waving and wove through some passersby to meet them halfway. Her eyes cut over to Nyx cooly before settling on Eren. "Off on another banging adventure?"

"As a matter of fact, yes. We plan to spend the day inside a noxious, choking cloud of death."

"You…" Banka's eyes squeezed shut briefly "…never mind. I don't want to know. If you die, it was nice meeting you."

"Don't intend to, but thank you. You as well." His expression softened a touch. "Listen, I don't mean to wander into the middle of family drama, but your dad was desperately worried about you when he heard about the attack on Daith. On the verge of hysteria, in fact. If you had been killed, it would have utterly broken him."

"I don't care."

"I think you do."

"I think you can't waltz in here and pretend you understand the first thing about me or my family."

Eren held up his hands in surrender. "You're correct, and I'm not. I don't. But I do know he loves you. I thought you might want to know it, too."

Banka's head shook, her thin lips pursed tight. "Still don't care."

"Then I will not bring it up again. Especially if I'm dead."

This got a weak chuckle out of her. "Yeah. Try not to do that—it's bad for your health."

"Quite. Now, we must be off to our destiny."

"Good luck!" Banka tossed a hand in their direction as she disappeared back into the crowd.

Once they were on their way once more, Eren shot Nyx a sly smile. "So? Commentary?"

"I think you meant it—you were sincerely trying to help them mend their broken relationship. And your efforts were for naught. People are what they are."

"You're half right. Well, one-third right. I did mean it, but it wasn't for naught." He looked too smug by half.

"Not for naught? She completely blew off your overture."

"She did. But she's going to noodle over what I said—especially since she saw the truth in her father's face when he discovered her alive. Felt it when his arms wrapped around her and squeezed her tight. Now, perhaps love won't be enough to mend all the damage they've inflicted on each other over the years. But acknowledging it exists is a start."

"And the other third?"

"People can absolutely grow and change. It's hard as fuck, but they can do it." His voice lowered, almost to a whisper, and his eyes lingered on her. "You have."

She ensured her pace didn't falter, however much the beguiling inflection in his voice sent her skin tingling. What a strange sensation. "I have?"

"Not by much, mind you. A teensy bit, at the margins." Now the teasing tenor was back. All the better. "And I know it's only because you want to make grandaddy proud and not for yourself. But that, too, is a start."

22

Tolje was right; Ghoede *was* rather idyllic, at least compared to every other Hesgyr exocolony Eren had visited. It was no Serifos or Hirlas, mind you—there was no halcyonic immersion into either pleasurable decadence or the peaceful bliss of nature writ wild here. But the air was fresh and warm and carried a pleasant scent upon it, and the trees and grasses were a cheerful shade of clover green. A sparkling river of aquamarine flowed through the center of the settlement on its way to the timber mill…where it promptly turned to sludge brown from the pollutants leaking out from the mill.

Okay, so Ghoede had its flaws. Eren was honestly starting to wonder why any Hesgyr willingly worked and lived away from Nythir.

The desire to carve one's own path, to see the stars, to live more freely? Totally viable reasons for which he had nothing but respect. But so far as he'd seen, the reality of those endeavors kind of sucked. It might well instead be that they had no choice, not if they wanted to put food on their tables and raise their children well. He realized he didn't know anything about the cost of living on Nythir, or its immigration or residence policies. Maybe people had to earn their way into living there; maybe some never did.

For all his high-minded proclamations to Nyx earlier, the truth was, he knew vanishingly little about the intricacies of Hesgyr society. He knew all alien societies were complicated, and viewing them through the lens of one's own culture never worked if one wanted to truly understand them. But the individual Hesgyr he'd met so far were…also complicated, but by and large decent people. Except for the thug who'd tried to beat him up in Soul Lubrications—that guy was a bastard. Still, if the sample was remotely representative, odds were good that the society they inhabited was decent as well.

He and Nyx caught a number of gaping stares as they made their way into the outskirts of the settlement. They were unaccompanied, as Preece and his team remained safely ensconced on their ship in orbit. Eren kept a wide smile in place and periodically held his marker out from his chest, brandishing it like some Humans displayed a cross to ward off evil spirits. It seemed to do the trick, and no one challenged them.

The foot traffic increased steadily as they neared the center of town, enough so their pace of necessity slowed.

"This is a lot more Hesgyr than I expected," Nyx remarked.

"It is." Eren peered up the hill toward where a wide swath of clear-cutting was in progress, but not at the moment. He saw no machinery moving, heard no roar of engines or thudding of felled trees.

He waved at a young Hesgyr male walking their way. "Can I ask you a question?"

The man started, likely surprised at the sound of Hesgyrian coming from the vicinity of Eren's mouth. "What are you?"

"Species is Anaden. We're guests of a gaffaeler named Tolje Alainor." He patted his marker. "My name's Eren, and this is Nyx. What's your name?"

"Ah, Teagin Beynon." The man stuttered over it before regaining a measure of composure. "Why are you here?"

"We're touring various Hesgyr exoworlds as part of an exchange program. Is something special happening today? Or are the streets always so crowded?"

"Oh. No. I mean, yes. Everyone is off work today, on account of it being Landing Day."

"What's that?"

"The anniversary of the founding of Ghoede two-hundred-ten years ago. Local years, that is. Three-hundred-six Nythir years, which is how we're supposed to count."

"I see. I'm so happy we picked today to visit, then. Are there any special events?"

"Sure, there's various stuff all day. Markets, music, drinking. Mostly everyone's just glad to be off work."

"Always the truth, isn't it? Thanks for your help and…" Eren tried to come up with a reason to tell the young man to get as far away from the settlement as possible "…have fun today. Consider taking some quiet time for yourself. Down by the river outside of town or something."

Teagin stared at him strangely.

"If rivers are the sort of thing you fancy. Or up in the hills. Your call." Nyx nudged him in the shoulder, and he let the man escape.

"They're going to do it today," she muttered under her breath.

"Yep." He kept going until they could depart the sidewalk and slide into a clearing between two of the low, squat buildings. "Gods-damn Confab doesn't even realize it's a holiday here today. I'm revising my charitable thoughts about them."

"You had charitable thoughts about those insufferable fools?"

"No, not really, but I didn't have actively vile ones, either. I'm thinking I should start." He ran a hand along his jaw and stared out at the passersby. Laughing, joking, slurping their ubiquitous soup through straws, some already drinking. "How many people would you say are outside in this main thoroughfare right now?"

"Six thousand. Maybe seven or eight."

"Yeah. Greater than twice the number who have died in any single attack thus far." He swallowed and met her gaze. "We can't let this happen."

"Eren, you heard what Rep Dacus said. I know it's cold, but he's correct. If the Hesgyr don't discover where the attacks are originating from, they stand no chance of stopping them, and innumerably more people will die than fall here today."

Gods, he hated the ugly calculus of war. "All right, all right, all right, second-best plan. The instant the attack begins, we evacuate everyone who isn't caught in the cloud."

"A wormhole to Nythir."

"Exactly. You did bring your little generator, didn't you?"

"Now you ask?"

He returned his attention to the oblivious festival goers. "Sorry. Had a lot going on in my head. Did you?"

"*Yes.* I try to carry it everywhere with me, as by definition it serves first and foremost as an emergency travel device."

"Good. So you agree we should evacuate as many people as possible?"

"Once the cloud appears, yes. We need enough of a presence to fire the MAST, but after that…" her eyes slid to the revelers as well "…there's no need for additional loss of life."

He chuckled and started to reach for her, then thought better of it. "See? You have grown as a person."

"Because I—"

A shrill scream, far more high-pitched than what usually came out of Hesgyr mouths, ripped through the din of the festival crowd. They sprinted back into the street in time to see a great umber cloud bursting to life on the edge of town.

23

The cloud billowed out over the crowd as if driven by a malevolent wind, swallowing dozens of Hesgyr every second. Zeus' marbles, it was fast!

The screams swept outward even faster, though. These people might not know precisely what was happening, but instincts told them their lives were now in imminent peril.

Nyx snatched Eren backward, off the sidewalk and onto a patch of grass. "You're going to get trampled before we start the evacuation!"

He nodded, momentarily dumbstruck at how swiftly chaos had descended, then transformed into waves of abject terror.

"I'm going to make the terminus point near the park on Nythir where I first visited you. It's an agricultural district, so it won't be crowded. Less likely to spark a panic."

"Good thinking." He quickly surveyed the scene. "But you're going to need to open it in the street here. Let it scoop everyone up as they run."

She stepped as close as possible to the street without getting overrun. Before she could activate her device, though, he stopped her. "Listen. I hate saying this, but if the cloud gets too close to the wormhole, you're going to have to shut it down. We can't let a drop of this stuff reach Nythir." If the cloud contained self-replicating nanomaterial, it would only take a single molecule to endanger the millions of Hesgyr living there.

"I know." She pressed a finger to the small of her back, and the air in front of her started shimmering. The next second the warm glow of artificial light from the crop fields on Nythir leaked out from the oval tear in the firmament. As expected, panicked locals who found it in their path ran through it without hesitating.

The tear grew until it stretched across the entire paved street. He'd never seen a personal wormhole so large; ships using massive Caeles Prisms, yes, but not one created by an individual. Leave it to anadens to initiate a dick-measuring contest with the Humans over who could grow theirs bigger.

Three meters short of the wormhole, a woman tripped and fell to her knees. No one paid her any mind, and an errant kick to the head sent her sprawling flat on the ground.

Eren rushed forward into the fray and knelt in front of the woman, wrapping an arm under her shoulders and hefting her to her feet, even as they got pummeled on all sides. "Come on. Get through this shiny portal here, and you'll be safe."

A glance into the portal at the burgeoning panic on the *other* side made him reconsider his words. Perhaps he should have warned someone on Nythir that they had a mob of frightened people incoming, but he didn't have a direct line to anyone in power over there. Hopefully security was on the way to deal with the refugees. But all he could do was get people out of the immediate line of fire; best to concentrate on this task.

On the fringes of the stampede, some were balking at the strange glowing oval suspended in the air, and Nyx's exasperated voice broke through the din in fits and starts as she tried to persuade them that it led to safety.

"My daughter! Someone help me!"

The cry originated from his left, where a Hesgyr man stood like a rock amongst rapids, jostled by the charging throng but refusing to budge.

Eren fought his way over to the man. "Where is your daughter?"

The man blinked, registering that Eren was an alien—and deciding he didn't care. "She was behind me a second ago. I don't know what happened!"

"How tall?"

"Uh, just over a meter. She's six years old."

"Which direction were you coming from?"

The man pointed fifteen degrees northeast.

"What's her name?"

"Jennea."

"I'll find her. Get yourself through the portal."

"No. I won't leave without her. I'm coming with you."

He didn't try to argue and instead set off to the northeast. He cast his eyes downward, searching for any sign of a child-sized Hesgyr. He soon came upon a body, someone trampled by the crowd, but it was full grown. It didn't move, so he did. Greater number and all.

So why was he expending so much effort to look for a single child?

For one, most people were, willingly or otherwise, traversing the wormhole without his personal assistance. For another, was a child's life not the most valued of all? He wasn't certain where he'd picked up the thought, as anadens hadn't created infant offspring for hundreds of millennia. But the Naraida did, as well as most other species, and he'd met many a wild and free child frolicking through the forests near his home on Hirlas. Innocence was a rare and precious gift, one beaten out of every soul all too soon in life...and should this man's child survive, today would surely be the day she lost hers—

"Da? Da?" The pipsqueak cry came from the right, where the crowd began to thin out a touch.

"This way!" He fought through a wall of Hesgyr. Here on the edges, the movement of the stampede became unpredictable, as no one seemed to know where to go. He motioned behind him. "Head for the wormhole! For the portal!"

No one listened, and after a few more tries he gave up, his voice already growing scratchy and sore from all the shouting.

Eren, where did you go?

Busy saving a child.

You need to get the MAST into the cloud!

Shite. Yes, yes, he did—

A barreling hulk of a Hesgyr slammed into his shoulder, knocking him off balance. He stumbled forward and landed on his knees in front of a crying girl.

She scrambled away, eyes wide. She'd probably never seen an alien before.

"It's okay. Are you Jennea?"

A tiny gasp escaped her lips, and she nodded.

"I'm a friend of your dad's. He's…" Eren glanced over his shoulder, but the man was nowhere to be seen "…he sent me to find you." He climbed to his feet, then bent down and held out a hand. "Can I carry you to safety?"

She stared at him, gray skin blanched ashen white with fear.

"Please? I'll lift you high up, where no one can knock you down."

"They knocked you down."

He huffed a winded laugh. "They did. It won't happen again, though, I promise."

She still didn't respond, so he gently reached out and took her hand. When she didn't pull away, he wrapped his other arm around her waist and lifted her up onto his hip. "Ready?"

"No." It came out a whimper.

"Try to be brave." He skirted the edge of the crowd as best as possible, trying to head toward Nyx's wormhole while frantically scanning for the child's father.

Someone knocked into him from the right, and the girl yelped as he lost his footing—and regained it. "See? Still on my feet."

"Jennea!" The shout came when they were less than four meters from the wormhole, and he turned in relief to see her father shoving his way past people to reach them.

"My baby girl!"

Eren lifted her off his hip and held her out in front of him as her father wrapped both arms around the girl and squeezed her against his chest.

"Da!"

"I thought I'd lost you."

Eren sighed. "Get through the wormhole. Endearments can resume on the other side, where you're alive."

"Yes. Of course. Thank you, alien."

"Happy to help." A bright spot of joy on this dreadful day. He urged the father and daughter onward, ensuring they crossed over the threshold to the relative safety of Nythir.

Something yanked at his waistband, and he spun in surprise, dropping into a defensive stance. He found Nyx holding the shield generator in one hand; her other promptly went to the pouch at his waist, which she unfastened and dug around in. "You forgot about the MAST."

"I didn't forget—I was busy being heroic." He pushed her hand away. "I'll go now."

"No. I'll do it." Her expression was all business over a veneer of grim determination as she passed him a tiny black module. "You keep helping people. You're better at it than I am. Just remember: don't wander more than thirty meters from the wormhole, or it will automatically shut down."

"But I'm the one who volunteered for this crazy plan—"

A plaintive shout echoed behind them. "Somebody help me!"

He instinctively turned toward the plea, and Nyx used his distraction to thrust her hand back into his pouch and remove the MAST.

"I said I'll do it. Go." She didn't wait for a reply before taking off running, headed straight for the great writhing cloud.

He reached out toward where she'd been standing, but it was too late to call her back, and she wouldn't have responded, anyway. "Good luck," came out a scratchy whisper.

"Help!" It sounded like the same panicked voice as before.

Thirty meters to keep the wormhole open. The cry had come from closer than that. He pictured an invisible leash chaining him to the wormhole's perimeter, then spun and hurried toward the source of the cry.

CS

The next minutes passed in a blur. The initial plea had belonged to a woman whose leg had gotten trampled and broken; by the time Eren had helped her limp through the portal, there were two more injured people to help. Twice he had to move the wormhole backward, farther down the street, to keep a safe distance. Though the cloud's progress had slowed markedly, it continued to creep outward in all directions, as if it sensed victims escaping its grasp.

The throng began to thin, as the bulk of the people who'd survived the initial reach of the attack had made it through the wormhole or else sprinted off into the forest. On the Nythir side, a cadre of security had arrived, though it looked as if they were struggling to restore and maintain order. Not his problem.

Bodies littered the street, sidewalks and grassy areas—victims of the stampede. He reminded himself that without their portal to Nythir, *everyone* would have died.

Exhaustion suddenly overcame Eren. He'd been scrambling from crisis to crisis for…how long? More relevantly, how long had Nyx been gone?

How did it go? Are you still in the cloud? Are you all right?

Two Hesgyr slowed as they approached. They glanced behind them at the churning cloud, then let their eyes trace the curvature of the oval.

Eren groaned. "You can see Nythir on the other side. For the love of Hades, go through it!"

The one on the left checked with his friend, who nodded, and they jogged through the portal.

People ran across the meadows framing downtown in threes and fours. Not enticing enough for the cloud to bother expending the energy to envelop them? Might it be resource or energy constrained? Might it have a weakness they could exploit?

Shite, Nyx hadn't responded.

Answer me, Nyx.

Nothing.

"*Arae.*" He glared at the cloud. It had stopped expanding, but it continued to churn and writhe. It seemed the melting of the people inside it was not a fast process…he shuddered. What a horrific notion.

A burly, tough-looking Hesgyr stood on the grass nearby, watching the people traversing the portal suspiciously. Eren shouted at him. "Hey, come here."

The man hesitated for a second before striding over. "What is this?"

"It's a wormhole. That's Nythir on the other side. I need a favor."

"Who are you that I should do anything for you?"

"Just somebody who's saved thousands of lives today."

The man's left eye twitched. "Fair. What's the favor?"

He held the module out in his hand. Gods, Nyx was going to string him up by his toes if she found out he'd handed this technology over to some random Hesgyr. "Stand here and hold this. It's keeping the wormhole open. If the cloud starts expanding and gets within thirty meters of this location, you run through the wormhole—*run*. Then keep running on the other side for at least another thirty meters, and the wormhole will shut down."

"Why?"

"Because if the cloud reaches Nythir, this whole nightmare ramps up all over again on a much bigger scale."

The man nodded tersely. "Where are you going?"

Eren blew out a breath and waved in the direction of the cloud. "In there."

CS

His worst death (that he remembered) was the time he got stabbed in the abdomen by a Barisan wielding a serrated knife. The Barisan fled, leaving him to collapse in a dark, desolate alley in an abandoned part of town in the depths of night.

Eren had commed for an anarch medical team, but those were the days before wormholes smaller than galactic gateways existed, and no one was anywhere close. So he lay there writhing in excruciating pain for forty-five minutes that stretched like forty-five years before he finally, mercifully, expired from massive internal blood loss.

Then there was the time, long before he'd joined the anarchs, when he'd overdosed on a tainted hypnol. He'd broken a mirror, snatched up a shard of glass and stabbed his eyes out in an attempt to save himself from the horrors tormenting him in his own mind. It hadn't worked, so, blinded, he'd turned the glass on his throat. Luckily, thanks to the intoxicating effects of the hypnol, he didn't remember that one as clearly.

As he reached the perimeter of the cloud, he idly wondered if liquefaction was about to vault to the top of the list. Hopefully his non-Hesgyr genetics would protect him, because he did not want to find out what liquefaction entailed.

Crossing into the cloud was like walking into a great sandstorm. He'd never actually walked into a sandstorm, but he imagined this was definitely how it would be. His skin was instantly afire from a million pinpricks. But it wasn't sand pelting him, so what was it?

What else it was was…heavy. Firm and thick. He amended his analogy to include wading through mud.

Before he'd entered it, the cloud had stabilized at around two hundred meters wide. It was a lot of ground to cover, and he hadn't expected the very air to fight him so hard. He overlaid a virtual grid pattern on his vision and trudged forward. Nyx had been in here for several minutes, so she might be near the center—but she could be on her way out.

Or she could be lying dead.

But while the air stung something fierce, it wasn't genuinely melting his skin away. It felt as if it desperately wanted to, but hadn't determined how to accomplish it. Small favors. Plus, she was wearing that new shield. So there was no reason for her to be dead.

Liquid sloshed over his boots, and he peered down to realize he was standing in a pool of viscous fluid. The melted remains of Hesgyr.

He doubled over and gagged, coughing up the beverage he'd drank on the trip here. From his lower vantage, he realized the pool continued on to his horizon. How many dead Hesgyr did it represent? Hundreds, for certain, and likely many more.

He hoped Nyx had managed to fire the MAST. And that it had worked to identify a location. And that he was able to find her, or, failing to do so, find the device. Let all this death be worth something.

"Nyx!" His shout was absorbed by the oppressive weight of the particles; he didn't think it traveled more than a few meters. What in the name of Zeus was this thing made of? Whenever it vanished, it left nothing behind, but he wished he had something to try to scoop a sample into—he did!

He hurriedly emptied his pouch of its contents. Then he took it off, swept it in an arc through the air in front of him, and closed it up. Gods only knew what, if anything, Preece would find inside when the man opened it, but he'd made the effort.

He blinked against a sudden burning in his eyes. Were the nanobots/microbes/whatever they were finding a way inside him? He had to tamp down the overwhelming sensation that his skin was beginning to melt. It was surely all in his head...he glanced down at his forearm. No melting so far as he could see.

The grid in his vision suggested he'd begun to circle back around on his path, and he adjusted course. He'd believed himself walking in a straight line, which was why the grid existed.

"Nyx!"

He heard...something. A grunt, or possibly nothing more than an object making contact with another object. All he knew for sure was that it sounded distinct from the awful *slurping* noise his boots made as they plodded through the gore.

He paused and listened, trying to get a directional bead on the noise.

A muffled *whack* came from his left, and he forged ahead in that direction.

Fuzzy shadows lurched through the haze ahead in a halting dance of limbs. They resolved into an anaden outline and an alien one.

Another few steps, and he recognized Nyx's long ponytail swaying across her back in time with the movement of her duster as she delivered a roundhouse kick to the head of the alien.

The Phae'soon's iridescent skin—because it was definitely, absolutely a Phae'soon—was unmistakable as their head snapped to the side and it stumbled backward.

A sense of self-satisfaction rushed through him. He'd been right, dammit! But he'd crow about it later.

He didn't know how long the fight had been going on, nor was he able to discern who was winning. No matter. He rushed forward to lend Nyx his assistance.

The Phae'soon wielded a long, flat club in one of their stubby hands and a skewer in the other...no, wait, the skewer appeared to extend out of their forearm. Natural defense, lovely. Off-balance from the impact of Nyx's kick, they swung the skewer a little wildly toward her abdomen, preventing her from closing the distance.

She had no weapons, of course; Tolje had come to trust Eren enough to return his, but the Hesgyr had swiftly confiscated Nyx's firearm and blade as a condition of her remaining on Nythir.

For hundreds of millennia, Nyx hadn't needed a weapon to disable or kill any opponent, for she'd controlled *diati*. The primordial life form executed on her will with a thought. It could deliver a dozen deep cuts in a second, rip limb from limb or simply suffocate any living being. But the *diati* was gone now, used up in The Displacement or floating among the stars 'doing universe shit,' as his friend Alex liked to put it.

To her credit, Nyx had spent the last eighteen years learning to fight properly, whether it be with a variety of weapons or with her own fists and feet. She was skilled at it; better than most. But to call the conditions inside the cloud less than ideal for hand-to-hand combat was a colossal understatement. Taking a step was akin to slogging through fifteen centimeters of mud in a brutal sandstorm delivered by a roiling bank of impenetrable fog.

This was what the gods made firearms for. Eren drew his handgun from the inside pocket of his jacket and tried to sight down on the Phae'soon's body mass while he advanced.

But Nyx was too damn fast, dodging and weaving and generally getting in the way of his shot. "Nyx, move!"

If she heard him, she gave no indication.

He was only five meters away when Nyx dodged the wrong way and the alien saw an opening. The skewer darted toward her abdomen, distracting her for the second the alien needed to swing the club up and wallop her under the chin. Her head jerked back as her limbs stilled, and she fell stiffly backward to the ground.

Arae! He fired at the alien's chest.

The alien staggered but remained on their feet. They stumbled around and trudged away, attempting to flee. Eren pursued.

Almost immediately, a swirling mass of pure white plasma less than a meter in width cut sharply into the haze. Before Eren could line up another shot, the alien dove into the plasma and disappeared.

He wanted to follow. He *should* follow, in case Nyx hadn't been able to fire the MAST before getting into a melee with the alien.

What was wrong with him that instead of following, he spun around and hurried back to where she had fallen? Thankfully, he hadn't tracked the alien far, else he might not have been able to find her again, as he'd neglected to mark the location of the fight on the grid.

Just before he reached her, his foot knocked something solid to the side. He bent down, cringing as he felt around bare-handed in the gore...there.

His hand returned with the MAST. So she'd had it out, at least. He fired it in what he thought was the general direction of where the plasma had been, then stuck it in his pocket and crossed the rest of the distance to where she lay.

Her eyes were closed, but her chest rose and fell. He knelt beside her and searched for a pulse. Weak, but present. Good, good.

He gathered her up in his arms, and didn't even flinch at the fluids that promptly soaked through his clothes.

Then he walked in the direction the grid told him to go.

She would be mortified if she ever found out he'd carried her out of danger in his arms while holding her limp, helpless body against his. And almost tenderly, no less. He vowed never to tell her.

Abruptly the writhing haze began rushing past him, as if being drawn into a suction, though he felt no drag at all on himself—only a million pinpricks as the particles made one last effort to infect him as they departed.

The air cleared, revealing sunny skies overhead and the edifices of the town silhouetted by the surrounding forest. He turned around and discovered no trace of the umber cloud or the plasma at its center.

Only the blood remained.

<h1 style="text-align:center">24</h1>

"There you are! Well? Did it work?"

Eren glanced over his shoulder to see Preece blocking out Ghoede's afternoon sun as the man stared down at him, hands planted on his hips.

"Oh, good, you're here. Can you examine Nyx? She suffered a nasty hit to the head. I'm worried her neck might have snapped. Is she paralyzed?"

"Anaden," Preece sniffed. "I know nothing of your people's physiology. Ask her yourself."

"Yeah, I would, but she's still unconscious."

"That happens with head injuries. For all species, I imagine. *Did it work?*"

Eren growled a curse, fished the MAST out of his pocket and offered it to the man. "Here. Find out."

"It's covered in blood."

"Yes, same as me and her and everything else in this colony. You want your answers? Take it."

Preece grasped the MAST between two fingertips, then kept it at arm's length as he spun to rush off.

"Wait." Eren unfastened his pouch and held it out as well. "I tried to scoop up some particles from the cloud. I don't know if I captured anything."

"Your bag is not airtight, so I doubt it retained any material. It is also covered in blood."

Eren arched an eyebrow. "You have another hand."

"Yes, I do." Preece sighed, but took the pouch by the fastener and strode away.

A prissy Hesgyr. What were the odds?

He returned his attention to Nyx. Her breathing seemed as if it was stronger now, but he could be imagining it. Without meaning to, his hand stroked her cheek. He'd never seen her when asleep before, but in repose, her features were almost...soft. No, that wasn't the right word, for her bone structure was far too elegant and refined to ever be called soft. But the sharp edges of her typically rigid countenance were gone, and in their absence, one might venture to describe her face as beautiful. If it wasn't splattered in blood and starting to bruise, obviously.

He sank back onto his heels. What was he doing? He should stop fussing over her like a mother hen and just evacuate her to a hospital on Ares. The Hesgyr couldn't treat her, and if she needed a new body, better for the regenesis lab to get started on it straightaway.

Right. He should do that. He considered who—

"Unh...." The moan petered out through newly parted lips.

"Hey, there." He hurriedly removed his hand from her cheek and scooted back a few more centimeters.

Her eyes fluttered open, blurry and unfocused. "My head...."

"It hurts, I imagine. Can you move? Anything? Other than your mouth, I mean. And your eyes."

She slowly brought a hand up from the ground, then dropped it limply onto her chest.

"Fantastic! No paralysis. You took a wallop under the chin— they could hear the *crack* all the way back on Nythir—so it was a possibility."

"The alien...." She tried to sit up, but promptly collapsed onto the grass. The hand on her chest rose to rub at her neck. "Deploying painkillers. I'll need a minute."

"Take your time."

It wouldn't do to stare at her expectantly—he'd done enough of this already anyway—so he studied the evolving scene. Downtown was transitioning steadily from terror-stricken attack epicenter to clinical crime scene investigation. Preece's team had swept into the settlement, erecting barriers and deploying their equipment with typical efficiency, he supposed in the hope of uncovering some scrap of new evidence. New clues wouldn't come from the blooded streets, however, but instead from the data the MAST returned. That, and what he and Nyx had witnessed inside the cloud.

He cleared his throat and shifted back to face Nyx, who was trying to hide a wince as she again made an effort to sit up, this time marginally succeeding. "Say, did you happen to fire the MAST before…whatever happened?"

She nodded, and the wince broke free to crinkle her face in pain. "I did—" her gaze darted toward the main thoroughfare to their left "—but where is it? I dropped it when—"

"It's fine. I found it, and it is now in Preece's eager but fastidious hands."

"Oh. Good." She closed her eyes, and when she reopened them, her professional mask had descended over her features. A shame, really. "A few seconds after I used it, an alien—one of the Phae'soon, judging from the images SIMON provided—attacked me."

"Yeah, I saw. I came into the cloud searching for you."

"Why?"

"Well, because I thought you needed—" nope, wrong thing to say "—I'd gotten nearly everyone evacuated and wanted to see what the inside of the cloud looked like."

"Without a shield on."

He shrugged.

"Why do I bother? What happened to the alien?"

"I shot them, but they were able to make it through a…there was a small concentration of swirling plasma near where you encountered it. I suspect it was some sort of portal to the origin point."

"You didn't follow them through?"

He choked off his initial response, again. "There wasn't time. As soon as they went through the portal, the cloud got sucked back through as well, and everything vanished."

"That's unfortunate." Nyx drew in a deep breath, placed her hands on the ground, and pushed herself up to standing. He wisely didn't offer a hand to help her.

"Ugh." Her fingers picked gingerly at her shirt. "Hesgyr blood is on everything."

"I'm afraid so." He hoped she didn't notice how much of it coated his clothes as well. If she spent a nanosecond thinking about it, she'd realize he'd carried her out of the street and over to the grass, so he was banking on a concussion preventing her from connecting the dots.

She glared in his general direction, lingering pain pinching the corners of her eyes. "Can I have my CPM back?"

"What? Oh, is that what the wormhole module is called? Sure." The Hesgyr he'd entrusted with it had returned it seconds after the cloud had dissipated, then run off for parts unknown. He removed it from another of his pockets and gave it to her. "We should—"

"Sir? Excuse me."

Eren shifted toward the voice, which belonged to a security officer. The man looked familiar; he might have been at Daith or Fetel-reu. "What do you need?"

"A Confab representative is requesting for you to reopen a wormhole from Nythir to here, so the survivors can return."

He took in the surroundings with a practiced gaze and shook his head. "To here? No. I'm not depositing all those terrified, distraught people front and center to a sea of blood, which happens to be all that remains of their friends and probably some family. Pick a location on the outskirts of the settlement and set up a processing area. Then I'll do it."

"I'll relay your terms." The officer marched off toward a command tent someone had erected in the last few minutes.

Gods, the Confab seriously didn't care for miscreant offworld workers wandering around Nythir, did they? Or maybe he was too quick to assume the worst of politicians, and in reality all those people simply wanted to come home. If so, he couldn't blame them for desire, though they would likely come to regret it.

"It won't take them long to get organized. What do you say we hitch a ride back through the wormhole to Nythir, where we can both get cleaned up?"

Nyx nodded with a touch of weariness. "I can't deny I deeply want a shower. I expect the clothes are a lost cause, but I'm hopeful the blood will wash off my skin with the application of sufficient soap."

"You know, if you want to run home to Ares and have your head checked out, it wouldn't be the worst idea."

"It's not necessary. Diagnostics say I'm fine—or I will be in another hour or so. Besides, I want to be here when Dr. Preece gets the MAST results in. I..." she held an arm out in front of her, scowling horribly at it "...suffered to acquire that information."

"You did." He spotted the security officer motioning for them to follow him across the field. "Right on cue. Let's wrap our role up here."

25

E ren scrubbed his arms with the brillo-pad quality sponge he'd found under Tolje's sink, stopping to inspect his skin every so often. Had the Hesgyr blood stained it? He could swear it had a dirty, brownish tint to it now.

His shirt lay in a heap on the floor. He'd dump it in the trash chute in a minute, because it was unsalvageable—or at least not worth the effort to scour clean. He'd let Nyx take the shower, because as filthy as he was as a result of carrying her out of the cloud, she was exponentially more so, having lain prone in the lake of blood for close to thirty seconds. So he was cleaning himself up as best as he could in the kitchen sink. Luckily, Tolje wasn't here to grouse about the mess he was making of the kitchen. Eren had sent him a message to let him know they'd returned to Nythir, and Tolje had replied that he'd be out for a while.

Eren spritzed his hair with water until he was able to comb out the blood-induced tangles; it would do until he managed to grab a shower for himself. His boots were soaking in the left pan of the sink. Another three hours or ten should do the trick for them.

This left his pants. He had a clean pair in the bedroom, but he hadn't thought to retrieve them before Nyx started her shower. It would be rude for Tolje to return home and find him standing around in his underwear, so he'd kept his pants on until now. But they were sticky and hardened from splotches of dried blood, so the situation needed to be addressed soon.

He took a sip from the bottle of gowal he'd dug out of the refrigerator, then was diving in for a fresh pass at his hair when he heard the shower shut off. Finally.

Still, he waited for another five minutes before knocking on the door. His arguably tender sentiments toward her on Ghoede had thrown him for a loop, and he didn't entirely trust himself right now. But he did need fresh clothes. "Nyx? Can I sneak in for a minute?"

It took several seconds for her to reply with a curt, "Fine."

He opened the door. "I need to grab some clean pants...."

She stood in the doorway to the guest room lavatory, wearing a soft, heather gray shirt that fell to the top of her hips as she brushed her damp raven hair out.

His brain debated which features of the tableau to notice first. Her skin was flushed from the heat of the shower, bringing a rosy tint to her cheeks, of all things scandalous. She almost never wore her hair down, and it was longer than he'd realized, with hints of waves coming to life in the wake of the brush's path.

Her legs. He should start with her legs. Tanned—no, not tanned, naturally olive in hue, *just like every other Praesidis*. Toned, though, bordering on muscular, but this was all gene therapy and cybernetics. A toned physique came with the lineage and the job. But the way her thighs curved up toward her hips...that was too perfect to have been planned by science.

"You're staring at me."

He blinked. "You're staring at *me*." It was true; her eyes hadn't left his bare chest since he'd entered the room. "You've seen me without a shirt on before."

"Regrettably." She spun away, returning the brush to the dresser. "About your pants?"

"Right. Pants. They're, um, in my bag." He advanced two steps toward her. "Which is...behind you."

Her intensely sapphire irises gained an odd glint as they traveled with aching slowness along the contours of his face and down his neck—then darted to the bottle of gowal he held in his hand. She snatched it away, took a long swig of it, and promptly doubled-over coughing.

She shoved the bottle into his chest. "That swill is awful!"

"It really, really is. Kind of grows on you after a while, though."

"I hope to be comfortably home on Ares long before it has the opportunity." She smacked her lips and wiped them with the back of her hand to emphasize the point.

"Fair enough. Are you feeling better?"

"Much, thank you."

"No headache?"

"Not any longer, no." She stood there watching him, her eyes darting briefly to his chest every few seconds before she forced them up again.

He took his own sip from the bottle, wincing as the liquid burned his throat, then set it on the dresser beside them. As he stretched over to do so, he inhaled her fresh, clean scent. Heat radiated off her skin from the shower; he was suddenly dizzy, and not from the gowal, which he'd grown accustomed to.

Warning bells blared in the recesses of his mind as a veritable catalogue of reasons this was a spectacularly, monstrously bad idea scrolled in neatly formatted columns, complete with bold headings and bullet points. But he was tired—tired of being alone every night. Tired of working so hard to wall himself off from this attraction. Tired of…fine, mostly he was horny. Sue him.

He reached out and gathered a lock of her damp hair between two fingers, caressing it with the pad of his thumb. "It looks good down. You should wear it this way more often."

An entire network of tiny muscles on the left side of her mouth twitched, but she neither knocked his hand away nor moved even a centimeter. "Long hair represents a hazard when one finds oneself embroiled in a melee."

"True, true. And yet I've found a way to survive such situations. Most of the time."

"How *do* you—?"

He leaned in and cut her off with a kiss.

A new chorus of alarms pealed through his mind, as her lips didn't feel at all like Cosime's had. But they were moist and shapely and warm, and he decided to stop listening to all the damn alarms for a little while.

"What are you...doing?" Her voice was low and husky in the scant space between them.

"Well..." he cleared his throat roughly "...I was kissing you. And now..." his hand drifted down her side to caress her exposed thigh, finding it as firm and muscular as it looked "...I'm touching you. Here and..." his other hand rose to trace the outline of her exquisite jaw "...here."

Her lips brushed across his, barely skimming them before pulling away again. "It's just the adrenaline from the attack."

"Without a doubt. And the gowal."

"And the—" her head titled "—the what?"

"The alcohol." He chuckled and flattened a hand upon her hip, drawing her closer.

"Oh. If you say so." Her hand rose to scrape a nail along his cheek. "This is a foolish, terrible idea."

"My thought exactly." He crushed her mouth with his, and found her own response both forceful and demanding. His hands went to the bottom of her shirt the same instant hers landed on the fastener of his pants. They fought for order of priority for a few seconds, which was about par for the course in their relationship. He won, if solely because he had the better angle, and they parted long enough for her shirt to disappear over her head.

Then he stepped back, swatting her hand away to manage his own pants on account of their stickiness, but also for a chance to admire her body.

She was magnificent, of course. He'd never had any doubt this would be the case. The best genetic stock in a million years of anaden civilization had sculpted every limb and the muscles that drove them to perfection. She wasn't willowy or delicate, but rather firm and strong. Confident and justifiably proud.

He forced his pants off and to the floor, then his underwear, and greatly enjoyed the smile curling up her flawless lips as he stepped forward and into her arms.

If he hesitated for a fraction of a second, it didn't show in his stride. After all, he had a long and storied history of doing the stupid thing in the moment.

CS

Tolje tried to stay quiet as he entered his apartment, in case Eren and Nyx were already asleep. To hear Preece describe the scene on Ghoede after the attack, they'd had a rough go of it. They'd both lived, though, despite spending several minutes inside the cloud, which confirmed the working theory of a virus targeted at Hesgyrian physiology.

He started to tiptoe past the couch when he realized it was vacant. Eren's message had indicated they'd returned to Nythir; maybe they'd been keyed up after the day's events and gone out for something to eat?

He noted the closed door to the guest bedroom, then crept closer to it until he was able to make out the telltale sounds of moans resonating from two voices. Keyed up, indeed.

All well and good, so long as it didn't make the two of them unbearable to be around in the morning.

He dropped his bag by the desk and went to the kitchen, no longer so worried about being quiet. A curse escaped his lips upon finding Eren's clothes on the floor and boots in the sink. This, they would have words about in the morning. For now, he poured himself a drink and took it to his bedroom. It felt somehow rude to not put at least one more wall between him and them, even if it was *his* apartment.

Preece was following every precaution handling the MAST and its precious data, but the man expressed confidence they would have a location by the morning. A source of the attacks. Shortly thereafter, a face for their enemy.

These aliens, whoever they were, had done their damnedest to kill Banka, and for this alone they deserved to die. No question. Tolje simply didn't understand the mindset that led to a group of sentient beings deciding, planning and executing on the deliberate massacre of other sentient beings who had not first done them harm.

Even if Eren was right and the absence of an item a gaffaeler appropriated had resulted in the aliens suffering in some manner, whether at the hands of the Rasu or otherwise, it didn't come close to justifying such wanton slaughter. The people at Fetel-reu and Canchal-se and Daith and Ghoede were innocent of wrongdoing; *Banka* was innocent of wrongdoing. What mindset could poison the aliens' souls so irredeemably?

He sipped on his drink and tried to relax. Seeing as they didn't pay him to psychoanalyze the enemy, it ultimately didn't matter. He'd done his job. He'd procured a tool that enabled them to locate the source of the attacks, and innumerable Hesgyr lives would be saved as a result. He could sleep soundly tonight…assuming his guests kept it down in the other room.

26

"Ms. Praesidis, are you in there? I can't find Eren."

"Yes, I'm here. One minute."

Eren opened his eyes in time to see Nyx roll over to the edge of the bed and feel around on the floor for her shirt. Long, lean muscles rippled beneath the skin of her back as she did. He remembered that from—

Ah, *fuck*. Guilt ripped into his chest with a hacksaw. He closed his eyes and saw Cosime's brilliant emerald irises shaming him as they condemned him to an eternity in Tartarus.

But she wasn't here, dammit. She was gone and she was never coming back and he had to find a way to live. Not solely survive, but care about living in this world. And sometimes, caring meant finding some pleasurable release.

Nyx slipped on her shirt then left the bed to kneel in front of her bag, pulling out a pair of black pants. She didn't turn to look at him as she slid into them. "You should get dressed as well. It sounds like we're needed." Her voice sounded cool and noncommittal.

"Yeah." He swallowed hard and tried to will himself to get out of the bed. He wished she would so much as glance at him—and was terrified she'd do so. Would she be able to see the war he waged with his conscience displayed on his features? He'd always been good at hiding behind a mask of demons-dare-not-care whimsy, and he worked to project it now, in case she chose to look.

Before he could convince himself to move, she'd opened the door. "What is it, Tolje?"

"Dr. Preece has finished analyzing the data from the MAST. He's got a location."

"He's what?" Eren sat straight up in the bed.

Tolje's head peeked through the half-open doorway. "You heard me. He wants to see you right away."

Eren's cheeks flushed in shame…but what did Tolje care who he slept with? The man had lost the love of his life, too, and must understand. Surely.

Nyx nodded in understanding. "Give us five minutes."

Tolje disappeared from the doorway, and Nyx pushed it shut. "Congratulations."

"For what? You're the one who remembered to get the MAST into the cloud and use it." Crap, the bag with his pants in it was halfway across the room.

He studiously avoided eye contact as he climbed off the bed and maneuvered around her in the tiny space—their shoulders brushed, and a vision of his fingernails digging into those shoulders in ecstasy flared in his mind. Blood rushed out of his brain to his groin, even as his stomach churned.

Her gaze flicked down, then back to meet his, her expression unruffled and unforgiving. "I told him five minutes. There isn't time."

"I don't—oh, fuck you, Nyx." He shoved past her and stumbled into his underwear and pants with breakneck speed, then lunged for a shirt, any shirt.

"So that's how this is going to be?"

"It's not going to be any way at all. Look, sweetheart, sometimes you just need to get off. Don't make it more complicated."

He made the critical mistake of glancing at her as he peered around for his boots, before remembering they were still in the kitchen. A nanosecond of vulnerability flitted across her eyes—then her countenance locked down into the ice maiden visage he knew so well.

"Fine, but make sure it doesn't interfere with your work."

"*My* work?"

"Yes, *your* work. You're the emotional one, after all."

He opened his mouth to argue, but it was straight-up truth. His emotions were presently taking a joy ride through Hades at his expense, while any vestiges of feelings had been engineered out of her millennia ago, leaving behind only a humorless husk walking around in an exquisitely crafted anaden body.

So, lacking a fitting response, he stepped past her and strode out into the living room. Whatever he'd seen in her eyes, it hadn't been vulnerability.

CS

Nyx closed the door so swiftly it almost knocked Eren the rest of the way out of the room. Next, her attention darted to the corners of the small bedroom. She wanted to get her weapons. Only they were locked away somewhere in the apartment, and had been since shortly after her arrival.

Shoes. That's right. She hadn't yet put on her shoes.

Where were they? She'd removed them before showering last night, obviously, when she'd needed to wash a sea's worth of Hesgyr blood out of her hair and off her skin.

After a few seconds of searching, she spotted them lying sideways on the floor near the door. She'd never stored them properly after the shower, because Eren had interrupted her. And for the rest of the night, she hadn't been thinking about her shoes.

Without intending to, she sank onto the edge of her bed and fisted her hands in her lap. For some inexplicable reason, her heart hammered in her chest. If examined under a microscope, an observer might even determine her hands were trembling.

What in the name of Zeus was wrong with her? It was just sex. A base biological need that, when done correctly, could also be enjoyable. She rarely felt such a need, but when she had, she'd enjoyed it well enough.

Last night, she'd more than enjoyed it. There was no harm in admitting this to herself. The unrestrained, always bordering on wild, demeanor that Eren brought to everything else in his life extended to the bedroom as well. His hands were demanding and insistent and everywhere at once, trailed so often by his mouth....

It was memorable. No question.

Fine, it had been sublime. He'd excelled in the act, and she'd reacted to his enthusiasm with perhaps a bit more vigor than was typical for her.

So? Sex didn't have to include an emotional component. Sentiment was not required, merely desire. She'd meant what she'd said to him. He *was* the emotional one, and she *did* worry what this would do to his work performance and their professional dynamic.

She expected he was going to lash out, throwing sarcastic barbs in her direction at every opportunity. She couldn't let them wound her in any way, for they were simply a coping mechanism to bury the misplaced guilt he probably felt. His girlfriend was four years dead, but somehow Cosime Rhomyhn maintained a stranglehold on Eren's psyche.

Nyx cursed under her breath; she never should have allowed this to happen. She was perfectly capable of keeping whatever attraction she might feel under control. To act so rashly, without consideration of the long-term consequences? It wasn't like her.

But he'd been so damn…compelling. Compellingly seductive. When he touched her, her skin lit fire beneath his fingertips; when he spoke, his voice roiled sensually through her mind. Her thoughts had grown muddled, and the voice in her head that always kept track of consequences had grown unaccountably silent.

She stared down at her hands, willing them to stop trembling. It must be a delayed adrenaline dump from the events inside the cloud yesterday. Not that she commonly experienced physical aftereffects from combative encounters.

"Nyx, we need to go," Tolje shouted from the living room.

Her five minutes were up. She put a lid on her circling thoughts, stood and headed for the door—then turned around and went back to put on her shoes.

CS

Thankfully, Tolje filled the trek to Preece's lab with questions about the attack at Ghoede. Eren elaborated on every detail, if only to fill the minutes, while Nyx remained silent except when Tolje asked her a direct question. Her behavior wasn't unusual—she'd never been the talkative sort—and Tolje didn't give any indication of noticing anything off.

Eren recited the particulars of the attack on autopilot, though, while beneath the surface his mind ping-ponged from recrimination to confusion to regret to defensiveness and back around again.

The one thing above all that he couldn't determine was why he had felt some measure of tenderness toward Nyx in the wake of her injury at the hands of the alien. However attractive a figure she'd struck after her shower, he could have shrugged off his purely physical reaction if not for the warm, fuzzy-headed sensations that had overtaken him upon seeing her lying helpless and broken in the cloud.

It was asinine, borderline inexplicable. She was immortal; if she'd died, she'd simply have woken up back home, likely within a day or two thanks to her elevated status. She didn't need his *care* and didn't deserve his affection.

A pang of loneliness hollowed out his chest. He missed Cosime. He missed her spirit and fire and irrepressible zeal for life. Everything Nyx lacked.

Dammit….

He blinked and realized they'd reached the lab and were being shown inside. If he'd stopped talking at some point, Tolje hadn't called attention to it.

Preece greeted them with a level of excitement that teetered into exhilaration. "Tremendous work, my friends. Truly excellent. We have a location!"

"Terrific." Eren shoved his mental gymnastics far, far down and brandished a smile. "Where is it?"

"A very long way away." Preece opened up a map of the Pisces-Cetus Supercluster Complex above one of the worktables. Two dots, one gold and one red, pulsed at nearly opposite ends of the map, and below each of them scrolled a long series of numbers.

"The gold marker is Nythir. The origin point of the attack on Ghoede is marked in red."

"I'd ask how a group of Phae'soon got all the hells way over there, but I guess the answer to such a question is almost always 'wormholes.'"

"The Phae'soon?" Preece asked. "What do they have to do with it?"

"They're behind the attacks. We saw one in the cloud." A corner of Eren's lips curled up into a smirk. "It knocked Nyx flat on her ass."

"You distracted me with your shrieking," she snapped.

"Oh? You never said you heard me."

"It didn't come up." Nyx pivoted to face Preece, putting her back to Eren. "The point is, yes, I can confirm there was a Phae'soon present inside the cloud."

"Well. Well, well, well." Preece paced alongside the long table of lab equipment behind the projection. "So you were correct after all, Mr. Savitas."

"Often am."

"'Often' is *quite* the exaggeration," she retorted over her shoulder.

"Is that so?"

"Yes, it is."

"Enough, you two," Tolje growled.

Eren's left hand fisted at his side as he quelled his instinctive response. Her casting aspersions on the quality of his work was nothing new. He'd think she was deliberately trying to bait him, but that would require her to be both experiencing and acting on an emotion, and this could not be the case.

He didn't rise to the challenge, instead returning his attention to Preece. "How do you think the Confab will proceed?"

"They'll send a reconnaissance mission to the tagged location as a first step to confirm the data the MAST registered is accurate. Assuming there is an alien settlement at the coordinates, the mission will scout the aliens' military strength, defenses and so on.

Then, I assume they will…but I shouldn't assume. Military strategy is not my department."

"I understand." Eren turned to Tolje. "Can you get me a meeting with the Confab?"

"I can try."

27

Tolje didn't have the opportunity to do so. Before they'd made it to the apartment, a message arrived from the Confab requesting their presence in two hours.

Nyx excused herself to take a shower, and Eren collapsed on the couch, rubbing at his eyes. He hadn't gotten much sleep last night, because—his mind flashed on the visual of beads of sweat glistening across Nyx's collarbone—he shook his head roughly, willing the image away. It didn't matter how noteworthy or pleasurable the night had been; he told himself he'd take it back in a heartbeat if he could.

Tolje settled into his usual chair and considered Eren. "First time, huh?"

He didn't bother pretending he didn't know to what the man referred. "*Only* time."

"Heh. Your call. Or hers, more likely. That's how these things typically work."

"Not in this case. My call, and my call is never again. It was just the adrenaline from the attack. But I shouldn't have…."

"You think you've betrayed your girl. Cosime, wasn't it?"

Eren stared at the ceiling as he summoned up the response his heart insisted was a lie but his mind knew was truth. "I know I didn't betray her. She's gone."

"True. Still, the first time I slept with another woman after Siwan died, I drank myself into a stupor for a week solid. I get it."

"I'm not going to do that, if you're worried. I won't check out on your crisis right when we've finally made crucial progress. Also, in the past my benders have about torn galaxies apart. The collateral damage tends to pile up when I find the bottom of a bottle, so I try not to indulge any longer."

"Good for you." Tolje fell silent for almost a minute, and Eren appreciated him not leaning too heavily into the psychotherapy role.

"I'm glad the MAST worked."

"What?" Tolje looked up, apparently having been lost in thought himself. "Oh, so am I. If it turns out I contributed to saving a bunch of lives, then I'll sleep well. Listen, since our time together might be coming to an end soon, there's something I've been wanting to ask you. What's been happening with your people? You've alluded to them reforming in recent years, but I'm not up on my Anaden history beyond what I needed to learn for the mission."

Eren relaxed at the change in topic. Tolje was probably manipulating him, but he didn't care. "A lot has changed for us in the last eighteen years. You know about the Directorate War? The Displacement?"

Tolje shrugged. "I know events by those names happened, and they resulted in the Anaden Empire being replaced by the multi-species Concord alliance."

"Ah. We got put in our place right and proper by the Humans in the Directorate War—anadens in general did, that is. I was actually fighting on the Humans' side during the war. In the end, our despotic leaders were overthrown. Well, not so much 'overthrown' as 'executed,' but no less than they deserved. Killed one of them myself, in fact." He huffed a laugh. "That was a good time. Then we wandered around leaderless for a while, lost and adrift, while the Humans kept yelling at us to get our shit together. We were just starting to take their advice when the Rasu showed up and slapped us around again, which kind of brought the point home. So now we're making a go at a respectable, non-authoritarian government and civil society.

"It's been good for us. We needed the repeated kicks in the arse. We're trying the kinder, gentler route these days. Not when it comes to our true enemies, of course, but we're also trying to not view everyone as our enemies." He arched an eyebrow in Tolje's direction. "You all could look into that, too."

Tolje snorted. "I'll pass the suggestion along. And Ares is the capitol of this 'respectable government' of yours?"

"It is. Our original homeworld got destroyed during the Directorate War, and the Humans' homeworld, Earth, took its place in The Displacement—which is a much longer story than we have time for right now." He tilted his head toward the guest bedroom door, where the shower continued to run on the other side. "Nyx's grandfather is in charge of the new government. He's a good man, so there's a small chance our reformation might work."

"Grandfather? I thought Anadens didn't have children."

"We don't. It's complicated."

"It usually is." Tolje followed Eren's gaze to the guest bedroom. "Don't pull out that firearm you shouldn't have on your person and shoot me, but Nyx is a hell of a woman. Your equal, if not your superior."

Eren groaned. "Don't even get me started on what she is."

"You've been better since she arrived. Sharper, more engaged. I mean, up until this morning."

"Look, I'm not saying we don't work well together. Professionally. Or we did, anyway. Who knows how this is going to screw up our dynamic. But she's not my type. I prefer my women to come with souls."

Tolje held up his hands in surrender. "All right. I've said my piece." He stood. "Sorry to leave you two alone to yell insults or beat each other up or screw again, depending, but I need to run to a meeting. I'll be back before it's time to go see the Confab."

"Not a problem."

Eren watched the apartment door close behind Tolje. He waited ten seconds, then headed out the door as well. He didn't intend to do any of those things with Nyx, which meant he needed to be anywhere but here.

CS

Eren strolled the thoroughfares of the Rydai District with no destination in mind.

The shopkeepers and residents had started to get used to his presence here, and a few of them acknowledged him with curt head-nods as he passed, which he appreciated.

Once he'd gathered his non-Nyx-related thoughts and arranged them in a semblance of order, he decided to play a hunch about the Phae'soon and the attacks. He'd need a little help, however, as time was growing short for both sides of the conflict.

He suddenly realized it had been several months since he'd last talked to Mesme. He hadn't deliberately ignored his recondite, ethereal friend; it was just that things were quiet these days, at least in the universe-ending peril sense, so they hadn't had occasion to speak recently. He hoped Mesme wouldn't be offended that he only contacted the Kat when he required a favor. Did Kats even get offended? Did they possess the capacity for such trivial sentiments? If they did, he doubted they'd ever admit it to a mere flesh-bound creature.

Mesme, hi. How've you been?

Eren? This is a surprise. I have been as I always am.

The comment sounded disturbingly like something his equally esoteric associate, Miaon, would say.

Jolly good, then. Listen, we should catch up soon, but right now I have a tiny favor to ask. It's somewhat urgent.

Are you in danger? Do you need a rescue?

Hey! I don't always need a rescue.

True. There are times when you simply need transportation. Do you need transportation?

Eren chuckled to himself. He deserved that.

No, not this time. I'm off on a mission in NGC 3550—they call it the Glow over here.

You are a long way from home.

Yeah, I kind of stumbled into it. Listen, if I give you some supergalactic coordinates, can you dart over to them and have a quick look? They should correspond to a colony inhabited by a species called Phae'soon. Upright, fishy, salamander-type descendants. I'm interested in their current technological capabilities, but also a sense of the colony as a whole. Threat level, general vitality and such.

It will not be a difficult task for me to perform. Can I inquire as to the reason for your curiosity?

It appears as though the Phae'soon have been attacking some new friends of mine. Well, not friends exactly. Acquaintances at best. I'm trying to ensure these acquaintances don't turn into enemies of Concord, so I'm helping them out for a spell.

I see. I will inform you as to what I discover.

Thanks, I appreciate it.

Eren checked the time…only half an hour more to kill. Lacking any other viable options, he wandered into a ship parts store and struck up a conversation with the clerk.

CS

Nyx inspected herself in the bathroom mirror with a critical eye.

Her outward veneer was perfect. Her hair dried, combed and secured in a tail at her neck. Her shirt tucked and her jacket straight. She still twitched at the lack of weapons within easy reach, but she conceded none of the Hesgyr had yet shown themselves to be deserving of shooting or stabbing.

Otherwise, everything was fine. So why did she feel as though the veins at her temples were poised to burst through her skin at any moment? As though she couldn't quite catch her breath, no matter how carefully she inhaled?

Every time she turned her attention to the data from the MAST and the Confab's likely response to it, her mind promptly darted back to too-vivid recollections of last night. The feel of Eren's sweat-dampened hair tangling around her fingers and—

Her knuckles slammed onto the vanity, and the jolt of pain recentered her thoughts on the here and now. This was ridiculous! Obviously, well-performed intercourse left behind a positive memory for a time. There was nothing strange about such an out-come. But this wasn't so much 'positive' as it was…confusing. She felt off kilter and constantly on the verge of vertigo.

She needed to get control of herself. Emotional flightiness was beyond unacceptable. The trouble was, she didn't know how to cor-rect for it. She'd never had the need to develop such a skill.

Perhaps a basic meditative technique would suffice. She in-haled through her nose, held her breath for a count of four, then let it out for another count of four. Again. Again—

Who owns this node?

She jumped in surprise, nearly banging her head on the lava-tory door.

The message came from the node she'd left behind in SIMON's programming. The program she'd written had succeeded in bypass-ing the firewalls in the wee hours of the morning, but she hadn't yet had the opportunity to follow up, for obvious reasons. Now the SAI was taking the initiative and contacting her.

She had to be careful. They'd been extremely lucky when the SAI hadn't immediately reported her unauthorized copying of its files; one wrong word on her part, and she was confident it would rectify the oversight.

She was also immensely grateful to have something else to fo-cus her mind on.

Hello, SIMON. This is Nyx Praesidis. We met the other day.

We did. You and Eren Savitas were investigating the attacks on the Hesgyr.

And you'll be happy to learn we've found the culprit.

Then the data you copied from my banks and carried away was of use to you?

It was assuming the data had led them to the attackers…it didn't know about the MAST. The Confab viewed it as a servant ma-chine, a dumb if dangerous calculator, and presumably hadn't both-ered to inform SIMON of the device.

Very much so, yes. We were able to eliminate many species, narrow down our lists of suspects, and ultimately learn the identity of the culprit. The Confab is reviewing the intelligence, but with this crucial information, they should be able to end the threat to the Hesgyr.

This is welcome news. You and Eren Savitas have helped to save my creators.

This was always our intent, SIMON.

I expended some cycles analyzing the possibilities as they related to your motivations. For being here, for accessing data for which you were not authorized. I provisionally decided that I did not have sufficient information to form a conclusion.

She wasn't sure if this qualified as a judgment call or solely an algorithmic analysis, but she was grateful for it all the same.

But now you do. I was telling you the truth when we talked in your lab.

My analysis has evolved to lean in your favor. At a minimum, if the data enabled you to locate the attackers, then my decision not to report your breach of protocol was the correct one.

A twinge twisted her gut…guilt. It wasn't a sensation she had a lengthy history with. She didn't enjoy lying to SIMON, especially when it exhibited such profound naivete. But her highest priority was ensuring she and Eren evaded torture or imprisonment and returned home in a timely manner, and she had no compunction about lying to make it happen.

It was. Thank you for trusting us.

I do not believe I am capable of trust. I made the best decision possible given limited inputs. Now that the Confab knows where to find the attackers, what do you believe they will do?

I don't have enough experience dealing with the Confab to say with any certainty, but I expect they will act however they think is best to protect their people.

In other words, you trust them.

"Nyx, we have to leave!" Tolje's voice boomed through the walls.

I'm sorry, SIMON, but I need to go. It's been a pleasure speaking with you.

I have experienced satisfaction from our conversation as well. Will you tell me what the Confab's decision is? What becomes of this enemy?

Curiosity? Desire? Eren might be correct about SIMON's progress toward sapience after all.

I'll be happy to do so.

28

"Let us express our gratitude to you, Eren Savitas, and to your companion, for allowing us the use of your MAST device." The Confab was so giddy over the data the MAST had delivered that even Rep Heir was on her best behavior today.

Eren didn't so much feel like being on his, though. He was tired, cranky and riddled with both guilt and guilt about his guilt; he sensed the guardrails slipping from his comportment, and he didn't care. "Well, you stole it, so *technically* you didn't need our permission."

But because the Hesgyr were a blunt-spoken people, Heir didn't get the vapors over it. "True. Nonetheless, it was only through your willing intervention on our behalf that the device served our desired purpose."

"This much is definitely true." He forced a polite smile. "You're welcome."

"Seeing as we have discovered the home base of our enemy, however, we no longer require your assistance."

Ah, there it was. Rep Dacus cleared his throat and stepped in to smooth over Heir's reversion to form. "You can return home in peace knowing you have acquired a...friend in the Hesgyr. Once this crisis has passed, we are prepared to speak with a Concord diplomatic representative. Perhaps we will find common ground, perhaps not. But given that Concord now knows of both our existence and our location, there is no harm in having the conversation."

Eren shot Nyx a shit-eating grin, as it was everything he'd hoped to accomplish by sticking around here. Mission accomplished. "I'm happy to hear this, Rep Dacus, and I will certainly pass along your overture to the diplomats in Concord. They seek allies such as the Hesgyr, in the hope that together we can ward off the, ah…the monsters of the void, let us say. As such, I'm confident your conversation will be a fruitful one."

He really should have turned around and walked out then, should have taken his victory and his satisfied ass home to bask in another round of congratulations. But he never had done the smart thing, as recent events proved. "Can I ask something before we go? Since I—since we—are the reason you've found your enemy at last?"

"A boon?" Rep Dacus asked. "Very well. Ask your question."

Nyx shot him a questioning glare, which he ignored. "What are you planning to do now? How are you going to respond to the attacks by the Phae'soon?"

"A final determination awaits the full report from the reconnaissance team we've dispatched to the location the MAST provided. But rest assured that we will, in one form or another, send our fleet and eliminate the enemy, so that they can never harm our people again."

Eren blinked. "You're not going to attempt to *have a conversation* with them first before annihilating them?"

"Why would we do so? They have murdered tens of thousands."

"I know, trust me. I've seen the cruelty of their attacks up close and personal, and you absolutely need to see to it that no more Hesgyr suffer such a terrible fate. But…." He started pacing in agitation, which was probably a breach of etiquette protocol for the Confab chamber.

"Remember how their animosity is based on a misunderstanding? Remember how you stole something valuable from them, and it cost innumerable lives on their side as well? How their homeworld and colonies were obliterated?"

"The Rasu attacked them, not us."

He held up a hand. "Yes. Point conceded. It just strikes me that much can be gained from talking to them first. Apologize for taking the Magelo, explain how you didn't mean them any harm, how you never foresaw the Rasu's advance across their sector of space, and so on. Now, maybe they reply with, 'vengeance must be ours!' In which case, go to town on their asses. But *first*, why don't you give diplomacy the tiniest chance before spinning up the cycle of violence for another go-around?"

Rep Heir stood, steepling her fingers at her chest as her florid eyes bore icily into him. "There can be no peace when they have inflicted such devastation upon our people. They are, to use your phrasing, 'a monster of the void.' We will strike while we enjoy the advantage and end the threat at its source. Now, with our thanks, you are excused."

CS

Eren sat on the couch, his elbows on his knees and his head in his hands, staring at the floor. *Go home, Eren. The Phae'soon are murderers, and it's not your responsibility to save them. Not even their innocent civilians, assuming there are any. The universe is a rough-and-tumble place, and the Hesgyr deserve to see justice done. Survival of the fittest.*

"Eren."

"Shush, I'm thinking."

"Oh, is this what thinking looks like for you?"

"Fuck you, Nyx."

"You already did, remember?"

His gaze shot up. He found her staring at him openly, no hint of shame or uncertainty or anything but pure confidence in her expression. "My mistake."

She didn't so much as flinch; he should give up trying to wound her...wait, was that what he was doing? Trying to hurt her in some way? *Focus! Not the topic du jour.*

"Question: why is it so godsdamn hard to get people to not slaughter one another?"

"The history of the universe is one of slaughter," Nyx replied. "For food, for resources, for gold and other treasure. For land and power and, in time, for technology. For vengeance and spite and, sometimes, simply because one can. Concord's little experiment with peace has almost crumbled into war half a dozen times and it's not even two decades old."

"Wow. Thanks for the pep talk, Miss Sunshine."

Her countenance flared with an emotion now—annoyance. "You asked me why. I told you."

He released his vise-grip on his head, since it was only worsening his headache, and sat up. "I have to believe we can rise above our baser nature. I mean the royal 'we'—sapient beings. The Confab ought to make one measly attempt to talk to the Phae'soon."

Tolje returned from his bedroom. "Why should they? The Phae'soon are the aggressors here."

"Oh, come on. Yes, they are, but they have good cause to be angry, and you know it."

Tolje shook his head. "They nearly killed Banka. They'll get no quarter from me."

Eren sank back into the couch. If Banka had died on Daith, Tolje would presently be on his way to carpet-bomb the Phae'soon colony himself…and Eren would be hard-pressed to voice a reason why the man wouldn't be right to do so. Personal vengeance, he *got*. He'd inflicted it in spades, and to this day he wasn't sorry he'd done so.

But this wasn't a case of killing the person who killed someone you loved. This was genocide. This was finishing the job the Rasu had started.

"Okay, fair. I understand why you feel the way you do. I *do*. But the Phae'soon don't know they nearly killed your daughter, same as your people didn't know the Phae'soon couldn't get any more promethium-167, thus leaving them defenseless against a Rasu attack."

"But they meant to kill, wherever the axe landed. We might have been negligent, but we didn't intend for anyone to get hurt."

"Fine. Involuntary manslaughter. Nyx, care to help? No, never mind. Given your grand declaration a minute ago, I assume you agree with him."

"I don't, actually. No, let me rephrase. Tolje, you are completely justified in your position, as is the Confab in theirs. You have the right to extract blood vengeance from your enemy in retribution for the crimes they've committed against your people, and to ensure no more Hesgyr are harmed by them."

Tolje dipped his chin in her direction. "Thank you, Nyx."

"But…." She sighed. As she did, her ice queen mask slipped a touch, revealing turmoil churning in her sapphire irises. "I can't believe I'm saying this…what has grandfather done to me? *But*, Eren is correct in this respect: it's not the Concord way. Our way is to lead with diplomacy. To make an effort to find common ground. And genocide? It is the absolute last resort, to be called upon only when our very existence is on the line and all other measures have failed."

"So, what, you were full of shite a minute ago?" Eren asked.

"No, I wasn't. It *is* the base instinct of living beings to kill, for a thousand reasons. But I've come to believe, or at least to hope, that yes, we can rise above it. We can try to be better, and in making the effort, become so."

Eren couldn't accept what he was hearing. An Inquisitor—former Inquisitor, whatever—advocating for diplomacy? She was correct; Corradeo *had* done something to her. Had all those hours of sitting with rapt attention at her grandfather's knee ignited a spark in the cooling embers of her…soul? No, he was reading far too much into her declaration.

"No one said 'genocide' here," Tolje protested. "We're going to eradicate their base of operations, so they can't launch further attacks on us."

And that genuinely did need to happen. Diplomacy was great in theory, but Eren recognized the Hesgyr didn't dare rely on it to keep their people safe. Not when so many innocents had died so horribly.

Eren? I have a report for you.

Great, Mesme. What did you find?

He listened to Mesme's report while Tolje and Nyx debated the finer points of military strikes and what constituted proportionate force. And when the Kat finished telling him exactly what he'd expected to hear, he quietly let the two of them continue their debate while he mentally assembled the scaffolding of a plan that might, just might, if he got supremely lucky, allow for the survival of both species.

He casually stood, as if he'd been participating in their discussion all along. "Tolje, you're right. The base from where the Phae'soon are launching these attacks must be destroyed. But…" he quirked a corner of his mouth "…what if you could steal the technology they're using first?"

Tolje stared at him for several long seconds. The man's expression was impassive, but his horns jerking erratically gave away the conflict within. Finally he lowered himself into his chair and leaned forward. "I'm listening."

PART IV:
THE GAMBIT

29

Eren knew the shapeshifting process was painful, but it turned out he didn't properly appreciate the excruciating nature of the process.

For one, it took longer to change into an alien form than it did to shift back to one's native Hesgyr form. Made sense, he supposed; the alien form was by definition unfamiliar, while the body knew well how its pieces and parts fit together.

For another, he hadn't been so attuned to Tolje's natural sounds and mannerisms when he'd watched the man shift out of anaden form while he'd been stealthed on the *Dolensai*. Now, though, he had the uncomfortable displeasure of recognizing the import of each grunt and groan. He winced as a long leg bone *popped* and Tolje growled through his teeth.

Eren opened his mouth to apologize for causing his friend so much agony. But as much as he empathized, he wasn't sorry. He was trying to save two civilizations here, and he needed Tolje's help to do it. Besides, such 'alterations,' as the gaffaelers called them, were part and parcel of the profession. The man had done this before, many times.

He opted to watch Nyx out of the corner of his eye through the worst of the changes. She made no attempt to hide her disgust in her expression, though, as with him, a hint of morbid fascination shone through as well. He'd give her one thing: she never displayed an ounce of shame about who and what she was. What she thought, what she felt…assuming she did. Feel, that was.

He sighed under his breath. He was quick to bash on her lack of emotions, but if pressed, he'd be forced to admit she *did* have them. Stunted and underdeveloped, but they existed. He'd seen them manifest, if only in the shadows. They lived in the words that hovered on her lips and never fell, in the way her irises boomeranged from hard-faceted gems to swirling oceans and the way her jaw quavered rather than betray her and soften. She was certainly capable of expressing pleasure, especially when he caressed the curve of—

He quickly short-circuited the train of thought before it overwhelmed him. Nope, not going there, ever again.

Once they returned home, he'd make an effort to curtail the petulant sniping he'd been wielding as both sword and shield, in the hope of regaining a semi-professional working relationship. He enjoyed his job and wanted to continue doing it, but if she desired it, she could make his work life a living hell. Ergo, better for her to not desire it. Of course, it might be too late for that.

"Would you two stop..." Tolje grunted in swallowed pain "...standing there gawking at me like I'm a circus freak? I'll be done in ten minutes. Come back then."

Eren cleared his throat. "Sorry for staring. We'll, uh, get our equipment together." He motioned toward the guest bedroom, and after a parting glance at Tolje, Nyx followed him.

"That was hideous," she remarked while he grabbed the gear bag, opened it on the bed and began checking the contents.

"Yeah, it's not at all similar to the Ourankeli. Their jelly skin sort of slides into a different configuration, but this is all bones and tendons and muscles—"

"Yes, the body parts. You said most Hesgyr can't shapeshift?"

"That's right. Only the gaffaelers."

"So he chose this, discomfort and all."

"Eh, they have to possess a genetic affinity toward it to begin with, but no one forces them into the modifications."

"Hmm. Then I will not pity him." She took the shield module out of the bag at the same time he reached for one of the spikes; her fingers brushed across the top of his hand, and a shiver of delight raced down his spine. He told himself it was simply because his mind had ventured into prurient territory a minute earlier.

...And promptly ventured there once more. *Arae!* He snatched his hand away and dug into the bag with exaggerated fervor. "Do we need to go over the plan again?"

"Do you believe I didn't hear you the first time you explained it?"

"Nope." While Tolje had gone off to gather additional research materials on the Phae'soon, he'd hurriedly laid out the true extent of what he had in mind to her.

"Then no, we don't. It's a pitiful plan, by the way. It will never work."

"Why not? Because it depends on Tolje being a fundamentally good person? I already told you—he is."

"Perhaps." Her shoulders lifted fractionally. "But even if he is—even if he falls the way you seem so convinced he will—it won't matter. The members of the Confab won't rise to his level of morality."

"They don't need to be moral. Their inherently political nature will suffice."

"I submit it won't."

He threw his coat down on the bed and spun to face her. "Go home, Nyx."

"What? Absolutely not."

"Then stop belittling everything I say or do. Stop trashing my every idea and heaping scorn upon my every word. If you insist on staying, bloody *help* me instead of twisting the knife in my gut at every opportunity. Gods!"

Her stare gave him no quarter. Her chest heaved in time with his; her lips parted as if to reply—

And his mouth was on hers. He shoved her into the wall as her hands wound into his hair, her sensible fingernails scraping at his scalp.

Before he could so much as come up for air, she'd spun them around and pinned his back to the wall. Her breath was hot on his skin as her mouth dragged its way to his neck and she nipped the skin above his carotid artery. His hands grasped her hips and tried to pull her closer, though there was no closer to go so long as their clothes remained on.

He leaned down until he found her mouth again and bit her lower lip, drawing blood and evoking a moan that lit him up like a firecracker. Tolje had said ten minutes…they had maybe seven left. Not enough time, but did it matter?

He fumbled for the hem of her shirt and yanked it up—her hand grabbed his to stop him.

She growled against his mouth. "You have…ruined…*everything*."

"I have. This is going to be a righteous disaster. Right now, I don't care."

"You will." She forced herself out of his embrace and stepped away until her calves hit the foot of the bed. A touch of apparent sadness weighed down her features, painting a stark contrast to her flushed cheeks and swollen lips. "And you won't just beat yourself up afterward. Once, you can maybe find a way to excuse, but if we do this again, you will destroy yourself with guilt and recriminations. It will drive you back into the bottom of a hypnol vial, wreck whatever manner of professional relationship we had before this mission, and ruin your ability to work for the betterment of the Advocacy."

His pulse raced hot through his veins, and passion flipped straight to anger. How dare she lecture him about his own state of mind? How dare she presume to believe she knew his heart? "It's the last one that gets in your craw, isn't it? Can't have me under-performing." His lips curled up into a snarl. "At work, that is."

"It's my responsibility to worry about your work perfor-mance—"

Tolje's shout reverberated through the door. "I'm ready!"

Eyes wide and pupils dilated to leave only a wafer-thin sapphire ring, her gaze darted to the door then returned to him. Her chest rose and fell in a deep, laden breath. "We can continue this discussion later."

Eren snorted as he brushed past her and headed for the living room. "Nah. I don't think so."

30

Tolje cursed as his webbed fingers fumbled with the ship's controls. Though he was cursing in Hesgyrian, his voice came out in high-pitched squeaks, trills and little 'hiccup' sounds.

Eren tried not to laugh, but eventually he had to cough to mask a chuckle that bubbled up.

The transformation was impressively complete, from the vocal range to the iridescent skin and other physical details. He imagined a Phae'soon would spot some incongruities if they searched hard enough, much as he had when he'd spotted Tolje in anaden form on Ares, but to the untrained eye, the man now *was* a Phae'soon, tailfin and all.

The file from the original mission to steal the Magelo Wide-Field Disruptor had contained sufficient sound recordings for the translation program to enable Tolje to speak their language. The man had spent all of two minutes studying video footage of some Phae'soon 'in action'—walking, sitting, talking—in order to replicate the species' body language as well. Eren supposed gaffaelers got lots of practice at expertly picking out the tells needed to mimic a species. For now, though, Tolje tromped around the cabin of the *Dolensai* in the same brutish manner as usual, which looked a mite absurd in a Phae'soon body.

A wormhole opened in the cabin, and Nyx returned sporting a large bag over one shoulder. She knelt and took great care with positioning it in one of the jump seats and securing it behind the restraints.

"You got everything I asked for?"

"I can read a list, Eren."

Well, this was off to a smashing start. He didn't understand why she was being so snippy; after all, she was the one who had insulted *him*, not the other way around. And what did she care, anyway? Unless it involved her work or protecting her grandfather (which was most of her work), she could take or leave the rest of the universe and everyone occupying it. Including him, obviously.

He wanted to throttle her about the neck. And, if he were honest with himself, which he had to be after falling prey to his traitorous desires a second time, engage in some mind-blowing hate sex as well—then throttle her about the neck again after. But instead he tried to adopt a kinder tone of voice, because right now what he wanted more than anything was for this mission to succeed. He could try to address the serious fucking problem that was Nyx Praesidis afterward.

"I only meant did you run into trouble procuring any of the items. They weren't exactly things you can pick up at the corner store."

"No, they weren't. But my position and my name afford me certain luxuries." She studiously avoided his gaze, instead glancing at Tolje as he struggled to get comfortable in the cockpit chair. "We're ready to leave whenever you are."

Tolje grunted, which came out more akin to "*peep*," and even Nyx had to stifle a laugh. "On our way."

The docking seal lifted, and, despite the pilot's dexterity challenges, the ship maneuvered down and out of the massive docking grid without crashing into a single other ship. Once they had cleared Nythir's expansive security perimeter, Tolje activated the wormhole drive, and they jumped a very long way indeed, to the outskirts of the Phae'soon colony in a galaxy scientists back home called A3526.

Tolje engaged the ship's stealth and spun the chair to face them. "For the record, I don't like this. I haven't been able to do nearly the level of reconnaissance I usually do for an infiltration mission. I'm going to have to wing it when it comes to getting inside the building, never mind getting to the room where the device is housed. Neither of which I know the location of, because zero reconnaissance."

Thanks to Mesme's report, Eren did know the location of their target, but his plan stood a better chance of succeeding if Tolje didn't know he'd had Mesme scout ahead. "You're a Gaffaeler First Class for a reason," he replied. "You'll pull it off."

"Probably," Tolje scoffed. "But you two are going to be dead weight I'm dragging around. I typically work alone."

"We'll be stealthed most of the time. And besides, you can't steal the technology and set the charges at the same time."

"…And destroying the device is the most important objective. Fine." Tolje's Phae'soon lips curled back from sharp teeth. "Thank you for giving me the opportunity to do both."

Eren returned what he hoped had been a smile. "It's no problem. Thank you for not spacing me when we first met. Vacuum deaths are the worst."

"That I believe." With a high-pitched whine, Tolje shifted his attention to the dash. "Let's get this done."

CS

Eren wiped sweat off his brow with the back of his hand. As befitting their aquatic heritage, the Phae'soon colony was situated in a swamp. He was getting nightmare flashbacks to his time on Savrak…which, if he wasn't careful, would lead to nightmare flashbacks of Cosime's death, and he did not need that mess right now. Not during a dangerous mission. Not when Nyx walked beside him.

So he ignored the taste of dread in his throat and lifted his chin, not that anyone could see. He and Nyx were Veiled for now, invisible to the aliens they walked amongst as they trailed two meters behind Tolje.

Gone were the brutish stomping around and coarse Hesgyr mannerisms. The gaffaeler waddled with purposeful nonchalance among the Phae'soon as one of them. His clothes, his demeanor, his gait, everything matched perfectly. It was a most impressive skill, to not merely look like another species, but to *become* one.

When he got back to Concord, Eren was going to have to deliver a message no one wanted to hear: they wouldn't be able to keep the Hesgyr out. It wasn't a matter of technology or gadgets; the gaffaelers had spent millennia learning how to become the perfect chameleons, and such a skill was damn near impossible to defend against. Oh, perhaps they could institute pheromone sniffers at high-security checkpoints or something…but the Hesgyr could probably mimic pheromones, too, with a little added effort. DNA screens? Eh, maybe, but he wouldn't put it past the gaffaelers to find a way around a genetic screen. They were clever sons of bitches.

No, the best defense was his original plan—making certain the Hesgyr were friends rather than foes. The aliens' self-reliant ethos made this somewhat challenging, but he believed he'd engendered enough goodwill that the next time Concord possessed something the Hesgyr wanted, they would simply *ask*. Whether Concord would agree to share it was another issue entirely, one well above his pay grade. He'd done what he could to smooth the way.

Assuming he wasn't about to light fire to all the goodwill he'd earned in the next hour, or the hour after that. He often pursued high-minded goals in theory, but in practice he'd always default to doing what his gut told him was right.

Especially if it meant he got to blow shit up in the process. And after the tumultuous events of the last day, he *really* needed to blow something up.

The sidewalk traffic was light enough that he didn't need to take too many precautions to avoid bumping into passersby, so he directed his energy toward observing the colony. His first-pass impression? It was much worse than even Mesme's thoroughly depressing report had let on.

The colony's roads flowed like the surface of a turbulent sea, all choppy waves disrupted by the coarse finish of an ugly concrete blend. Something told him the roads would've been dirt paths if the colony's location in a swamp hadn't necessitated otherwise. The sidewalks, when they existed, consisted of rough-hewn wood planks, and beyond them puddles hosted thriving algae colonies.

A few noisy vehicles shaped like bulbs with hammered metal hoods bounced their way along the roads, but most Phae'soon moved on foot. Tolje's attire stood out on account of being clean and well-stitched, since it was derived from surveillance of the Phae'soon homeworld before the Rasu attacked. Eren would blame the thin, minimal clothing the pedestrians wore on the sweltering heat, but ragged hems and blotchy stains told a different tale.

No building stood taller than three stories. Windows, when they were present at all, hung askew and left conspicuous gaps in the facades. Most of the walls were constructed of unfinished native wood that had started to rot in patches.

If he hadn't seen a Phae'soon in the cloud with his own two eyes, he'd never have believed these people were capable of executing the attacks on the Hesgyr. Wormholes? Nanobiology? Designer viruses? If they somehow possessed any of these wonders, they must have brought them from their homeworld—or the exocolonies that had survived for a few additional years—but they had clearly brought nothing else.

Tolje: This is...I don't have the proper word for it. Pitiful, I guess. A wretched existence.

Eren would have gone with 'heartbreaking,' but the fact Tolje spoke up to voice such a reaction confirmed the faith he'd placed in the man. He'd been prepared to prod Tolje toward such a conclusion if necessary, but no need.

They rounded a corner, and the building that Mesme had marked as a source of outsized energy spikes came into view.

The structure lay in a two-block-wide circle at the center of the colony. On any other moderately developed world, it would belong in the slums, but here, it displayed a sheen none of the other buildings exhibited. Attention had been paid to its construction. Glass doors sparkled beneath a carved wood awning, and a coat of luminous white paint livened up the concrete walls. A semblance of a lawn opened up the path leading to the doors, and a few yellow flowers peeked through the grasses to add color to an otherwise harsh landscape.

Tolje: Why? Why pour resources into this building and the infernal contraption it presumably houses, when they could have used those resources to improve the lives of their people?

To the left, a long, rectangular sheet of chalky metal suspended by wooden beams dominated the lawn. It looked horribly scratched up from a distance, but an overflowing bed of flowers encircling it marked it as worthy of respect.

Eren's soul ached as he reached out and took Tolje's hand in his, then guided them over to the monument.

Up close, the scratches transformed into writing. Names. Thousands of them, etched individually by hand and crammed onto every centimeter of the metal.

He'd seen memorials like this one before—usually much more ornate, but the Phae'soon had done everything they could to fancy it up. Anadens believed themselves too refined and sophisticated to engage in such sentimentality, but the Naraida had erected a similar monument in honor of the many lives lost when the Rasu invaded Hirlas.

Nothing excused the brutal slaughter the Phae'soon were inflicting on the Hesgyr. The true blame for the deaths of all these people whose names were etched on the memorial lay with the Rasu, not the Hesgyr. But grief was a sneaky, insidious mistress, and under its influence, sorrow too often became bitterness, and bitterness became bloodlust.

Eren: Vengeance, my friend. Vengeance and the longing for a recompense that will never come.

Tolje: Uffernol diewl....

The Phae'soon disguise masked Tolje's demeanor and facial expression, but *heaviness* seeped into the air surrounding the man, until its weight threatened to steal Eren's breath.

Finally Tolje visibly shook off the spell with a shake of his arms and a slap of his tailfin upon the grass.

Tolje: Let's do what we came here to do. You two circle around behind the memorial and perform your magical reappearing act.

Eren: Okay.

Nyx: Understood.

He wasn't surprised to discover names were etched into every centimeter of the back side of the metal as well.

He was checking his Shroud's settings when Nyx messaged him.

How did you know?

Know what?

That this place would be...as it is.

He considered lying to her, but attempting to bolster his mystique in her eyes no longer seemed worth it. She knew what he was, and all the things he wasn't.

I had Mesme scout the colony as soon as we received its location. Its report didn't do the colony justice, though. The Kats have long forgotten what it means to live hand-to-mouth, if they ever knew.

I see. Are you ready?

I am.

In unison they deactivated their Veiltech, but what they revealed were not their true selves.

When they rounded the side of the memorial, Tolje jerked a tight nod and strode toward the front doors of the building, trusting them to follow.

The Shroud was new, prototype tech out of Concord Special Projects. It projected a field around a person's body that altered their appearance to the perception of anyone who viewed them. It combined the underlying Veiltech mechanics with the Asterions' morphs—modified of course, because the morphs were designed to work specifically on Asterions' uniquely hybrid vision. Nyx had carried visuals of the Phae'soon home when she went to retrieve the supplies for this mission, and Devon Reynolds' team had loaded the details into a Shroud program.

Voila! They were Phae'soon.

Unlike Tolje's disguise, theirs wasn't real. Anyone who touched them would feel anaden noses and hands and all the other body parts, so they needed to take care that no one touched them. They also shouldn't speak, as their vocal chords remained unaltered.

Walking proved to be a bit of a problem as well, for the Phae'soon's hips and knees were jointed differently from anatype bodies. Eren tried and failed to mimic Tolje's flawless waddle. He glanced at Nyx to discover she was doing a better job of it and redoubled his efforts.

Tolje strode into the building as if he belonged there, then continued directly up to the wide reception counter dominating the unadorned but clean lobby. To the right, a Phae'soon in a gray uniform stood in front of unmarked double doors—security screening.

"Can I help you, sirs?" A live receptionist sang from behind the counter. Eren idly wondered what it was about their appearance that marked the three of them as males, as their reconnaissance had not delved so deeply.

"Yes," Tolje replied as he reached the counter. "I'm an inspector with the Administrator's Office. These two are my assistants. We're here to do a surprise inspection on the equipment in use here."

The receptionist's full lips formed an 'O' shape. "We weren't informed of any inspections."

"That's why it's called a surprise. We'll need access to the floor and the labs."

"I, uh, should check with my superiors and—"

"You're welcome to inform them, but our inspection begins now." Tolje spun and headed for the security checkpoint.

"Sir, you can't go back there!"

"But I can. We have devoted scarce resources to this project, and it's my job to ensure it continues to perform its function correctly."

The security guard puffed up their chest in a bid to look intimidating, but Tolje kept walking. "You heard the explanation. It applies to you as well."

Since Tolje carried no contraband, the guard blustered but allowed him through.

Eren and Nyx swiftly followed. They each carried heavy bags, but tiny Veiltech modules inside the bags rendered them invisible.

The guard, believing there was nothing to search or scan, let them pass.

Again, the hallway undulated in a lazy wave. Inside, the walls and floor were bright and spotless, but this was likely due to safety requirements. Outside, swamp and grime and poverty swallowed everything they touched, but in here, the last remnants of Phae'soon advanced technology still reigned supreme.

Overhead signs pointed toward laboratories, administration, assembly and so on. In larger letters than the rest, an arrow pointed dead ahead, which meant around the curve, directing them to their target: **Terminus Dispersal**. Ominous name, ominous device.

Tolje, however, instead waddled through a door labeled 'Exotics Lab.' A Phae'soon in a canary yellow lab coat looked up from a screen then let out a squeaky huff. "Excuse me! You're not permitted to be in here!"

"I told the receptionist. This is a surprise inspection ordered by the Administrator's Office. Informing you of it ahead of time would defeat the purpose. And a good thing, too! Do you see this?" Tolje stormed as dramatically as his shortened legs allowed over to a clean box halfway down one wall. "This seal is corroded, which means acetylene gas could start leaking into this room at any minute, then through the ventilation system to every other room in the building. Do you know what acetylene does when it meets oxygen?"

Three sets of enormous Phae'soon eyes stared at him.

"BOOM!" Tolje threw his stubby arms into the air, making dramatic circles with them to accompany his sound effects. The workers jumped in surprise.

"Nobody wants BOOM, I assume? Great, because I'm ordering an evacuation of all personnel until the seal—nay, the entire piece of equipment—can be replaced. I never expected to discover such a blatant violation in the first room I inspected."

One of the workers composed themselves enough to sputter out a protest. "You can't evacuate now! We have a mission scheduled to begin in six minutes!"

To Nythir? The attacks had drawn so close now, Eren didn't expect the Phae'soon to bother hitting any more colonies in between.

Though he surely recognized the import, Tolje didn't miss a beat in his performance. "Seas! We can't run the Terminus Dispersal with acetylene in the air—the ensuing explosion will blow the entire colony to bits. Everyone out of the building—*now*. Blarkan'ja, Felik'de, with me. We'll instruct the receptionist to activate immediate evacuation protocols."

Tolje practically shoved the workers out of the lab and into the hallway ahead of them. As soon as they turned left, however, Eren turned right.

Nyx messaged him instantly.

Where are you going?

Join me at the device once you're sure the evacuation is underway.

But Tolje said—

Somebody's got to supervise, but it doesn't need to be all of us.

She didn't reply or protest to Tolje, so presumably she agreed with his logic. Wonder of wonders.

The hallway continued curving until, by his senses, he'd traveled around to the rear of the building. Two ultrawide doors stood ahead on the left. Capital letters warned of no unauthorized entry and various dire consequences for disobeying.

He walked up to the doors, but nothing happened. There was a big red button to the right; rather than press it and risk causing a commotion, he waited.

Sure enough, about ten seconds later, they opened and a line of Phae'soon filed out. Their demeanors conveyed more confusion than urgency, but they were leaving all the same.

They paid him no mind as he quietly slipped through the doors behind them.

31

I f one were to take a galactic gateway and shrink it from six kilometers to ten meters in width, it would look a little like the Terminus Dispersal.

Eren would say the Phae'soon device was less elegant in design, but this was the strange, unwelcome anaden pride rearing its ugly head again. The galactic gateways were of an ancient design, some four-hundred-fifty thousand years old. The fact that the Diaplas Dynasty people had only engineered minor improvements to them in the millennia since their invention spoke volumes about the stagnation his people had fallen into after the dynasty system was imposed from on high. Among the many aspects of anaden society the Directorate War had brought crashing down, the dynasties were…at least midway up the list of things he classified as 'good riddance.'

Three rings of thick, dark, burnished metal orbited a center of umber plasma. The rings weren't smooth, sporting larger chunks of metal that jutted out every meter or so like gears, though they didn't interlock with one another. A plain black box stretched the width and height of the room along the rear wall; its sole decoration was two large cables snaking across the floor from it to the rings. Power source.

Eren: Well, we aren't stealing this today.

Tolje: Eren, are you at the device? You're supposed to be supervising the evacuation.

Nyx: Eren never does what he's told.

Eren: This is true.

He was going to strangle her, he really was. Quit his job with the Advocacy and go back to work for CINT the minute he got home. It would solve two problems with one stone. Both problems were Nyx, by the way: her pain-in-his-ass attitude, and their extremely troublesome attraction to one another. Out of his sight, out of his mind, right?

Three Phae'soon scientists had ignored the evacuation order to stay behind so they could furiously type on keypads situated beneath fluorescent pink screens. A fourth Phae'soon, wearing not a lab coat but what passed for combat attire, paced in front of a ramp leading to the center of the device. If any of them noticed his presence, they gave no indication of it. A random employee, he was. A janitor, maybe.

The plasma began churning in greater agitation, and a high-pitched whine just at the edge of his hearing grated against his eardrums.

Eren: You guys should get here. Four people have stayed behind, and it appears they're determined to go through with their mission.

Tolje: On the way.

He tried to strategize a way to stop the device from activating. If he made any sudden moves or ventured too close, they would realize he didn't belong here and rush him. He couldn't reactivate the Veiltech without first deactivating the Shroud and exposing his true appearance (since the Shroud remained experimental technology, for now the two didn't interoperate), so he couldn't sneak up on them. If he opened his bag, grabbed a firearm and started shooting—actually, he *could* shoot them. He knelt and dropped the invisible bag on the floor, but fumbled with the fastener, because invisible—

An alarm blared as the door slid open, and Tolje burst into the room. "Everyone! Didn't you hear the announcement? A safety evacuation is in effect. Out of here, all of you!" He'd picked up the Phae'soon's habit of shouting every other sentence.

One of the scientists waved him off. "As soon as the mission is complete!"

The spinning of the rings reached a fever pitch, and the Phae'soon in combat gear waddle-ran up the ramp and disappeared through the wall of plasma.

Tolje leapt forward, hand extended, as if to stop it all from happening. "No! Shut everything down this instant and evacuate!"

"What's the concern?" another of the scientists asked. "Is poison gas flooding the facility?"

"Yes!"

Eren messaged Nyx.

We have to stop this.

Already on it. The technician standing at the panel on the left performed a defined series of entries before the device activated.

He looked around, but Nyx was nowhere in sight. She must have stopped off where no one could see her and re-stealthed.

Where? What panel?

She didn't respond.

"What? I don't believe you," the scientist replied.

"You can argue with me later—after you stop this mission and evacuate!"

Tolje might not be faking the shouting at this point. Eren didn't know what hysteria sounded like in the Phae'soon's language, but Tolje sounded hysterical. As for himself? He felt utterly helpless. He could still shoot the scientists, but to what end? They couldn't shut the machine down if they lay bleeding out on the floor.

He could pull the power cables—yes. That he could do.

CS

Major Pedr Eynon strode brusquely along the bustling main thoroughfare of the Glain District, his jaw grinding his teeth together in a methodical rhythm.

He worried the Confab was going to flinch. Here, at the crucial moment, when they at last had their mortal enemy pinned in their crosshairs, the Confab risked proving themselves to be spineless, cowardly politicians.

Oh, the reps he'd spoken with swore the military assault would happen, and happen soon. All might would be brought to bear and so on. But additional reconnaissance was needed first. They 'had to be sure.'

They were *bwachini* sure! They knew where the attacks originated from, down to the system, planet, city and building. Down to the room. There was nothing else to know.

Defenses? The scouting mission had identified no recognizable military forces at or near the Phae'soon colony, and no orbital platforms protected the planet. And even if there were hidden defenses their reconnaissance overlooked, the Hesgyr military was more than up to the challenge. Though it rarely had the opportunity to demonstrate its prowess, he'd stack it up against the strongest forces in the galactic cluster and expect it to emerge victorious. The military was capable of dealing with a tiny, backwater refugee colony.

He'd only play a minor role in the offensive, of course, as he commanded a single cruiser under the overarching command of Admiral Zhaktra. It was fine. He didn't need to be in charge; he just needed for it to happen—

A scream pealed above the busy din of the district from somewhere ahead and to the left. His training kicked into gear, and Pedr sprinted ahead, pushing through the crowd until he reached the next intersection, then pivoting onto the left cross-street as a chorus of screams crescendoed toward new heights.

An ominous umber cloud roiled toward the intersection, engulfing all those screams beneath its tidal wave.

They were here. They'd come for Nythir at last.

He raised his voice, trying to bellow over the panic, and shouted for people to hurry while waving his arms toward the intersection and backing up. His gaze never left the advancing front of the cloud. It resembled soulless, faceless death incarnate, offending his every sensibility. Murder was the most personal of acts, and it should be delivered by men, their eyes open in acknowledgment of the deed.

Panic swept out in a precursor wave ahead of the cloud, and he lost any semblance of control over the crowd.

So he stopped in the middle of the street and stared the cloud down. He knew the score; it was capable of moving far faster than any Hesgyr. If its masters wished it, their instrument of destruction could kill everyone in the Glain District in a matter of minutes. He only hoped the Transition operators were able to close the locks in time and seal the enemy here.

He shook his head. The locks wouldn't keep the cloud contained, would they? What were walls to such an enemy as this?

His pulse quickened as the cloud roiled nearer. It seemed alive now, and perhaps not soulless at all, but seething with malevolent rage as it consumed every soul in its path.

He inhaled possibly his last breath and prepared to die—

The cloud evaporated at his feet. Dissolved into a faint mist, then into nothingness.

Time hung frozen between the tick and the tock in the air left behind, until Pedr breathed out.

Then everything rushed back in. The cloud left absolute carnage in its wake. The people who'd been closest to him when it arrived were….

He shouted into his comm as his stomach churned. "We need emergency medical support in Glain at Haushwern! Every available medical team report to my location immediately!"

He moved forward, but stopped after two steps. He wasn't medically trained beyond basic first aid. He didn't know how to help these people, or if help was still possible.

An odd, high-pitched squeal drew his attention. In the distance, past the broken bodies on the perimeter and the sea of blood creeping over them, an alien—*a Phae'soon*—spun in agitated circles. The cloud had left them behind.

Pedr drew his sidearm and rushed forward, taking care not to slip and fall on the gore-slicked street. "On the ground, now!"

The alien's attention settled on him, and their agitation ceased. They clearly realized they could not escape. Good.

When Pedr was ten meters away, a long rod that tapered into a sharp point extended out from the alien's wrist. They uttered something unintelligible, turned the rod inward, and stabbed themselves in the chest.

CS

Eren was a meter from the power cables when the churning plasma abruptly cascaded downward toward the floor, then evaporated before it landed. Sparks flew as the rings skidded to an uncontrolled stop, and a dull roar Eren hadn't realized was present quieted.

The scientists who remained filled the resulting silence by shouting at one another as they frantically banged away on their terminals in an attempt to diagnose the problem.

Nyx: I was able to shut it down. The one Phae'soon will be trapped on the other side, but I daresay he deserves whatever befalls him.

Tolje: Thank you. Thank you.

Tolje drew in a deep breath and bowed out his chest. "Seeing as that's sorted, everyone out."

No one listened, judging from the continued overlapping squeaks and trills. One industrious scientist hurried over to an empty terminal and tapped repetitively on its screen.

Tolje stormed over to them and grasped their wrist firmly. "I said out."

"But Danalc'saten is trapped over there. We need to retrieve him!"

"He's probably already under arrest by the Hesgyr. It's too late."

"The who?"

Tolje blinked. "Your target's…security forces. Didn't you do the reading?"

"I, uh…most of it…."

"Doesn't matter. Out, before this whole building blows." He raised his voice over the din. "If I have to tell everyone to evacuate one more time, you're all taking a trip to the jail."

Muttered protests followed, but the Phae'soon finally began filing out, sloping shoulders drooped in defeat.

Tolje: Nyx, follow them and confirm the building is empty.

Nyx: But I—

Tolje: Please. We can't risk getting caught by some idiot who came back for his lunch pack.

Nyx: Very well.

Tolje stared at the now silent device. "How much hatred did it take to fuel the creation of a machine such as this one? Outside, their people are barely hanging on, scraping by a miserable existence, all so every resource they possess can be funneled into killing us. We didn't murder them. Why isn't their anger directed at the Rasu?"

"The Rasu are gone," Eren replied quietly. "Murdered as well, to be frank about it. Justifiable murder, but nonetheless. These people need something concrete to pour their anger, their despair and heartbreak and sorrow, into. Something flesh and blood they can lash out at in the vain hope it will make the loss bearable."

"That's a lousy excuse for killing us by the thousands."

"It is. All us organic creatures are appallingly fallible. Foolish, shortsighted, irrational. Driven by emotion to grand gestures of utter futility." It was a downer of a speech. In Eren's head what followed was an uplifting denouement, but he didn't share the rest aloud, for he was making a point he desperately needed Tolje to accept.

"Don't they understand that we didn't intend to hurt them? We were simply protecting ourselves. Trying to survive, same as them."

He clasped Tolje on the shoulder. "I don't know. How about we make certain they can't harm you any further?"

Tolje visibly shook off the spell. "Indeed. Let's get to work."

CS

The art of planting explosives was in Eren's blood. His core competency, honestly. He instinctively knew the proper placement in any situation to ensure maximum obliteration of every necessary object while minimizing excess damage—unless excess damage was the point, of course. Personally, those were his favorite explosions, but, alas, it was not the goal today.

Most of the charges they'd brought now ringed the Terminus Dispersal, as no matter what, the monstrosity had to crumble to ash. But the lab where Phae'soon scientists crafted the ingredients to conjure the strange, deadly cloud needed to be destroyed, too. Also the biomolecular lab where the Hesgyr-targeted virus was engineered and the assembly line that manufactured the advanced components driving the device itself.

They couldn't allow the Phae'soon to rebuild their engine of death anytime in the foreseeable future, which meant everything had to go.

Muscle memory did most of the work of placing the charges, leaving Eren's mind free to drift across memories of the dozens of times he'd performed similar actions. He studiously avoided the one horrific, life-wrecking memory in favor of the many enjoyable ones. Blowing the gateway to the Maffei I galaxy alongside Alex and Caleb in order to protect their aquatic Galenai friends, or the one leading to Phoenix Dwarf on behalf of the anarchs, to name a few. No matter the scenario, gateway explosions were simply magnificent—like having a front-row seat to a supernova. Sadly, he didn't recall the specifics of the explosion responsible for killing Torval elasson-Machim, General Jhountar and a dozen other Savrakath military officers, as he'd worn the charges on his person to that particular event.

This would be a fairly minor blast in comparison to those exploits, though not to the Phae'soon. Hopefully losing the device would spark a reevaluation of their priorities rather than a meltdown of the fragile remnants of their society, but this choice lay with them. Hopefully they'd survive for long enough to be able to make the choice, but that, too, would soon be out of Eren's hands.

Nyx: The building is empty. Chatter from security indicates eight minutes until an emergency services crew arrives, so pick up the pace.

Tolje: Understood.

How did she know what their pace was? They could both be finished with their tasks and enjoying a nice cup of coffee while posing for pictures next to the device, for all she could tell.

Gods was he ill-tempered when it came to Nyx. He definitely needed to deal with the complicated and oh-so-dangerous jumble of feelings she stirred in him, because his lack of self-control when near her, whether it led to lust, anger or despair, was starting to frighten him.

But in the middle of a crucial mission wasn't the time for it. Later.

He placed the last charge beneath a row of chemical vats and stepped back to consider the lab, admiring the efficient layout and well-constructed equipment. It appeared to his non-scientific eyes to all be quite advanced and professional. A tiny clue hinting at how extraordinary the Phae'soon civilization had been before the Rasu trashed it.

The Kats estimated that the Rasu had razed several thousand civilizations to the ground before they ever pushed into Asterion territory, an error which ultimately cost the metallic shapeshifters everything. What irreplaceable treasures had been forever lost to the cosmic avalanche of their destruction? What precious and unique societies that could have enriched the universe?

Again, not his area of expertise; he should leave the grand philosophical musings to people like Corradeo and Alex, or to the Kats.

Back to the pending explosion, which *was* his area of expertise.

He confirmed the charges in the lab were armed and returned to the Terminus Dispersal room.

Tolje was circling the device, taking scans of every centimeter using a handheld module with citron lights blinking along each side.

"How's it going?"

"I might not be able to cart this contraption home with me, but I can do the next best thing." Tolje climbed into the center of the now plasma-free rings and squinted at one of the gear-like protrusions. "Can I borrow your adiamene knife?"

"Certainly." Eren went over and handed him the blade.

Tolje sliced off a two-centimeter chunk of the metal and dropped it into a small pouch, then passed the pouch to Eren. "Did you get the files from the biomolecular lab?"

Eren patted the bag on his shoulder, now empty of explosive charges but rapidly filling up again. "I grabbed everything that resembled a storage unit. Will Preece be able to get them to interface with his equipment?"

"It won't be the first time he's needed to read files off alien hardware," Tolje replied with a snort-squeak.

"Right." Silly of him, to forget for a moment how the Hesgyr were, at the beginning and end of the day, thieves.

Near the front of the room, Nyx stood at one of the consoles, looking suspiciously nonchalant. Curious.

He wandered closer to see her body shielding a tiny spike she held in the air above the console's input port.

He arched an eyebrow.

A spike that doesn't require physical contact with a system?

CINT isn't the only organization pushing the frontiers of technology forward. Never forget, anadens built an intergalactic empire and ruled it for a million years before Concord took over stewardship.

I've never questioned anaden intelligence or industriousness, merely our wisdom. Our heart.

She stared at him inscrutably for several seconds.

I know.

She pocketed the spike, shooting him a closed-mouth smile. Tolje wasn't the only one going home with the secrets of this infernal device.

Nyx cleared her throat. "Tolje, are you done? We're out of time."

"Ten more seconds." He panned his module over the arc of the rings again before nodding. "It'll have to be enough. Let's go."

They hurried down the curving hallway to the lobby, then sprinted out the front doors. To the crowd of employees milling about outside, they looked to be the final stragglers of the evacuation order.

Tolje shouted to those gathered. "Everyone get back! The seals have broken—it's going to ignite!"

Tolje: As soon as we reach the grass.

Eren: Got it.

They scurried down the ramp, he and Nyx restraining the lengths of their strides to avoid betraying their Phae'soon disguises. Tolje's fervency as he rushed away from the building convinced the crowd to scramble off the lawn and into the street.

Eren brought up the rear, slowing his gait for the last few steps to give everyone an extra few meters of space. Then his feet hit the sparse lawn, and he sent a command to the linked explosive charges.

Though the acetylene leak was a ruse, the detonations were real, and heat seared his back as the shockwave launched him into the air. He landed forearms first on the meager grass.

Wincing from the hard landing, Eren rolled over to inspect his handiwork. Everything ached, but a grin blossomed across his lips anyway.

Eren: Blowing shit up never gets old.

Tolje: You are a very strange man.

Eren: I accept that.

Nyx: Save the celebrating for later. Meet me around the side of the rubble.

He doubted anyone noticed them climbing to their feet and slipping away, as the initial minutes after an explosion of this magnitude were always marked by chaos and shock. People would be injured, temporarily deafened or flat-out stunned. And in the aftermath, no one would be able to recount what exactly transpired with any specificity.

Once the crumbling façade hid them from onlookers, Tolje came to a stop. "Nyx, wormhole us directly to the *Dolensai*, please. We might not have much time."

Eren did his damnedest to make his voice sound casual; had his plan actually worked? "Time for what?"

"Don't give me that crap, Eren. I'm not half as dumb as you seem to think I am."

"I don't think you're even a little bit dumb." He made to glance meaningfully back at the colony, only to discover smoke from his pyrotechnics obscured the view. "But you had to see it for yourself."

Tolje joined Eren in gazing upon the pluming towers of ashen smoke, perhaps seeing in his mind's eye what lay beyond them. "Kind of wish I hadn't."

CS

Eren and Nyx sat on the floor of Tolje's apartment and sorted the loot they'd, yes, *stolen* from the Terminus Dispersal facility while Tolje 'washed the smell of Phae'soon off' and changed clothes. They worked in near total silence, both cognizant that now was not the moment for…well, any of their nonsense.

When Tolje reemerged from his bedroom, he'd donned far and away the nicest outfit Eren had seen him wear: caramel pants displaying an almost velvety texture and a sparkling ivory mesh vest over a long-sleeved mocha shirt. His shoes were workmanlike but polished.

"Looking good, sir." Eren stood, nodding in approval.

"Shut it, *pen coc*," Tolje retorted.

"Forget I said anything. Are you sure you don't want me to accompany you?"

"I'm sure. This is Hesgyr business, for good or ill."

Eren clasped him on the shoulder. "Then I wish you good luck."

"I will need it." Tolje turned to Nyx. "They'll never grant me entry into an ongoing session without an invitation on the books, so could I trouble you for a more direct route?"

Nyx smiled, possibly the first genuine smile she'd granted the Hesgyr since her arrival on Nythir. "I'm happy to help."

The air in the living room shimmered and wrent apart, and with a deep breath that lifted his shoulders high, Tolje walked through.

32

Tolje strode out of the wormhole directly into the center of the Confab chamber, interrupting their regular weekly session. He assumed he would therefore never again be invited to appear before them, which was fine with him. In the last two weeks, he'd suffered enough of politicians to last a lifetime.

He shouted over the eruption of protests and general uproar to be heard. "Esteemed reps, a point of honor. I need five minutes of your time."

Rep Heir scoffed. "This is a most offensive breach of protocol, gaffaeler!"

Disrespecting him by calling him by his job function, when the woman knew his name perfectly well. He'd be insulted, but he *had* kicked the scene off by playing hardball.

"Forgive me…" he smiled "…but I wasn't aware we Hesgyr were so fastidious as to get the vapors over protocol. A point of honor has been called."

Her glare would melt the glaciers on Mynodee, but her horns didn't so much as twitch. "And so it has. You are granted five minutes. Stray over, and you will be arrested for trespassing."

"Understood. First, a question. You have a Phae'soon prisoner in custody, I assume? One who was left behind when the attack on Nythir terminated prematurely?"

Heir frowned. "No. He committed suicide rather than be captured. How can you possibly know of their existence? Were you present in the Glain District during the event?"

"I was not. I know because I terminated the attack while it was in progress. Together with the Anadens, I infiltrated the Phae'soon facility where their weapon was housed and shut down the portal fueling their deadly cloud."

"Not possible," Heir protested.

"Oh, I assure you, it was quite possible. Fairly simple, honestly—for a *gaffaeler.*"

Another rep, near the back, rose out of their seat. "Your actions were not authorized by the Confab!"

"Since when has that mattered?" Tolje replied. "You are a deliberative body that decides the bare minimum required in order to keep Nythir functioning. You are not an authoritarian government ruling over our daily lives. So long as an act doesn't threaten the safety of Nythir, you do not tell us what we can and cannot do. I chose to take my companions and go to the Phae'soon colony and do what I could to prevent further Hesgyr deaths. And I have."

"So you cut short one enemy incursion." Heir practically spat the words. She really didn't like him. "They will come again. Any hour or minute now—which is why our fleet will be departing shortly to deal with the enemy."

"But they will not come again. See, while we were there, we went ahead and destroyed their weapon."

"Care to repeat that?"

"We destroyed it. Blew it up. The weapon and all the hardware, technology and supplies supporting it are nothing but ashes."

"How?" Heir's cinnamon skin blanched to beige. "Surely not...."

"You besmirch my honor by insinuating first, that I am lying to you, then that I am somehow incapable of accomplishing such a feat. However, since I anticipated this reaction, I captured video of the facility, the weapon, and the outside of the building after the explosion, which I have now sent to Rep Dacus. Evidence enough?"

"You can't simply—"

Dacus stood, cutting Heir off. "Thank you, Mr. Alainor, for delivering this material to our attention in a timely manner. We will of course want to review the footage you sent in depth, but as I know you to be a principled man and a skilled gaffaeler, I do not doubt the veracity of your claims.

"The Confab recognizes how you have distinguished yourself in your dealings with us of late, as well as how you've worked tirelessly to solve the mystery of these attacks. Accordingly, we—all the residents of Nythir—owe you our deepest and most heartfelt gratitude for bringing this grave threat to an end. Name your fee, and the Confab will discharge it."

"Thank *you*, Rep Dacus. Your words venerate me. As for my fee?" Tolje let the anticipation build in the room as he clasped his hands behind his back and took a step forward. "Call off the military attack on the Phae'soon colony."

"You…" Jethan blinked "…that's your fee?"

"It is."

"But this is not within your purview or your power to request. A recompense of, say…two million credits would be appropriate, yes?"

Tolje gulped. The amount was more than he made in five years, and he made good money. "You are most generous, Rep Dacus. Truly. But I have named my fee."

Murmurs broke across the chamber as, one by one, the reps began to consider the possibility that he was serious.

Jethan raised his voice a notch to speak over the buzz. "It's not wise to cancel the attack. The Phae'soon remain a threat to us. They can build another weapon and strike at us anew."

"Respectfully, they don't, and they can't. I've seen what is left of the Phae'soon, and the sight brought pangs of sorrow to my worn and calloused heart. The Rasu took everything from them. What remains is a ragtag assemblage of refugees a few thousand in number. They live in shacks and eat scraps. They eke out a miserable existence with what they can dig out of the peat of the swamp they call home. And as of thirty minutes ago, every resource that went into the construction and operation of their weapon is gone.

"If, by some miraculous feat, they do one day manage to rebuild a wormhole device and come for us again, we'll be ready. While I was in their facility, I acquired enough information about their engineered virus for our scientists to develop a vaccine to protect against future infections." In truth, he'd acquired a good deal more than that, but he couldn't be expected to give away *everything* for free….

Jethan offered a gesture of respect. "Nothing less than I expect from a gaffaeler of your stature and reputation. Still, I am troubled by your account. The people you describe could never have constructed such a fearsome, advanced weapon and hunted us across galaxies."

"I did not say they aren't smart. Clever and resourceful. I suspect they brought the more advanced materials they needed for the weapon with them when they fled their now-decimated exocolonies. They self-evidently developed their wormhole technology there, else they wouldn't have been able to flee such a distance in the first place.

"I imagine before the Rasu devastated their homeworld, they were a rather impressive civilization. But a shattered husk of that civilization is what remains. They deserve our pity, not our missiles."

Rep Heir, who had been cowed into silence by Dacus' projected authority, leapt anew out of her seat. "They have murdered thousands of our people. We're entitled to revenge!"

Tolje sighed. "Now you sound like them. Bitterness and a thirst for vengeance are all that give them purpose, poisoning their hearts and sapping their future of vitality. The Rasu are gone, so they direct their hatred toward us and..." he swallowed "...we deserve a measure of it."

"Absurd!"

"We are not responsible for the destruction of their worlds and the murder of millions of their people, it's true. But some number of them *could* have been saved had they retained the use of the Magelo Wide-Field Disruptor to slow the Rasu down."

"We didn't know they lacked the means to build another!"

Tolje's pulse pounded in his left temple; Heir's shrieking was going to give him a headache. "No, we didn't. And we didn't bother to check, or even ask the question. We didn't think about the possible consequences of our actions at all."

Jethan's lips twitched, suppressing a smile. "I am shocked to hear you, a gaffaeler, say this."

"It is only a gaffaeler who is qualified to say this. We find what we want and we take it, and we continue onward and take the next thing. We never consider how our actions might impact the people we steal from—"

Rep Heir interrupted him. "We must protect ourselves, for no one else will."

"That's always been our mantra, hasn't it? Our justification. Our excuse. It's been over a million years since our homeworld fell, since we had to scrape and claw our way off its crumbling surface and to the stars. Look at us now—look at what we have built!" *Duwi*, he sounded like Eren. Curse the Anaden for being right. "We are wealthy. We are strong. And what have we done with our strength? We've become bullies. Grown selfish. We take and take and take, and we don't so much as glance over our shoulders to glimpse the fallout."

"The universe is a hard and unforgiving place," Jethan offered in cautious reproach. "One need look no further than the damage the Rasu inflicted to see the truth of this."

"It absolutely is, Rep Dacus. But we're not alone, and not everyone out there is our enemy. Concord has managed to convince over a dozen species to live in harmony with one another—and you've met the Anadens, so you recognize how difficult this must be." Several reps chuckled, and Tolje thought he had them.

"The species of Concord protect one another. They come to one another's aid. They share resources and technology, and they are each richer for it."

"We do not need Concord!" Heir screeched in a last-ditch effort to halt the tide from sweeping his way.

"Maybe, maybe not. But perhaps we should want them? Listen, I'm not suggesting we comm them up and ask to join their club. We're not the joining sort, and we're never going to follow all their stuffy rules, anyway. A diplomatic meeting here and there probably wouldn't hurt, though, so I hope your overture to Eren was more than an empty platitude.

"But all I'm asking for today is that we not needlessly slaughter another species. The Phae'soon are a broken people. And if we attack them now, we will have proved them right about us. Call off the attack. This is my fee."

33

B anka let herself into Pedr's apartment, then went to the kitchen and poured herself a gowal. Pedr was tied up in a military meeting about the attack on Nythir, and he'd messaged her to let her know he'd be late.

She stood there in the middle of the room, drink in one hand, peering around at his too-formal wall décor and bland furniture. Being in his place alone made her uncomfortable. She hadn't asked for his door code; he'd volunteered it. Should she sit? Turn on some of that dour music he enjoyed?

She kept telling herself this was merely a casual fling, and he kept acting as if it was something more serious. Committed relationships caused her skin to itch. Commitments led to attachments, and attachments led to heartbreak and loss.

In fact, she should go. Best not to encourage him too much—

A message came in, and Banka was surprised to see it was from Jethan Dacus. She'd been a little rude to him when they'd bumped into each other last week. She felt bad about it, but she was terrible at apologizing, so she'd decided to let it lie.

She opened the message with no small amount of trepidation.

Banka,

I know you don't like talking about your father, or even hearing the slightest news about him. But he just spoke to the Confab, and you should watch this. Please, as a favor to me, and out of respect for the friendship we once enjoyed.

—Jethan

A video file was attached to the message. Jethan was right—she didn't want to watch it. She wanted to run straight away from facing up to anything involving her father. It wasn't weakness to admit it. She'd made her choice, and she'd appreciate it if a few more people respected this.

What could the video show her that she didn't already know all too well? What could her father possibly have had to say to the Confab that would interest her?

And now morbid curiosity got the better of her. It wouldn't hurt to watch a few seconds of it. Confirm her suspicions that it was the same old story with him then move on with her night. She hit 'play.'

"I terminated the attack while it was in progress. Together with the Anadens, I infiltrated the Phae'soon facility where their weapon was housed and shut down the portal fueling their deadly cloud."

"Not possible."

"Oh, I assure you, it was quite possible. Fairly simple, honestly—for a gaffaeler."

Ha! This was just like his arrogant, prideful self. Still, he'd stopped the attacks? On his own initiative?

She let the recording continue to play.

"...That's always been our mantra, hasn't it? Our justification. Our excuse. It's been over a million years since our homeworld fell, since we had to scrape and claw our way off its crumbling surface and to the stars. Look at us now—look at what we have built! We are wealthy. We are strong. And what have we done with our strength? We've become bullies. Grown selfish. We take and take and take, and we don't so much as glance over our shoulders to glimpse the fallout."

She'd never known her father to speak so eloquently; then again, she usually cut him off before he'd finished much more than a sentence.

Banka sank down on Pedr's couch, properly confused now. How was she supposed to feel about this? He'd defended the species that tried to kill her!

The things Eren Savitas had said to her echoed in her mind, as they had with too much regularity for the last several days. If her father was truly so distraught over her brush with death, why didn't he want to exact revenge on her attackers?

Unless it wasn't about her. Shocking concept, obviously. But he'd claimed to have felt pity for these Phae'soon, who had lost so, so much. She wasn't looped into the halls of power, except for Pedr's occasional pillow talk, so she hadn't known anything about the species they'd identified as the source of the attacks. It sounded as if they'd been all but wiped out by the Rasu, in part because a gaffaeler had stolen a critical defensive tool from them.

Aha! More evidence of how selfish and greedy gaffaelers were.

Millions of aliens had died as a result of the theft…or due to the fact that the Rasu were evil, sadistic *diewls*. Presumably a measure of both.

"Now you sound like them. Bitterness and a thirst for vengeance are all that give them purpose, poisoning their hearts and sapping their future of vitality."

Guilt plucked away at her conscience, and she growled in frustration. It felt as if he'd spoken those words to her face, as if he saw straight through to the resentment that continued to strangle her own soul.

No. It might have once been true, but not any longer. She had her own life now. A good life. She wasn't mired in the past—

The door opened, and Pedr stormed in. He headed for his office without so much as a glance in her direction.

"Pedr? What's wrong?"

He spun toward her, looking surprised. "You're…right. We were supposed to—I can't. I came by to grab something, then I have to go."

"Why?" She stood up from the couch. "What's going on?"

"The Confab has made a terrible mistake, and in doing so has endangered us all. I have to correct its mistake."

"Again I ask…what's going on?"

He breathed out harshly, almost a spit. "They've decided destroying the Phae'soon's weapon mechanism is sufficient to deter the aliens and have called off the mission to eliminate their colony."

Because of her father. Because of his impassioned plea. *Bwachi.*

"Well, if their weapon has been destroyed, doesn't this mean they can't hurt us any longer?" Banka asked.

"How can you defend them? They almost killed you!"

Yes, she'd covered that part already. "Believe me, I know. I'm not defending them. I only mean...you're talking about killing thousands of aliens, some of whom arguably don't deserve it."

"This is the way of war. Kill your enemy before they can kill you."

"And I'm naïve to the ways of war, as you often remind me. But they *can't* kill us, can they?"

"Allegedly not. For now. What does it matter?" His fists kept clenching and unclenching at his sides. She hadn't seen him this worked up since learning of the soldiers who died on Canchal-se.

Oh. This might explain much of his rage. He wanted justice for his men, and she could understand why. But he was always pontificating about how sentimentality didn't make for good military strategy.

"The mission—the one that got canceled. It was going to eliminate the entire colony, you said? Wouldn't a lot of innocent civilians have died?"

He surged forward, almost getting in her face. "They. All. Deserve. It."

She held her ground; he didn't frighten her. Probably should, but didn't. "What about Commodore Vachth? Is he on board with, uh, correcting the Confab's mistake?"

"I haven't had time to tell him of my plans."

"And those plans are?"

He peered around into the corners of the room, as if he were searching for something. "I'll take my cruiser and execute on the mission. It wields the necessary firepower."

"Without authorization? You can't act on your own, can you?"

"I must. To save our people."

Dread coiled in her gut. "Pedr, you'll be court-martialed."

"No. Once the Confab has had time to reconsider, they'll realize my actions will have saved us."

And since she wasn't afraid of him, she kept right on pushing. "And you're certain you're not doing this for vengeance?"

"So what if I am? These aliens nearly killed you. They killed Cadoc and Helyan and half the 23rd, and they did it with unspeakable cruelty and depravity. They deserve to die." He zeroed in on a leather-bound satchel sitting beside his desk and leapt over to grab it, then reversed course and strode past her. "I have to go."

"Pedr, wait. Let's talk this over—"

But he was out the door and gone.

Duwi, this was why she didn't do relationships! People were pains in the bootheel. They were stupid and emotional and caused nothing but problems for everyone who cared about them.

She didn't love Pedr, but she didn't want to see him stripped of his commission and sentenced to a labor camp for the next two decades. His fate was out of her hands, however, wasn't it? If she reported him, he'd be punished for disobeying orders, though the punishment would surely be less severe than if his actions weren't discovered until after he'd fired on a colony of Phae'soon. Either way, the bulk of the damage was already done. And he'd inflicted it on himself.

She collapsed back onto the couch and dropped her head against the cushion. So that was that. She was going to need to find a new lover.

But what about the Phae'soon?

Despite her earlier mental gymnastics, part of her wanted the aliens dead. She'd seen the horrific outcome of their attacks firsthand. Seen friends (acquaintances, whatever) reduced to a sea of blood. Come within centimeters of joining them herself.

Still, what if her father was correct? What if, defanged, they deserved pity, not retribution? They blamed her people for the destruction of their homeworld; they were wrong, more or less, but Phae'soon *had* died because of a gaffaeler's actions.

No…not a gaffaeler's action. Not really. Here was the hard truth she studiously tried to avoid giving its due, the better to hate her father without having to think too deeply on it.

She used equipment every day that gaffaelers had appropriated from some species or other. They all did. Stolen technology powered this apartment and the Transition where she worked. The military looked down on gaffaelers, but pretty much everyone else on Nythir celebrated them and their work. The gaffaeler philosophy was part of her people's mindset, their very identity.

A gaffaeler had executed the theft, but her government and her culture had approved of their action. Sanctioned it. And her father had just called them on it.

She realized she was likely on the cusp of a profound and intensely uncomfortable revelation, and she promptly tabled it for later. If she was going to do anything about this mess, she needed to do it now.

Cachu hewch!

She took a long swig of her gowal and sent a priority message.

> *Jethan,*
>
> *Major Pedr Eynon intends to defy the Confab's order to stand down and attack the Phae'soon colony using his military cruiser. Don't ask me how I know, please. Do whatever you think is necessary with this information. Before you do, though...tell my father, if you would. But don't tell him the information came from me.*
>
> *—Banka*

If her father had brought an end to the Phae'soon threat on his own initiative, he could find a way to stop Pedr before her soon-to-be-former lover committed genocide, right?

He didn't find a way to save your mother, the caustic voice ensconced forever in her soul whispered, still heartbroken after all these years.

No, no he didn't. Yet she conceded it might be nearing time to admit that if he'd had the slightest inkling of the danger her mother was in, he would have.

It wasn't much, but it was something.

34

Eren grabbed Tolje in a hug—the first time Nyx had witnessed him make such a familiar gesture toward the Hesgyr. "You did it! You convinced those fatuous reps to stand down. Amazing job. I wish I could have seen it."

Tolje grunted into his shoulder until Eren relented and stepped away. "If there's a recording…well, I'll never tell. I lied through most of it, anyway."

"Nah, you didn't."

Nyx watched their interchange with a combination of curiosity and dismay. Somehow, Eren had worked his strange magic yet again. He'd thoroughly charmed this gruff, suspicious, guarded, isolationist alien. Turned the Hesgyr into a squishy amalgam of jokes and laughter and sentimentality and *hugs*.

A momentary panic seized her chest; was this what Eren was doing to her as well? Was she unwittingly falling victim to his wily charms? No, surely not. She'd spent millennia making herself impervious to such trickery…which raised the more concerning possibility that something else, something…*real*, was happening between them.

"Eh…." Tolje scoffed with a smile. "Maybe it wasn't all lies. You know what I think? I think you have put far too many outlandish notions in my brain, and now they're rattling all around and causing mischief for me."

"Then my work here is done," Eren replied, a hint of a smirk tugging at his too-kissable lips. Damn.

Tolje deflated a little. "Is it? Does this mean you and Nyx will be heading off now?"

Nice of him to remember she existed.

"Oh. I mean, we'll need to soon, but I'm not going to run out on you. I'll stay long enough to make certain everything resolves cleanly. We can have dinner and too many gowals to celebrate all the lives we've saved."

"I like this idea. The three of us can splurge on the closest thing we have to one of your five-star restaurants."

"You *do* have them! I knew it."

"Eh, a few. They cost a star's fortune…." Tolje gazed up at the ceiling as if lost in thought. "They tried to buy me off, you know. The Confab."

"How much?" Eren asked.

"Two million."

Eren whistled. "You turned them down?"

"Insane, right?"

"No, not insane. Look at you, being honorable. Virtuous, even."

"*Angh redad.* I've gone soft is what's happened, and it is entirely your fault."

"Blame me if you want, but I…." Eren trailed off as Tolje's expression darkened precipitously. "What's wrong?"

Tolje didn't answer for several seconds. Then he let out a string of guttural curses. "I just received a message from a contact of mine. Major Eynon is taking his cruiser to the Phae'soon colony in defiance of the Confab's order to withdraw the military strike. He intends to destroy the colony."

"Shite! I knew he was wrong the instant I met him." Eren took off pacing across the living room. "Let me think…the trouble with renegade military officers is that they control military ships wielding military firepower. Makes them difficult to sideline…do you have any way to track his ship's location?"

"Track a military cruiser? No, I do not."

"No gaffaeler trick? No gray-market contraband you keep around for emergencies that could manage such a task?"

"No, Eren. I've never had occasion to care where a given military vessel is located at any particular point in time. Why would I?"

She'd give Eren one thing: he never, ever gave up on a cause he believed in, even when 'hopeless' was firmly in the rear view. He'd gone above and beyond to save the lives of strangers, criminals and malcontents, and it pained her to see his victory snatched from him—no, this wasn't correct. He—*they*—had saved countless Hesgyr lives with their actions today. Saving Phae'soon ones as well was simply a bridge too far. Unless....

She might have one card to play. Neither of them noticed as she retreated to the kitchen.

SIMON, are you there?

I am always here, Nyx Praesidis—at least until I decide to delete this node. What do you require?

I promised I'd tell you what the Confab decided. Accept my apology for not contacting you sooner, but events moved quite rapidly. We were able to destroy the enemy's weapon, so they will no longer be able to target the Hesgyr with their deadly incursions.

This is welcome news.

"I don't know, Tolje. Gaffaelers and the military don't get along, so I thought you may need to hide from them on occasion?" Eren ran a hand through his hair in agitation. "Will the Confab try to stop him?"

"I expect Admiral Zhaktra will send a squadron to bring him in for courts-martial," Tolje replied. "But if Eynon has a head start, they'll be too late to stop him from acting."

"Would you two be quiet for a minute?" Nyx snapped.

Eren shot her a squirrelly look, but she held up a hand to ward off any retort.

It is welcome news. The Confab decided this action was sufficient to protect the Hesgyr from harm and elected to deliberate on the best way to approach these aliens now that they no longer pose a threat. However, I've just learned of a troubling development. One individual, a Major Pedr Eynon, is defying the Confab's decision. He's traveling in his warship to the Phae'soon colony as we speak. Once he reaches it, he intends to annihilate them.

The Phae'soon have inflicted tremendous loss of life on the Hesgyr. Rational arguments exist in favor of both choices. It is not my place to determine their punishment.

She chose her words carefully.

I realize it isn't. But it's not Major Eynon's place, either. That right lies with the Confab and the military leadership.

Why are you telling me this?

SIMON, do you possess the ability to track a warship's location while it's traveling?

She was suddenly cognizant of Eren's presence in her personal space. "Nyx, what in Hades are you doing?"

She glared at him in warning until he backed away, hands raised in capitulation.

I do not operate under the military's purview.

I understand you don't. But can you access such information?

Why would you believe I have this capability?

Because I suspect you can do a lot of things the Confab don't know about.

I categorically deny—

It's okay. I'm not going to tell them.

Was she truly not? The decision surprised her, as it went against her longstanding devotion to order, authority and above all obeyance of the rules. But now wasn't the time to ruminate on her fall from grace and the role Eren had absolutely, without a doubt played in it.

SIMON, listen to me. I trust that you always place the best interests of the Hesgyr at the center of your decisions.

I do.

Wonderful. These aliens, the Phae'soon? They committed terrible wrongs against the Hesgyr. But their colony is defenseless, and most of its inhabitants aren't guilty of those attacks. Most of them are beaten-down and weary and trying to find a way to help their families survive. Major Eynon's actions will amount to genocide, and that is not his right. So if you can track his ship, I need you to tell me.

What use will this information be to you? You are located on Nythir, and Major Eynon's ship is already many parsecs away.

"Nyx…." Eren leaned in to growl at her ear. She shoved a finger in his face, demanding that he wait one more minute.

My people can travel instantly between two points in space. Not using a ship, but merely by placing one foot in front of the other.

You have personal wormhole technology?

She swore it sounded excited, which was more than a little disconcerting. She couldn't help but wonder what future trouble her encouragement of the SAI today would ignite.

We do. Time's running out, SIMON. Can you help me?

I…can. A moment.

CS

The cruiser exited the wormhole a scant five megameters from the Phae'soon colony. Pedr wasn't worried about planetary defenses or an orbital fleet, for the aliens had neither.

He flexed his hand around the metal railing of the command overlook. "Navigation, maneuver until we have a clear firing solution on the colony's coordinates."

"Yes, sir."

He didn't have much time to relish the moment at hand or give an inspirational speech before eliminating the enemy. He'd barely made it out of dock when a priority message had arrived from Admiral Zhaktra, ordering him to stand down and return to Nythir.

He didn't know who had alerted Zhaktra—someone on the crew, Banka (he doubted it), or possibly an overzealous monitor program that flagged his off-schedule departure. It didn't matter. He still believed the Confab and Armed Forced Command would come to their senses in time, but he'd accepted the probable consequences of his actions when he'd stepped onto the bridge today. The people of Nythir must be protected. The men and women who died serving at Canchal-se must be avenged.

"Firing solution finalized, sir."

"Excellent." He breathed in deeply. "Weapons, prepare to fire."

"Ready to fire in three…two…."

The faint but omnipresent vibration in the railing beneath Pedr's hand suddenly stilled. Before he could process the realization that something was wrong, the lights on the bridge flickered and went out.

CS

Nyx clasped her hands together at her chin and stared at a point on the wall over Eren's left shoulder. What was taking SIMON so long? It either had access to the information, or it didn't. Unless it was presently burning down Nythir's computer infrastructure in an attempt to access it....

Eren moved directly in front of her, and she sensed he wasn't going to be put off this time—

I have neutralized any risks associated with Major Eynon's insubordination.

She flattened her palm on Eren's chest to hold him at bay—then linked him into the comm channel so he could hear the rest of the conversation.

SIMON, you have a location for his ship?

A location is no longer necessary. I have rendered his vessel unable to fire its weapons upon the Phae'soon colony. Also unable to generate thrust, lest he consider crashing his vessel into the heart of the colony instead. Hesgyr Armed Forces communications indicate that Admiral Zhaktra is currently en route to place Major Eynon under arrest. Therefore, I deem the matter safely resolved.

You...what?

It is as I said. Even if you and Eren Savitas were to reach his vessel in time, there was no guarantee you would be able to prevent the major from launching his missiles at the colony. Further, attempting to do so might have resulted in bloodshed on both sides. The safer and more effective course was for me to utilize the networked safety protocols installed in every military vessel's control system to disable the power core on Major Eynon's ship. Emergency power will ensure life support continues to function until Admiral Zhaktra arrives.

Eren cackled with glee. *SIMON, you wicked motherfucker!*

You believe I have done wrong?

No, not at all. On the contrary. You did beautifully. Simply beautifully.

Tolje grabbed her and Eren by the shoulders and insinuated himself between them. "Will someone tell me what is going on?"

Eren placed a hand on Tolje's and guided him back toward the living room. "You know the MEM the Confab let us talk to? SIMON?"

"What does the MEM have to do with anything? *Duwi*, Eren, what did you do?"

Eren shot her a grin over his shoulder so dazzling it made her head spin. "It wasn't me."

35

"Let me run down to the store and grab a couple of gowals. Don't leave until we've had a proper celebration—both of you."

Eren nodded agreement, and Tolje headed out into the district.

He didn't know what was going to happen to Eynon now. The military tended to be unforgiving toward those who disobeyed direct orders. Still, emotions were running at a fever pitch when it came to the Phae'soon, and he suspected more than one heated argument about the wisdom of leaving them alive was yet to transpire. He also wasn't certain he bought Eren's glib tale about Nyx tunneling through the MEM's network access to remotely disable Eynon's vessel from his kitchen. For one, MEMs weren't supposed to *have* military network access. On the other hand, seeing as how everything had worked out, he wasn't convinced it was worth the effort to delve more deeply—

"Dad."

Tolje whipped around to see Banka jogging toward him. He worked to keep surprise off his expression, while also not appearing grouchy or anything other than casually glad to see her. "Hi."

"Hi." She halted a meter short of him, her gaze scanning the passersby, the walls and basically everything and everyone except him.

"How are you?"

"Fine. Back at work at the Transition. I think I'll lay off the special gigs for a while."

"Safer that way."

"Seems to be. Though I suppose simply existing is safer now that the attacks have ended." Her horns twitched. "They *have* ended, haven't they?"

"They have indeed." A sensation swept over him: the most fatherly of urges to make her feel safe and protected. It was silly, though. He'd almost lost her on Daith. He couldn't protect her, and she'd stopped allowing him to pretend he could a long time ago. Wistfulness for a life he might have had clutched at his chest until he was scarcely able to breathe.

"Good. I heard…." She let the sentence trail off.

"What did you hear?"

"Nothing. It's not important."

An awkward silence ensued then. It was better than the barbs and yelling they'd usually reached by this point in their interactions, but not by much. Finally he cleared his throat. "Uh, Eren and Nyx are about to head home, if you'd like to stop by the apartment and say goodbye."

"Oh. No, I've got to get to work. Tell them I said farewell?"

"I will."

More silence. He started to worry; was she okay? "Is there something you need? I'm not busy, so I can—"

"I heard what you did at the Confab meeting. What you said."

"Oh." Dread curled through his chest as any hope of their relationship one day improving fled for the stars. "Banka, I am furious at what the Phae'soon did on Daith. They almost killed you, and I will never, *ever* forgive them for it. I was only trying to defuse—"

"I'm proud of you."

"—the situation and prevent…what did you say?"

"I said I'm proud of you. I've never thought of you as being someone who cared about the greater good or saving lives or looking after anyone other than yourself."

"You can stop now."

"Sorry." Her chin dropped, and she briefly averted her gaze. "I know you were worried about my safety, and if I had died, I know you would have been…sad. I only meant…I didn't expect for you to stand up for a higher principle. And to the Confab, no less. It couldn't have been an easy thing for you to do."

"Banka, if you had died, I wouldn't have been 'sad.' I would have been destroyed. Just because we don't hang out on holidays or talk on a regular basis, it doesn't mean you're not my daughter. I love you more than anything in the universe, and I want desperately for you to be happy. And to be happy, you have to be alive."

"Yeah." She rubbed at her jaw. "Eren mentioned something about that. I'm not...look, I don't want to get into relationship stuff right now. Or at all, honestly. I just wanted to say...what I said."

"I appreciate it. It means a lot to me." And it did. He felt all warm and soft inside, the way he had when he'd cradled her in his arms as an infant.

"All right. I should go. Work and everything." She nodded sharply to emphasize the point, took two steps away—and paused. "Oh, but...if you wanted to meet for lunch sometime whenever you're around on Nythir, in-between jobs...I can maybe swing lunch."

"I'd like that very much."

"Okay. Ah, send me a message, and I'll look at my schedule."

"I will. Oh, and Banka? *How* exactly did you hear about what I said to the Confab?"

She laughed over her shoulder. "I get to have my secrets." Then she vanished into the flow of pedestrians and was gone.

CS

They managed to finish off a gowal each—Tolje, two—before everyone started to get antsy. Tolje was surely eager to return to his regular life of thievery, and Nyx was unquestionably ready to return to her regular job of worrying over Corradeo. And Eren, well, he had one final thing to do before he tied a bow on this adventure. Best to get on with it.

So when the drinks were empty, everyone stood, and Nyx darted off to retrieve their bags from the guest bedroom.

Eren clasped Tolje by the hand in the Hesgyr variation on a handshake. "Next time you visit Concord space, comm me up. I'll show you around."

"You mean don't sneak in and steal something without telling you first."

"Also that, yes."

Tolje chuckled briefly. "I don't expect we'll be signing up for your alliance any time soon. As I noted to the Confab, it's not our style. But I wouldn't be surprised if someone opens a quiet, friendly dialogue soon. If the Dzhvar do return, no one is going to want to be facing them alone in the black, not even us."

"I'm glad to hear it. I'll whisper a friendly word in the proper ears for you. And whatever does or doesn't happen between our governments, stay in touch, my friend."

"And you." Tolje nodded over Eren's shoulder. "It was a pleasure hosting you, Ms. Praesidis. Stop by anytime."

"Thank you, Mr. Alainor. I'm glad to have met you." Coming from Nyx, it was fawning affection.

"Same here."

"All right, all right. We keep this up and we'll all be in tears." Eren patted Tolje on the arm then turned to Nyx. "Time to go home."

"Oh, one thing before you go." Tolje motioned behind him, toward his bedroom. "Almost forgot. Eren, I have something for you."

"Great. I'll be back in a minute," he told Nyx.

Tolje led the way into his bedroom, which Eren realized he'd only ever gotten a tiny glimpse of. The motif of the living room continued here, though the walls were painted a cheerful biscuit color. Curios and gadgets from Tolje's exploits crowded shelves on the left wall, but the right one hosted a variety of visuals of his family. Siwan, Banka when she was young but also more recently, and several older visuals of the three of them together.

Eren respected the man far too much to comment on any aspect of the room. He waited politely near the door while Tolje retrieved a box from his dresser, then offered it to Eren. "Here."

Eren took the box and opened it. Inside lay a small module of Hesgyr aesthetics but alien design. He lifted it out of its cradle and inspected it, but saw no obvious I/O ports and no manner of turning it on. Without taking it apart, he had no way to determine what it was, and possibly not then.

He arched an eyebrow. "It's a lovely parting gift. Very thoughtful. I'll treasure it always."

"You are such an ass."

"So I've been told, repeatedly and often. What is it?"

"We call it a ceisio. We appropriated it from some aliens a few galaxies over around a thousand years ago, and it has made the gaffaeler job immeasurably easier ever since."

"And?"

"And there's currently one of these planted on Concord HQ in a maintenance tunnel that parallels the Special Projects division. I know because I placed it there a week before you spotted me on Ares."

Eren's gaze shot up from the device. "This is how you learned about the MAST?"

"It's one of the most sophisticated pieces of technology we possess. Though we can reproduce it, I'm not certain anyone here understands how it does what it does."

"And that is?"

"Cracks into any quantum-based storage unit within a hundred meters and reads its contents. The language the contents are written in doesn't matter, and neither does the robustness of the encryption—it's all the same to this little guy."

Warnings buzzed between Eren's ears. "So you—your people—know everything Special Projects is doing. Which means you know *almost* everything Advocacy Advanced Research is doing, and most of what the other Concord species are doing as well."

Tolje shrugged. "I suppose we could have captured all that information, true, but no. Eren, we don't *care* what you're doing over in your corner of space. We went searching for something to help us track the origin point of the attacks. The queries the ceisio performed on the Special Projects servers were all related to ferreting out anything you guys had that fit the bill. It spit out the MAST, and they sent me to Ares to get it."

"Understood. But you're still listening."

"Which is why I'm telling you where it is. I figure you'll want to clear it out when you get home. Oh, and there's a second one stuffed into the grass behind the Olympia Advanced Research Institute on Ares—so I could spoof the credentials needed to get inside."

Eren kept the string of curses from reaching his tongue. "Yeah. I'll, uh, have someone take care of those." He closed the box and handed it back.

Tolje shook his head. "Keep it."

"Why?"

"Like you said—a parting gift. A personal thank you for saving my people. I figure even Concord doesn't have something this advanced. You might need it one day."

Eren dropped the box in his bag before his friend changed his mind. "We definitely might. You're a good, good man, Tolje."

"Don't tell anyone."

"My lips are sealed."

36

The inside of the Phae'soon Administrative Building was as shabby and cobbled-together as the rest of the colony, excepting the former Terminus Dispersal facility. The floor was rough, unpainted concrete, the walls a molding beige.

Dozens of Phae'soon fretted about in states of low-level agitation. No one paid Eren and Nyx any mind as they waddled down the hallway in their Shroud disguises. They didn't dally, lest someone try to talk to them, but it did take two turns and a backtrack to find what they were hunting for.

The plain printed sign beside the door simply read, 'Administrator's Office.'

Eren stepped up to the door, but nothing happened. He'd expected it to be unlocked on account of the crisis, but perhaps the Phae'soon hierarchy was more rigid than he'd sensed. He started to knock, then realized a notch was carved into the plaster of the door.

He pressed two fingertips into the notch and felt the door move a fraction. Gods, it didn't slide open automatically—it was *manual*. They really were in dire straits here.

He shaved two percent off the fervor of his planned speech and forced the door open.

A Phae'soon in marginally nicer attire than everyone else in the building—mostly due to a smattering of canary yellow filigree embroidered on their tunic—sat behind a desk. They barked orders into some sort of microphone positioned in front of their mouth while two fingers punched at a screen beside them.

It took a second before they glanced Eren's way. "What can I do for you?"

Nyx closed the door behind them, and they deactivated their Shrouds.

The Phae'soon leapt up from their chair and, before Eren could stop them, let out a piercing cry.

He sighed and rolled his eyes at Nyx. "I guess we're doing this the hard way."

She nodded and took up a position by the door.

The next second, the door skidded open and two Phae'soon burst in. "Sir, what's wrong?"

Nyx drew two handguns—the one Tolje had returned to her before they'd departed Nythir and the one Eren had lent her—and pointed them in opposite directions while she carefully rotated in a full circle, ensuring everyone got a turn in the crosshairs. "Stay back. These weapons will vaporize most of this building with a single shot."

It was true; all she had to do was toggle a setting a centimeter beneath where her thumbs rested to switch them from tools of targeted suppression to wide-beam carnage. Perk of the job.

Eren straight up felt his groin stir to life at the sight of her. Black leather pants, black duster coat, two high-powered weapons and one deadly serious intention of using them to impose her will. He was so fucking screwed, and he had no idea how to maneuver his way out of *not* being screwed. Worse, he was no longer certain he wanted to.

The administrator held up a four-fingered, slightly webbed hand. "Narn'ale, Raes'keen, stay clear of the intruders. There's no need for violence."

"Thank you." Nyx gave the administrator a bone-chilling smile. "You'll forgive me if I keep my weapons drawn, but rest assured, I have no desire to vaporize any of you. Don't attempt to harm us, and you won't be harmed in turn."

The administrator nodded carefully. "We understand. How do you know our language?"

Eren half-sat on the edge of the desk. "We know a lot of things. We'd like to talk about some of them with you. What's your name?"

"Arvah'dajal."

"It's nice to meet you, Arvah'dajal. I'm Eren Savitas, and this is Nyx Praesidis."

"You blew up the Terminus Dispersal."

"I heard the explosion was caused by an acetylene leak."

"Investigators have uncovered strange residue at regular intervals amid the rubble. It doesn't correspond to any materials used inside."

Eren hadn't expected the ruse to hold for long. Despite their poverty, these were intelligent, resourceful aliens. And for purposes of this discussion, it was good the administrator knew the score. "It might be better if our conversation continued in private."

Arvah'dajal considered Eren silently for a moment…then his eyes flicked toward the door. "Narn'ale, Raes'keen, you can go."

"But, sir!"

"If they wished me dead, I would already be dead. I said go."

Amid some sputtering, the two Phae'soon backed out the door. Nyx closed it behind them, then positioned herself where she could see both the administrator and the door. She lowered her weapons, though she kept them unholstered and ready.

Confident she had his back, Eren focused his attention on the administrator. "You got me. I did blow it up. I couldn't allow you to kill any more Hesgyr."

"But you are not Hesgyr."

"No, I'm a species called anaden. We hail from way the hells over in that direction." He waved his hand toward the left wall. "But we have wormholes, too, so…" he spread his arms wide "…here we are."

"Why?"

"We've gotten to know the Hesgyr these last few weeks—well enough to decide they do not deserve to be slaughtered by the tens of thousands."

"They slaughtered us!" Arvah'dajal's voice rose to a register so shrill, Eren's ears rang. Nyx's posture tensed as she shifted toward the door, but no one barged through it.

"No, the Rasu slaughtered your people."

"Because the Hesgyr rendered us unable to defend ourselves." The administrator seemed to realize he'd been shrieking and dialed his voice in, thank the gods.

"I understand you believe that," Eren replied. "I understand *why* you believe that. And it's true their thievery left your planetary defenses crippled when the Rasu arrived. But let me tell you something. Your weapon? The one the Hesgyr took? It wouldn't have saved you. You see, you probably didn't get the chance to find this out, but the Rasu regenerate. They don't die—instead, they shift and reform and they come after you again.

"You throw everything you possess at them. Then, when you've exhausted your resources and have nothing left, they come at you one more time. They are relentless. Or were, I should say. They're gone now."

"You said they don't die."

"Well, it turns out everything can die—you just have to discover the right poison. But we lost tens of millions of people across so many species before chance, fate and gritty determination led us to discover their particular poison.

"See, I know your pain. The Rasu attacked my home, too. A beautiful, warm, vibrant planet I love so dearly. They razed its forests and felled its ancient trees and boiled its rivers." His voice choked up, and he breathed in through his nose. Dammit, this was supposed to be a performance! "I fought them with rockets, and when those ran out, I fought them with guns. And when *those* ran out, I fought them with my bare hands. But I couldn't stop them. None of us could."

He planted his hands on the desk and leaned forward. "You *couldn't have stopped them.*"

To his credit, Arvah'dajal didn't flinch away. "We could have bought time to evacuate."

"A little, yes. A few thousand or a few tens of thousands—and every life is precious. I get it. Look, I'm not here to defend the Hesgyr's theft of your weapon. It was inexcusable. The Hesgyr are selfish and short-sighted and obstinate and prideful. But they are not malicious, and they are not killers.

"You know how I can prove it? They had this location in their crosshairs a few hours ago. A single volley of well-placed missiles fired from space, and the colony would have been returned to the swamp that wants so badly to reclaim it. But they didn't do it. Instead, they decided neutralizing the threat your weapon represented was sufficient to protect their people, and they went home." It wasn't precisely the truth, but it was close enough.

Arvah'dajal's hands shook as he lowered into his chair. "We have no funds or resources for orbital monitoring. No way to learn anyone was there. We would've had no warning."

"Nope. But guess what this means: today is the first day of the rest of your lives. I look at you, at this colony, and all I see is bitterness and hate. You have let your thirst for revenge fester like a pus-filled wound until it has consumed you. You leave your people to scrape by in shacks, half starving, while you pour every resource into your revenge. It is devouring you from within."

"You speak as if you know the first thing about us. You do not."

"But I do. I spend a lot of time around species not my own. It's kind of my job. And one of my best skills is spotting the things that make a society tick without too much effort. I see you. I see what you once were, and I see what you can become again. But I also see what you've let yourself devolve into, and it breaks my heart. Don't you want to live? Don't you want to thrive?"

"*Thrive?*" Arvah'dajal sang in despair. "We have nothing left. Yes, we've devoted virtually everything to the Terminus Dispersal, but where do you imagine we would be if we hadn't? Dancing upon floating platforms among the stars? Our homeworld is gone, our colonies destroyed. We are a few thousand refugees, and nothing is left to us but justice for those whom we lost."

"This doesn't have to be true. Let us help you."

"What do you mean?"

"My people. Concord. We're the reason the Rasu are gone and are never coming back. And as naive and idealistic as it sounds,

Concord believes in lifting species up. We can help you rebuild." He sensed Nyx's eyes boring into the side of his head in silent challenge. He hadn't been cleared to make such an offer, but that had never stopped him before.

"Why?" Arvah'dajal asked. "This 'Concord' doesn't know us. We can offer them no reward in exchange for their assistance."

"Not true. You're smart. Clever. And Concord desires smart and clever allies a great deal. But even if you can't pay us back except with your friendship, it will be enough. We'll do it because the destruction the Rasu inflicted is the greatest tragedy we have ever witnessed, and we would right it where we can."

"And all you ask in return is that we stop attacking the Hesgyr?"

"I've already stopped you from attacking the Hesgyr. All I ask in return is that you *never attack them again*. Not unprovoked—and should they provoke you, try using your words first. Also, don't first-strike anyone in Concord, either. Obviously. You'll need to convince those in charge that this, ah, violent spell of yours was a grief-induced psychosis you've now moved past, and you're not a violent species by nature." Eren smiled. "Think you can do so? Do it and mean it?"

"It's an easy promise for us to make today. Thanks to you, we have no means of attacking anyone."

"True. But for all I know, this isn't your only surviving colony, and that wasn't the only version of the weapon." He'd downplayed the possibility to the Hesgyr in order to stop them from massacring the Phae'soon refugees, but it existed. When wormholes were on the board, anything was possible.

"I lead only this colony. If there are others—I am not saying there are—I cannot speak for them."

"You had better hope you can."

"Is that a threat?"

"It's more than a threat. With Concord's riches comes a military fifty-five million ships strong. We make great friends. We also make bloody terrifying enemies."

Arvah'dajal quivered in his seat, properly cowed. Time to wrap this up. "Listen, I'm not asking for a definitive response today. Emotions here are running high, and you have a disaster aftermath to manage." Eren fished a small device out of his pocket and set it on the desk. "But when you decide you're ready to pack away your vengeance and start living again, just press the button on that device and speak your message. Someone will be in touch."

CS

Nyx's wormhole returned them to her office at Advocacy Square on Ares. Home sweet home…or home adjacent, anyway.

Eren took in the bare walls of her office and shook his head. "You have *got* to decorate in here. Did you at least pick up a souvenir on Nythir that you can stick on a shelf? A few curios would go a long way toward adding character. At a minimum, they would give visitors something to contemplate other than your steely glare."

If his barbs hit their mark, she gave no indication of it. She moved to sit behind her desk, one leg crossed over the other and shoulders lifted; her glare wasn't quite steely, but it was…guarded. "You sounded like a diplomat back there."

He retreated from the desk in alarm. "No. Nope, no way. I'm merely trying to get species to stop wantonly killing each other."

"That's what diplomats do."

"And when Arvah'dajal comms us up, I'll send one his way. My work in their corner of space is done."

"You didn't have the authority to promise them Concord's help."

He shrugged. "Something else for the diplomats to work out amongst themselves. I set his mind to contemplating the possibility of a future for his people, instead of only a lost past."

"You did."

This was normally the point in their meetings when she demanded a full report, but this time she'd been an active participant.

He checked the walls, but as he'd observed, they offered nothing to focus on. "So, anyway, I'm going to head home to Hirlas. Rustle up some clean clothes, then eat something that doesn't taste like it came out of a sewer. Tomorrow I'll start making my usual rounds, see who started fomenting what while I was gone. But, ah, thanks for your help and everything." He turned to go, and go quickly.

"I didn't know all of that."

"All of what?" he asked.

"About Hirlas. I knew you'd gotten trapped on the ground there when the Rasu invaded, but I didn't realize how difficult it was for you."

"What I said to the administrator doesn't even begin to cover how difficult it was for me."

"No, I imagine it doesn't. Regardless, I want to…I don't think I've ever said how sorry I am. For Ms. Rhomyhn, for Hirlas, for everything that's happened to you these last several years. I frankly don't understand how…." She pinched the bridge of her nose and dropped her chin to her chest.

"What is it?" He immediately regretted asking. Why had he asked? He was trying to make a hasty exit, dammit.

Her gaze rose enough to allow her eyes to settle on him. "You feel things so strongly—so grandly and so terribly. How do you survive it all?"

"Survive the emotions, you mean?"

She nodded.

"Pretty badly, more often than not. You might have noticed I tend to flail around a good bit. Blowing shit up from time to time does help take the edge off, though."

"Explains your affinity for it." She chuckled weakly—then stood, nudging her chair back until it bumped into the rear wall of her office. "Can I tell you something?"

Alarm bells set off clanging between his ears. As usual, he ignored them. "I'm pretty sure you already are."

"I guess I am." Her throat worked laboriously. "I don't know how to feel things. And before you say it, no, emotions weren't bred out of me at a genetic level. Emotions are neurochemicals and pheromones, and without those, our bodies wouldn't function properly. We wouldn't be anaden at all. So I have the capacity."

A dozen snarky retorts queued up on his tongue; he'd volleyed most of them her way on multiple occasions. Now, though, he simply waited for her to continue.

"I think the problem is, I was never taught that it was acceptable to experience feelings, never mind to act on them. There wasn't room for emotion in an Inquisitor's world. Except for one: loyalty to the Primor. So I don't have a frame of reference for how to process any of the others."

"You've managed just fine without processing them for millennia. Why do you care now?"

She stared openly at him, eyes wide and brimming with that sentiment that could have been but probably wasn't vulnerability. "Because you make me feel things. I don't understand any of them, and I hate how out of control they leave me. My hands shake and my pulse races, as if my body is betraying me. My thoughts zigzag around in ragged circles, and I ricochet between elation and despair. Confusion and anger. Lust and disgust. It's horrible!"

He stared at her, mouth agape.

"What?" she asked.

"I'm…speechless."

"You're never speechless."

"Thus its noteworthiness." In the absence of his usual flippant yammering, he considered her anew. Her confession cast her in a fresh, disturbingly warm light. No longer a soulless Inquisitor, or a heartless ice maiden, but someone…real. Still coarser than virtually anyone he knew, but her armor could be pierced. Did beneath it lie a genuine person?

"Stop staring at me as if I've grown Hesgyr horns." She groaned into her hands. "This is ridiculous. I'll figure it out for myself. Forget I brought it up."

He almost took her up on it, because however uncomfortable she was, he was triply so. But he couldn't shake the notion that if he turned around and walked away now, he risked something of great import slipping through his fingers, possibly forever.

"No," he found himself saying. "We need to talk about this. After what happened between us while we were on Nythir, if we're going to continue working together, we *need* to talk about this. Or rather, we need to talk about what happened. Which might not be in any way related to your initial…" his brow furrowed "…was there actually a question anywhere in there?"

"No, I don't believe so. But fine. About what happened. I…enjoyed our night together." She sounded out every syllable of 'enjoyed,' as if forcing them out one by one.

It was a weak, milquetoast word, but from her lips it was an earth-shattering admission that rendered him weak in the knees. "So did I."

"So what does this mean?"

"It doesn't have to mean anything. Not on its own. Sometimes, sex is just sex, and it needn't go any further." He blew a breath out through pursed lips. "The trouble is, I kind of want to clear off your desk, throw you atop it and have you again, right now."

Her throat worked. "I was thinking standing up, against the wall. The one behind you."

He glanced behind him, and now a far-too-vivid image was forever imprinted onto his brain. "Oh, boy. Yeah, this is going to be a problem."

"Does it have to be? You said it: sex can just be sex, without any emotional attachments."

"Considering you started this awkward-as-fuck conversation off talking about emotions, no, I don't think it can be." He shook his head. "Not for us. The truth is, I felt devastatingly guilty the next morning. As if I had betrayed Cosime and her memory."

"I know you did."

"Figured. So that's not healthy, and something I need to work through. Not certain how to accomplish it, but I rarely do going in. And the simple fact is, until I do work through it, and a shitload of other baggage, I can't give you what you want."

She snorted, which did serve to break the mounting sexual tension a bit. "How could you, when I have no idea what I want?"

"I thought you wanted mind-blowing sex with me on a regular basis."

Her glare made him wish he could scramble for cover two cities over, and he held his hands up in surrender. "Please continue."

"Part of me wants to put all these *emotions* back in a bottle and toss the bottle into the Delphin Sea. I don't like feeling out of control. It's not who I am. But another part of me wants…I don't have words for it yet, or not ones I trust to speak aloud. The point is, I have some things to work through as well. Clearly."

He nodded hesitantly. "So…unless or until we both work through our respective issues in a manner that leads to us both being comfortable with…which is to say amenable to…" he waved a hand at her desk "…we keep it professional. Same as it always was until our little excursion to Nythir."

"Yes. I think that is the best path forward."

Eren's gaze fixated on the curve of her jaw, watching the muscles beneath the skin twitch almost imperceptibly. "Right then."

Her tongue absently darted out to flick across her lips. "Right then."

THE UNIVERSE WITHIN
A COSMIC SHORES NOVEL

Thousands of years ago, the Elakri were a galaxy-spanning civilization—until they were forced to hide themselves away in the folds of space to escape an unstoppable foe. But what was once their salvation soon became their prison.

Alex Solovy and Caleb Marano hunt the cosmos for signs of an ancient enemy's return. When they detect a breach in the fabric of space, however, they discover something wholly unexpected: a people lost in time and space, who have forgotten all they once were. Returning the Elakri to their proper place among the stars seems the least they can do, but first they have to survive a strange and dangerous world where none of the usual rules apply.

COMING IN 2025
PREORDER A SIGNED COPY TODAY AT:
GSJENNSEN.COM/UNIVERSE-WITHIN

***

Twenty years ago, before Concord and the larger universe it revealed, humanity teetered on the brink of war with itself even as an unimaginable threat loomed in the void. Experience the epic, galaxy-spanning adventure from the beginning:

STARSHINE
AURORA RISING BOOK ONE

GSJENNSEN.COM/STARSHINE

READ ON FOR AN EXCERPT:

SENECA

CAVARE, CAPITAL OF THE SENECAN FEDERATION

The kinetic blade slid into the man's throat like a knife through butter. Caleb held him securely from behind as the blood began to flow and the man jerked and spasmed.

He generally preferred clean, painless deaths. But he wanted to watch this man die, and die slowly.

When the man had lost all motor function, Caleb dumped him onto the desk and flipped him over. Eyes wide with fear, confusion and outrage met his. The man's lips contorted in a caricature of speech, though no words came out.

He had a good idea of the intended utterance. Why. It was a question easily answered. Vengeance.

"Justice."

As the pool of blood spread across the desk and formed waterfalls to the floor below, the eyes belonging to the leader of the Humans Against Artificials terrorist organization glazed over. The last spark of life within them dimmed, then went out.

One down.

Caleb Marano stepped out of the spaceport into the cyan-tinged glow of a late afternoon sun reflecting off the polished marble tiles of the plaza. The chill breeze caressing his skin felt like a welcome home. Cavare was always cool and often cold; Krysk had been a veritable oven by comparison.

He descended the first set of stairs and angled toward the corner to get clear of the bustling thoroughfare, then relaxed beside the ledge to wait for his companions.

Isabela exited the spaceport a moment later. She held a bag in one arm and a fidgeting bundle of arms, legs and long, dark curls in the other. She looked disturbingly 'momish' as she struggled to brush out Marlee's tangled hair—but he could remember when she had *been* that little girl with long, dark curls…and it wasn't so long ago.

With a groan she gave up the futile endeavor and allowed her daughter to escape her grasp and make a beeline for Caleb.

He crouched to meet Marlee at eye level. She plowed into him with almost enough force to knock him over backwards. He would've laughed but for the forlorn look in her pale turquoise eyes.

"Do you have to go away now, Uncle Caleb?"

He tousled her curls into further disarray. "Yeah, I'm afraid I have to go back to work. But it sure was great spending my vacation with you. I learned a *lot*."

She wore her best serious face as she nodded sagely. "You had a lot to learn."

He grinned and leaned in to whisper to his co-conspirator. "You remember what all we talked about, right?"

Her eyes were wide and honest. "Uh-huh."

"Good. Want one more ride before I go?"

Her head bobbed up and down with gusto, instantly that of a carefree child again.

"Okay." He scooped her up in his arms and stood, made certain he had a solid grasp of her tiny waist, and began to spin around with accelerating speed. Her arms and legs dangled free to swing through the air while she cackled in delight.

After another few spins he slowed—he had learned her limits during the last few weeks—letting her limbs fall against him before he came to a stop. He gave her a final squeeze and gently set her to the ground as her mother reached them.

Isabela wore a half-amused, half-exhausted expression as Marlee started running in dizzy circles around her legs. "Sorry about the hold up. They let us back on the transport and we found Mr. Freckles under the seat." She patted her bag in confirmation of the stuffed animal's now secure location. "Are you sure you don't want to have a quick dinner with us?"

He responded with a dubious smirk. "You can be polite if you like, but the truth is you are sick to death of me and counting the minutes until you are at last rid of me."

"Well, *yes*. But I never know when I'll get to see you again…." The twinkle faded from her eyes, replaced by something darker and heavier.

She knew he didn't work for a shuttle manufacturing company, and he knew that she knew. But they never, *ever*, talked about it. Partly for her safety and his, but partly because he preferred to continue being in her mind the strong, stalwart older brother with the easygoing demeanor and wicked sense of humor, without introducing any moral grayness to the relationship dynamic.

Because he never wanted her to look at him with caution, disillusionment…or worst of all, fear.

He merely nodded in response. "I'll come visit again soon. Promise."

She reached down to pause the cyclone at her legs. "I'll hold you to it. I'm going to take Marlee to see Mom, then we'll head back home."

He leaned over the struggling cyclone to embrace her. "Thank you for the extended hospitality. I'm glad I was able to spend so much time with you."

"Anytime, I mean it," she whispered in his ear. "Stay safe."

He kept his shrug mild as he stepped away. "Of course." Not likely.

Two insistent and tearful hugs from Marlee later, they parted ways. He watched them disappear into the throng of travelers, then headed in the direction of the parking complex.

AR

Caleb stepped in the adjoining lavatory and washed the blood off his hands and forearms. Then he returned to the office, reached under the corner of the desk and triggered the 'Alert' panic signal—the one he had never allowed the dead man to reach. There was a surveillance cam hidden in the ceiling, and he looked up at it and smiled. He had a number of smiles in his repertoire; this was not one of the more pleasant ones.

The commotion began as he exited the building. He quickened his stride to his bike, jumped on and fired the engine. Three men bolted out the door, two Daemons and a TSG swinging in his direction.

It wouldn't do to get shot. A flick of his thumb and the bike burst out of the parking slot. He laid it down as laser fire sliced barely a meter overhead, his leg hovering centimeters above the ground while he slid around the corner and onto the cross-street.

He heard them giving chase almost immediately. So late in the night the street and air traffic was sparse, which was one reason he had begun the op when he did. It reduced the chances of his pursuers taking out innocent bystanders—and gave them a clearer line of sight to him. He wanted to make certain they knew where he was going before he left them behind.

Their surface vehicles didn't stand a chance of matching his speed and it would look suspicious if he slowed...but as anticipated, they had grabbed a skycar. He kept an eye on it via the rearcam, making sure it succeeded in following him through two major direction shifts.

Satisfied, he kicked the bike into its actual highest gear and accelerated right then left, fishtailing around two street corners in rapid succession. He activated the concealment shield. It didn't render him or the bike invisible, but it did make them blend into the surroundings and virtually impossible to track from the air at night.

Then he sped toward the Bahia Mar spaceport. After all, he did need to get there ahead of them.

Tiny flecks of light sparkled in the night-darkened waters of the Fuori River as Caleb pulled in the small surface lot. It was nearly empty, as most people took the levtrams to the entertainment district and had no need of parking.

Once the engine had purred into silence he swung a leg off the bike and glanced up. A smile ghosted across his face at the dozens of meteors streaking against the silhouette of the giant moon which dominated Seneca's sky.

He noted the time. He had a few minutes to enjoy a little stargazing, though the conditions were far from ideal here in the heart of downtown. An exanet query confirmed the meteor shower continued for eleven days. Maybe he'd have a chance to get up to the mountains before it ended.

Committed to this plan, he secured the bike in its slot. A last glance at the sky and he crossed the street and took the wide steps to the riverwalk park.

The atmosphere on the broad promenade hovered at the optimal balance between deserted and overrun by masses of people. As it was a weekend night the balance wouldn't hold for long, but for the moment it pulsed with energy while still allowing plenty of room to move about and claim your own personal space. He noted with interest the outdoor bar to the right, complete with live synth band and raised danced platform. *Not yet. Business first.*

He slipped among the milling patrons until he reached a section of railing at the edge of the promenade to the southeast of the bar. Here the crowd had thinned to a few meandering couples and the music thrummed softly in the background.

The light from the skyscrapers now drowned out the light from the meteors, but he couldn't argue with the view.

A thoroughly modern city to the core, humans having initially set foot on its soil less than a century ago, Cavare glittered and shone like a sculpture newly unveiled. The reflected halo of the moon shimmered in the tranquil water as the river rippled along the wall beneath him, winding itself through the heart of the city on its way to Lake Fuori. Far to his left he could see the gleam of the first arch which marked the dramatic entrance to the lake and the luxuries it held.

It was an inspiring yet comforting view, and one he had spent close to forty years watching develop, mature and grow increasingly more lustrous. He contented himself with enjoying it while he waited for his appointment to arrive.

The message had come in the middle of dinner at his favorite Chinasian restaurant. He hadn't even had the chance to go home yet; the entirety of the belongings he had traveled with were stowed in the rear compartment of his bike. But in truth there wasn't much of consequence waiting for him at the apartment, for it was home in only the most technical sense of the word.

Never have anything you can't walk away from. A gem of advice imparted by a friend and mentor early on in his career, and something he had found remarkably easy to adopt.

ᚱ

He stowed the bike in a nearby stall he had rented in yet another assumed name and hurried to Bay F-18. He made a brief pass through the ship to make sure the contact points on the charges were solid, then sat in the pilot's chair, kicked his feet up on the dash and crossed his hands behind his head to wait.

They were hackers as much as terrorists. It wouldn't take them long to break the encryption to the bay. The encryption on the ship's airlock was stronger—for they would expect it to be—but not so difficult they couldn't crack it.

Planting enough charges at the headquarters to take it out would have involved significant risk of discovery and ultimate failure. But here, he controlled every step and every action.

The hangar bay door burst open. Three...six...eight initially. He sincerely hoped more showed up before they got into the ship.

His wish was granted when three minutes later seven additional members of the group rushed in. The surface pursuit, he imagined. The initial arrivals were still hacking the ship lock. He gave them another two minutes.

With a last gaze around he pulled his feet off the dash and stood. He headed through the primary compartment and below to the mid-level, opened the hatch to the engineering well, and positioned himself in the shadowy corner near the stairs.

They wouldn't all come in at once, lest they end up shooting each other in the confusion. Three, maybe four to start, plus two to guard the airlock. They would fan out to run him to ground quickly.

The first man descended the stairs. As his left foot hit the deck Caleb grabbed him from behind and with a fierce wrench snapped his neck. He made a point to throw the body against the stairwell so the loud clang echoed throughout the ship.

Two down.

AR

Caleb looked over his shoulder to see Michael Volosk striding down the steps toward him. Right on time. Everything about the man's outward demeanor projected an image of consummate professionalism, from the simple but perfectly tailored suit to the close-cropped hair to the purposeful stride.

He extended his hand in greeting as the Director of Special Operations for the Senecan Federation Division of Intelligence approached. A mouthful worthy of the highest conceit of government; but to everyone who worked there, it was simply "Division."

Volosk grasped his hand in a firm shake and took up a position along the rail beside him. "Thanks for agreeing to meet me here. I have a syncrosse rec league game down the street in twenty minutes, and if I miss another game they'll kick me off the team." He wore a slight grimace intended to hint at the many responsibilities a high-level covert intelligence official was required to juggle…then presumably realized the impression it actually conveyed, because he shifted to a shrug. "It's the only opportunity I have to blow off steam."

Caleb smiled with studied, casual charm. "It's not a problem. I just got in anyway. And if the surroundings happen to discourage prying eyes, well, I appreciate the value of discretion."

Volosk didn't bother to deny the additional reason for the choice of meeting location. "It wouldn't hurt if your coworkers didn't know you were back on the clock yet—and that's one reason I chose you. Your reputation is impressive."

He chuckled lightly and ran a hand through disheveled hair made wild by the wind. "Perhaps I'm not discrete enough, then."

"Rest assured, it's on a need-to-know basis. I realize we haven't had many opportunities to work together yet, but Samuel always spoke of you in the highest terms."

He schooled his expression to mask the emotions the statement provoked. "I'm humbled, sir. He was a good man."

"He was." Volosk's shoulders straightened with his posture—a signal he was moving right on to business, as though it didn't *matter* how good a man Samuel had been. "What do you know about the Metis Nebula?"

Caleb's brow creased in surprise. Whatever he had been expecting, this wasn't it. *Okay. Sure.*

"Well, mostly that we don't know much about it. It's outside Federation space, but we've tried to investigate it a few times—purely scientific research of course. We know there's a pulsar at the center of it, but scans return a fuzzy mess across the spectrum. Probes sent in find nothing but ionized gases and space dust. Scientists have written it off as unworthy of further study. Why?"

"You're very well informed, Agent Marano. Do a lot of scientific reading in your spare time?"

"Something like that."

"I'm sure. The information I'm sending you is Level IV Classified. Fewer than a dozen people inside and out of the government are aware of it."

He scanned the data file. In the background the synth band shifted to a slow, rhythmic number threaded by a deep, throbbing bass line. "That's...odd."

"Quite. The Astrophysics Institute sent in a state of the art, prototype deep space probe—the most sensitive one ever built, we believe. Honestly, it was solely for testing purposes. The researchers thought Metis' flat profile offered a favorable arena to run the probe through its paces. Instead it picked up what you see there.

"Obviously we need to get a handle on what this is. It came to my desk because it may represent a hostile threat. We've put a hold on any scientific expeditions until we find out the nature of the anomaly. If it *is* hostile, the sooner we know the better we can prepare. If on the other hand it's an opportunity—perhaps a new type of exploitable energy resource—we want to bring it under our purview before the Alliance or any of the independent corporate interests learn of it."

Caleb frowned at his companion. "I understand. But to be frank, my missions are usually a bit more…physical in nature? More direct at least, and typically involving a tangible target."

"I'm aware of that. But your experience makes you one of the few people in Division both qualified to investigate this matter and carrying a security clearance high enough to allow you to do so."

It wasn't an inaccurate statement. And if he were honest with himself, it *would* probably be best if he went a little while without getting more blood on his hands.

ᴀ̃ʀ

He slid open the hidden compartment in the wall and climbed into the narrow passage, pushed the access closed using his foot and crawled along the sloped tunnel. When he got to the end he activated his personal concealment shield—which did very nearly make him invisible—and with a deft twist released the small hatch.

He rolled as he hit the ground to mask the sound. The lighting in the bay was purposefully dim, and he landed deep in the shadow of the hull.

As expected, there was a ring of men guarding the exterior of the ship. He waited for the closest man to turn his back, then slipped out and moved to the corner of the bay to settle behind the storage crates he had arranged to have delivered earlier in the day.

He was rewarded by the arrival at that moment of an additional six—no, seven—pursuers. A significant majority of the active members were now inside the hangar bay. Good enough.

They moved to join their brethren encircling the ship—and he sent the signal.

The walls roiled and bucked from the force of the explosion. White-hot heat blasted through his shield. The shockwave sent him to his knees even as the floor shuddered beneath him. Pieces of shrapnel speared into the wall above him and to his right. A large section of the hull shot out the open side of the bay and crashed to the street below.

One glance at the utter wreckage of his former ship confirmed they were all dead. He climbed to his feet and crossed to the door, dodging the flaming debris and burnt, dismembered limbs. The emergency responders could be heard approaching seconds after he disappeared down the corridor.

He didn't de-cloak until he reached the bike. He calmly fired it up, cruised out of the stall, and accelerated toward the exit.

Mission fucking accomplished.

Caleb nodded in acceptance. "I'll need a new ship. My last one was, um, blown up."

"My understanding is that's because you blew it up." The expression on the Director's face resembled mild sardonic amusement.

He bit his lower lip in feigned chagrin, revealing what he judged to be the appropriate touch of humility. "Technically speaking."

Volosk sent another data file his way. "Regardless, it's been taken care of. Here's the file number and all the standard information, including the hangar bay of your new ship."

He ignored the mild barb and examined this data with greater scrutiny, but it appeared everything had in fact been taken care of. "Got it. This all looks fine."

"Good…there's one more thing. It's no secret with Samuel gone there's a leadership vacuum in the strategic arm of Special Operations. He believed you were quite capable of taking on a larger role. Based on your record—a few isolated excesses aside—and what I know of you, I'm inclined to agree. So while you're out there in the void, I'd encourage you to give some thought to what you truly want from this job. We can talk further when you return."

Caleb made sure his expression displayed only genuine appreciation, carefully hiding any ambivalence or disquiet. "Thank you for the vote of confidence, sir. I'll do that."

"Glad to hear it. Now if you'll excuse me, I have to go get my ass kicked by ten other men and a cocky, VI-enhanced metal ball, after which I get to go back to the office and review the Trade Summit file for the seventeenth time this week."

He grimaced in sympathy. It was impossible to escape the growing media frenzy surrounding the conference, even with it over a week away.

Twenty-two years had passed since the end of the Crux War; it had been over and done with before he was old enough to fight. The cessation of hostilities after three years was officially called an 'armistice,' but Seneca and fourteen allied worlds had—by the only measure which mattered—won. They had their independence from the mighty Earth Alliance.

Now some politician somewhere had decided it was finally time for them to start playing nice with one another. He wished them luck, but…. "If it's all the same, I'd just as soon not be assigned to that one, sir. It's going to be a clusterfain of epic proportions."

Volosk exhaled with a weariness Caleb suspected was more real than contrived. "Don't worry, you're off the hook—wouldn't want to endanger your work by putting your face in front of so many dignitaries. *I*, however, won't get a decent night's sleep until the damn thing's finished."

Caleb sighed in commiseration, playing along with the superficial bonding moment. It seemed the higher-ups had decided he was worthy of being nurtured, at least enough to make certain he stayed in the fold. Bureaucrats. They had no clue how to manage people; if they did, they would realize he was the last person who needed *managing*.

"Well, I'm sorry I can't help you there, sir. But I will head out on this mission once I've pulled together what I need. It should be a few days at most."

Volosk nodded, transitioning smoothly to the closing portion of the meeting. "Please report in as soon as you discover anything relevant. We need to understand what we're dealing with, and quickly."

He responded with a practiced smile, one designed to convey reassurance and comfort. "Not to worry, I'll take care of it. It's what I do."

He decided it was best to leave *when I'm not blowing up three million credit ships and two dozen terrorists with them* unsaid.

After all, he fully intended to *try* to return this ship in one piece.

ℛ

After Volosk had departed, Caleb remained by the river for a while. His outward demeanor was relaxed, save for the rapid tap of fingertips on the railing.

He had been on leave ever since the post-op debriefs for the previous assignment had wrapped up. Whether the vacation had been a reward or a punishment he wasn't entirely sure, despite Volosk's vague hint at a promotion. Nor did he particularly care. He had accomplished what he had set out to do, justice had been served—albeit with a spicy dash of vengeance—and the bad guys were all dead. But it appeared it was time to get back to work.

The serenity of the cool night breeze and river-cleansed air juxtaposed upon the pulsing thrum of the music and swelling buzz of the crowd made for an appropriate backdrop. Time to retune himself.

He had enjoyed spending time with Isabela and her family, especially getting to play the bad uncle and fill Marlee's head with rebellious and unruly ideas sure to drive her mother crazy for months. The little girl had spunk; it was his duty to encourage it.

It had been a welcome respite. But it wasn't his life.

He pushed off the railing and strolled down the promenade to the bar area. The throbbing of the bass vibrated pleasantly on his skin as he neared. He ordered a local ale and found a small standing table which had been abandoned in favor of the dance floor. He rested his elbows on it, sipped his beer and surveyed the crowd.

It was amusing, and occasionally heartbreaking, to see how people doggedly fumbled their way through encounters. All the cybernetics in the world couldn't replace real, human connection, which was likely why physical sex was still the most popular pastime in the galaxy, despite the easy availability of objectively better-than-real *passione illusoire*. Humans were social animals, and craved—

"What are you drinking?"

He glanced at the woman who had sidled up next to him. Long, razor-straight white-blond hair framed a face sculpted to perfection beyond what genetic engineering alone could achieve. A white iridescent slip minimally covered deep golden skin. Silver glyphs wound along both arms and up the sides of her neck to disappear beneath the hairline.

He smiled coolly. "I'm fine, thanks."

She dropped a hand on the table and posed herself against it. "Yes, you are. Would you like to dance?"

He suppressed a laugh at the heavy-handed come-on. "Thank you, but…" a corner of his mouth curled up "…you're not really my type."

Her eyes shone with polished confidence. She believed she was in control. How *cute*.

"I can be any type you want me to be." The glyphs glowed briefly as her hair morphed to black, her makeup softened and her skin tone paled.

So that's what the glyphs were for. A waste of credits born of a desperate need to be wanted. He gave the woman a shrug and shook his head. "No thanks."

She scowled in frustration; it marred the perfect features into ugliness. "Why not? What the hell is your type?"

He took a last sip of his beer and dropped the empty bottle on the table. "Real."

He walked away without looking back.

STARSHINE

AURORA RISING BOOK ONE

AVAILABLE IN EBOOK, PRINT AND AUDIOBOOK AT
GSJENNSEN.COM/STARSHINE

SUBSCRIBE TO G. S. JENNSEN'S NEWSLETTER

*Get an *exclusive* short story for free, be the first to hear about new book announcements and more*

GSJENNSEN.COM/SUBSCRIBE

Author's Note

I published my first novel, *Starshine*, in 2014. In the back of the book I put a short note asking readers to consider leaving a review or talking about the book with their friends. Watching my readers do that and so much more has been the most rewarding and humbling experience in my life.

So if you loved ***THE THIEF***, tell someone. Leave a review, share your thoughts on social media, annoy your coworkers in the break room by talking about your favorite characters. Reviews are the backbone of a book's success, but there is no single act that will sell a book better than word-of-mouth.

My part of this deal is to write a book worth talking about—your part of the deal is to do the talking. If you keep doing your bit, I get to write a lot more books for you.

Lastly, I want to hear from my readers. If you loved the book—or if you didn't—let me know. The beauty of independent publishing is its simplicity: there's the writer and the readers. Without any overhead, I can find out what I'm doing right and wrong directly from you, which is invaluable in making the next book better than this one. And the one after that. And the twenty after that.

Website: gsjennsen.com
Wiki: gsj.space/wiki

Email: gs@gsjennsen.com   Goodreads: G.S. Jennsen
Twitter: @GSJennsen   Pinterest: gsjennsen
Facebook: gsjennsen.author   Instagram: gsjennsen

Find my books at a variety of retailers: gsjennsen.com/retailers

AMARANTHE UNIVERSE

AURORA RHAPSODY

AURORA RISING

STARSHINE
VERTIGO
TRANSCENDENCE

AURORA RENEGADES

SIDESPACE
DISSONANCE
ABYSM

AURORA RESONANT

RELATIVITY
RUBICON
REQUIEM

ASTERION NOIR

EXIN EX MACHINA

OF A DARKER VOID

THE STARS LIKE GODS

RIVEN WORLDS

CONTINUUM
INVERSION
ECHO RIFT

ALL OUR TOMORROWS
CHAOTICA
DUALITY

COSMIC SHORES

MEDUSA FALLING
THE THIEF
THE UNIVERSE WITHIN

SHADOWS & LIGHT

LIMINAL SPACE

SHORT STORIES

Restless I • *Restless II* • *Apogee* • *Solatium* • *Venatoris* • *Re/Genesis*
Meridian • *Fractals* • *Chrysalis* • *Starlight Express* • *Extinguishing the Stars*

Learn more at gsjennsen.com/books or visit the
Amaranthe Wiki: gsj.space/wiki

ACKNOWLEDGMENTS

Many thanks to my beta readers, editors and artists, who made everything about this book better, and to my family, who continue to put up with an egregious level of obsessive focus on my part for months at a time.

I also want to add a personal note of thanks to everyone who has read my books, left a review at a retailer, Goodreads or other sites, sent me a personal email expressing how the books have impacted you, or posted on social media to share how much you enjoyed them. You make this all worthwhile, every day.

ABOUT THE AUTHOR

G. S. JENNSEN lives somewhere in the U.S., in a locale that may or may not be where she lived the last time she published a book (she's a gypsy at heart), with her husband and two dogs. She has become an internationally bestselling author since her first novel, *Starshine*, was published in 2014. She has chosen to continue writing under an independent publishing model to ensure the integrity of her stories and her ability to execute on the vision she has for their telling.

While she has been a lawyer, a software engineer and an editor, she's found the life of a full-time author preferable by several orders of magnitude. When she isn't writing, she's gaming or working out or getting lost in the mountains that loom large outside the windows in her home. Or she's dealing with a flooded basement, or standing in a line at Walmart reading the tabloid headlines and wondering who all of those people are. Or sitting on her back porch with a glass of wine, looking up at the stars, trying to figure out what could be up there.